Dragon Magic

Books by Alexandra Ivy

ETERNAL MAGIC
DRAGON MAGIC

Ares Security
KILL WITHOUT MERCY
KILL WITHOUT SHAME

Romantic Suspense
PRETEND YOU'RE SAFE
WHAT ARE YOU AFRAID OF?
YOU WILL SUFFER
THE INTENDED VICTIM
DON'T LOOK
FACELESS
UNSTABLE
DESPERATE ACTS
THE MURDER CLUB

Historical Romance
SOME LIKE IT WICKED
SOME LIKE IT SINFUL
SOME LIKE IT BRAZEN

And don't miss these Guardians of Eternity novellas
TAKEN BY DARKNESS in YOURS FOR ETERNITY
DARKNESS ETERNAL in SUPERNATURAL
WHERE DARKNESS LIVES in THE REAL WEREWIVES OF
VAMPIRE COUNTY
LEVET (ebook only)
A VERY LEVET CHRISTMAS (ebook only)

And don't miss these Sentinel novellas
OUT OF CONTROL
ON THE HUNT

Published by Kensington Publishing Corp.

Dragon Magic

By Alexandra Ivy

LYRICAL PRESS
Kensington Publishing Corp.
kensingtonbooks.com

KENSINGTON BOOKS are published by

Kensington Publishing Corp.
900 Third Avenue, 26th Floor
New York, NY 10022

The K with book logo Reg. U.S. Pat. & TM Off

ISBN: 978-1-5161-1209-8 (ebook)
ISBN: 978-1-5161-1210-4

The authorized representative in the EU for product safety and compliance
Is eucomply OU, Parnu mnt 139b-14, Apt 123
Tallinn, Berlin 11317, hello@eucompliancepartner.com

154969777

Chapter 1

Maya Rosen was bored. A shocking realization for the powerful mage. Usually she was running around like a maniac trying to keep up with her endless to-do list.

After all, in the past few months she'd acquired a vampire mate, Ravyr. She'd taken on the training of potential mages who equally inspired and frustrated her to the point of exhaustion. And she'd completely remodeled the deep basement beneath the Witch's Brew coffee shop in Linden, New Jersey.

The basement had started off as a barren hole in the ground, but now it was a luxurious apartment with elegant furnishings and high-tech gadgets that Ravyr used in his security-for-hire business. She'd also replaced the vault she used to protect her vast collection of magical charms, amulets, relics, and a stockpile of potions with a massive steel safe that could withstand everything from an earthquake to a magical tsunami, and even the fire from a dragon.

Not that everything had changed, of course. The Witch's Brew still looked the same. The small bakery still had white tiled floors and lavender walls lined with shelves of pastries and round tables set near a large front window that offered a charming view of the street. It still oozed with the fragrance of freshly baked muffins that lured in customers by the hundreds. It was still attached to the shadowed bookstore where a customer could settle in a leather chair and become lost in a cozy world far removed from their own. And there was still a private office at the very back of the building where Maya negotiated contracts with the local demons.

As a powerful mage she had the ability to create curses and love potions, track down missing relatives, and create short-term illusions.

It was her main source of income and business had never been better. New York City was the epicenter of a pool of magic that throbbed deep in the earth called a Gyre. At one time the spot had been the lair of a dragon, but since their retreat from the world, it was used by both goblin and fey creatures to tap into their ancient powers.

The Gyre was currently under the rule of the vampire named Valen. The Cabal maintained control of all the Gyres spread across the world. Something that annoyed the hell out of Maya, despite the fact she was currently mated to a vampire. And why she chose to remain in New Jersey at the edge of Valen's territory. She didn't need the power. She had her own wild magic flowing through her veins.

Another thing that hadn't changed was the fact that when she needed help, she reached out to the mages who were the sisters of her heart.

Peri Sanguis was currently standing next to her as she hid behind the steep stairs that led to the basement. The young mage was without a doubt the most powerful magic user born in the past millennium. The beautiful woman had lush, dark curls and vivid blue eyes and was mated to Valen, the local Cabal leader. Maya had also called on Skye Claremont, a clairvoyant who was mated to Micha, the Cabal leader of New Orleans. Skye was currently MIA. A fact that had Maya on edge. She wasn't worried about her friend. Skye had proven she could not only take care of herself, but could prevent the world from being consumed in endless flames. But she needed Skye's gentle soul.

Clearly as bored as Maya, Peri leaned against the side of the staircase, stifling a yawn. Peri was wearing a pair of cutoff shorts and a Green Day T-shirt with her hair pulled into a high ponytail. It had been a punishingly hot day in New Jersey and the August heat hadn't faded as the sun set. In fact, it had thickened to an unpleasant soup of damp humidity.

"Explain again why we're kidnapping a child," Peri demanded.

Maya clicked her tongue. She'd chosen a loose black caftan that fell to her ankles. The air in the basement was cool and silk felt good against her skin. Besides, she had a reputation for her flawless elegance. Just because she was setting a trap for a mysterious thief was no excuse not to look her best.

She smoothed back her dark, silky hair that was cut just above her shoulders. "We're not kidnapping anyone."

"No?" Peri arched a brow. "When you demanded that Valen—"

"Asked," Maya corrected. "I asked."

"Okay, when you very aggressively *asked* for Valen to spread the word that an extremely dangerous artifact had been discovered in New York City and then he'd asked you to keep it hidden in your vault. And then you *asked* me and Skye to join you in setting a magical trap to capture a child. I'm not gonna lie, it seems weirdly close to kidnapping."

"We're catching a thief." Maya made a sound of impatience. "And where is Skye? She said she'd be here an hour ago."

"Her plane was late and now she's stuck in traffic. Finish telling me why we're kidnapping a child."

"For the last time, it's not kidnapping. It's...an intervention."

"Intervention. Right."

"Look, I don't have a choice. The supposed child has been spotted from Miami to New York stealing magical objects."

"From what Valen could discover, they were mostly junk. The kind of stuff that you sell to tourists, not to serious magic users."

Maya pressed her lips together. She'd been just as dismissive when she'd first started hearing the rumors about a kid sneaking into magic shops and even onto a few covensteads. Human magic wasn't that dangerous. Not like the charms and potions that were created by mages and demons.

She remained indifferent even after she'd viewed the security video sent to her of a young girl with a round freckled face and big brown eyes. She looked like a harmless child. Who cared if she was taking a few baubles?

But when the rumors became more frequent and the vaults that she began to enter were owned by mages and demons that were heavily protected, she reluctantly conceded that she had to do something.

Which currently included crouching next to the staircase, in the dark, listening to her friend bitch and gripe.

"I don't care what she's stealing. I care about the fact that she's been able to slip in and out of some of the most secure safes, vaults, and repositories in the country. The next thing she steals might not be a harmless trinket."

"Fine." Peri heaved a resigned sigh. "Is she a demon?"

"No one knows. She's been captured on security video, but she doesn't leave a trace of her presence. Not fingerprints or footprints or even a scent. Like she's a ghost."

"Then she must be a mage."

Maya shook her head. A mage began life as a human with a mother who had some ability to use magic. A witch, a fortune teller, a midwife. As she became an adult, her powers would manifest as the wild magic seared through her blood, transforming her into a mage. The powers ranged from Peri, who was off the charts, to some mages who could barely sense their magic. But the one thing that was universal was the initial rush of wild magic.

"She's too young to have come into her powers."

"I was young."

"In the video she looks about twelve."

"Looks can be deceiving," Peri insisted.

Maya shrugged. She didn't have her friend's skill with illusions, but she understood that things weren't always what they seemed to be.

"Which is why I want to meet her face-to-face. If we discover she's a harmless kid, then I'll let her go about her business."

"It still feels excessive," Peri groused, more out of habit than annoyance at being called to help. The young mage had always been headstrong and fiercely independent. It kept their relationship interesting. And by interesting, Maya meant snarky. "This isn't because Sinjon has called a meeting of the Cabal in Greece and you were lonely, is it?"

Maya clicked her tongue. Although Ravyr wasn't an official member of the Cabal, his years as a spy for Sinjon, the current leader of the vampires, meant he was often requested to attend the meetings.

"I spend my days with a half dozen mages in training who snipe and snarl and indulge in epic meltdowns on a regular basis. I swear it would be less stressful to try and tame a pack of hyenas," she said dryly. "Certainly it would be quieter. That doesn't include keeping the Witch's Brew running smoothly and fulfilling the contracts I've signed with several impatient demons. I can promise you that I would far prefer to spend the next few nights alone, soaking in a hot bubble bath with a glass of wine and utter silence. Which is exactly what I would be doing if I hadn't spotted the kid hanging around the shop when I was cleaning up." She reached up to touch the perfect emerald that hung on a chain around her neck. The gem held her magic if she needed an extra boost. "The trap has been baited and the prey is on my doorstep. I have no choice but to spring it."

Peri studied her, as if sensing the tension that vibrated through Maya. "You really are worried."

"I don't understand how she's slipping through the magical barriers. That should worry all of us."

Peri wrinkled her nose. "For once I wish Joe was around."

"I'm not that desperate," Maya growled.

Joe had been a part of Maya's existence since she set up the Witch's Brew years ago. He hung around the shop, looking like a street person with a bushy beard and velour tracksuit, but Maya had eventually realized he was the mysterious Benefactor who'd offered her protection for her business while at the same time demanding that she perform small tasks for him. Like a mob boss on steroids. More than one of those tasks had nearly gotten her killed. Eventually he revealed himself to be the Watcher, an even more mysterious creature who was the ultimate guardian over the vampires, demons, and dragons.

Whether he'd been in his disguise as Joe or the Benefactor or the Watcher, he'd been a pain in the ass.

"Come on," Peri teased. "You have to miss him at least a little."

"Like I miss an infected toenail."

"That's very...graphic."

Maya shrugged. "He had his uses, but there is enough testosterone in my life. He's welcomed to pester someone else."

"I wonder where he is," Peri mused. Then without warning her magic tingled in the air. "Someone's coming," she whispered.

Maya thought she heard the soft sound of footsteps, but didn't have Peri's talent for sensing who or what was approaching.

"Human? Demon? Mage?"

"I don't know."

"Damn, I wish Skye was here."

Peri looked confused. "We're two of the most powerful mages in the world. We could take down a vampire if necessary. Why are you worried?"

"Skye has something we don't."

"What's that?"

"The patience to deal with a child."

"Yeah. Good point," Peri agreed. "She's a lot nicer than we are."

Maya didn't know if it was Skye's brutal upbringing at the hands of demons or the dark visions that haunted her, but whatever the cause, Skye possessed the most gentle, empathetic soul she'd ever known.

Maya's thoughts were shattered as the steel door leading down to the basement was slowly pushed open. She exchanged a glance with Peri. Earlier they'd both cast layers of magic that would keep out a horde of demons, not to mention set off a dozen different alarms.

There'd been nothing to indicate the Witch's Brew had been breached. Not a peep.

Maya and Peri remained hidden in the shadows as footsteps crept down the stairs and a silhouette passed by, heading directly for the safe that was built into a concrete wall. Maya touched Peri's arm, keeping her from springing the trap. She wanted to see exactly how the girl was entering the vaults. Was it magic? An incantation? Did she have inside help? And just as importantly, how did she know the safe was hidden behind the shelf of books?

Maya barely dared to breathe as the intruder lifted a hand and waved it in a circle, as if she were conducting an orchestra. In response, the shelves swept aside and the door to the vault swung open.

There was no tingle of magic. No blast of power. Nothing.

Next to Maya, she could feel Peri tense in surprise. Was the younger mage finally realizing that they weren't dealing with a sticky-fingered brat?

A minute passed, then another. This was no smash and grab. The intruder was taking her sweet time. After what felt like an eternity the shadow reappeared and, chanting in a soft voice, Maya released the spell she'd cast onto the floor. At the same time, Peri dropped her own spell from the ceiling, wrapping it around the shadow.

"What the..." The intruder briefly struggled against the invisible bands wrapped around her, then as if realizing that each movement made them tighter, she made a sound of disgust.

"A snare?" The girl's voice floated through the darkness. "Really? Super original."

Maya reached to flip on the light switch. The soft glow flooded the formal sitting room decorated in dramatic shades of black and silver with low glass coffee tables and metal works of art that shimmered with a cold beauty. It was what most people expected when they visited the lair of a vampire and a powerful mage. The private areas of the lair were far cozier, with deep couches and lots of soft, fuzzy pillows. It turned out, she liked to snuggle with her vampire. Honestly, no one was more surprised than she was.

Maya stepped away from the stairs, sweeping her gaze over the short, slender form that was no longer hidden by shadows. Up close the girl looked even younger than Maya had expected. Her round face was sprinkled with freckles and surrounded by a halo of brown curls that matched her wide eyes. In defiance of the sweltering heat, she was wearing an oversized winter coat with large silver buttons and baggy sweatpants with sneakers.

There was no aura around her that would mark her as a demon. Red for goblin or green for fey creatures. And the girl certainly wasn't a vampire. There were less than a hundred leeches in the entire world and they were exclusively male. Just like all mages were females.

Maya's attention turned to the swirling mist that formed over the girl's coat pocket as well as the black bag she clutched in a tight grip. The snare was designed to reveal magical objects as well as any spells or curses attached to her captive.

"She's carrying some magical artifacts."

Peri nodded, moving forward to grab the black bag before reaching into the coat pocket.

"What are you doing? Leave me alone." The girl slapped at Peri's hand. "Stranger danger! Stranger danger!" she screamed in a piercing voice.

"Hush." With a wave of her hand, Maya placed a weave of air over the thief's lips.

The girl glared at her, but her eyes widened as she caught sight of the silvery scars that ran the length of Maya's jaw. It was possible she was simply bothered by the disfigurement, but Maya suspected that girl had belatedly recognized her. The rumors of Maya's battle with a demented vampire had become the stuff of legends over the past forty years. In the demon world there were few creatures who weren't a little afraid of the mage with a scarred face.

"These are yours," Peri said as she strolled back to Maya and handed her the bag.

Maya peered inside. It felt oddly heavy. A lead lining? Interesting. She tilted the bag to the side, studying the three crystals that held minor curses and a vial of truth serum.

"Out of all the magical objects in the safe, this is what you decided to steal?" Maya demanded in confusion.

"This was in her pocket." Peri handed Maya a small round stone with a hole drilled in the center of it.

"What is it?"

"There's some sort of magic, but I don't recognize it."

Maya smoothed her thumb over the stone. It looked like something you could pick up anywhere, but there was a tingle of power that warned it wasn't just another rock.

"There's magic in it," she murmured, gathering a small tendril of power. "But the only way to figure it out is to trigger the spell."

"Don't!" the girl snapped, easily breaking through the web Maya had placed over her lips. "You're going to ruin it."

Maya cut off her magic, like turning off a faucet. There was an edge of urgency in the girl's voice.

"What is it?" Maya demanded.

"My private property is what it is." The girl stuck out her hand. "Give it back."

"Fine, I'll figure it out myself." Maya held up the stone, as if preparing to probe it with her magic.

"No!" the girl said in frustration. "It's an opener."

"An opener?" Maya scowled. "What does that mean?"

"I don't know how to explain it. It's...like a garage door opener."

"What does it open?"

"Everything."

Maya continued to study the stone. She'd never heard of a rock that doubled as a garage door opener. There were demon relics that allowed them to pass through magical barriers, and a rare few that also opened locks, but they had been banned by the Cabal for centuries. And the one she'd confiscated from a goblin ten years ago had been a seven-foot crystal figurine that glowed with a crimson power. They weren't exactly user friendly.

Was it possible that the demons had managed to create a new artifact that was smaller and less conspicuous? A daunting thought.

"How does it work?" she demanded.

"Magic, I guess," the girl said. "I just know when I'm holding it, the stone lets me go into places most people can't get into."

"Like locked vaults?"

The girl continued to hold out her hand, snapping her fingers at Maya. "Can I have it back?"

"No. Where did you get it?" Maya demanded.

"I found it. Don't ask where. I don't remember."

Maya narrowed her eyes. Normally she admired a young girl with confidence. She didn't even mind a little cockiness. How else would women ever change the world? But there was spicy attitude and you're-wearing-on-my-freaking-nerves attitude.

"Do you think this is a game?"

The girl gave an angry toss of her curls. "I think two old ladies lured an innocent child into a trap and now you're holding her against her will. It's called trafficking. Google it if you don't believe me."

Peri leaned against the side of the staircase, her lips twitching as if she were enjoying the show.

"Told you," she murmured softly.

Maya sent her fellow mage a chiding glance. With friends like that, who needed enemies? With a click of her tongue, she returned her attention to the thief.

"We are not old."

"Okay, boomer."

Maya paused, forcing herself to count to ten before she did something stupid. Maybe she *was* getting old.

"Where did you get this?" She nodded toward the stone lying in the center of her palm.

"I told you, I found it."

"Where?" Maya tightened the bonds of the snare. Not enough to cause pain, but a physical warning that she was in charge of the situation. "And don't tell me you don't remember."

"Fine." The girl sniffed. "It was in some junk I found when I was walking through the Everglades."

The mention of the Everglades prompted a memory of the complaint that Maya had received last summer from a witch who demanded that Maya do more to track down and punish thieves. It was an early warning that something was wrong. Unfortunately, Maya had been too busy dealing with the demons from her past to check into the complaints. After that, she'd been caught up in her new school for young mages and joining her life with Ravyr, not always an easy task.

Now she regretted letting the child continue her stealing spree. Obviously she'd managed to get her hands on objects that were far more powerful than Maya had assumed. Some of them might be dangerous in the wrong hands.

"You didn't find it," she corrected the girl. "You stole it from the Celeste Coven."

The brown eyes widened. "Coven? Does that mean it was from a bunch of witches? Cool. No wonder it has some weird-ass magic."

Maya ignored the girl's fake astonishment. The thief might look and smell human, but there was something very suspicious about her.

"What were you doing in the Everglades?" she asked. Maybe if she could get the girl talking, she would give away some useful nugget of information.

There was a short silence, the girl's face suddenly grim, as if she were attempting to break free of the bonds. Then, clearly unable to escape the snare, the thief forced her clenched muscles to relax, a mocking smile curving her lips.

"I was there on vacation. Not my idea. Honestly, it's pretty lame unless you like mosquitoes and skanky water." She wrinkled her freckled nose. "The alligators were legit, I guess, but the heat was smothering. Like being stuck in a sauna. And not the good kind of sauna, the stinky kind."

Maya arched a brow. "You were on vacation?"

"Yup."

"With who?"

"Mom, who else?"

Maya didn't believe a word coming out of the girl's mouth. "And does your mom know about your crime spree?"

"Crime spree?" The girl snorted. "Are you serious? I stole a few worthless doohickies and sold them on eBay. So what? I hoped I might eventually find something worth real money, but so far there's been nothing but a bunch of bottles filled with weird stuff and crystals. Plus a few necklaces and bracelets but they were all butt ugly. I'm not wasting my time trying to pawn that junk."

"How did you choose which vaults to break into?"

"The stone." The dark gaze flicked toward the seemingly harmless rock. The words coming out of the girl's mouth were no doubt lies, but her hunger for the stone was very real. "I'd walk around and it would start glowing when there was a big safe I could sneak into." She stretched out her hand again. "Now give it back and I'll be on my way."

"I don't think so." Maya curled her fingers around the stone, hiding it from view. "Where's your mother?"

"None of your business."

"No problem." Maya glanced toward Peri. "Call the police. I'm sure they'll be interested in—"

"Wait." The girl lowered her arm. "If you must know, my mom's in the hospital. Happy?"

"Why?"

"Are you dense? Obviously she's sick. Why else would she be in the hospital?"

The overhead lights flickered as Maya struggled to control her temper. She'd encountered annoying kids before, but she'd never let them get under her skin. This one...argh.

"What's wrong with your mother?" she managed to ask in a voice that was just short of a growl.

"The doctors said that she has some sort of rare cancer. I brought her to New York because I heard they have a new treatment to help. I didn't know how expensive it was going to be."

Maya studied the round face and big brown eyes. She didn't trust the girl, not for a second, but was it possible she really did have a pressing need for money? A need that might explain why she was such an annoying little shit?

"That's why you're stealing?"

"It's not like I want to—"

The girl snapped her lips together as the sound of footsteps lightly running down the stairs had them all turning to watch Skye Claremont make her belated appearance.

The clairvoyant didn't look much older than the thief, with her golden curls corkscrewing around her heart-shaped face and her deep, midnight eyes. At least until you took a closer look. Those eyes were as ancient and mysterious as time itself.

"Sorry I'm late," Skye said as she reached the bottom step. "You wouldn't believe the traffic. Did I miss anything?" She blinked as her gaze landed on the girl trapped in front of the safe. "Hello."

"This is our midnight bandit," Maya explained as she moved to stand next to her friend.

"Wait." Skye furrowed her brow. "You said it was a child."

Maya studied Skye's confused expression. "I don't know if she's entirely human, but she's most certainly young."

"No." Skye abruptly stepped back, as if she sensed an unseen danger. "She's old. Very, very old."

"What?"

"Sucker." Without warning the thief pounced toward Maya. Why the aggravating...snot. She'd been pretending she was stuck in the snare while waiting for her chance to escape. Before Maya could react, the girl had snatched the stone along with the lead-lined bag that Maya had forgotten she was holding. Then, with a blinding speed, she was racing up the steps and disappearing.

Peri moved to peer up the stairs. "What just happened?"

Maya hissed in fury. Well, that was embarrassing. The creature had not only waltzed through her layers of magic as if they weren't there and stolen her belongings, but she'd fooled Maya into thinking she was an obnoxious child. Hell, Maya had started to fall for her sob story about her mother being in the hospital. Gah.

"I have no idea."

Chapter 2

Wynn raced out of the Witch's Brew and darted into the alleyway across the street. Once out of sight, she leaned against the brick wall and struggled to catch her breath.

Dammit. She'd been careless. For the past two centuries she'd trained herself to wait until she'd devised a meticulous, detailed plan before executing a job. It sometimes took years to properly prepare herself. But tonight she'd plunged into the most obvious trap ever set. It was embarrassing.

Then again, it wasn't like she had much choice. She was no longer in the position to wait to create the perfect heist. Hell, the way the magic was consuming her, she was beginning to wonder if she had more than a few weeks.

Right now she had to gamble on finding what she needed, even if it meant risking the wrath of the mages. She was trusting that she had the skill to stay one step ahead. Or if not skill, then maybe dumb luck would be on her side.

Sucking in a deep breath, she took a quick glance around to make sure she was alone. There didn't seem to be anyone hanging around, but a prickle of unease crawled over her skin. It was late enough for the humans to be tucked in bed, and since it was outside the Gyre, it wasn't a hot spot for demons or vampires. Not unless they were there to purchase a magical contract with the mages. But over the past week, she couldn't shake the sensation she was being stalked by an unseen enemy.

The sensation was wearing on her already raw nerves.

Telling herself that she was imagining things, Wynn rubbed her thumb over the stone. She'd lied about what it was, of course. She always lied. Ever since she'd awakened on the banks of the Thames River nearly two hundred years ago. It was the only way for a young woman on her own to survive.

A familiar tingle sparked to life. Closing her eyes, Wynn felt the magic rush through her. Not her magic—she didn't have any—but she could tap into the spell contained in the stone. Once she felt the familiar tingles of power, she visualized the thin, shimmering thread of power that appeared in her mind. It wound its way through the empty streets of New Jersey and across the bridge until it stopped in a narrow alleyway in the Bronx.

Once she was certain that she was firmly anchored, she released the magic binding her to the stone in her hand. It wasn't as simple as picking up a stone and dropping another one. At least not for her. She had to carefully make sure she held firmly onto one thread of magic while gently releasing the other thread before the spell could activate. Otherwise, she would either be torn in two by the competing powers, or she'd lose contact with the stone she was trying to use as an anchor and she'd be stuck taking the bus.

Something she very much hoped to avoid.

At last, Wynn removed her thumb from the stone and dropped it into her coat pocket. A second later the magic lashed out, snapping along the thread. As it went, it curled around Wynn, whipping her from one place to another.

It wasn't like soaring through the air. Or skimming over the ground. It was as if she blinked out of existence and was shoved through a black hole into another location. She didn't understand exactly what happened. And if she was being honest, she'd admit that a part of her worried that she was being dissolved and re-formed each time she used the magic. If that was true, then it seemed possible that if something went wrong, she might not reform with all her parts in the correct place.

But when she was in the middle of a job there was nothing more important than being able to disappear without a trace. That was how she'd managed to remain a mere shadow over the years.

So abracadabra and zip-a-dee-doo-dah...time to go.

The darkness consumed her before spitting her out on the other side. Lurching forward, Wynn rammed into the nearby dumpster as she struggled to regain her balance. At the same time, the stench of rotting trash and human vomit assaulted her like a punch to the face.

Grimacing, Wynn forced herself to bend down and grab the small stone that she'd hidden behind the dumpster and slipped it into her pocket with the first stone. Then, straightening, she headed down the alley. A few minutes later she was climbing the wooden steps connected to the back of the shuttered pawnshop. Halfway up, she paused long enough to glance around, once again feeling the gaze of the unseen Watcher.

As always, there was no one in sight, and with a muttered obscenity, she forced herself to continue up the staircase.

She felt the brush of magic as she stepped through the barrier wrapped around the narrow brick building, but it slid past her without harm. The spell wasn't nearly as potent as the complicated weaves that protected the Witch's Brew. Just as the lock on the door was nothing more than a mere inconvenience.

Shoving her way into the apartment that was crammed to the ceiling with wooden boxes and plastic totes, she carefully inched her way through a narrow opening to where a goblin was standing near an open window, as if checking to see if she'd been followed. Seemingly assured that she was alone, he turned to reveal the narrow face that was framed by long, stringy hair and crimson flames that had been tattooed along the line of his jaw. He was wearing faded jeans and a leather vest that revealed more than she wanted to see of his bare chest.

He stepped forward, his pale red aura weaving around him. The dullness of the glow revealed he was a pedestrian demon, his bloodline diluted over the centuries.

She'd been dealing with Hexx since she'd first discovered her talent for...acquiring...magical items. At the time, he was peddling an elixir that could cure everything from the plague to the lack of manly vigor near the docks of London. After he'd been run out of the city by the Cabal leader for accidentally poisoning several members of a royal demon clan, he'd set up shop in New York.

"Did you find it?" the demon demanded as he held out his hand.

"No, but I got these." Opening the bag, Wynn spilled the contents onto the male's palm.

Hexx sniffed, studying the objects. "Low-grade stuff."

Wynn reached to take them back. "If you don't want them—"

"Slow your roll." Hexx wrapped his fingers around the objects. "I didn't say that. I can move them, but it's going to be for pennies."

"A thousand US dollars."

Hexx widened his eyes. "Are you deaf? I just said this stuff is crap."

Wynn snapped her fingers. This was a familiar song and dance they'd performed a hundred times over the past century.

"Then give them back and I'll sell them to Virgil."

"Virgil Magyari?" He spit the name out like a curse. "That bastard? He might claim he's some sort of expert in black market magic, but he's nothing more than a hack who regularly steals, cheats, and bullies his customers. Only the most desperate idiot would go to him." Hexx pursed his lips. "You know what? I'm in a generous mood, so I'll give you three hundred. You're welcome."

"You would cheat a poor girl just trying to survive?" Wynn pressed a hand against her chest, her eyes filling with tears. "What about my poor sick mother? Nine hundred."

Hexx snorted. "If you're a poor, helpless girl, then I'm the Easter Bunny. Three fifty."

With a chuckle, Wynn shattered the illusion she'd created for her various heists. The child with freckles and bouncy brown curls was replaced with an angular face and stunning lavender eyes. Her features were finely chiseled, with high cheekbones and a narrow nose. Her lips were wide and full, as if they were offering a sulky invitation. Or at least that's what one hopeful lover had told her. She didn't know what that meant, which was probably why he'd never gone from hopeful to lover.

Her silky blond hair was pulled into a tight braid that hung down her back, and beneath her coat she wore black spandex that made it easy to disappear into the shadows.

At a glance she looked to be in her mid-twenties, although Wynn honestly had no idea how old she was. At least 198 years, but it could be more. It could be a lot more. Just another mystery in her crazy life.

"Seven hundred fifty dollars and not a penny less," she said.

"Five hundred. Final offer."

Wynn rolled her eyes. "Fine. But only because I'm in a hurry. Those curses are worth five hundred apiece."

"Why are you in a hurry?" Hexx reached into his back pocket to pull out a wad of bills, counting them off with meticulous care.

Making a sound of impatience, Wynn reached forward to snatch them out of his hand.

"A good question." She shoved the money into the pocket of her coat. It was the one thing that hadn't been a part of her illusion. Five hundred dollars was less than she used to spend on a nice bottle of wine, but beggars couldn't be choosers, and this would give her some breathing space for a few days. "You have a relationship with the Witch's Brew, don't you?"

Hexx stilled, belatedly sensing Wynn's seething annoyance. "Relationship?"

"You know the owners?"

Hexx's ratlike features twisted with disgust. "If you mean the trio of bitches who've made my life a living hell, then yeah, I suppose I know them. Why?"

"Because I walked into a trap tonight."

"A trap?" Hexx stared at her. "Are you kidding?"

Wynn held out her hand, hovering above one of the crystals that held a nasty curse.

"You tell me, Hexx. Do you think I'm kidding?"

"Okay. Simmer down." Hexx might not have known exactly how her magic worked, but he understood she could release the curse to spill over him. "I didn't have anything to do with it. I swear those mages are the bane of my existence."

"Pretending that they're your bane would be a perfect cover if you were working with them, right?"

Hexx stuck out his bony chest. "I'm an independent contractor. I don't work for anyone. And even if I did I would never be with them."

"Exactly what a spy would say," Wynn insisted, even though she truly didn't think the demon had betrayed her. Hexx was many things. Devious, immoral, and willing to sell his soul for a few bucks. But he wasn't a poker player. Any lie would be etched on his face. "You told me that there was an item with enormous powers hidden at the Witch's Brew, deliberately leading me into their trap."

Tossing the crystals on a nearby tote, Hexx licked his lips. "Look, I was just repeating what I heard. If you want to blame someone for the false information, then..." Hexx abruptly gasped. "Shit."

"What?"

"I overheard two fairies talking about the item when I was at the Dead Badger. I thought they were talking kind of loud about something that was supposed to be a big secret." He grunted. "And now that I think about it, I'm pretty sure one of the fairies works for Valen."

A genuine stab of fear pierced Wynn's heart. She didn't live in New York City, but she traveled through the area often enough to recognize the name. You'd have to live under a rock not to know who he was.

"Valen the vampire? The local leader of the Gyre and one of the most powerful members of the Cabal?" she hissed. "That Valen?"

"Yeah." Hexx fisted his hands as his eyes darted from side to side. As if he were expecting something to leap out and attack. "They set you up, not me. Which means they're probably chasing you right now. Dammit. Get out of here."

"Don't be such a baby. No one followed me here." Wynn reached into the pocket of her coat, brushing her fingers over the stones.

It was supposed to be a reminder that she'd taken all the necessary precautions to avoid being tracked. A promise that no one could know she was in this dingy apartment. But instead of the confidence that she was seeking, a wave of dread cascaded through her.

Had the Cabal realized who she was and what she was doing? Did they have some means of tracking her that she didn't know about?

That would explain why she'd felt as if she were being stalked since arriving in New York.

"Shit," she breathed.

"Wynn? What's wrong?"

Hexx's sharp question cut through the panic that threatened to cloud Wynn's mind. Right now it didn't matter who set the trap. All that mattered was getting back to her lair before she could be captured. Once she was safe she could reconsider her current plan of action.

"You know what? I think you're right," she said. "We should run."

Giving in to the abrupt impulse to flee, Wynn ignored the door behind her and instead leaped forward, clearing the nearby stack of totes.

"What?" Hexx watched her race past with wide, frightened eyes. "Dammit, Wynn. If those leeches—"

She didn't hear the end of his threat as she crashed through the windows and plummeted to the sidewalk. She landed awkwardly, pain jolting up her legs and into her lower back. Unlike demons and vampires, she didn't have superpowers. If she broke her ankle, she was going to be incapacitated until she could steal a healing potion.

The knowledge usually made her avoid performing any daring feats. She left that to amateur thieves who loved the drama. Tonight, however, speed was more important than caution.

Reminding herself of that fact, Wynn limped down the street. Within a block she felt the familiar sensation of being watched.

"Leave me alone," she growled, wincing as she picked up her pace.

Tomorrow she was going to be too sore to move. Always assuming she made it to tomorrow.

A fresh surge of adrenaline raced through Wynn, giving her the strength to dart down an alleyway and through a rusted door she'd left wedged open. Just because she was forced to ad-lib her current plans, didn't mean she was completely reckless. She had her escape in place before entering the Witch's Brew.

"Stop!"

The male voice sliced through the darkness, edged with a ruthless command. Along with it came a blast of compulsion. The power wrapped around Wynn, stroking over her skin with a shocking heat. That wasn't a leech. Their magic was frigid. Like being touched with an icicle.

This was...

Hell, she didn't know. She'd never felt anything like it.

The realization sent her scurrying across the cement floor slowly crumbling to dust. The building had once been a fish market, but it'd been stripped down to the studs several years ago. Best of all, the ceiling was sagging and the entire structure leaned to the side, slowly losing its battle against gravity. No one was willing to enter when there was a risk of a total collapse, not even the humans who spent their nights on the street. It made it a perfect location to stash one of her skipping stones.

Limping through the shadows pierced by moonlight from the holes in the ceiling, Wynn paused long enough to bend down and touch the ground. She closed her eyes, shuffling through the various strands of magic that twirled through her like a spiderweb, weaving and unweaving as if seeking to claim her attention. It usually created an explosion of sparkles that enchanted Wynn. Who wouldn't enjoy watching their own personal lightshow? But lately, one of the strands had become thicker and darker than the others.

The pulsing crimson thread was not only a distraction, but she had no idea what magic it was connected to. The only thing for certain was that since it appeared she'd been tormented by nightmares that left her shaken and drenched in sweat. Eventually she feared that she would get to the point where she was too afraid to sleep.

Then what would happen?

She would collapse from exhaustion.

Shaking her head, Wynn forced herself to focus on the paler strands, choosing a blue one. Mentally plucking it away from the others, she allowed it to coil through her body and out the tips of her fingers. The magic shuddered, as if struggling to work. She clenched her teeth. It wasn't unusual for the magic she'd acquired to fade. Sometimes she used it once and it was gone. Other times she kept it with her for decades, like the skipping stones. It all depended on the power held inside the object and how much magic she absorbed.

Or at least, that's how it used to work. Now the strands could work fine one minute and then give out a second later. Or twist into a spell that she'd never seen before.

Yet another reason she was increasingly concerned that the new, mystery strand was causing damage in her body.

At last the magic flowed through her, attaching to the cement before spreading up to the sagging ceiling and from side to side to form an invisible barrier. It wasn't large, but it provided enough protection for her to scurry to the corner and grab the stone she'd hidden earlier in the day.

Plucking it off the dusty ground, she rubbed her thumb over the smooth surface, hissing in frustration as the magic refused to ignite. At the same time, the heavy tread of boots sent jolts of alarm through her.

"You can't hide in the corner, little mouse," the rich male voice chided.

Clutching the stone in a tight grip, Wynn forced herself to turn. She didn't mind people thinking she was a thief or a liar or a swindler. She was all those things. But she'd be damned if she'd let them label her a coward.

Pretending she wasn't completely unnerved by her creepy stalker, Wynn tilted her head high and squared her shoulders.

Bam.

Warrior-woman mode activated.

Then the male stepped into a pool of moonlight and her world shattered. Just like that. One minute she was Wynn, thief extraordinaire and the next everything she'd known and believed in was being stripped away and she was catapulted into a new, startling reality.

A reality that included a sexy, outrageously decadent creature who stepped up to the barrier and laid his hand against her magic. A gut-punch of power suddenly thundered through the empty building.

Wynn couldn't breathe. Couldn't think. She didn't understand what was happening. Why was her heart thundering and her stomach twisting into a tight knot of delicious awareness?

It had to be some sort of sorcery, right?

Okay, he was drop-dead gorgeous. His hair was dark and thick and glossy. Like a swath of silk that rippled to brush his shoulders. And sure, her fingers itched to run through the strands just to see if it was as soft as it looked. Then there was his face. It was narrow, almost delicate, with the sort of features that were too perfect to be real. They should have softened the impact of his raw male beauty, but instead they emphasized the hint of savagery. And his eyes...

They were astonishing. In the shadows they shimmered with a silvery mist. But as he realized that he couldn't force his way through the barrier, they darkened to the deepest black, swirling like storm clouds.

Stalking along the shield, he kept his hand pressed against the magic, sparks dancing around his fingers. He moved like a dancer, all elegant grace and supple muscles that rippled beneath his silky black shirt and black slacks. A sleek predator on the hunt.

Wynn shivered. The male terrified her in a way she'd never experienced. And at the same time, she'd never been so mesmerized. As if something inside her understood that she'd been waiting for this moment all her life.

Desperately rubbing the stone still clutched in her fingers, Wynn tried to ignore the heat that seared through her. She might have succeeded if it'd just been lust. That was expected. The male walked straight out of her deepest fantasy. But the tingles of awareness weren't just a hunger for sex. They were a weird sense of recognition. As if the magic inside her was reacting to his presence.

What was he? Not a leech. Which meant he had to be a demon. But she'd never encountered one without an aura. And never one with the sort of power that made the ground tremble and the hair on her nape stand up in fear.

"Who are you?" The question came out as a croak. Honestly, she was just glad she got the words past the lump in her throat.

"Azh." He dipped his head, as if they were formally introducing themselves. "And you're Wynn." The sparks danced around his slender fingers. "Let me through your shield, sweet Wynn."

Said the spider to the fly...

"Yeah, I don't think so."

"You like to play games? Very well." He tilted his head to the side, the eyes returning to a shade of misty gray. "I've been trying to figure out exactly what you are. You don't smell human."

Wynn blew out a shaky breath. She didn't know what the male wanted from her, but she didn't intend to stay around long enough to find out.

"What I am is none of your business." She leaned against the wall, pretending a bored nonchalance as she continued to rub the stone. "I assume you're the one who's been stalking me. Do you want to know where you are on the scale of creepiness?"

He ignored her question. "What are you?"

"A low-level mage just trying to survive." A tiny thread of power ignited inside the stone. *Please work, please work, please work...*

"No, not a mage. I would be able to sense your wild magic."

Wynn didn't have to pretend her annoyance at the mention of her inability to create her own spells.

"I already admitted I was low level. Yeesh. Want a little salt to rub into the wound?"

"I didn't say you aren't blessed with magic. But it doesn't flow in your veins. And you don't have the scent of a mage."

Wynn focused on the thread connecting the stone in her hand to the one she'd placed several blocks away.

"Then what is my scent?"

His nostrils flared, as if he were absorbing her very essence. "Old. And..." The misty smoke in the strange eyes swirled, as if he'd been caught off guard. "What have you done?"

Wynn licked her lips, continuing to tug on the thread of magic even as she studied the dangerously addictive male.

"Do you recognize it?"

"That has yet to be determined."

"What do you mean?"

"Where do you come from?"

Wynn hissed in frustration. "I asked you a question. Do you recognize the magic?"

His lips pulled into a taunting smile, the flames coating his fingers suddenly charring the shield in a silent warning.

"Let's get one thing straight, Wynn. I'm the one asking the questions, and you're the one answering them. Now tell me where you come from."

Wynn rolled her eyes. Okay, so much for her brief hope he could give her the answers she so desperately wanted. Gorgeous or not, he was just another male spewing out orders like he ruled the world. Time to bounce.

"You want my life story? Fine. I was born on a small island in the South Pacific." She launched into one of her well-rehearsed stories, focusing her concentration on connecting the thread of magic from one stone to the other. "My mother was the local medicine woman."

"Medicine woman?"

"Yes, she was a great healer who was adored by our entire village, but we were forced to flee after a volcano destroyed our home. Since then I've been doing whatever necessary to provide for my family."

His jaw tightened. "Have you always had this power?"

"Not when I was a child. It only emerged after the eruption of the volcano. You see, we were surrounded by lava and I had to lead my family into a nearby cave to survive. When I woke up we'd been miraculously protected."

"Protected by what?"

"I don't know. I think there was magic in the cave and it followed me when I fled the island."

"What does it do?"

"Nothing. I know it's there, but it doesn't help."

His dark, heavy brows furrowed. He didn't like her answers. Tough luck.

"When did this supposed volcano erupt?"

"A few years ago."

"How many years?"

"I don't know. Ten years. Maybe more." Her voice was distracted as she snapped the thread tight, the magic humming through her. She was almost there. "My memories are fuzzy."

"Then why haven't I sensed the magic before now?"

Was he talking about the magic that was currently ruining her life? It had to be, although it hadn't just appeared. It'd been plaguing her for over a year. Wynn hesitated. She wanted answers so damned bad. And if this male...

No.

With an effort, she shoved aside temptation. This male had already refused to answer her questions. And more importantly, he was dangerous. She could feel it pulsing in the air. The sooner she could get rid of him, the better.

"That sounds like a *you* problem, not a *me* problem," she taunted. "Maybe you're not very good at sensing magic."

"Let me through." The flames climbed up the barrier, the spell wavering as he attempted to sear a hole through the shield.

"No."

"If I touch you I can determine the source of your magic."

"Touch me?" She scrunched her nose, refusing to acknowledge the white-hot excitement that blasted through her. If he tried to touch her she was going to punch him, right? She most certainly wasn't going to melt into a puddle of breathless need... Wait. No, no, no. She hissed in frustration. "You think you're the first guy to use that line? You're just like all the other perverts."

The air pulsed with a choking heat, a strange shimmer of power floating behind him. What was that? Wynn narrowed her eyes, trying to focus on the iridescent outline. It looked like some sort of transparent silhouette. Then, with a loud curse, the male turned and the shimmer expanded as he raced toward the door, stretching out like...wings?

She was still trying to focus on the bizarre illusion when the magic from the stone abruptly snapped into place, jerking her into the void. A second later she reappeared in yet another alleyway. This time, however, she was smart enough to maintain her grip on the thread.

The stranger had been running out of the building with the confidence of a male who knew exactly where he was going. Or worse, exactly where *she* was going.

Her caution was rewarded when a dark shape appeared at the end of the alley, stalking toward her with blatant impatience.

Shit. Fumbling through her strands of magic, she created a hasty barrier. It wouldn't withstand a direct assault, but she just needed a second to regain her balance before she skipped back to the abandoned building.

The male halted directly in front of her, no doubt assuming he had her pinned against the back of the alley. The glittering illusion of wings had disappeared, replaced by an aura of anger that heated the air until sweat dripped down her face. It wasn't the aura of a demon. It was more like he was surrounded by white-hot flames.

"Stop running, damn you," he growled. "I just want to talk to you."

"Liar." She rubbed the stone. "You already admitted you wanted to touch me, you creeper."

"Was your story true?"

"What story?"

"About the volcano."

"Right. That one." She shrugged. "Of course not."

"Then how did you gain the power?"

The heat curled around her, wrapping her in a tangible cloak of power. Was it a warning? She didn't think so. She wasn't sure he realized he'd been able to penetrate her shield.

She trembled, something inside her yearning to be immersed in that luscious warmth. Like a lioness bathing in the sun.

"It was a gift," she forced herself to retort, squashing her bizarre reaction to the male. Obviously her sleepless nights were starting to take a toll.

"From who?"

"A genie."

The smoky eyes darkened to a metallic gray. Still annoyingly beautiful. "A genie?"

"Yup. I was wandering through a cave and I stumbled across a magic lamp. One good stroke and poof, out popped the genie."

As she said the words, Wynn frantically rubbed the stone. She had only minutes to make the jump back before the thread vanished.

"I don't believe in genies," he growled.

"Then maybe it was a leprechaun. Or a unicorn."

He studied her with a grim expression. "Do you know what I find interesting?"

"My sparkling personality?"

"In both stories you mention a cave."

Wynn froze. Shit. He was the first to notice. Yet another reason to disappear ASAP.

"I have a lot of stories."

"Is that where you encountered the magic?"

"Seriously I have no idea what you're yakking about."

The eyes lightened back to mist, his power brushing over her skin like a caress.

"If you give it to me, I swear I'll allow you to walk away and never bother you again."

Maybe she wanted to be bothered... No, no, no. She wanted to get the hell out of there.

"*Allow* me to walk away? Who made you the boss?"

His gaze moved to the brick wall behind her. "I'm the boss because you're trapped."

"You say trapped. I say momentarily inconvenienced."

He heaved a loud sigh. As if she were being unreasonably difficult. "I've been watching you for days, you know."

"You mean spying on me, creeper."

"So I know your tricks."

Wynn felt the thread tighten, preparing to yank her back. She flashed a mocking smile.

"Stupid male. You should never tell a woman she's lost her mystery. No wonder you're forced to stalk and corner strangers in dark corners to get your yee-haws."

Something flared in the misty gray eyes, but it wasn't anger. It was something perilously close to fascination.

"You truly are unique," he murmured, his gaze sweeping over her.

Wynn snorted. "That's the only thing we can agree on."

He studied her for a long moment, as if he were silently reminding himself she was the enemy. It seemed to work, as he lifted a hand and laid it flat against the barrier. Instantly sparks danced around his fingers, his magic sizzling against her shield.

"I'd hoped we could keep this civil. I'm not a barbarian despite the reputations of my people."

"Your people? You mean vampires?"

She threw out the question, already knowing he wasn't a leech. Just as she somehow sensed he wasn't going to like being mistaken for one. She was right. His breath hissed between clenched teeth.

"Dragons."

"Dragons?" Wynn laughed. "Yeah, right. And I'm the tooth fairy..." The words died on Wynn's lips as the clues belatedly fell into place. Like pieces of a puzzle. The magic that was reaching out to shroud her in a smothering heat. The flames that even now coated his fingers. The smoky silver eyes. The explosive power that could easily grind her into dust. And the strange illusion of wings when he'd turned around.

Of course.

How the hell had she been so blind?

"Holy crap. You are a dragon."

Chapter 3

Azh kept his hand pressed against the barrier as he watched Wynn process the fact she was face-to-face with one of the most powerful beasts to ever walk the world. Most creatures would have collapsed in terror. Dragons might have been gone from the world since the Ice Age, but the memories of their savage battles with both vampires and demons lingered. They were considered nightmares that were better left to myth and legend.

Not this woman.

Tilting her head to the side, she ran a bold gaze down his body, her fresh, floral scent untainted by fear. He wasn't surprised. He'd been following her for days. Ever since he'd been stirred out of hibernation by the sensation of dragon magic moving through the world.

He'd watched with bemused curiosity as she'd scuttled through the city, creating a strange network of magic, like a spider weaving a web. Tonight he understood what she'd been doing. She was a thief, and the magical web was her escape route.

His dangerous fascination had only deepened as he followed her, but his reason to linger in this world wasn't just because she was the most beautiful, unique creature he'd ever encountered. It was the trail of potent magic she was leaking.

When he'd first awakened, he'd assumed the queen had escaped her prison and was once again attempting to break the treaty. Over a year ago, she'd used her powers to reach into this world and manipulate a demon to destroy the key keeping them locked in hibernation. Since then, the ancient dragon had been carefully locked behind a powerful wall of magic. It'd kept her physically sealed in place, but that didn't mean she didn't have other devious plots set into motion.

But instead of his queen, he'd found this delicate slip of a female with her air of human fragility and unexpectedly potent abilities. Add in the dragon magic and it was a bewildering combination.

He needed to discover exactly what she was, how she'd gotten ahold of the magic, and what she intended to do with it.

Something easier said than done if the current standoff was anything to go by.

"I didn't know you guys could look like humans," she at last said, returning her attention to his grim expression.

Azh shrugged. "We have many forms. I dislike being in this one, but it was the only way to follow you."

"You mean the only way to stalk me."

"Follow you," he insisted.

She snorted, but she didn't press the issue. "I thought the leeches locked you in the pits of hell?"

"The leeches have no power over the dragons," he retorted, his tone edged with arrogance. He'd be damned if he allowed her to think the bloodsuckers made decisions for his people. "We are currently in hibernation. Once the terms of the treaty have been met, we will return to our place in this world."

She pursed her lips. "So if you're in hibernation, then why aren't you snoozing?"

"I was awakened by the feel of mysterious magic moving through this world. The sort of magic that could tilt the balance of leadership among the demons."

"Okay. So go find it and leave me alone."

A growl rumbled in his chest. Leave her alone? Never.

He ignored the dangerous thought. "Where did you get it?"

"Get what?"

"The magic?"

She clicked her tongue, but her expression was suddenly distracted, as if she were concentrating on something more important than the dragon who had her cornered.

"I don't know what you're talking about. If I had some sort of mysterious power, why would I be stealing junk to survive?" she demanded. "I'd just take over the world."

He burned a hole in the barrier. She was up to something. He'd bet his favorite treasure hoard.

"A good question." The hole was slowly spreading. Too slowly. "Why are you stealing trinkets? And another question. Why did you have such an elaborate escape plan if you were just..." The truth hit like a lightning strike. You didn't work that hard to steal worthless baubles. But you did steal worthless baubles to hide the truth of why you were sneaking into vaults. "Ah. Of course. You're searching for something else. What is it? A potion? A charm? A rare artifact?"

Azh felt a stab of juvenile satisfaction as the astonishing lavender eyes widened in shock. He was right. She *was* searching for something. Obviously something she didn't find in the mage's vault.

"I have everything I need." She blatantly lied, holding up her hand that held the stone. "And it doesn't include meddling dragons. Mind your own business."

With a dramatic wave of her hand she disappeared. Just like that. One second she was there and the next she was gone.

Azh heaved a sigh. He could sense her magic, which meant that she was still in the city. But it was becoming a genuine pain in the ass to waste his time chasing her from one spot to another.

Turning on his heel, Azh prepared to track down his prey, only to come to an abrupt halt as a form appeared at the entrance to the alley.

"Stop, Azh." The deep male voice echoed through the air, bouncing off the brick walls and resonating inside Azh like a drum. "We need to talk."

Shit. Azh was frozen in place as the form strolled toward him. "That's supposed to be my line," he muttered.

The unwelcomed intruder stopped a few feet in front of Azh, wearing what looked like a pair of flannel pajamas with fuzzy slippers on his feet. His head was covered by an old-fashioned night cap that he had pulled down to his eyes with a fuzzy ball dangling from the tip. His lower face was hidden beneath a bushy beard giving him the vibe of a human Santa Claus.

He should have looked ridiculous, but there was nothing funny about the green eyes that blazed with an ancient magic or the displeasure that slammed into Azh with the force of a freight train.

"Why have the dragons broken their treaty?"

Azh held his ground. He'd never been face-to-face with the Watcher, but he recognized the elusive creature. With a godlike strength the male maintained the peace between leeches, demons, and dragons. Eons ago, the bloodbath created by the constant warfare had nearly caused a total collapse of all three species. That was when the treaty had been created, forcing the dragons into hibernation until it was their time to once again roam free, and the leeches would become dormant.

A glorious thought.

"No treaties are broken," Azh argued. "My people remain in hibernation as you commanded."

The green eyes smoldered with ruthless authority. "And you?"

"The dragons are allowed to investigate if they fear a threat to their safety. It's written in the treaty. And the reason there was an opening in the barrier for me to enter this world."

The strange male scrunched his nose. "You didn't create the opening?"

"Of course not. I've pledged to uphold the treaty. The opening was there when I awakened."

The Watcher considered his answer for a long moment. Then he shook his head, the fuzzy ball on the end of his cap bouncing.

"What is the threat?"

"Don't you feel it?"

"Fah. I feel many things. Be more specific."

"It feels like..." Azh's words faded. How did you explain a pulse of magic that was familiar and yet intoxicatingly mysterious? As if it had been created by his deepest fantasies.

"Yes?" the male prompted.

Azh shrugged. "I can't explain it. But it calls to me."

The Watcher tilted his head to the side. "The magic or the female calls to you?"

Azh jerked. The male had obviously been watching him for a while. An unpleasant realization. And a sharp reminder that he'd been doing the same thing. No wonder Wynn had been so pissy with him. It was unpleasant to discover that someone had been spying on him from the shadows.

"Both," he admitted between clenched teeth.

The Watcher made a sound of exasperation. "Return to your slumber. I'll deal with this latest complication."

"Not a chance in hell."

Azh's fierce refusal was still on his lips when the world dissolved around him. A heartbeat later he was standing at the edge of the thick mist that formed a barrier between the dragons and the rest of the world.

Dammit.

Clenching his hands, Azh stormed through the marble corridors of the dragons' hidden lair, his footsteps echoing through the thick silence. Most of his people preferred to sleep through this time of hibernation, restoring their strength and repairing wounds from their last battle against the vampires. On occasion they would awaken and move around the lair, some of them spending time with mates or polishing their fighting skills in the vast arena beneath the lair. Azh preferred to devote his time in the massive library that held treasures far greater than any in his hoard.

But first, he had to reassure himself that the magic he'd felt hadn't been a trap devised by Zanna, the former Queen of Dragons.

Turning into a side hallway that led to a forbidden area of the lair, he stepped through the layers of magic that blocked the crystal cell. No one could go in or out of the space. No one but him.

Once inside the prison, Azh blinked at the shimmering glow that filled the space. This area was devoid of power, but unlike many of his brethren he'd been unwilling to leave the traitor in complete darkness.

Not that Zanna deserved his sympathy.

She'd driven her dragons into a war with the leeches that had threatened their very survival, and refused to negotiate until her people had openly revolted. Even after she'd signed the treaty, she'd spent centuries plotting to break the agreement and destroy every living creature in the world.

That was when Azh had been forced to take a more dramatic action.

He'd allowed her to roam freely through the lair even if she had become a queen in name only since they'd entered hibernation, now she was locked in the crystal cell, cut off from her magic as well as any dragon foolish enough to try to help her escape.

His only concession to the arrogant female's various demands was giving her the gem-encrusted throne that she'd sat on for thousands of years. Until the hibernation ended and a new leader was chosen, it was a meaningless chair. Why not let her have the thing?

He strolled around the cell. It was too sparse and brightly lit for anyone to be hidden in the space, but he wanted to make sure there were no objects of power that had been smuggled in, and more importantly, no changes to the crystal walls. Only when he was confident that the queen had no means to touch the outside world did he turn to face her.

She was currently perched on the throne in her human form since the cell was too small for her dragon. As usual she was wearing the heavy black shroud she'd requested as a symbol of her martyrdom, but Azh wasn't fooled. She hadn't given up her raw ambitions. Even now her flame-red hair was braided and coiled to resemble a crown on top of her head while the aura of her beast blasted around her like solar flares around the sun.

Meeting the dark female gaze that held a ruthless arrogance that could never be diminished, Azh offered a respectful bow of his head. No matter what had happened, Zanna had devoted an eternity to leading her people. She'd earned his respect if not his trust.

"Well?" she demanded in impatient tones, the reflective bronze tint to her skin hinting at scales. "Did you find what you were seeking?"

Azh shook his head. "No."

"Then why did you return?"

Frustration smoldered through him. He should be with Wynn. Everything inside him screamed at the thought of leaving her alone and vulnerable. He told himself it was a natural reaction. How could he investigate the ancient dragon magic that pulsed around her from this prison? Or discover why she fascinated him in a way that felt dangerously like destiny.

"I didn't. I was forced back."

"Forced? How?" Zanna's nostrils flared as if she'd caught a nasty whiff. "No, don't tell me. There's only one creature who could impose his will on a dragon. That bastard," she hissed. "I knew he intended to destroy us. I warned you that the treaty had to be broken before he handed our world to the leeches on a silver platter. We're sitting ducks here."

Azh arched a brow. "Ducks?"

"You know what I mean," Zanna snapped. Her sense of humor had never been great. Now it was nonexistent. "The Watcher has us trapped in this place. There's every reason to assume he will leave us here to rot. Or worse, allow the vampires to enter and destroy us."

"This has nothing to do with the Watcher." He refused to take her bait. Zanna's grievance with the creature who'd forced them into hibernation had driven her over the edge.

That was why she was sitting on an empty throne in a crystal cell.

"Then what is it?"

"I'm not sure."

She made a sound of disgust. "I thought you were our most powerful hunter? The male who has been chosen to replace me?"

"No one has been chosen to replace you. Not until the treaty has come to an end. I only seek to protect my people."

"*Our* people."

"Yes, our people." He held her smoldering gaze without apology.

She waved a slender hand. "Tell me about the power. You must have discovered something."

"Not as much as I hoped. There is a female who seems to echo with our magic, but she is most certainly not a dragon."

"Echo. What does that mean?"

"It's in her, but not fully a part of her." Another wave of frustration rolled through him. "I need to return."

"The opening remains?"

"No."

"Ah." Zanna's lips twisted into a mocking smile. "Then you intend to bend the rules to suit your ambitions? Like I did?"

Azh shook his head. "I trust it will open again. The Watcher is unaware of the danger, but the magic of the treaty will ensure that I'm allowed to protect us." Azh turned to leave the cell. "First, however, I have some research to do."

"Research on what?"

"Kazak."

"Kazak? Our mythical homeland?" A sharp laugh echoed through the cell. "Only a fool would believe that's anything but a fairytale."

"Maybe it's a fairytale, maybe not." He shrugged. "I chose to believe the warnings of our forefathers."

"Trust you to waste time with looking through moldy old books instead of taking action against our true enemy, the Watcher," the queen taunted. "You've always been more a scholar than a warrior."

Azh halted at the barrier, turning to regard the older woman with a vague sense of regret. There'd been a time when dragons had exalted in their brutality. They delighted in battling each other as much as they did their enemies. The bloodshed had eventually been contained by Zanna's cunning leadership, directing their violent tendencies to destroying anything that wasn't a dragon. Vampires, demons, and the increasing tribes of humans.

The future, however, wasn't going to belong to those stuck in the past. As technology expanded and times changed, they would need intelligence to survive, not mindless cruelty. The only way to continue as a species was to adapt. He truly believed that.

Still, looking to the future didn't mean forgetting their history. His earliest ancestors had warned of a darkness that remained a threat to his people. And that there would come a time when they would have to prepare to battle back the evil with an ancient magic that would be returned to the dragons when it was most needed.

He had no idea if the female was somehow involved in the warning, but he was going to make sure he'd searched through every damn book in their vast library that referred to the mysterious magic.

"Knowledge is a formidable weapon," he assured his companion.

"Might makes right. Never forget that..." Zanna deliberately paused, her black gaze searing over him. "Son."

Azh bowed. "I'll keep that in mind...Mother."

He stepped through the barrier and left behind the female who might have given him life but had never seen him as more than a competitor for her position as queen.

* * * *

Wynn was running on empty by the time she plodded up the stairs leading to Hexx's apartment. She'd managed to return to the abandoned building with the skipping stone, but her magic had been sputtering on empty.

The only good news was that there'd been no stalker waiting for her in the darkness.

She huddled in the corner of the old fish shop for over an hour, assuming that he was waiting for his moment to pounce. When nothing happened, she'd slowly inched her way out of the building and down the silent streets.

Could she have finally gotten rid of him?

She grimaced.

She wasn't overly modest. She knew that she was smart, quick to adapt, and capable of making the hard choices. That had been the only way to survive. But she was no match for a dragon.

Dragon...

A shiver raced down her spine. She was too tired to try to wrap her brain around the fact that there was a mythical creature roaming the streets of New York City. But wait. He wasn't just roaming the streets. He was following her around like a hunter stalking his prey.

Her luck had been trending south lately, but this was ridiculous. Strange nightmares, weird magic she couldn't control, and now a dangerous, sexy, majestic...had she mentioned sexy...dragon chasing her?

Releasing a harsh sigh as she reached the top of the steps, Wynn pushed open the door. There was no surprise when it easily swung inward. Hexx was a true rat. As soon as he sensed a sinking ship he'd bailed. Which was why she was there.

Unless she got a few hours of sleep she was going to pass out.

Once she was rested she would try to figure out what she'd done to attract Azh's attention, and more importantly, how to get rid of him. He might be the most gorgeous male she'd ever encountered, but he was a complication. A huge, delicious, sexy...there it was again. Sexy.

No, no, no.

She sternly banished any thought of Azh and his sexy complications.

Entering the apartment, she crept through the stacks of boxes and totes, her muscles tense as she prepared to flee at the least hint of danger. By the time she reached the recliner set near the window, she had convinced herself she was alone. If there was anyone or anything hidden in the cramped space, she couldn't detect it.

For now that was good enough.

Flopping into the chair, she winced as a rusty spring jabbed into her butt. Hexx had worn the cushion as thin as a pancake. Unfortunately, beggars couldn't be choosers and she was too exhausted to try to find something more comfortable.

With a deep sigh, she pushed back the chair until it was in full reclining position and closed her eyes. With a speed that would shock anyone that had never been sleep deprived, physically exhausted, and magically drained, Wynn tumbled into a welcomed puddle of nothingness.

She drifted in the abyss for what felt like a second but might have been several hours before the nightmare found her.

It started as a regular dream. She was strolling through the streets of London, enjoying the sound of the nightly crowds spilling out of the local pubs. She didn't know where she was headed, and it didn't matter. It was enough to share the vibrant sense of joy that oozed from the locals. Humans might not be immortal, but they made up for their shortened life span by embracing each moment.

She turned the corner, belatedly realizing that she was heading to the small magic shop at the end of the block. It was owned by Axton and his clan of goblins who sold knock off cauldrons and crystal balls, as well as rare spices and herbs to the local coven. He was a regular customer who bought the low-ticket items she managed to steal.

Halfway down the block, Wynn abruptly stopped, hit by a nasty wave of magic. It felt like someone had tossed a bucket of filth from above. The magic poured over her and she abruptly realized that she was frozen in place. It was like her feet were stuck to the cobblestones and invisible bands were wrapped around her body. Tilting back her head, Wynn parted her lips to scream, only no sound came out.

She was completely helpless.

Her heart thundered in her chest, a layer of sweat coating her skin as she watched Axton step out of his shop, surrounded by a dozen lesser demons. None of them were particularly dangerous. The auras surrounding their bulky bodies were a dull red despite the fact they were living in the center of a powerful Gyre. But Wynn sensed a foul perversion wrapped around them. As if they were coated in evil.

Slowly they walked toward her, none of them speaking or even acknowledging each other. As if they didn't know anyone else was there. The silence made their slow advance creepy as hell. Then they moved through a pool of light from a streetlamp and the creep factor was cranked from high to a sizzling sense of panic.

Each of the demons was staring at her with hungry expressions and eyes that glowed with a sickly green light. As if they were infected by a putrefying disease.

Or possessed.

Horror beat through Wynn, her body bowing into a painful arch as she struggled to break free of the ruthless bonds. She couldn't budge. She was well and truly trapped.

Wynn silently screamed as the demons marched closer and closer, stretching out their hands. No! She couldn't let them touch her. She didn't know exactly what would happen, but she knew it would be bad. Really, really bad.

With a last desperate effort, Wynn bit her tongue hard enough to draw blood. The sharp pain was enough to shatter the nightmare, allowing her to wrench open her eyes and suck in deep gulps of air to fill her starved lungs.

It was getting worse, she silently acknowledged. The dreams were more vivid and the sense of danger more intense. As if the nightmares were learning how to transform into reality.

It was terrifying.

With an effort, Wynn pulled her fingernails out of the arms of the chair where they'd dug into the leather and forced herself to her feet. Her knees were shaky and her face drenched in sweat. She needed a shower and fresh clothes, but right now it was the sharp pangs of her stomach that demanded attention.

Squeezing through the stacks of boxes, Wynn stepped into the narrow opening where Hexx had a micro-fridge and microwave precariously perched on a wooden counter. She opened the fridge to discover a jug of sour milk and a couple containers of moldy takeout along with a six-pack of beer. With a grimace she shut the door and opened the cardboard box on the counter.

One glazed donut remained.

"Score!" she breathed, grabbing the pastry and shoving it in her mouth.

It was stale and the glaze stuck to her fingers, but it tasted like nirvana as she licked the sugar from her lips.

Unable to find anything else edible, Wynn was turning toward the nearby totes to grab a few items she could sell for some quick cash when the creak of the door hinges warned her that someone was entering the apartment.

Shit. She'd hoped that Hexx had been frightened enough to stay away for a few days. Now she'd have to deal with the idiot.

Licking the last of the stickiness from her fingers, she prepared to confront the approaching form, her brows knitting together as she realized she couldn't sense the creature. It wasn't a demon, that was for sure. Which meant it wasn't Hexx.

Was it her personal stalker? Probably.

Pretending she didn't notice her pulse picking up speed and her stomach fluttering like she was a teenager in one of the rom-coms she secretly adored, Wynn stepped toward the approaching form, her head held high.

"Are you back? I told you to stop spying on me, you creep."

"Creep? Who are you calling a creep? Rude." The chiding voice echoed through the cramped apartment. "At least, I'm not the one stealing from Hexx. Or eating his pastries. Good grief, woman. Taking a demon's last donut is downright cruel."

Wynn's eyes widened as the intruder stepped into the faint sliver of dawn sneaking through the skylight. He was short and squat with a big bushy beard and piercing green eyes. There was a weird cap stuck on his head with a dangling fuzzy ball and he was wearing...

She didn't know what the baggy pants and loose flannel top were supposed to be. PJs? Yes, it had to be pajamas, she decided, since he'd matched the bizarre outfit with a pair of furry slippers.

It would have been easy to mistake him for a confused human who'd wandered off the streets through the unlocked door. There were dozens of the poor souls in search of shelter. But one glance into those eyes spoke of an ancient wisdom and a power that couldn't come from a mere mortal.

"You're not the dragon," Wynn muttered in confusion.

"Nope."

"Or a vampire."

"Nope."

"Or a demon."

"Again...nope."

"What are you?"

The creature spread his arms, the scent of copper filling the air. "I'm like you. Unique to this world."

Wynn instinctively stepped back. There was no overt threat from the intruder, but the magic that leaked from him warned her that he could squash her like a bug without even trying.

Time to be moving on. With a practiced smile, Wynn leaned back against the counter, trying to look casual.

"Cool. Are you an alien?" She slowly inspected his bizarre clothing. "You look like Santa Claus."

"Ah." He touched a finger to the tip of his nose. "It's my special power."

"Is it? Do you have any others?" Wynn kept her smile intact as she focused on her inner strands of magic. She couldn't use the skipping stones, but she did have a thread that would make her invisible for a few minutes. Just long enough to escape. Assuming it bothered to work.

"I have an endless array of powers."

"Yeah, me too."

Finding the strand she'd been searching for, Wynn mentally wrapped it around her. Then, with a gentle push, she spread the magic from her head down to the tips of her toes. Goosebumps crawled over her skin, assuring Wynn it was working.

Thank the goddess.

Still, she forced herself to wait until she was certain that she was completely invisible before she cautiously edged her way around the stranger, keeping as much space between them as possible. Not easy considering that Hexx had the place crammed with his cheap-ass inventory.

The male stood calmly at the edge of the opening, waiting until she'd almost inched past him before his hand snapped out to grab her arm.

"I don't think so." He firmly tugged her back to the spot where she'd started. "We aren't done chatting."

Her illusion vanished with a puff of smoke, leaving Wynn exposed and pissed off.

"I'm done." She jerked her arm, trying to break free of his light grasp. "Let go of me."

"Not until I've had a little peek."

Wynn frowned as the creature leaned forward. What did he mean "have a little peek"? She arched back, her hips digging into the wooden counter as he stretched out his hand, clearly intending to touch her.

"Ew. I thought the dragon was the perv. You're—"

"Be quiet," he muttered, the green eyes unfocused as if he were looking through her, not at her.

"Hey." She hissed as his hand cupped her cheek, his touch gentle. "Stop it."

She tried to angle away, but the moment she felt the soft touch of his fingers, she was surrounded by a white mist. Was this an illusion? Or had she been transported to another dimension?

Holding herself perfectly still, Wynn cautiously glanced around. At first there was nothing to see beyond the shimmering fog. It swirled around her, as if it was dancing on a breeze she couldn't sense. Then, slowly the outline of a tall, broad-shouldered male began to form.

Wynn tilted back her head, her muscles clenching. She had no way to know if it was more dangerous to stay or to flee through the strange fog. All she could do was wait and see what happened.

The mist swirled again, parting to reveal the male standing directly in front of her.

The stranger was gut-wrenchingly beautiful, with smooth, bronzed skin and the features of a Greek god. His eyes glowed with a brilliant emerald power and his reddish-gold hair fell past his shoulders.

Wynn might have been impressed if she hadn't already encountered the dragon. Now she acknowledged that this male was too perfect. Too aloof. His power too extreme.

All in all, he was just too...much. He would pulverize her with his presence.

Plus, he didn't make her palms sweat and her blood sing with awareness, a voice whispered in the back of her mind.

Lost in her inane thoughts, Wynn wasn't prepared for the sudden scent of copper that laced through the mist. Wait. Her mouth dropped open, her terror replaced by shock as she realized that this was the same creature as the bizarre, bearded intruder in Hexx's apartment.

Was this his true shape? Probably. It was no wonder he went around the world as a scruffy vagrant. Hordes of women, along with hordes of men, would be following him through the streets, begging for his attention.

"What are you?" she at last managed to croak.

Indifferent to her amazement, the creature studied her with a piercing curiosity. "That's not the question."

Wynn's mouth felt oddly dry. "It's not?"

"No. The question is"—he lifted his arm to point at something in the distance—"what is that?"

A chill inched down Wynn's spine. She didn't want to see what he was pointing at. For some reason, the mere thought of it made her entire body shudder with fear. But the stranger gave a wave of his hand, and the mist ruthlessly parted, revealing the gaping hole in the floor that bubbled with a repulsive green goo.

"No, don't go over there," she rasped, horror racing through her as the stranger strode forward.

He was wearing a white robe that flowed around him like a river of satin, his hair floating on a sudden breeze. Like a god striding through the heavens.

The sight should have given her confidence. Instead she slapped her hands over her mouth as she fought the urge to scream. Even at a distance she could see the greenish goo bubbling and churning, clearly reacting to the presence of the stranger.

"Don't," she breathed. "Please don't."

The words had barely left her lips when the slime struck out, tendrils of magic snapping around the stranger. With a blinding speed the male was wrapped from shoulders to knees in the thick coils.

At the same time a blinding white light abruptly surrounded the stranger as he fought against the swift attack, forcing Wynn to squeeze her eyes shut. The ground shook beneath her feet, the stench of decay threatening to choke her.

"What's happening?" she demanded.

"Run."

"What?"

Shading her eyes, Wynn forced herself to look directly into the ball of light. She could vaguely make out the shape of the male who'd brought her to this place. He'd managed to break free of the tendrils and was spreading his arms wide as if trying to contain the brewing, toxic sludge that continued to strike out. But even as his magic pulsed outward, the greenish goo crept toward him, surrounding his feet in a circle of evil.

Wynn's mouth was dry, her heart struggling to beat. She didn't know what was happening, but the male had told her to run.

So she did.

Chapter 4

Wynn had no idea how long she fled through the silvery mist. It felt like an eternity, but she refused to stop, even when her knees threatened to collapse and her lungs screamed from sucking in the thick air. The green sludge had looked exactly like the glow in the eyes of the demons in her nightmares. That couldn't be a coincidence.

Not unless this was a nightmare too...

Locked in the weird fog, Wynn frantically searched for a way to escape. It wasn't until a hand reached out of the mist to grab her shoulder and give her a sharp shake that she abruptly snapped open her eyes to discover she was lying flat on her back in the middle of Hexx's kitchen.

Had it been a nightmare? She wasn't in the recliner, but maybe she had been sleepwalking to escape the creepy demons chasing her.

"Shit," a familiar voice moaned. "Now what have you done?"

With an effort, Wynn focused on the demon crouching next to her. Hexx looked like he'd spent the night hiding in the sewers. His hair was tangled, his clothes wrinkled, and there were streaks of dirt on his rat face. Plus, he carried a distinct whiff of something vile.

"Me?" she croaked, carefully pushing herself into a seated position. A wave of dizziness washed over her, but she managed to stay upright. She was taking that as a win. "I didn't do anything."

"Then what's that?" Hexx pointed toward the edge of the stacked boxes.

Wynn's heart sank as she grudgingly forced herself to glance toward the lump of flannel. She hadn't been sleepwalking. There really had been an intruder, and he'd really transported her to a misty dimension where the green sludge was lashing out of a cesspit.

And now he was passed out on the floor, probably trapped in the fog.

"He attacked me." She shakily rose to her feet, squashing any sense of guilt for leaving the creature alone with the bubbling evil.

She hadn't been the one to force him into the fog. And she certainly hadn't asked to be taken with him. If he was stuck, then that was his own damned problem, right?

Hexx shoved himself upright and moved to study the unconscious male. "Well, get him out of here."

"You get him out."

"Who is he?"

"I thought he was a sad homeless man looking for shelter. Now I don't know." Wynn rubbed her hands over her coat, trying to get rid of the dust. Had Hexx ever heard of a mop? The entire place needed a good scrubbing. "He might be a god."

"A god?" Hexx scowled, tentatively tapping the sleeping male with his toe. "He looks like Santa Claus."

"If he's Santa Claus, then he has enough power to walk between dimensions and to force me to go with him." Wynn shuddered. "I can assure you that he's not going around delivering presents to good boys and girls. He's destroying civilizations and wreaking havoc on lesser beings. Like Hercules or Thor, only with fewer hammers."

"Argh. Why? What have I done to deserve this?"

"I have no idea, but you might want to look into getting your chi cleansed." She walked forward, slapping the demon on the back. "Time to get going. Good luck, old friend. I'll be seeing you around."

"No!" Hexx grabbed her arm. "Don't you dare leave. Not without taking your creature with you."

"He's not mine."

"What am I supposed to do with him?"

She yanked out of his desperate grasp, moving to grab a filthy tea towel off the counter and throwing it over the sleeping male's face.

"There. Problem solved. See you around."

"Not if I see you first," Hexx said, watching her walk away with a jaundiced glare.

Wynn strolled through the narrow pathway, pretending a casual confidence that was at complete odds with the nausea rolling through her stomach and the sweat trickling down her spine. Right now all she wanted was a dark hole to crawl into so she could sleep in peace for the next month.

Reaching the front of the apartment, Wynn was pulling open the front door when she heard Hexx call out.

"Hey. Where's my donut?"

Wynn rolled her eyes. "Men and their donuts."

* * * *

Azh spent the next hours searching through the ancient scrolls stored in a forbidden area of the library. They weren't kept off limits just because they were fragile. Many of them contained prophecies and omens that a cunning dragon could use to terrify and bully the others into submission.

Dragons like his mother.

Azh wasn't a believer in prophecy. He understood that there were clairvoyants who claimed to have glimpses of the future, but they were so vague that any attempt to use the vision was a wasted effort. But among the scrolls was the earliest history of the dragons.

Many of his brothers and sisters dismissed them as myth. They didn't believe that dragons had once roamed another world, or that they'd been forced to flee, becoming refugees in this place. They were too proud to consider the possibility that they could be anything less than conquerors. And unfortunately, their violent past meant that the dragons who'd written the scrolls had been destroyed during various battles.

Translating the text without adding in his own prejudices to make it fit what he wanted to believe was a necessary but tedious task. A task that he was eager to put aside the second he felt the crack forming in the barrier.

Yes. He knew the opening would return. Not that he was happy that the Watcher hadn't managed to end the danger, he sternly told himself, scurrying through the silent lair to the outer courtyard. But he was increasingly convinced that the dragon magic wasn't a new threat. Instead, it was a very old enemy that had been lurking and waiting for a chance to strike.

It was going to take a dragon to piece together the clues from the past and stop the mysterious adversary from destroying them.

And if he was being honest, he was eager to track down the female who'd first lured him from his sleep.

Wynn and her mysterious dragon magic.

Stepping through the barrier, Azh tilted back his head and breathed in the muggy air. It was early evening and the backstreets of New York City were ripe with the scent of street food, potted flowers, and the trash cans overflowing onto the narrow sidewalk.

It should have assaulted his sensitive senses, but Azh felt pleasure rush through him. Unlike many dragons, he didn't disdain humans. Or even the demons who lived hidden among them. If he was chosen to become king, he intended to discover a way to live in harmony with the fragile creatures once they left their hibernation.

A worry for later.

Catching the unmistakable tingle of magic, Azh cut through the maze of alleys, at last locating his prey hidden in a mundane ranch-style home with a For Sale sign stuck in the front yard. He circled the property, searching for any hidden traps before he stepped onto the cement porch and boldly yanked open the front door.

He braced himself for a torrent of furious magic. Or even a physical attack. Wynn might not have the power of a dragon or vampire, but she was far from helpless. When nothing happened, he cautiously inched his way through the empty living room to the bedroom at the end of the narrow hallway. He felt a brush of magic as he stepped through the open doorway, but as far as he could tell it was nothing more threatening than a shield to keep out any nosy human who might be wandering around.

His wariness was replaced by genuine concern as he silently crossed the yellow shag carpeting to study the delicate form curled into a tight ball in the corner.

Was she hurt? The thought sent a blast of fury through Azh. If anyone dared to lay a hand on this woman he would...

The murderous thoughts were abruptly interrupted by the sound of a groggy voice floating through the darkness.

"Dammit. Are you back?"

"Like a bad penny."

Azh should have moved forward to tower over her huddled form. He needed to know how Wynn had crossed paths with the dragon magic. And every second that passed might put his people in danger. Instead, he remained in the center of the floor.

He told himself that it was no use forcing the information out of her. Not when her skill with magic was only surpassed by her skill in lying.

He didn't trust a word that came out of her mouth. He had to find a way to convince her to tell him the truth.

But there was also a part of him that refused to treat her as his enemy.

Until she proved she was a threat to the dragons, he intended to savor the fierce attraction that sizzled between them.

With an obvious effort, Wynn shoved herself into a standing position, her back braced against the wall.

"More like a bad dream."

Azh breathed in her fresh floral perfume threaded with a deeper, more complex scent, attempting to discover if she was injured. He couldn't smell blood or inner damage, but there was a distinct stench of copper clinging to her.

"The Watcher," he breathed, unthinkingly stepping toward her. "What did you do to him?"

Her eyes widened, almost as if he'd frightened her. Azh scowled. This woman had been spitting in his face just a few hours ago. Even after she discovered he was a dragon. What had changed?

It wasn't until her gaze swept over him, almost as if she were seeing him for the first time, that he realized he hadn't bothered to mute the dragon aura. The flares of gold and silver could blind a human. And even those with demon blood would find it overwhelming.

At last she licked her lips as if they were dry and stiffened her spine. "What are you talking about?"

Relief raced through him as Wynn at last managed to send him a bold glare, as if she refused to be daunted.

"The Watcher," he repeated. "I can smell his scent on you."

"I've never heard of one."

"He is supposed to be the referee who keeps the dragons and leeches from descending into a violent, chaotic war."

She looked genuinely confused. "There's an actual referee?"

"Yes." Azh shrugged. "According to my queen he is biased toward the leeches."

"And according to you?"

He moved forward, careful to leave space for her to escape from the corner. There was nowhere she could go that he couldn't find her.

"I'm more concerned with you."

She shoved her hands into her pockets, glaring at him in frustration. "Concerned or obsessed?"

"It could be both," he admitted. "Why do I smell the Watcher's scent?"

She clicked her tongue. "I don't know anything about the Watcher."

"Who have you been with?"

"Nobody...wait." She furrowed her brow, as if trying to pinpoint a memory. "There was a weird dude who attacked me in Hexx's apartment."

Heat seared through the air, like the blast from a furnace, as Azh moved to stand less than an inch from her. He swiftly searched for any hidden wounds that he might have missed.

"He attacked you?"

She lifted a hand, pressing it against his chest. "Okay, maybe he didn't attack me. But he somehow reached into my mind and then we were in this misty place with the yucky green sludge spreading out to wrap around him and... You know what? That all sounds crazy now that I'm saying it out loud. Probably it was just a nightmare."

Azh studied her for a long moment, then he shook his head, containing his angry heat. The Watcher was yet another problem for later. Right now, he needed to discover the source of the dragon magic.

"Tell me where your power comes from."

Her eyes narrowed at his command. "I'm not talking until you back up and give me some room."

"No."

"I can't think when you're crowding me."

Azh slowly smiled, pleasure sizzling through him. He planted a hand against the wall and leaned forward. So much for his promise not to intimidate her.

What was that human saying about the "road to hell and good intentions"?

"I have that effect on most females," he murmured.

"Gross." She made a sound of disgust, but her cheeks were flushed and the scent of her desire threaded the air. She might not like it, but the fierce awareness sparking between them was too powerful to deny. "Could your head get more bloated?"

"Probably." He held her wary gaze. "Where did your powers come from?"

There was a tense silence before she heaved a resigned sigh. "Fine. My mom was a fortune teller in a traveling circus and—"

"Stop," Azh interrupted the ludicrous story. "Tell me about the cave."

"A specific cave. Or caves in general?"

"The one that always is included in your wild tales."

She flashed a taunting smile, but she lowered her lashes to hide her stunning lavender eyes. "I don't know what you mean. There's never been a cave in my charming folktales."

Azh lowered his head, brushing his cheek over the smooth blond hair. Someday very soon he was going to release those satiny strands from her braid to watch them fan over her naked body.

"Stubborn." His voice was rough as his body hardened with need. It'd been a very long time since he'd indulged his most primitive passions. He had no doubt when he finally claimed this woman it was going to be epic.

"Not stubborn...bored," she insisted, pushing against his chest. "Time for me to move along."

He chuckled, skimming his lips down her cheek before burying his face in the curve of her throat. Flames danced over his skin as he absorbed her essence.

"You don't smell bored."

"Gah. Don't sniff me."

"You smell...hungry."

"Impossible. I just ate a yummy donut."

"It's not food you're hungry for."

Her lips parted to deny his claim, but the violent shiver that raced through her body ruined her pretense of indifference.

"You're burning me," she instead accused.

"No I'm not. My fire is created for pleasure, not pain. If you're overheating it's not my fault." He licked the skin above her pounding pulse at the base of her throat. She tasted of warm female temptation, rich magic, and dragon. He didn't know how it was possible, but it was an intoxicating combination. "Or maybe it is my fault."

Her head tilted back, as if inviting his touch. But before Azh could wrap her in his arms, she sucked in a sharp breath, as if suddenly coming to her senses.

"No," she rasped.

Azh didn't hesitate. Stepping back, he allowed his flames to fade. The finest treasures were always the most difficult to obtain, and he didn't doubt for a second that Wynn would be worth any amount of effort.

Besides, he couldn't allow himself to become distracted by his intense attraction to this woman. His people depended on him to keep them safe.

"This is the last time I ask nicely. Tell me where you got the power."

She stuck her chin in the air. Defiant to the end. "I don't know anything about the magic or the power you're looking for. I'm just an average woman trying to scrape by. Something that would be a lot easier if you would leave me alone."

He folded his arms over his chest, pleased when her eyes widened as his muscles rippled beneath his silk shirt.

"If you're not lying—which seems unlikely since you lie about everything—I would think you would be eager for my assistance."

She rolled her eyes. "I've been taking care of myself for a very long time. Why would I need your assistance?"

"I have the answers to the origin of the magic."

"If that was true, you wouldn't be harassing me."

He shrugged. "Fine, I don't have answers, but I do have a theory."

Her brows snapped together, but he sensed her sudden interest. "This is a trick."

"Allow me to prove my claim."

He turned to the side, pointing to a spot on the wall. Then moving his hand in a slow circle, he created a spinning circle of smoke.

"An illusion," Wynn muttered.

"You aren't the only one with tricks."

"Can you breathe fire?"

He glanced toward her, a slow smile curving his lips. "Only if you ask very nicely."

"Lame." Her frown abruptly deepened. "Wait. Are you creating a magic hole?"

A laugh was wrenched from his throat. "Magic hole?"

"What do you want me to call it?"

"A small window that allows you a glimpse into our private lair."

She warily watched the smoke spread to reveal the towering shelves that held countless books and scrolls and precious manuscripts protected by layers of magic.

"No weapons," he assured his companion. "Nothing more dangerous than a book."

"Like books aren't the most dangerous weapons in the world."

Azh jerked at her soft words. She understood. This aggravating, stubborn, unpredictable, completely glorious woman understood. Was it any wonder that he'd been immediately fascinated by her? It wasn't just her rare beauty. Or the way she stirred his passions. Dragons enjoyed companionship with lots of partners over the endless centuries.

But this one...

It was as if she touched a part of him that no other creature had ever managed to reach.

His beast stirred, waking from the deep slumber of hibernation. It studied the tiny wisp of a woman in bemusement. Ah, so this was what the fuss was about, it sleepily acknowledged. Good. He was pleased. She was a tasty morsel.

With an effort, Azh ignored the rumblings of the dragon.

"You're right. They are dangerous. This one, however, is dedicated to the history of my people."

He felt a portion of her tension ease. "A history of dragons? You didn't come here to bore me to death, did you?"

"There are a few images I think you'll find interesting."

"If I let you blabber about the dragons for a while, will you leave me alone?"

"Probably not."

She glared at him, but there was something that might have been curiosity shimmering in the lavender eyes.

"What is it?"

"The histories speak of a time when the dragons lived in another place."

"You mean like another country?"

"Another realm." Azh wasn't concerned that he was revealing the dragons' deepest, darkest secrets. Most of his people had forgotten their distant lore. "It's referred to as Kazak. Or the homeland."

"So why did you come to this world?"

"According to legend we were fleeing a corruption."

"A corruption. What does that mean?"

His jaws clenched. That question had been a source of annoyance to him for eons. He'd gone through every scroll, manuscript, book, and even personal diaries he could find, but there'd been nothing to reveal the exact nature of the "corruption." He didn't know if it was a powerful enemy that had driven the dragons to this world, or a toxic destruction of their homeland, or a disease that had forced them to flee. And the fact he couldn't find information to understand their ancient foe had been a thorn in his side. Unlike most of his people, he wasn't willing to dismiss the fact their past was shrouded in mystery. Without the truth of where they came from, there was no way to guarantee their mistakes weren't being repeated.

"Again the histories are vague and different scholars have a variety of explanations."

"Wait." She blinked. "Dragons have scholars?"

Azh flinched as her disbelief scraped against a raw nerve. Dammit.

"Why is that shocking? Do you assume that all dragons are brainless savages?"

Chapter 5

Wynn sighed. She hadn't meant to insult him. At least not that time. But she was struggling to think clearly.

She'd found this empty house after fleeing Hexx's apartment. It was small, nondescript, and tucked into a human neighborhood far from the nearest demon lair. The perfect place to disappear. After creating a protective barrier, she managed to fall into a deep sleep for the first time in forever. She didn't know how long it'd lasted, but night had obviously fallen again, so at least twelve hours. Was it any wonder she was fuzzy when Azh had woken her?

Then, just when she managed to clear her brain of the cobwebs, she'd gotten her first good look at the aggravating creature.

It had felt like an earthquake was ripping the ground from beneath her feet, dropping her into a void of stunned bewilderment.

Her first encounter with Azh had been unnerving. He was without a doubt the most obscenely gorgeous, ruthlessly sexy male she'd ever met. But now...

But now he was earthshattering.

Wynn's mouth felt weirdly dry and her heart pounded as she took in the blazing, devastatingly flawless beauty of the male standing in front of her. The thin blade of a nose. The sharp cheekbones and the lush lips. It was as if he'd removed a dampening spell to reveal the pure precision of his lean features and the smoky gray eyes that burned with a tumultuous power. His skin was smooth, but it shimmered with a silvery hint of unseen scales. And his aura...it raged around him like a fiery tornado. Solar flares of magic brighter than anything she'd ever seen.

It was spectacular.

This was the real Azh. Even if he was in human form.

Wynn cleared the lump from her throat, struggling to follow the conversation. She sensed it was important.

"I never really thought about dragons or their schooling," she admitted. "I thought you were a myth."

The magic of the Gyre pulsed beneath her feet, as if reacting to his annoyance. "Can I continue?"

She instinctively wrapped her arms around her waist, struggling to stand her ground against the raw blast of his male presence.

"Go for it."

He took a moment, as if gathering his composure. Then, with a twist of his hand, he gestured toward the hole he'd created in the air. A thick leatherbound book on the highest shelf floated forward, moving through the opening and floating in front of Azh. With a casual motion he grabbed the heavy tome and bent down to lay it on the floor, as if indifferent to the years of filth embedded in the shag carpeting.

Curious in spite of herself, Wynn watched in silence as he flipped open the book and stepped back, the heat of his magic swirling through the air.

Pleasure sizzled down her spine as the magic washed over her like a caress. Had it been on purpose? Or had she got caught in a rogue wave of power? Not that it mattered, she sternly warned herself. The only reason she wasn't trying to escape was because he promised her answers.

Once she knew what the magic was and how to get rid of it, she was going to take a tip from the dragons and find herself a hidden lair and hibernate for the next month. Maybe the next year.

Thankfully unaware of her intense reaction, Azh released his magic with a sharp motion. A mist swirled over the book and the detailed illustrations that were painted onto the yellowed pages began to glow. Almost as if they were coming to life.

Wynn instinctively froze as the image of a silver dragon suddenly hovered in midair. She was a breathtaking creature with delicate wings spread wide and a solid body that narrowed to a long, elegantly curved neck. Slowly the mist widened, allowing Wynn to view the illustration behind the dragon. She was soaring through an open sky with her head tilted toward the two reddish suns and her mouth open to reveal her rows of lethal fangs. As if she were screeching a challenge to the gods.

"There is endless speculation on how we arrived in this world, but all historians agree that we were led here by Gabriela, our most fierce warrior." Azh broke the silence.

"Awesome. She sounds like a kickass female. My favorite. But what does it have to do with me?"

"There's also a universal agreement that we were fleeing an unknown evil," he continued, ignoring her interruption. "Most books refer to it as some sort of corruption."

Wynn frowned. "And?"

He waved his hand and the mist swirled to reveal a different engraving of the silver dragon. She was no longer soaring through air. Instead, she was wedged into a large cave with her head bent low as fire bellowed from her parted mouth.

"Gabriela created the rift to bring us into this world and then sacrificed herself to block the opening so we couldn't be followed by the mysterious enemy that was chasing us."

"Wait." A knot twisted Wynn's gut as the mist cleared to reveal a bright green slime, oozing over the floor of the cave. It was horrifyingly familiar. "That's the corruption?"

Azh sent her a curious glance. "It's an artistic representation. I'm not sure how accurate it is. Why?"

Wynn licked her dry lips. "I don't want that nasty crap coming here."

"Neither do I. Which is why I've been following you."

"Are you suggesting I've been corrupted?"

He narrowed his smoky gray gaze. "No, but your reaction is interesting."

Wynn snapped her lips together. Her shock at seeing the glowing green had made her reckless. She was giving away too much. With an effort she folded her arms over her stomach and heaved a resigned sigh.

"Well, I'm glad I'm interesting, because you're not. In fact, you're starting to bore the hell out of me."

"You don't want to hear the story?"

She hunched a shoulder. "Fine, yes. Just get it over with."

His lips twitched. He wasn't fooled. "After Gabriela closed the rift and sealed out the evil, she transformed herself into a statue that was left to stand guard at the rift," he said. "There are some who believe it was left as an early warning in case the corruption attempted to follow us. There are others who claimed that Gabriela had foreseen the day the evil would enter this world and that she left her magic to battle against it."

Wynn returned her attention to the image in the swirling mist, her heart missing a beat. A statue. That might very well be what had been the start of her misery. She waited, expecting the image to change. When it remained on the dragon, she sent Azh an impatient glare. The spurting fire thing was impressive, but it didn't give her the answers she needed.

"What did the statue look like?"

"No one is certain." The mist abruptly evaporated and the book slammed shut, the scent of brimstone wafting through the air. "There are some who swear it was shaped like a small dragon, and another one claimed it was a tall woman with a sword over her head, and there's those who were certain it looked like a plain stone so no one could find it."

"Seriously?" Wynn felt a pang of annoyance. "No one knows for sure?"

Azh shrugged, bending down to pick up the book. "The dragons were still traumatized and in a hurry to flee from the rift in case their enemy attempted to follow them. They didn't bother to sketch the statue."

"So go back and find it. Surely you'll know what it's intended to do once you hold it?"

"That's impossible."

"Why?"

Azh gestured toward the small opening into the dragon lair. Moments later a long leather coat appeared. Shrugging into the well-worn jacket that reached past his knees, he tucked the book in a pocket. Then, with a wave of his hand, he shut the opening.

"Because the location of the rift was erased from the minds of the dragons," he at last admitted, as if he'd been deciding how much to reveal. Fair enough. It was dangerous to divulge that his people had a secret kryptonite. "All they could recall was running through a deep cave and at last finding a tunnel leading to the sunshine."

Wynn's frustration deepened. "Why was it erased?"

"Those who were fleeing said that it was a last act of magic by Gabriela. I presume it was to make sure that no one was foolish enough to try to open the rift and return to Kazak."

And that was that, Wynn acknowledged with a burst of disappointment. Even if she had somehow stumbled across the mysterious statue, she had no way of knowing where or even what it looked like.

She was back to square one. Only now she had an aggravating dragon pestering her every move.

"A fascinating story, but I still don't know why you've been stalking me."

"I sensed the dragon magic beginning to stir a few months ago. At first it was nothing more than a brush across my mind. Like a caress. It woke me from my slumbers."

Wynn rolled her eyes. Her luck really had gone south if she'd managed to wake this male from his hibernation just by walking around. What else had she woken? The question doubled the size of the knot in her stomach.

"What makes you think the magic has anything to do with the..." She bit off the word corruption. She didn't want to explain why she was obsessed with the green goo. "Gabriela?"

"I didn't at first. I assumed a dragon had escaped from hibernation."

"Escaped like you?" she taunted.

"It's my duty to protect my people." There was an edge in his voice that hinted he didn't like the direction of the conversation. As if he had something to hide. "Once I caught sight of you I realized that you weren't a dragon. Which meant the power must have come from somewhere else. The most logical answer is that the magic was hidden in a relic that you possess."

"Even if I did have a magical relic, it doesn't mean it's linked to Gabriela," she insisted.

He shook his head. "The magic resonating inside you is old. The oldest I've ever felt." He stepped forward. "Where is it?"

There was a sudden, crushing wave of compulsion, as if his patience had snapped.

Wynn sensed the magic slam into her, but astonishingly, she didn't shatter beneath the blast. In fact, she managed to meet him glare for glare.

How dare he try to force her to bend to his will?

"It's not here," she said in cold tones.

"Then take me to it."

"You're not the boss of me."

The magic vanished, along with the obnoxious arrogance, leaving behind a male who'd reached his limit.

"Dammit, Wynn, this isn't a game," he rasped. "Dragon relics are unique. The magic inside them can't be used by demons or mages or witches. Those who try are eventually destroyed. But only after they are driven to madness."

Wynn sniffed at the warning, acting like his words hadn't touched a raw nerve. Was he right? Had she stumbled across an item that was infused with dragon magic and it was taking control of her? And were the nightmares a form of encroaching insanity?

"You're trying to scare me," she said.

"If I wanted to scare you, then I'd threaten to torture the information out of you." It wasn't a warning. Just a plain statement of fact. He was physically stronger than her, even in his human form. And if he decided to shift into his dragon...well, she would be toast. Literally. She couldn't squash her instinctive shudder and he clicked his tongue. "Wynn, I have no desire to hurt you. Or to see you hurt," he assured her. "All I want is the statue."

She forced herself to meet his fierce gaze. He was right. This was no time for games. She needed to return to her search for the source of the magic plaguing her. And she needed to do it without Azh breathing fire down her neck.

"I don't have it."

"Then where is it?"

"I don't know."

"Wynn." Her name came out on a low sexy growl.

Heat swirled through her, but she pretended her toes weren't curling in response. "I truly don't know, I swear."

"Then how are you tapping into the magic?"

"I'm not," she insisted. "I have no idea what it can or can't do...wait." Wynn's protest faltered as she felt a familiar tugging inside her. As if the skipping stones were being activated. "What's happening?"

Azh's brows snapped together as he reached out, clearly intending to grab her arm. "Don't you dare leave."

"I'm not doing this. It's the stupid dragon magic. It keeps doing weird things."

"Wynn!" he snarled, his fingers brushing her arm just as the magic snapped into place and she was jerked through the darkness, hurtling to...

Hell, she didn't know.

* * * *

Tia clicked her tongue as she stood in front of the Witch's Brew. Really. The place might delight the local humans, they seemed to adore all things cutesy-cute and downright sappy, but how could any self-respecting mage create such a travesty? From the glowing neon light above the door to the front windows painted with bright flowers and butterflies to the smell of blueberry muffins, it screamed with a cloying sweetness.

In contrast, her own lair near Pike's Peak in Colorado was an imposing castle surrounded by towering mountains and thick woods, not to mention guarded by a dozen demons.

She was one of the most powerful mages in the world, who ran a multimillion-dollar empire. She expected her lair to reflect the status she'd earned in blood, sweat, and tears.

It was a shame that Maya didn't share her appreciation for creating the proper image. Her one-time friend could be living in a mansion or a penthouse suite. Especially now that she'd mated with a nasty leech. Instead she continued to run a coffee shop and live in the basement like a savage. If she'd stayed with Tia all those years ago, they could be ruling the world. Or at least the parts of the world worth ruling.

With another click of her tongue, Tia laid her hand on the door and used her powers to smash through the protective layers of magic. Over the past year she'd started the painful process of forgiving Maya for abandoning her just days after they'd defeated the monster who'd held them captive for decades. And they'd started the tentative process of rebuilding a friendship.

Tonight, however, she was in a hurry and in no mood to play nice.

Stepping inside, she closed the door, glancing around the shadowed shop. She hadn't really expected to find the male she was searching for sitting at one of the tiny tables sipping a cappuccino and nibbling on a pastry, although she wouldn't put it past him. He was the most aggravating, unpredictable, elusive creature she'd ever encountered. It would be just like him to fall off the face of the earth and then reappear, eating a blueberry muffin as if nothing had happened.

Focused on her dark thoughts, Tia abruptly cursed as an unseen magic brushed over her. The touch was as light as a feather, but she wasn't fooled. She knew a snare when she idiotically stepped into one.

"What the hell?" Tia stood stiffly in the center of the tiled floor, refusing to embarrass herself further by struggling against the tentacles of magic wrapping around her. Instead she sent a silent command to Maya. "Release me. Immediately."

Seconds later the steel door at the back of the room was shoved open. Tia's talent as a dream teller meant that she could easily create a mental connection with anyone, although it made it easier if she was familiar with them. At one time she and Maya had often communicated without speaking.

The younger woman moved toward Tia, wearing a pair of white slacks and a yellow silk shirt despite the late hour. Her black hair was silky smooth as it framed her pale face, brushing against the scars that marred her jawline.

Scars Maya had received saving Tia's life.

"Tia." Maya arched her brows in surprise, although it was obvious by her clothing and the powerful snare that she'd been expecting company. "What are you doing sneaking around my coffee shop?"

"Clearly I'm here to see you," Tia said in cold tones.

"Have you heard of knocking? Or better yet, sending me a text to warn me that you're about to break-and-enter my lair?"

"Just release me."

Maya ran a suspicious gaze over Tia, lingering on the white tunic dress that hugged her tall, slender body and the priceless pearl choker around her neck before lifting to study Tia's narrow face dominated by dark eyes and stern features emphasized by her silver-gray hair pulled into a tight bun.

As if satisfied this wasn't some sort of trick, Maya waved her hand in an impatient motion, releasing the snare.

"Fine. Now tell me why you're here."

"That exasperating male," Tia muttered.

Maya arched a brow. "Ravyr is currently in Greece, so I assume you're referring to some other exasperating male?"

"Joe."

"The Watcher slash Benefactor slash pain-in-my-ass Joe?" Maya demanded.

Tia sniffed. Joe was a pain in the ass, but it bothered her that he'd been a pain in the ass to Maya first. It wasn't jealousy. It was... Well, she wasn't sure what it was, but she didn't like it.

"That's the one," she said between clenched teeth.

Maya shrugged. "He left here after Ravyr moved in. The place wasn't big enough for both their egos."

"No crap."

"Why are you looking for him?"

"He's in trouble."

"Joe?" Maya shook her head. "I don't believe it. That guy is indestructible."

Tia might have agreed if Joe hadn't spent the past months popping in and out of her castle as if he were a welcomed guest. Slowly she'd become accustomed to his presence, and if she was being honest, even looking forward to the nights he would magically appear to lessen the echoing emptiness of her castle. And during those nights she'd caught glimpses of the vast sense of duty that he shouldered and the relentless attacks against the peace he was struggling to protect. He might be close to a god, but he wasn't impervious to danger.

"He pretends to be indestructible," she agreed, "but he's not."

Maya stilled, staring at Tia in confusion. Then suddenly her eyes widened. "Wait. Are you two—"

"No," Tia snapped, battling the revealing blush that threatened to stain her cheeks. It was nobody's business if she spent her nights fantasizing about what she would do if she ever got the delectable male in her bed. "You know my feelings about domineering, arrogant jerks who think they can control a woman."

Maya's lips twitched. "But you rushed here from Colorado to check on him?"

"Because he won't get out of my head." It wasn't a lie. The whispers had started last night and continued through the morning hours. At last she'd ordered her jet to be prepared so she could track down the bothersome pest. "He keeps saying the same word over and over and it's driving me nuts."

"Okay. What's he saying?"

"Run."

"Run?"

"That's all I could make out, but there was pain in his voice, as if he's being attacked."

Maya's amusement faded. She understood the danger, just like Tia did. It was one thing for the mysterious Watcher to be annoying. It was another for him to be in a situation that was causing him genuine pain. What could hurt a god-adjacent creature who had seemingly limitless powers?

The answer couldn't be anything good.

"Can you contact him?" Maya asked.

Tia shook her head. "No, and when I try there's a weird static hum. Like something is interfering in our connection."

"You can't determine if it's a demon or vampire that's creating the interference?"

"It doesn't feel like it's coming from an individual creature. It's almost as if he's being smothered by layers of magic that's continuing to spread. Which is why I have to find him. The sooner the better."

Maya nodded in sharp agreement. "What makes you think he's here?"

"I'm following the static inside my head."

"That's a sentence you don't hear every day."

Tia ignored the woman's teasing. "It brought me to New York. Naturally, I assumed he might have returned to visit you," she grudgingly admitted, once again feeling a pang of emotion that was definitely, absolutely not jealousy.

"I haven't seen him."

Tia glanced toward the front window, futilely hoping to catch a glimpse of Joe, looking like a harmless drifter as he leaned against the lamppost. There was nothing.

With a shake of her head she returned her attention to Maya. "Has anything happened in the area that would have attracted his attention?"

"Not really. I..." Maya's gaze narrowed. "Wait. You said there was some sort of interference?"

"Yes. Does that mean something to you?"

"It might. There's been a series of burglaries up and down the East Coast."

Tia made a sound of disappointment. She wasn't going to waste her time chasing a petty criminal.

"I doubt Joe would be interested in a thief. He has more important worries."

"This wasn't a regular thief," Maya insisted.

There was no missing the edge in Maya's voice. Tia arched a brow. "It sounds personal."

Maya pinched her lip, confirming Tia's suspicion she held a personal grudge against the burglar.

"She hit Witch's Brew last night. I had a trap set for her but she managed to walk through my magical locks and shield as if they weren't there."

Tia blinked in surprise, recalling the painful bonds of air that had wrapped around her just moments ago.

"The same one you set for me tonight?"

"Well, it wasn't intended for you, but it was the same spell." Maya deliberately paused. "Along with help from Peri."

Tia's attention was fully captured. Peri's wild magic could hold a feral vampire captive. If there was a creature out there who could bust through both Maya's and Peri's combined strength, then she needed to know about it.

"What did the mystery thief steal?"

"Junk." Maya waved her hand toward the open door that led to her private lair. "I have a hundred powerful charms, potions, and spell books in the vault but she grabbed the least valuable objects. I think it was on purpose."

"Why would she do that? It doesn't make sense."

"Yeah, well, it makes even less sense that I tracked her to a nearby alley where her trail disappeared."

"Did she leave anything behind?"

Maya reached into the pocket of her slacks to pull out a small plastic bag. "A strand of hair. I tried a locating spell but there's an annoying buzz that blocked me. It might be the same interference you're experiencing."

Tia held out her hand, watching as a silvery-blond strand floated out of the plastic bag to land in the center of her palm. It looked human, but there was no way to tell for sure. Not without using her magic. Right now, however, she was more interested in whether or not it could lead her to Joe.

Closing her eyes, Tia tapped into the tumultuous power that flowed through her blood. The magic sizzled and snarled, demanding to be released even as she grimly wrestled for control. Every mage was different when they spoke of their magic. For some it was a sweet, gentle surge. For others it was a bubbling pool. For Tia it was a crushing avalanche that cascaded through her, threatening to explode the moment she was distracted.

It was a dangerous, intoxicating sensation, but it demanded her full concentration to avoid disaster.

With care not to destroy the strand of hair, Tia released a trickle of power, forging a mental connection. Almost immediately the image of a woman with pale hair pulled into a braid and startling lavender eyes formed in her mind. Tia had never seen her before, and even with her magic blasting through her it was impossible to determine if she was a demon or a mage.

Locking on the image, Tia called up her memories of Joe. His long, coppery hair and elegantly sculpted features with eyes that burned with an emerald fire. And his tall, muscular body that was too perfect to be human.

The image of the unknown woman blurred before re-forming to reveal her standing in the center of an apartment.

"There she is."

"You found her?"

With an effort, Tia widened the vision to take in a filthy room that was stuffed with boxes. In the background was a male goblin with long hair and a pale red aura.

"I can see her standing next to Joe," Tia said, unable to determine if she was witnessing an image or a memory. "There's a demon there. It looks like he has something tattooed on his face. Flames?"

"Hexx." Maya spit out the name like a curse. "You've got to be kidding me. He's like the plague. He just keeps coming back no matter how many times I try to scrub the streets of his annoying presence."

"You know where to find him?" Tia demanded.

"Unfortunately. I'll grab my satchel."

Tia didn't bother to respond, heading outside to where her car was waiting. Lynch, a large goblin who'd been her personal bodyguard for years, was behind the steering wheel, showing no surprise when Maya quickly joined Tia and they slid into the back seat.

Maya gave Lynch the address before leaning back against the plush leather seat, content to allow the silence settle between them. It was nice, Tia decided with a pang of surprise. She'd been so angry with this woman for so long. For decades she blamed Maya for walking away when they could have combined their powers to make themselves invincible. But in truth, she'd been angry that her friend had abandoned her when she needed her the most.

A half hour later, the car swerved toward the curb and stopped in front of a single-story brick building mashed between a liquor store and a pet grooming salon. There was a blinking neon sign that promised easy credit loans although the large front window was dark and empty.

"This is it."

Tia tilted back her head, opening her mind. This time she didn't try to connect with anyone. She simply absorbed the thoughts and emotions that drifted toward her.

She brushed away the nearby humans walking down the sidewalk arm in arm. And the handful of fairies stumbling out of a nearby bar. Impatience blasted through her, and it was only years of training that kept her from leaping from the car and charging into the building.

There was no point in alerting anyone that she was searching for Joe until she knew his exact location. Surprise might very well be her only advantage.

At last she felt a familiar mental pattern, easing the icy fear that had somehow wrapped around her heart.

"He's here," she announced, opening her eyes. "But his power is muted."

"Maybe he's trying to stay incognito," Maya suggested. "I assumed he was a homeless man for years."

"Maybe." Tia had been around Joe when he was in one of his human disguises, but there'd never been this strange static that continued to buzz in her head like an angry wasp. "But this feels different." Reaching out, she shoved open the door, glancing toward her companion. "Ready?"

A smile of anticipation curved Maya's lips. "Always."

Tia returned her smile as they climbed out of the vehicle. This was the Maya Rosen she'd known and loved when they'd been imprisoned together in Batu's lair. The woman who always had her back and never retreated from any challenge, no matter what the risk.

Moving in silence, Maya led Tia around the side of the building and up a narrow flight of stairs to an upper-story apartment. The younger mage paused to pull a glass vial from her satchel, pouring it over the door to reveal any hidden snares.

Tia ground her teeth. It was smart to make sure they weren't charging into a trap. But she wasn't in the mood to be smart. She wanted to bust through the door and kick the ass of whoever was hurting Joe.

As if sensing her seething impatience, Maya sent her a warning glance before opening the door and stepping over the threshold. Once again, she halted, this time to bend down and create a web of magic that spread over the floor. It would reveal anyone who might be inside, even if they'd created an illusion to hide their presence.

"Empty," Maya at last announced, straightening to switch on the overhead light. A bare bulb hanging from an overhead wire sparked to life, spilling out a dull yellowish glow. "But you're right the thief was here." Maya reached out to grab the crystals that had been left on top of a plastic tote, her expression suddenly grim. "These were stolen from my vault."

Tia couldn't sense the thief, which was weird, but she did feel something. A power signature hummed through the air, as if it was so powerful that it'd engraved itself in the very fabric of the building, continuing to vibrate long after the creature had disappeared.

"Something else too. A dangerous power," she breathed, reluctantly squeezing between the stacks of boxes to search the disgusting apartment. Whatever had been there might very well be responsible for...

Her thoughts were shattered as she caught sight of the crumpled form lying motionless on the floor. Even with the ridiculous pajamas and a towel thrown over his head, she knew exactly who it was.

"Joe!"

"Tia, no." Maya grasped her arm, trying to keep her from rushing forward. "We don't know what happened to him."

"He's in trouble." Jerking her arm free, Tia moved to kneel next to the unconscious male, shoving aside the towel as she laid her hand on his chest.

"Dammit, Tia," Maya muttered.

Tia ignored her friend, concentrating on the steady beat of Joe's heart. He was alive, thank the goddess. And seemingly uninjured. At least physically.

Which meant that the attack was on a psychic level.

Tia didn't hesitate as she opened her mental connection with the unconscious male. Whatever was attacking Joe had to be incredibly strong. Far stronger than a mere mage, but she was a dream teller. This place was her specialty.

On cue, Tia found herself standing in the middle of a swirling mist, the coppery scent of Joe settling around her. She sucked in a deep breath, allowing his presence to ease the fear that had scrubbed her nerves raw. Only when her emotions were tightly under control did she use his scent to lead her through the mist to discover him bound from head to foot in thick tentacles that glowed with a sickly green light. The same green sludge bubbled in a large pool near his feet.

Tia halted, her fear returning with a blast of urgency. What the hell was that? It looked like a malignant goo, but she sensed a cunning awareness in the foamy depths. Whatever the thing was, it was alive and aware of what it was doing.

"Joe, can you hear me?" she rasped.

There was no answer. Hardly a surprise. The male was hidden from head to toe by the tentacles. It was only the epic crash of powers that battled against one another, rattling the ground beneath her feet and thickening the air, that reassured her that he was holding his own against the evil slime.

So what could she do? Right now it felt as if they were at a stalemate, but the balance was so fragile any distraction might cause a disaster.

Paralyzed by a sense of helplessness, Tia abruptly froze as an unexpected heat brushed against her back. It wasn't a physical touch, but someone had passed by with an enormous amount of magic. Spinning around, she studied the mist. She couldn't see anything, but she wasn't fooled. There'd been a presence behind her. A powerful creature who'd been close enough to set off her instinctive warning bells.

"Who's there? Show yourself," she commanded, her voice echoing eerily through the vast emptiness. The mist continued to swirl, stubbornly hiding whoever was lurking just out of sight. A shiver raced through her even as she straightened her spine. She'd wondered how she could help Joe. Now she knew. Remaining in the mist, she reached out to her companion. "Maya."

A second later Maya appeared, glancing around in confusion. "You rang?"

"I need to remain here and protect the Watcher."

Maya's gaze at last landed on the green pile of slime, her eyes widening as she realized that it was Joe being smothered under the thick tenacles.

"Dear goddess," she muttered. "What is that?"

"I'm not sure, but we don't want it getting loose."

"No shit." Maya shuddered. "What do you want from me?"

"It's too dangerous to try and interfere in Joe's battle, but I've sensed a presence in the mist."

Maya arched a brow. "Now?"

"It's able to stay hidden from view, but I felt a pulse of their power just moments ago. The fact that they're lurking out of sight means that they aren't here to do anything good." Tia moved to stand as close to Joe as she dared, slowly lowering herself to sit on the ground. "I need to stay here, but that leaves me vulnerable."

Maya nodded. "I'll weave a layer of protection around the building. Nothing's going to get in or out without me knowing."

Tia held her friend's gaze. "It will be stronger if we weave the spell together."

"You're right," Maya agreed without hesitation. "I'll start outside and weave it toward the roof before adding another layer around the apartment." She paused, her brows pulling together. "Be careful."

Breaking their mental connection, Maya disappeared, and Tia impatiently waited for the younger mage to tap into her magic. Once she felt the familiar tingles, Tia released a burst of power to join with Maya, working together with an ease that only came from years of practice. Patiently they weaved the delicate strands of magic to form a shield that should be able to keep out any enemy. Then, with one last burst, they sealed the barrier in place.

Once she was done, Tia released her magical link to Maya and heaved a harsh sigh. It hadn't been that difficult, but she was more frustrated than she wanted to admit that she could do nothing to stop the violent magic that was crushing Joe. What if he didn't survive? What if...

"*Tia.*"

Clearly sensing her rising panic, Joe's voice whispered through the air, easing the knots that had formed in the pit of her stomach. With an effort, she squared her shoulders and scooted so she was facing the mist.

She was Tia. The most feared mage in the entire world. She didn't give in to hysterics. Joe was going to defeat the nasty, slimy evil. And she was going to make sure nothing happened to him while he did his thing.

"I'm here, you annoying pest. I've got your back," she assured him. "Just take care of your business so we can go home."

Chapter 6

Wynn was shocked when she reappeared in the alley across from the Witch's Brew. The glitches in her magic usually meant a spell didn't work or that it repeated itself over and over. It didn't often do something completely unexpected.

Leaning against the side of a Chinese takeout joint, Wynn waited for Azh to make his appearance. It was becoming a familiar trend. She disappeared and then he followed. Even if she hadn't actually intended to disappear on this occasion.

But as the minutes ticked past she slowly accepted that he wasn't coming. Either her impromptu vanishing act had hidden her trail too well to follow, or he'd lost interest now that he realized she didn't have the mysterious dragon statue.

Telling herself she was happy that the intrusive male wasn't around to pester her, Wynn darted across the street and pressed her way through the layers of magic wrapped around the Witch's Brew. Last time she'd been in the building she'd been focused on finding the vault where the powerful relic was supposedly being hidden. She didn't have time to stop and enjoy the yummy treats that filled the shop with a mouthwatering scent.

Her stomach rumbled with anticipation as she entered the coffee shop and silently crossed the tile floor to the walk-in fridge. She paused, listening for the sound of footsteps. Silence. As far as she could tell there was no one in the building.

Determined to take full advantage of the unexpected opportunity, Wynn grabbed a couple blueberry muffins along with the last of the flaky croissants. Then, heading to the door at the back of the shop, she cautiously pulled it open.

Once again she paused, making sure she was alone before heading up the stairs to enter one of the empty bedrooms. She assumed they had once belonged to either Peri Sanguis or Skye Claremont, the two mages who'd helped Maya try to capture her, but thankfully they'd moved out long ago.

Munching on the treats, Wynn searched the closet and the dresser for something that she could use. Either a magical artifact she could pawn or cash left behind. She didn't find anything of value, but she did score with a pair of cutoff shorts that looked like they would fit her along with a New Jersey Devils T-shirt.

Polishing off another muffin, Wynn headed into the attached bathroom and hopped into the shower. She was hot, sticky, and in dire need of a good scrubbing.

A half hour later she was squeaky clean with her hair pulled into a fresh braid and wearing fresh clothes. She dumped her old stuff in the trash, except for the coat that she pulled back on despite the heat. It was heavily spelled to prevent her accidentally absorbing any unwelcomed magic from items she might brush against. It'd had happened more than once in the past, overwhelming her with an influx of power she didn't understand and wasn't prepared to use.

Allowing herself one more muffin, she brushed off the crumbs and headed out of the building. As much as she'd loved to stay and clean out Maya's sweet inventory, she finally had a lead to follow.

If she believed Azh—and that was still a big if—then it was possible that she'd absorbed the magic of a dragon. More specifically, the magic from Gabriela. She still had no idea where or when it'd happened, but if there were dragon artifacts out there, then someone had to know about them.

They were too rare and too precious not to have attracted the attention of the most exclusive collectors. Which meant that the black market brokers would be buzzing with interest.

One broker in particular.

Strolling through the dark streets, Wynn took the train into Manhattan. Then, avoiding the crowds that flocked to Times Square, she took the side streets to Lenox Hill. The elegant shop she was searching for was in a cream building sandwiched between a high-end boutique and a cigar bar. As she neared, she could make out the gold lettering on the glass door:

Hamilton Brothers Gallery

The lights inside were dim, but Wynn wasn't worried that the place was closed. Unlike the more famous auction houses in the area, this shop catered to the demons and vampires spread throughout the world. A few came to browse through the glass display cases filled with rare crystals and ancient artifacts, but the large majority were interested in the quarterly auctions held in the private rooms hidden beneath the shop.

It was there that the finest, most exclusive objects of magic were sold to the highest bidder. Items that moved through the black market and were usually outlawed by the Cabal.

Pushing open the door, she stepped into the shop, a welcome wave of cool air washing over her. It was well past midnight but the air in the city was still hot and thick enough to make her uncomfortable.

Releasing a sigh of relief, Wynn swept her gaze over the low, steel-and-glass display cases that shimmered with layers of protective spells. Next to the cases were soft leather seats for those who wanted to spend some time with the various objects before forking over the enormous price tag. Overhead, an expensive chandelier spilled out a soft light, while classical music played in the background.

Everything about the place screamed money. A hushed, exclusive atmosphere that was only for the very rich. Wynn felt a pang of regret. This was the sort of place that she'd become accustomed to patronizing. High class. Sophisticated. After years of begging on the streets for every scrap, she'd fought and clawed her way to the top.

It was utterly unfair she was once again scrambling for a living.

Squashing her futile burst of self-pity, Wynn at last spotted the male she'd come to find at the back of the gallery.

Albert Hamilton looked like a traditional English gentleman. He was short and stocky with thinning silver hair that was meticulously brushed to cover his bald spots. He was dressed in a tailored suit with a white shirt and conservative gray tie. It wasn't until he rose from behind the antique rolltop desk that she could see the glint of ruby cufflinks that matched the deep red aura pulsing around him.

"Wynn. This is a pleasure." Striding across the thick silver carpet that matched the wallpaper, Albert grabbed her hand and pressed it to his lips. "I heard you were in town. I'm so pleased you stopped by."

Wynn pulled her hand free. This male might possess the polished veneer of a gentleman, but his heart was pure demon. He was cunning and ruthlessly immoral. There were rumors that he had a goon squad spread around the world to track down rare artifacts, using intimidation or violence to get his hands on the item. He used those same goons to shut down any demon stupid enough to try to open a gallery in New York. He didn't seem to mind the black market dealers who sold cheap knockoffs, but he wasn't going to allow any direct competition.

"How did you hear I was in town?" she demanded. Then she gave a sharp shake of her head. "Hexx," she muttered, answering her own question. "That demon needs to keep his mouth shut."

"Don't be too hard on him," Albert drawled. "If he wasn't willing to gossip, he'd never get any free drinks. Poor soul."

"I'll deal with him later."

"Come. Sit down." Albert motioned toward a nearby leather chair, waiting for Wynn to grudgingly perch on the edge of the cushion before lifting his hand toward an armed guard who was hidden in the shadows. "Tea? Or perhaps something a bit stronger?"

"No thanks."

With a shrug, Albert moved to elegantly sink into the chair angled to face her, smoothing his hand down his silk tie.

"So, Hexx mentioned you were in the city for something... How did he say it?" He pretended to consider his words. "A big score?"

Wynn swallowed a curse. She was going to wring Hexx's skinny neck. She might as well have announced her plans on a billboard in Times Square.

"It fell through."

Albert studied her for a long moment, his expression impossible to read. "Unfortunate."

"It happens."

"True. But you must have found something." A faint smile curved his lips. "As much as I'd like to think it's my charming personality that draws you to my humble gallery, I assume you have a prize you hope to sell."

She glanced toward the chandelier hanging overhead. "Hardly humble."

"True enough. Still..."

She licked her lips, knowing she was taking a risk. She didn't trust this male. Okay, she didn't trust anyone. But she really, really didn't trust this demon. Unfortunately, when it came to collectors and sellers and thieves in the black market world, he was the unrivaled expert. If there were rumors of what she was searching for, Albert would know.

"I'm not here to sell," she informed him. "I need information."

"A shame." He didn't bother to hide his disappointment. "Information about what?"

"A statue."

He held out a large hand with manicured nails and a gold wedding band studded with rubies.

"Show me."

"I don't have it with me."

He grunted in annoyance. "Describe it."

"Actually there are three possible descriptions," she admitted. "One is a plain stone. One is a small dragon, and another one is a tall woman with a sword over her head."

"And?" He snapped his beefy fingers, clearly impatient. "I have to have more information than that."

Wynn hesitated. She didn't want to include Albert in her hunt for the statue, but she had to find it. The sooner the better.

"It's possible the statue contains dragon magic."

"Dragon?" Albert released a low whistle, leaning toward her as his aura flared with a visible lust. "You're sure? Where is it?"

"Who knows? All I have is vague rumors about a dragon statue in the area. That's why I'm in town. But without more information I can't pinpoint the precise location. That's why I thought of you. I wondered if you had stumbled across any mention of the statue in your research. If I know more about it, that might narrow my search."

"It's possible. Very possible." He studied her with an unnerving intensity. "Of course, I won't know until I see it."

Wynn frowned. "You haven't heard about any dragon relics being sold on the black market? Or recently stolen?"

"No, and I'm certain I would have if they'd gone through the usual suspects." He pursed his lips, his dark eyes smoldering with an eagerness that sent a chill down her spine. "In fact, the only way to keep something like that a secret would be if they were being hidden by the Cabal."

Wynn laid her hands on the arms of her chair, preparing to get to her feet. Unless Albert was playing some strange game, he had no idea where she could find the statue. Which meant that she was wasting her time.

Again.

"Vampires have no use for magic," she pointed out the obvious.

"No, but they could offer them to their pet mages."

"I already looked. There was nothing inside Maya's vault. At least nothing with dragon magic."

He leaned closer. "So you say."

"What?"

Albert's hand shot out, his fingers wrapping around her wrist. "Where are they?"

Wynn felt a stab of annoyance. She had a few nasty spells to make this male regret touching her without permission, but she didn't want to make him an enemy. At some point she hoped to get rid of the troublesome dragon magic so she could get back to her previous life. Which meant dealing with exclusive brokers like Albert Hamilton to keep her in the luxury she was accustomed to.

"Don't be stupid. If I had them, why would I come here for answers?"

His fingers tightened until they dug into her wrist. "You know what I think?"

She tried to yank free. "Actually I really don't care."

"I think you got the statues but you don't know how to use them," he said. "Now you're looking for someone who can help you tap into the power."

"Believe whatever you want." She surged to her feet, still struggling to break free of his grasp. "I'm out of here."

"I don't think so."

He glanced toward the back of the room where the guard was obviously waiting for his cue. The bald goblin dressed in a black uniform moved forward, revealing that there were three more guards behind his massive form. They spread out to cover the exits, making sure Wynn would have to fight her way out.

"You can't be serious?" she questioned in annoyance.

"Hand over the statues and you can walk away," Albert warned. "No fuss, no muss."

Wynn glanced down at the fingers wrapped around her wrist, searching through the strands of magic humming inside her. Ignoring the pulsing red strand, she grasped the slender blue thread of magic. A cool tingle of power fizzed through her like a fine champagne.

"Oh, there's gonna be a muss when you're splattered across the wall," she informed him, releasing the magic in one solid burst.

The magic sizzled through the air, coalescing into a solid ball as it slammed into Albert. She'd hoped to knock him on his ass or at least make him stumble off balance. Anything to create a distraction so she could escape. But the renegade strand of red magic once again decided to interfere, shooting out to join the small blast. It wasn't content to shove the goblin to the ground. Instead, it wrapped around him and lifted his massive form high in the air. Albert screeched in fury, glaring down at her with foam at the edges of his mouth. As if his anger at being manhandled was making him rabid.

Wynn smiled, watching with pleasure as the magic gave the goblin a disdainful jerk before tossing him across the room. For once she didn't mind the unpredictable strand adding the extra umph of power. Not when it was sending the treacherous demon sailing through the air to land on the nearest display case.

There was a loud crash as the glass shattered and the steel frames buckled beneath Albert's impressive weight. Swearing in a language that Wynn didn't recognize, the demon forced himself to his feet and hastily backed from the various crystals, amulets, and orbs infused with ancient spells that were now exposed. The pulse of their power spilled through the air, raising the hair on Wynn's nape. She could determine that at least one of them was a dangerous curse and another glowed with a white-hot heat. Not dragon magic, but a fey lightning rod.

"What are you waiting for?" He glared toward his goons even as he dug out a handkerchief to wipe the sweat from his face. "Get her."

The guards cautiously moved forward, no one wanting to be the first to get close, despite the fact they each had at least a hundred pounds on her and glowed with the crimson aura of pureblooded goblins. After witnessing her pick up their leader and toss him across the room like he weighed nothing, they had to wonder what other nasty tricks she might have waiting for them.

Not that she could depend on their hesitation. Albert's hands were already curling into fists of frustration, as if he were preparing to thump some courage into his employees.

Wynn's gaze skimmed the room. The obvious exits were cut off, but maybe she could reach the narrow window on the far side of the gallery. The trick was keeping the guards away long enough to make her escape. A task easier said than done.

Inching to the side, Wynn moved to stand next to the shattered display case. Instantly she felt the magic wash over, trying to penetrate the shields she'd woven into her coat. It was dangerous to stand so close to such powerful objects, but she didn't have any choice. There were only a few things that could frighten a goblin. Especially when they were in the center of a Gyre where they could touch the magic that pulsed beneath their feet.

Holding out her hand, she placed it over the crystal that glowed with a dull gray light.

"Stay back or I'll turn your manly parts into squishy grapes," she warned in a voice that brought the goons to an abrupt halt.

The three guards exchanged glances, licking their lips as they weighed their job against the potential of having their balls turned to grapes. The silence stretched as Wynn measured the distance to the window.

Then with a strangled growl, Albert stomped his foot. "Dammit. She can't curse all of you."

The largest of the goons took a hesitant step forward. Wynn sent him a taunting smile.

"You want to be first? All right, come and play."

"Do it or I'll have you flayed and tossed in the pit for the hounds to gnaw on," Albert snapped.

The male shuddered, but with a grim determination he forced his feet forward, motioning toward his companions to join him. Wynn's hand remained above the display case, but she shifted it to hover over the three-foot rod that glowed with a searing heat. She'd accidentally absorbed curses before. It wasn't an experience she was eager to repeat. She just wanted the goblins to fear they were going to be castrated to give her some time. The hope was that she could scare the guards to back away far enough to give her a shot at escaping.

Now it looked like she was going to have to fight her way out. She needed a weapon that could do more than scare the demons. She needed to be able to kill them.

Allowing the fey magic to flow through the palm of her hand, Wynn hissed as the heat scalded through her flesh and into her body. It was going to take a few minutes to finish absorbing the power and then allow it to settle into a visual strand that she could use. Until then she was vulnerable.

Unfortunate, but there wasn't much she could do about it.

Keeping her attention locked on the guards slowly closing the distance, Wynn ignored the heat that gathered around her. There was no way to absorb lightning without getting burned. That didn't make it any less painful.

It wasn't until a familiar voice whispered next to her ear that she realized it wasn't the rod causing the heat. It was her pain-in-the-ass dragon.

"Troubles, my elusive mouse?" he asked in a soft voice.

Relief blasted through her. She was cocky enough to pretend she was immortal, but she was well aware that she was in trouble. Really big trouble. That didn't mean, however, she was going to let her aggravating stalker know how happy she was that he'd followed her.

"You call me that again and I'll prove this mouse has teeth and isn't afraid to use them," she warned.

"Is that a promise?"

"Really?" She rolled her eyes. "Now?"

With a chuckle he moved to tower beside her, the blinding glow from his aura spreading through the gallery.

"It looks like you could use some help."

"Nothing I can't handle."

"Okay. Should I wait outside?"

She glanced up to meet his teasing gaze, her heart squeezing at the sight of his earth-shattering beauty. Would she ever get used to those stunningly perfect features or the smoky silver eyes?

Nope. Not ever.

And she certainly wasn't going to get used to the power humming around his lean body. Being near him was like standing next to a raging fire. Raw, seductive heat that in the end was terrifyingly lethal.

Her mouth was dry, but she managed a tight smile. "I'm not that selfish. You can share in the fun."

His smoky gaze swept over her face, lingering on her lips. "Very generous."

Wynn silently swore as awareness curled through the pit of her stomach. Good grief. He'd looked at her lips. Not a caress. Not a kiss. Nothing. Just a look. And she was shivering with sensual pleasure.

This male was going to be the death of her. One way or another.

"That's me. Ms. Generosity." She nodded toward the goon squad that had halted to regard him in confusion. No doubt they'd never seen anything like Azh with his nuclear aura. And then there was the fact he'd managed to appear from thin air. "Maybe you should concentrate on our companions."

"If you insist."

Sweeping his gaze over the guards, he casually stepped forward, moving toward the obvious leader.

"Who the hell are you?" The goblin grudgingly stood his ground, reaching behind his back to pull out a large knife from a hidden sheath.

The blade was at least ten inches long and shimmered with hieroglyphs that had been carved into the metal. It'd been hexed and laced with poison.

Wynn's lips parted to warn Azh to be careful only to snap shut when the dragon casually reached out to grab the demon by his thick neck. The guard's eyes went blank as his body spasmed, the knife dropping from his twitching fingers.

"Wrong question," Azh said, studying the male as if determining whether to kill him slow or fast. "You should ask 'What the hell are you?'"

"What are you?" the goblin obediently repeated, his voice dull as if he were under some sort of spell.

Was it compulsion or fear? Probably a combination of both.

"I'm your worst nightmare," Azh answered.

"Ugh," Wynn muttered.

He sent her a questioning glance. "Too much?"

"It's embarrassing."

With a sigh, he picked up the male and launched him toward the nearest goon. They both went down in a tangle of limbs.

"Better?" he demanded.

She clicked her tongue, but she didn't bother to answer as she felt the fey magic she was absorbing settle into place, creating a strand of deep jade. At last.

"Get them, now!" Albert bellowed toward the remaining guard, even as he backpedaled toward the door.

The coward was trying to escape.

With obvious reluctance the goblin forced himself to charge forward, his expression resigned as Azh easily grabbed him by the throat and lifted him off his feet.

Azh once again glanced back at Wynn. "Do you want me to finish up here or do you want a turn?"

"You might as well finish up since you're in the mood," she assured him.

The smoky eyes smoldered with a deliciously tempting invitation. "I'm always in the mood."

"Seriously, stop," she commanded.

With a chuckle he tossed the male on top of the others, waiting to see if he would be stupid enough to get up or if he'd play dead. Wynn was betting he was going to stay down. She was right. The male squeezed shut his eyes and lay motionless, no doubt praying to his god that he survived the next few minutes.

Wynn shifted her attention toward Albert, who was inching ever closer to the door.

She wavered between the desire to zap him with the magic sizzling through her and the acceptance that he wasn't worth the effort. He didn't have the information she needed. Better to focus on finding someone who could actually help, right?

Dismissing the goblin from her mind, she turned back to Azh, who was watching her with an expectant expression. No doubt the aggravating creature intended to follow her. They might as well pretend to be civilized and leave at the same time.

Her lips parted, but the words died on the tip of her tongue as she felt a nasty tingle in the air. A second later she watched as one of the goon squad surged upright. She wasn't shocked by the fact the goblin had found the nerve to face off against a male who could obviously destroy him with terrifying ease. It was the weird green glow that came from deep inside his eyes. As if there was something inside him peering out at Wynn.

"Azh." His name came out as a harsh gasp. "Behind you."

Easily sensing her fear, Azh whirled back toward the guards. With a curse, he moved to the side, as if intending to block the male shuffling forward. Wynn shuddered in horror.

"No. Don't let him touch you."

Keeping his gaze locked on the male, Azh obediently backed toward Wynn. "What is it? Magic?"

"Evil," she rasped, and instinctively moved closer to Azh as the other two guards rose to their feet, their eyes glowing.

Azh's aura snapped around him as he lifted a hand and pointed toward the approaching goblin. Heat seared through the air before a burst of flames abruptly surrounded the guard. Wynn gagged as the stench of burning flesh tainted the air, pressing a hand over her mouth.

She might have felt sorry for the goblin if he wasn't infected with the essence of evil. She didn't want the vile stuff spreading. She didn't know what it would do, but it couldn't be good. The flames danced and flared as if they were battling against an unseen enemy. Then the fire was extinguished to reveal a charred body with blackened flesh peeling off in huge chunks. The male was dead, but his eyes were still glowing and his feet were shuffling forward. And worse, behind him the other guards were rising from the floor.

"Have you seen this before?" Azh demanded, his power thundering through the air.

"In my nightmares." Her throat felt like it was closing as pure fear cascaded through her, threatening to stir a tidal wave of panic. "We have to get out of here."

"No argument from me."

They turned toward the front of the gallery, but the door was being blocked by Albert, who was clearly infected with the same evil as his goon squad.

Where had it come from? She hadn't sensed the venomous magic until the guards had suddenly started their glowing routine. Could it be coming from one of the artifacts in the broken display cases?

No. That didn't make any sense. If it was a magical item, then she would be infected too, wouldn't she?

Wynn shook her head. The guards were getting way too close for comfort. She would worry about the how and why later.

Right now, she had to concentrate on escaping.

Turning to the side, she lifted her arm and pointed toward the small window on the far side of the gallery. At the same time she released the fey magic she'd absorbed from the rod.

As always, she had no idea what to expect when she acquired a new strand. Especially with the recent interference from the dragon magic. Closing her eyes so she wouldn't be blinded, she felt the bolt of lightning leave her hand with enough force to knock her backward.

Azh wrapped his arms around her waist, keeping her upright as the magic exploded against the wall. The impact shuddered through the building, shattering display cases and buckling the floor beneath their feet. The smell of garbage suddenly perfumed the air.

With a grimace Wynn opened her eyes to discover the massive hole that had been blown into the side of the building. The window was completely gone along with most of the wall. She'd even managed to explode the dumpster that had been in the alleyway.

Well, that explained the putrid stench, she wryly acknowledged, glancing up as the ceiling popped and cracked. It was getting ready to collapse.

"Go!" Azh said, gazing back at the infected goblins.

Wynn didn't need to see the demons to feel their ruthless approach. The pulses of evil washed over her like a surging wave.

She ran.

Chapter 7

Azh allowed Wynn to take the lead as they raced out of the crumbling building and through the dark streets. He concentrated on creating a web of smoke around them. The thin layer didn't make them invisible, but it would mask their scent and hide any tracks in case someone was hunting them.

He didn't know what had happened to the demons. The plague. A curse. Dark magic. He'd never seen anything like it. But he did know that they were dangerous. And that they were somehow connected to Wynn.

Which meant they had to be destroyed.

The question was how.

Remaining on high alert as they left the elegant neighborhood and headed north, Azh was caught off guard when Wynn veered into the parking lot of a cheap motel. The single-story building stretched at an angle between a trailer park and an auto shop. The bricks had faded to a dull orange and the roof was missing several shingles. It looked like the sort of place where the dregs of human society would gather. Or demons who wanted to avoid the attention of the Vampire Cabal.

"Why are we here?" he asked, frowning as she halted in front of the door at the end of the building.

"This is my current lair." There was a tingle of magic before the steel door swung open.

Arching a brow, Azh stepped into the small square dominated by a double bed and a cheap dresser with a television precariously propped on top of it. There was a closed door on the far wall that he assumed led to the bathroom.

"Sparse," he murmured, silently noting the frayed canvas bag tossed in the corner. It was the only personal item visible.

Of course, she presumably had the ability to use dragon magic. That would give her the talent to hide dozens of items in the room. Or even on her person.

He had an assortment of weapons concealed by his weaves of magic, along with the history book he'd brought through the small portal.

Wynn snorted, heading to the fridge next to the dresser to pull out a bottle of water. She tried to act casual, but Azh didn't miss the pallor of her skin and the way her hands trembled as she lifted the bottle to her lips.

She was still freaked out by the glowing green demons.

Draining the water, she at last sent him a chiding glance. "We can't all have mysterious bat caves with fancy libraries and marble walls," she said, obviously taking full advantage of the portal he'd opened to peek into the dragon lair. "You probably have a dozen slaves to cater to your every need."

Azh resisted the urge to try to comfort her. Wynn didn't want to share her emotions. She wanted to be a tough, kick-ass warrior. Better to distract her.

"No slaves, but I do have a large harem."

As he hoped, she was immediately furious. "Ew, I knew you—"

"I'm kidding," he interrupted her looming tirade. "Dragon females are the most dangerous creatures in this world. Any potential lover goes in with the understanding that they don't take shit from anyone, including their mates."

Her temper eased and something flared through her amazing eyes. Was that...gratitude?

"Good for them," she retorted.

He folded his arms over his chest. She was still pale and shaky, but they couldn't waste time. He had to have the answers he was seeking.

"Are you going to tell me what's going on?"

"I don't know."

He made a sound of exasperation. "Wynn, it's too late for lies."

She tossed aside the bottle. "It's not a lie. If I knew what was happening I'd make it stop."

She sounded sincere.

"Okay then, where's the dragon statue?"

"I genuinely don't know." She spread her arms, glaring at him. "Look around if you don't believe me."

Azh didn't take her up on her offer. He wasn't in the mood for a game of hide-and-seek.

"I can sense the magic," he stubbornly insisted.

"Where?" Slowly she peeled off her coat and tossed it onto the bed.

He paused at her sharp question, forcing himself to concentrate on the hum of power. He'd assumed that it came from an object that Wynn was carrying with her. Or the residue of magic that clung to her because she'd been in close contact with a dragon relic.

Now that she'd removed her coat that was obviously layered with spells of protection, he could finally pinpoint the source of the magic.

"It's coming from inside you."

"Exactly."

Azh frowned. "How?"

"It's a long story."

"You aren't old enough for it to be very long," Azh pointed out in dry tones.

"I have no idea how old I am. Honestly I don't know *what* I am."

His frown deepened. "You lost your memory?"

"I guess." She shrugged. "I woke up one day with no idea of who I was or where I came from."

"Wait." Azh held up a hand. He was genuinely confused. Memories could be stolen. And sometimes altered. But only humans suffered from amnesia, and this woman most certainly wasn't a human. "Start at the beginning. What do you first remember?"

"I opened my eyes and discovered I was lying on the banks of the Thames on the outskirts of London."

"How long ago?"

"Two centuries." She wrinkled her nose. "Give or take a few years."

"And you have no memories of your life before you woke up?"

"None." Her tone was flat. Her eyes smoldered with frustration. "I managed to find shelter in London and for a while I assumed I was just another poor human woman who'd been attacked and left for dead. There was a lot of crime during that time."

"How did you realize you were something more?"

"When I started seeing auras around some people. I thought I must have brain damage when no one else noticed them."

His confidence that she wasn't mortal was confirmed. Humans couldn't detect the auras that surrounded supernatural creatures. Even mages didn't see them until the wild magic flared through their veins, igniting their primitive powers.

"I would say you have a trace of demon blood that you couldn't sense until you were inside a Gyre, but you don't have the scent of a goblin or a fey." He studied her with a brooding intensity. "That means you have to be a mage."

"I don't have any magic," she protested.

Azh stepped forward, careful to leash the heat that could singe her delicate skin. Why was she being so stubborn?

"You really do think dragons are stupid, don't you?"

She blinked, as if caught off guard by his burst of annoyance. "I mean I don't have magic in my blood. Not like other mages."

Azh forced himself to take a calming breath. He was more on edge than he realized. "A witch?" he guessed.

"That's what I hoped. I even sought out a local coven in London."

He didn't miss her shudder at the mention of the coven. As if the memory still caused her pain.

"That didn't go well?"

"They tied rocks around me and tossed me into the river. They wanted to drown me before I could attract attention that might get them burned at the stake."

Azh wasn't surprised. Witches had blamed mages for causing them to be hunted by both humans and demons from the beginning of time. Personally, he thought they were jealous of the rare members of their covens who were blessed with the ability to tap directly into their primal magic.

Still, if she wasn't a witch or a mage or a vampire or a demon or a dragon...then what the hell was she?

"How do you create spells?" he asked.

"From objects that hold magic. Amulets, crystals, charms, relics."

"But you need magic to tap into the spell or power."

"I don't tap into it. I absorb it."

Azh swept his gaze over her face, which had thankfully lost its pallor. This cramped room that reeked of mildew and echoed with the sounds of voices from next door appeared to give her some sense of safety.

Or maybe it's my presence that eased her fears, a hopeful voice whispered in the back of his mind.

His heat flared as a razor-edged excitement sliced through the layers of indifference that had wrapped around him since the dragons had gone into hibernation.

This woman. She fascinated him in a way he couldn't explain. Maybe because she remained such a mystery. He'd never encountered anyone like her. Of course, he'd spent the past centuries locked in his lair, he reminded himself. He could glimpse the world and keep track of the changes in society and technology, but they'd had no effect on him or his people.

Not until the dragon magic had stirred him fully awake.

The thought was an abrupt reminder that now wasn't the time or place to become lost in his obsession with this woman.

Later, however, he intended to indulge his desires. Vociferously and with exquisite attention to detail.

He smoothed his expression as he realized she was staring at him with a hint of suspicion. No doubt she'd sensed his dangerous distraction.

"You said you absorb the magic." He forced out the words. "There's a difference from what mages do?"

She slowly nodded. "I've never created a spell like a regular mage, but I know they use their magic to release the power stored in the object. When I am near one, the power simply seeps into me."

"And then you can use the magic?"

"Yes."

"How long does it stay?"

"It depends on the object. The more powerful the magic, the longer it stays. There are some spells that have been with me from my earliest days in London and other magic that disappears as soon as I use it."

"I knew you were unique, but this..." Azh was young in dragon years, but he'd been alive a very, very long time. Wynn continued to surprise him. "I've never heard of anyone who could store magic from another creature. Is it different if the object was created by a demon or a human?"

She considered the question, as if trying to recall if there'd been a notable variance in the powers she absorbed.

"Not that I can tell," she at last decided. "Witch magic isn't as strong and usually fades the fastest, but otherwise there's nothing to reveal who placed the spell in the artifact."

"What about potions?"

She looked confused. "They take magic to create, but anyone can use them. Even humans."

"Yes, but do you absorb the power from the potion?"

She shook her head. "No."

He stepped forward. He genuinely wanted to discover the source of her powers. But more importantly, he was eager to use any excuse to be closer to her. A realization that made him weirdly uncomfortable. He was a dragon with royal blood flowing through his veins. A male who was used to females making their desire obvious. Sometimes painfully obvious. Earning this woman's trust was new territory for him.

"What if you touch a magic user?" He ran a finger down the side of her face, his touch as light as a butterfly wing. "Like this. Can you absorb my magic?"

"No." She shivered, the lavender eyes darkening with the same heat that pulsed deep inside him. "There's nothing."

"There's something." Flames danced over his fingers. A kiss of fire that was a promise of pleasure to come. "And it's magic."

Her face flushed, but it wasn't from the flames. The sweet scent of her arousal perfumed the air.

"Azh." She lifted a hand to press it against his chest.

"I know, but I'm bewitched." His voice was husky with something that was more than hunger. Need? Yearning? Fate? "There something tantalizingly familiar about being near you. As if we've lived this moment a thousand times."

Her fingers stroked over his chest, as if unable to resist tracing the edge of his smooth muscles. "You're distracting me."

He lowered his head, skimming his lips over her cheek. Her skin was velvety soft and scented with a hint of citrus. Deep inside, his dragon breathed in the bright aroma, growling in approval.

"In a good way?" he asked, brushing a kiss over her lips.

Her fingers curled into his shirt, as if intending to pull him closer, only to abruptly push against his chest.

"In a dangerous way," she muttered.

"True." He reluctantly conceded defeat, taking a step back. When he finally took Wynn into his arms, he didn't intend to be standing in a sleazy hotel that smelled like mildew. "Where did you find the dragon statue?"

"I have no idea." She held up her hand as his lips parted. "I didn't have a clue I had dragon magic. Not until you started sniffing around me like a dog."

"Did you just compare me to a dog?" He arched a brow. "Are you completely fearless?"

"Probably senseless," she clarified.

He studied her with a vague sense of bewilderment. Dragon magic was the most dominant force in this world. It was what fueled the Gyres' power despite his people being in hibernation for thousands of years. It should have slammed into her with a shocking intensity. In fact, it was amazing that it hadn't crushed her mind and body.

"You genuinely don't sense the dragon magic that you absorbed?" he demanded.

"There's a strand of magic inside me that appeared nearly a year ago," she conceded. "It must have come from an artifact that I touched, but I have no idea when or where it happened."

"What does the magic do?"

Frustration tightened her features. "I haven't been able to use it. All I know for sure is that it's expanding and interfering with my other magic. And that the nightmares started after it appeared."

Her words sparked a memory. "You said that you'd seen the demons from the gallery in your nightmares."

"Not those specific demons, but I've had dreams where I'm being attacked by goblins with glowing green eyes."

"But it's never happened when you're awake?"

"No..." Her words trailed away as she furrowed her brow.

"You remember something?"

"I saw something similar when that creature in the crazy pajamas touched me."

"Creature in crazy pajamas?"

"At Hexx's apartment."

"The Watcher?" Azh demanded, recalling his own encounter with the powerful being.

"I guess." She shrugged. "He touched me and suddenly we weren't in the apartment anymore."

"Where were you?"

"I don't know. We were surrounded in a silvery mist." She paused, as if struggling to remember. "And he changed. He went from looking like a homeless man to a god."

A low growl of jealousy escaped Azh's throat before he could stop it. He didn't want this woman comparing another male to a deity.

"Not a god," he insisted. "At least not in this world. What did he do?"

"The mist parted to reveal a pit of bubbling green slime." She clicked her tongue as Azh stared at her in confusion. "I don't know how else to describe it. The stuff matched the demons' eyes and the weird magic that was leaking out of them."

Azh's jealousy was forgotten as he concentrated on her words. Obviously the Watcher had used his powers to tap into her mind. But had her thoughts led him to a specific location? Or was the magic being spread through various relics?

And did it have anything to do with the dragon magic he could sense?

"Did the Watcher recognize it?"

"I don't think so." She pressed her hands against her stomach, as if she suddenly felt nauseous. "The slime attacked him and he looked like he was struggling not to get sucked into the pit."

"Did he say anything?"

"He told me to run. So I did." Something that might have been regret rippled over her delicate features. "The next thing I knew I was back in the apartment with Hexx."

"What happened to the Watcher?"

"He was lying unconscious on the kitchen floor. As far as I know he's still trapped in the mist."

Azh turned to pace the cramped floor. What would be strong enough to attack a Watcher? The creature might not be a god, but he possessed the powers of one. And the fact that the male had followed the trail of magic while touching Wynn...

Fear pierced his heart.

"Green slime. Possessed demons. And dragon magic," he muttered in frustration. "It has to be connected."

Chapter 8

Wynn watched Azh stomp across the room, only to spin around and stomp back. In the dingy light she could see the shimmer of invisible wings tucked against his back and sense the tail whipping from side to side. He was still in human form but his inner dragon was venting its annoyance as they continued to come up with more questions than answers.

Wynn was equally annoyed.

If he was right and she did have dragon magic inside her, then why wasn't it helping her? As far as she was concerned it'd done nothing but cause her trouble. And if it was somehow related to the creepy green sludge, then it only made her more desperate to discover how and when she'd absorbed the stupid stuff.

"I just want it to go away."

Azh abruptly halted at her muttered complaint, turning to face her. "Maybe I can help." With cautious steps he moved to stand directly in front of her, lifting his hand as he held her wary gaze. "May I?"

She stiffened. "What are you going to do?"

"I want to try and identify the magic."

"How?"

"I need to peer into your mind."

Wynn hesitated. "The last time someone peered into my mind they ended up trapped by the evil magic."

"I'm not going to enter your thoughts," he assured her. "I'm concentrating on the dragon magic. It's possible I can determine how you managed to absorb it."

Wynn remained tense, but she gave a slow nod of her head. "Go ahead."

His fingers traced the line of her jaw before brushing down her throat and lingering over the racing beat of her heart. Wynn hissed as the heat from his fingers spread through her, warming places that had no business being warm. At least not when she was trying to figure out why her life had turned into a shitshow.

The gray eyes swirled with a smoky concern. "Am I hurting you?"

"No. Just..." She cleared the lump from her throat. "Just hurry."

His nostrils flared as if he'd caught the scent of her arousal. "Some things shouldn't be rushed," he murmured in soft tones.

"Argh." She glared at him. "Are you going to look for the magic or not?"

"Hold still."

Wynn shivered as his presence scoured through her. The blazing heat of his power was gloriously addictive. Like bathing in the summer rays of the sun.

"There," he at last announced in fiercely satisfied tones. "I found it."

Wynn was genuinely surprised. She knew that she imagined the magic as separate strands of power, but she didn't realize someone else could actually see them.

"Seriously?" She went from surprised to shocked as the magic began to flow out of her, the threads of shimmering color spreading through the shadowed room. "What's happening?"

"Dazzling," Azh rasped, turning to study the delicate filaments that swirled together, forming a complicated pattern before unraveling and forming a new pattern.

"The red strand." Wynn pointed toward the thickest strand that pulsed with a crimson glow. "That's the magic I can't control. Is it dragon?"

He edged toward the magic. "I don't recognize it."

"Is it dangerous?"

"Yes."

Wynn flinched. There hadn't been a second of hesitation. "Great."

"There's something about it..."

Azh stretched out his arm and Wynn sucked in a sharp breath. "What are you doing?"

"Trying to release it."

"Stop," she commanded, fear darting through her. Not for herself but for the aggravating male who seemed to think he was impervious to danger. "You don't know what it's going to do."

He glanced back, his expression somber. "Do you want to get rid of it or not?"

Wynn hesitated before giving a reluctant nod of her head. "Fine. But... be careful."

Bracing herself, Wynn watched as Azh allowed his fingers to graze against the crimson strand. She somehow expected to feel the light touch. As if he were reaching inside her to stroke the magic. Instead, the swirling spiderweb of colors seemed to be separate from her. A good thing, as the crimson strand abruptly sizzled with power.

"Azh. Watch out!" she rasped, watching in horror as the blast of glowing magic headed directly toward the male.

Azh lifted his hand, flames dancing around him in a protective barrier. Wynn could see the sudden shimmer of a bluish silver coating his skin. It looked almost like scales. Impressive. But was it enough?

The mysterious power washed over him like a tidal wave, but it didn't look like it was attempting to penetrate the flames. In fact, it swept past him and disappeared in a puff of smoke.

It wasn't until Wynn heard something hit the floor that she realized that the magic had pierced Azh's shield. With a frown, her gaze dropped to the heavy book that had appeared from seemingly nowhere. It looked like the same book that Azh had been showing her earlier. She assumed he must have kept it hidden beneath a weave of illusion.

"What's happening?" she demanded.

"I don't know." He allowed the flames to vanish as he glanced down. He made a choked sound of surprise. "Wait. Look. It broke the seal."

Wynn cautiously moved forward. The book had opened when it hit the nasty carpet, revealing the pages covered with elaborate illustrations.

"What seal?"

Azh squatted down, touching the picture of a dragon in flight with reverent care. "This part of the book has always been protected by Gabriela's magic. I've never been able to see what was on the pages."

"Then the magic is dragon," Wynn breathed, not sure whether to be glad she'd discovered the truth or terrified it was inside her.

Azh continued to study the book. "It's more than that. Only Gabriela or her magic could have broken through that seal."

"I thought she was dead?"

"She is. But the power you absorbed must belong to her." He glanced over his shoulder, his eyes a misty shade of gray. "That's why you feel so familiar. I've spent centuries searching for every scrap of information that survived the journey to this world."

Wynn flinched at the sharp burst of anger that exploded in the center of her heart. It shouldn't matter that his intense obsession had nothing to do with her and everything to do with some stupid magic from a female who'd died eons ago. It wasn't like she wanted him chasing after her, right? Once she'd gotten rid of the curse, then she was returning to her normal life and Azh could...well, go back to his damned lair where he belonged.

"Great." She sniffed, tilting her chin to a defensive angle. "Then you can get her out of me and the two of you can disappear back into hibernation where I'm sure you'll be very happy together."

The smoky eyes swirled with an emotion she couldn't read. "Are you jealous, Wynn?"

Yes. Yes, she definitely was. And it was pissing her off.

"I'm confused, exhausted, and angry," she hedged. "I want to be done with this. Can you get rid of it or not?"

He studied her for a long moment before returning his attention to the book. Then, with a wave of his hand, he lifted the illustrations from the page, allowing the image to coalesce in the middle of the room. Like a 3D model floating in midair.

Wynn dismissed her embarrassing stab of jealousy, stepping forward to watch the image of massive dragons soaring through an impossibly blue sky. She blinked in surprise as they swooped over towering mountains, realizing that there were two suns on the horizon.

"This must be an image of Kazak," Azh said, slowly walking around the edge of the illusion.

"Your homeland?"

"Yes." He sent her a quick glance. "If the statue came from there it would explain why I don't fully recognize the magic."

Wynn refused to contemplate the implications of having an alien magic inside her. Instead she concentrated on the dragons as they soared past the mountains and over a brilliant blue ocean.

"It looks like paradise."

"Our ancient histories claim it was a land of plenty where creatures lived in peace," Azh agreed.

Wynn snorted. She was willing to admit the landscape was enchanting, but she'd studied enough history to understand that there were always winners and losers in any society, and that those who succeeded were often the ones climbing on the backs of the less fortunate.

"Histories are written by those in power," she reminded him. "They rarely notice the creatures who don't have plenty or the ones being brutalized by those who claim it's in the name of peace."

Something that might be approval flared through Azh's eyes, as if he were pleased she'd bothered to read a book. Wynn clenched her teeth. She should be annoyed by the condescending ass. Instead a warm satisfaction settled in the center of her soul.

"You won't get any argument from me," he assured her. "The stories were written by dragons who were looking back to long-ago days. Their nostalgia no doubt added a rosy glow."

Wynn sniffed, determinedly kept her attention locked on the illusion as one of the largest dragons arrowed downward, landing on a sandy beach. Her heart missed a beat as she realized it was the silver dragon. The one that Azh claimed was Gabriela.

The massive creature barely touched the white sand before it was surrounded by a thick cloud of smoke. Seconds later, the mist cleared to reveal the creature's human form. She was tall and muscular with long silver hair and eyes that smoldered with crimson flames. Wynn couldn't see any clothing, but her skin shimmered with the lustrous beauty of a pearl as if she were coated in a thin layer of scales. There was also a silver crown perched on top of her head.

"Gabriela," Azh whispered in awe.

Wynn sternly ignored her prick of annoyance at Azh's obvious obsession with the dead queen. Or at least she tried to, even when the jerk stepped closer to the illusion to watch as Gabriela crossed the beach and climbed a wide staircase that she created out of layers of mist. Up and up she went, clouds beginning to form in the blue sky to surround her.

"What's happening?" she demanded.

Azh shrugged. "I'm not sure, but there has to be a reason this section of the book was protected by magic."

On cue, the clouds thinned to reveal a heavy stone pyramid that looked far too solid to be resting on air. There were two uniformed men standing next to a copper door engraved with complicated hieroglyphics. Gabriela never slowed her pace, waving away the guards as the door swung open. Was her presence some sort of trigger?

The illusion darkened as the dragon stepped into the interior of the pyramid, her skin releasing a soft glow that allowed Wynn to see she was walking through a huge room that looked surprisingly empty. Like a vast cavern.

Then she reached the back wall, pausing in front of another copper door set in the thick stone. She glanced over her shoulder, as if to ensure that there was no one around. Odd. Did she have some sort of secret hoard? Or was she just looking for some peace and quiet? Maybe a bubble bath and a glass of wine.

Being the queen to a bunch of arrogant, brutally violent dragons couldn't be an easy job.

The dragon lifted her hand, pressing open the door to reveal another vast space, only this one wasn't empty. In the center of the stone floor was a raised dais with a huge, gem-encrusted throne that sparkled with priceless perfection.

Gabriela walked with an elegance that made her appear to float on a breeze as she climbed the steps and slowly turned to settle on the throne. The gems flared with brilliant light in response to her presence, shredding through the shadows to reveal a wide crack in the floor filled with a thick sludge.

Wynn gasped. There was no mistaking the sickening green glow that suddenly came from the sludge, rising and spreading through the room.

"Azh," she breathed in shock. "That's the same magic that's infecting the demons."

Azh hissed, his brows pulling together as he watched Gabriela lean her head against the back of the throne, allowing the glow to wash over her. As if she were in a spa, not being infected with evil.

"The corruption." He stepped back, as if worried the toxic sludge might spill out of the illusion. "It has to be."

"It's supposed to be locked out of here." Fear trickled through Wynn, freezing her blood and sending goosebumps over her skin. Azh didn't have a lot of information on the corruption or how it worked, but he'd been very clear he suspected it'd destroyed the homeland of the dragons. What the hell would it do if it managed to spread through this world? "How did it get into the demons?"

Reaching down, Azh closed the book with a loud thump before speaking a word of power. Instantly, it disappeared.

"I have to speak to the Watcher," he announced in grim tones.

Wynn was already heading toward the door. "Follow me."

* * * *

Maya heaved a sigh as she tossed her cell phone on the worn counter. She'd known that Ravyr wasn't going to be pleased when she shared her latest update. He wasn't foolish enough to try to tell her not to protect Tia, but he made it clear he was going to be epically pissed if something happened to Maya.

Not for the first time, she wished he was there. His absence was like an ache she couldn't ease. As if a piece of herself was missing. And if she was honest, she could use the comfort of his presence. If he was there, she would be absolutely certain that nothing bad could happen.

Unfortunately, he was stuck in Greece for at least another week, and she was on her own.

No...wait. Not on her own. She could sense someone approaching the front door of the empty pawnshop.

Maya touched the emerald that glowed around her neck. The barrier that she and Tia had wrapped around Hexx's building should be strong enough to deter the most determined trespasser, but she had a lethal spell prepared if anything managed to break through.

Scooting off the high stool that was the only piece of furniture in the empty pawnshop, Maya walked forward to peer out the large front window. Her tension eased as she caught sight of the slender woman jogging across the street dressed in cutoff shorts and a tight T-shirt.

Peri.

Maya moved to open the front door, whispering words of power to allow the younger woman to step through the barrier.

Peri stopped in the doorway, studying the shimmering webs of magic with a lift of her brows.

"This isn't just your magic."

"No," Maya agreed. "It was a combined effort with Tia."

Peri's lips twitched. "You and Tia working together? A miracle."

"A minor miracle," Maya agreed. For over four decades she'd considered Tia her nemesis. The past few months had gone a long way to heal their old wounds, but their relationship was still a work in progress.

"I'll admit that I'm impressed," Peri murmured. "It's impossible to determine where your magic joins with Tia's. The weave is flawless."

Maya took a moment to admire her work. Peri was right. It was flawless.

"You're not the only mage with skills, although I'll admit I don't have your power."

"Yes, well. I am blessed." Peri batted her lashes before stepping through the weaves. "Still, the melding is beautiful."

Maya snorted. "Did you come here to admire my shield?"

"One of many reasons," Peri confessed, the amusement fading as she glanced around the shop that was now nothing more than an empty shell despite the residue of magic that lingered.

Hexx had spent over a century peddling black market spells and potions out of this store. Nothing short of burning it to the ground and salting the earth could get rid of the echoes of power.

Maya grimaced. She recognized that tone. "Oh no."

Peri held up a slender hand. "First, I'm here to make sure you're okay. Your text was pretty vague. What's going on? And why are you hanging around this god-awful place?"

Maya shared what had happened from the moment her trap had been triggered by Tia until she'd ended up twiddling her thumbs in the empty pawnshop. Peri listened in silence, more resigned than surprised. Over the past couple of years they'd endured rogue magic, the end of the world, and the return of pure evil from the dead.

Of course they were going to be forced to battle against some weird glowing slime.

"And you don't know where the stuff came from that's attacking Joe?"

"Not a clue. Yet another mystery on a long list of mysteries."

Peri wrinkled her nose. "That's the second reason I'm here."

Maya braced herself. "Has something happened?"

"I have a video I think you should see."

"Okay."

Peri pulled her phone out of her back pocket, moving to stand next to Maya so she could see the screen.

"I was sent this security footage from one of Valen's guards. He was on patrol this evening in Lenox Hill when he sensed a disturbance at a local demon gallery. There's been trouble there before, so he went to check it out."

Maya was confused. She was called in to help when a mage was involved in a local disturbance, but never demons.

"And?"

"I'll let you see for yourself."

Peri pressed her finger against the screen to play the black-and-white security video. Leaning forward, Maya watched as a young blond-haired woman strolled into the elegant shop, pausing in the center of the room as a large demon appeared from the back.

Maya sent Peri a puzzled frown. "Is she a human?"

Peri froze the video. "Look closely at her coat."

Maya jerked in shock. She'd recognize that oversized winter coat with large silver buttons anywhere.

"The thief."

"Yes." Peri touched the screen to allow the video to resume.

"There's no sound?" Maya demanded.

"No. We're lucky there's any security. Albert Hamilton is a black market dealer who's a constant pain in Valen's ass."

"Like Hexx?"

Peri snorted. "Hamilton only deals with the most rare and expensive artifacts. He probably makes more in a day than Hexx has earned in his entire lifetime."

Maya believed her friend. The gallery looked expensive. Clearly she would have to personally investigate the claims of illegal magical items once this was over. For now, she was more interested in the woman who'd so easily penetrated her defenses.

There was nothing but the coat to reveal this was the same person, but Maya was confident that they'd found the thief. It was in the proud tilt of her head and her swagger as she entered the building. Whoever she was, she didn't lack in confidence.

Focused on the thief, Maya didn't pay much attention to the demon. He had a deep crimson aura, but he was no stronger than a dozen others in the city. New York had become an epicenter of power over the past two centuries, attracting demons who could claim the purest bloodlines.

It wasn't until three guards appeared from the shadows to surround the thief that she realized this wasn't a simple exchange of stolen goods for cash. The woman was jumping to her feet as the demon reached out to grab her. The next thing that happened was the demon was flying through the air and crashing into one of the display cases.

"She's not making many friends in town," Maya muttered, her unease intensifying.

The stranger had to be a mage, right? How else could she have tossed the demon around like he was a twig? And not just a mage. But one of the most powerful magic users that Maya had ever encountered. So why hadn't she been able to sense the woman's magic when she was standing a few feet away from her?

Maya's thoughts were distracted as there was a movement behind the woman. Maya squinted. Was that a man? It was hard to see more than a fuzzy outline.

"Who's that?" She pointed at the screen. "And why is he out of focus?"

"I asked one of Valen's security men to look at the footage. His opinion was the male's aura is screwing with the camera."

"A demon?"

"If it is, then his powers are off the charts."

"Crap."

"Wait. It gets worse."

"Of course it does," Maya muttered, preparing herself for an explosion or earthquake or incoming meteorite. If Peri said something was getting worse, then it had to be really, really bad.

The video continued, revealing a battle between the fuzzy male form and the demons. He was clearly the superior fighter, as he easily overpowered the guards, but even as they prepared to leave, the thief was pointing toward the guard who was rising to his feet and shuffling toward them with weird, jerky movements. As if he wasn't in control of his body. And there was something wrong with his face...

"Wait," she breathed, her gaze shifting to study the other guards, who were moving with the same strange jerks. "Are those demons glowing?"

"That's what it looks like," Peri agreed.

Maya furrowed her brow. "A spell? A curse?"

"I've never seen anything like it."

"This is the only video available?"

"Unfortunately." Peri pressed her finger against the screen, freezing the action. "This is what I wanted you to see."

She zoomed the image until it revealed the thief's hand reaching toward a slender rod. The video was too grainy to make out the exact designs on the metal object, but Maya guessed that it was a fey lightning rod. Not an illegal relic, but they were frowned on by the Cabal.

"We already knew the thief has a habit of taking things that don't belong to her," she said, not sure what Peri wanted her to see.

Peri pointed to the woman's hand. "She's not stealing the rod. She's draining the magic."

Maya leaned closer, barely able to make out the shimmering threads of magic that connected the rod to the thief's open palm.

"She's a Void," she breathed.

"What does that mean?"

With a string of highly inventive expletives, Maya whirled around to discover the blond-haired woman standing in a corner of the pawnshop, her odd lavender eyes glowing with a sharp-edged curiosity.

Chapter 9

Wynn tightly clutched the skipping stone she had hidden in the pocket of her coat. She'd promised Azh that she would pop in and pop out, distracting the mages long enough for him to slip through the barrier they'd discovered wrapped around Hexx's pawnshop. But her promise had been given before she'd overheard the two women discussing the security video of her visit to Hamilton Brothers Gallery.

And before the dark-haired mage she recognized as Maya Rosen had called her a...what had she said? A Void?

"Don't move." Maya grabbed the satchel from the nearby counter and pulled out a vial.

Wynn widened her eyes, trying to look innocent. She didn't doubt the vial contained a nasty potion, not to mention the fact the mage she recognized as Peri Sanguis, the Cabal leader's mate, was busy weaving a spell that made the entire building tremble.

"I'm not here to steal anything," she promised.

Maya glanced around the empty shop. "Shocker."

"Yeah, okay. Fair enough. No one would come here to steal anything," Wynn conceded.

Maya's expression remained grim. "Who are you?"

"Wynn."

"That's it? Just Wynn?"

"Powerful women don't need more than one name."

Maya rolled her eyes, her impressive beauty only enhanced by the web of scars along her jaw.

"If you're trying to kiss and make up, you're doing a lousy job."

"Probably because I'm not trying," Wynn said. "I just want to talk."

"About?"

"Why I snuck into your vault."

Maya narrowed her bright green eyes while Peri casually moved to lean against the counter. Wynn wasn't fooled. Both of them were on full alert, prepared to strike at the first hint of danger.

She didn't know if they were there to protect the Watcher, or if they had another purpose for wrapping the building in layers of magic, but she did know she didn't want to do anything to spark a fight.

Not this time.

"I'm listening," Maya said.

"First." Wynn took a cautious step forward, her mouth dry. "Why did you call me a Void?"

The mage arched a brow. "I assume that's why you're absorbing the fey magic from the lightning rod instead of just using it."

Distantly Wynn sensed Azh's presence above her head. He'd managed to slip into Hexx's apartment. And thankfully, the mages appeared unaware of his stealthy entrance.

"I don't understand," Wynn admitted. "Why does a Void absorb magic?"

Maya frowned. "You don't know?"

"Would I be asking if I did?" Wynn snapped. She was trying to be polite, she really was. But it wasn't easy when all she wanted to do was grab the mage and shake the truth out of her.

Maya exchanged a suspicious glance with her companion before returning her attention to Wynn.

"I have no idea why you're here, but I can assure you that I won't be fooled again."

"I want answers." Wynn hesitated, then with an effort, spit out the word that she swore never to use once she stopped being a beggar on the streets. "Please."

Maya pursed her lips, her expression hard. "Fine. I don't trust you, but I'll answer your question." She returned the potion to her satchel, obviously trusting Peri to deal with any potential threats. Wynn didn't blame her. The younger mage was vibrating the entire block with the force of her pent-up magic. "You know the basics of a witch transforming into a mage?" Maya asked.

Wynn shrugged. Everything she'd picked up had been off the streets. She had no idea what was real and what was myth.

"I know that there are some witches that self-combust when they reach puberty. And that those witches become mages who can use magic without all the abracadabra nonsense."

Maya blinked. "Self-combust?"

"That's what it sounded like to me."

"Okay. That's a little dramatic." Maya paused, as if considering her words before she spoke. "More simply a mage is the daughter of a woman who is capable of tapping into magic. A witch, a fortune teller, a voodoo priestess, and so on. The original magic is in the DNA of the mother."

"So why don't all the daughters become mages?"

"No one knows for certain," Maya admitted. "And it's all but impossible to determine which daughter will become a mage. It's not until she reaches her late teens—for some it's earlier and for some it's later—the wild magic ignites and flows through her veins."

Wynn suppressed her stab of annoyance. It wasn't really an answer. "Okay. And?"

"Becoming a mage is rare. Extremely rare," Maya continued. "But even more rare are girls who have the wild magic flare through them, but their magic doesn't ignite."

Wynn's mouth felt dry. She had no memory of her youth, which meant she had no idea if she'd had magic exploding through her or not.

"Why doesn't it ignite?"

"Again I don't have an explanation. The witches and mages have been hunted by both humans and demons over the centuries. Their fear of exposure has meant they'd been forced to keep too much information hidden." Maya's jaw tightened with anger. Wynn sensed it was a fury that had burned inside the mage for a long time. "But what we suspect is that the power bursts through them with so much force it burns away their ability to hold on to the magic."

"So what happens to them?"

"The majority of them become Nulls."

There was a sadness in Maya's tone that sent a chill through Wynn. The other woman sounded like being a Null was a very bad thing.

"What does that mean?" she forced herself to ask.

"They can sense the magic flowing through their blood, but it remains out of reach. Usually it..." Maya's words trailed away.

"Tell me," Wynn insisted. Whatever she had to say couldn't be worse than the not knowing.

Maya slowly shook her head. "It drives them mad. They rarely live for very long after the failed transformation. I think they will themselves to death. It's tragic."

Wynn's heart squeezed at the pity in the mage's voice. It was obvious she'd watched at least one mage die from being trapped in a world where the magic was forever taunting them. But something about her explanation was off. At least for Wynn. She didn't have magic flowing through her veins, but she could still touch and manipulate the power she absorbed.

And thankfully, she'd never felt the urge to give up on her existence. In fact, her struggles had made her more determined to survive. Her shitty beginnings in the backstreets of London taught her how to fight, lie, and even cheat, to get to a better place.

"Is that what you think happened to me?" she finally asked.

"No. If you're a Void, then the wild magic flared and instead of igniting the power that flows through your blood, it creates a void."

Wynn studied her in confusion. "How's that different from a Null?"

"The Null can sense magic but is unable to touch it. But from the stories I've heard, a Void doesn't have magic inside them, but they're capable of absorbing magic and storing it to be used later. I'm not sure exactly how it works."

"Stories?" Wynn felt a stab of unease. "You never met one?"

"They are very, very rare. I don't think there's been one recorded in centuries." The mage paused, as if struck by a sudden thought. "Of course, they might not be willing to reveal themselves. As I said earlier, mages have been hunted by witches, demons, and vampires from the beginning of time." She studied Wynn with a curious expression. "If you're able to pass as a human it's much safer. Is that what you've been doing?"

"Hey, I'm just trying to survive," she said with blunt honesty.

"I can help." Maya circled around the corner of the counter, her movements slow, as if she were afraid of scaring Wynn. "When did you go through the transformation?"

Wynn rubbed the skipping stone, igniting the magic. She wasn't scared, but Azh was safely in the apartment and she suspected she had all the information she was going to get from Maya. She needed to get out of there before the mages realized what was happening.

"I don't remember anything about the wild magic going through me," she admitted, feeling the stone warm against her skin. It was preparing to jerk her away from the pawnshop. But first, Wynn had one more question.

"Could the transformation—or whatever you want to call it—scrub my memories?"

Maya looked baffled by the question. "I've never heard of it happening. Are you saying you don't recall transforming into a mage? Or that all your memories are gone?"

There was no reason not to confess the truth. "I woke up one day with no idea who I was or how I got there."

"How long ago?"

"Let's just say Queen Victoria was on the throne."

Maya's mouth dropped open. She was genuinely shocked by Wynn's answer. "And you've managed to survive with no mage to assist you?"

Wynn clicked her tongue, refusing to recall the nights she'd spent crying herself to sleep. The first few years after she'd awakened she'd been terrified, not knowing who she was or who she could trust. She would have given anything for a powerful mage to reach out an offer of help.

Now, she'd learned that she couldn't depend on anyone but herself.

She tilted her chin. "I don't need anyone."

"I'm not questioning your skills. Obviously you've managed to live a lot longer than many mages, but I could teach you to control the magic you absorb." Maya's voice softened, a tingle of magic floating through the air. It wasn't a hard blow of compulsion that a vampire could use to force creatures to bend to their will. Or even the grinding coercion that Azh had first tried to use on her. This was a soft enticement that lured Wynn into agreeing. "Plus, I could give you a home with no need to steal ever again."

"Yeah, thanks, but no thanks. I prefer my freedom." With a toss of her head, Wynn easily shattered the spell. "I'll never be caged. Not by a mage. Or a demon. And certainly not by a—" She cut off the word dragon, silently chastising herself for nearly exposing Azh's presence in this world. Dammit. She was getting sloppy. "By anyone," she lamely finished.

Something that might have been impatience flared through the green eyes. Maya Rosen was a woman accustomed to being obeyed.

"You said that you would tell me why you broke into my vault," she reminded Wynn in sharp tones.

Wynn smiled, but before she could assure the mage that it was stupid to believe anything that came out of her mouth, Peri was abruptly stiffening, her hand reaching out to grab Maya's arm.

"What's wrong?" Maya demanded, staring at her friend in concern. "Peri?"

"She's a diversion. There's something upstairs."

"Dammit."

Maya snapped her head around to glare at Wynn, who was giving them a mocking wave as her magic snapped into place.

"Buh-bye, suckers."

* * * *

Azh paused to glance around the dark apartment, a pang of irritation racing through him at the sense of Wynn in the empty space below him. She'd promised that she would distract the mages and then return to the safety of her lair.

Not that he was surprised.

Wynn would do what Wynn wanted to do when she wanted to do it. End of story.

With a shake of his head, Azh weaved his way through the maze of stacked boxes until he could see the motionless form wearing a pair of ridiculous pajamas stretched on the floor. Even at a distance it was easy to determine that the Watcher wasn't unconscious. He was in a deep stasis. His body was in this world, but his mind was locked in another plane of existence.

Azh's attention turned toward the beautiful, silver-haired mage kneeling next to him. Her head was bowed and her eyes were closed, but she wasn't asleep. He assumed she was trying to mentally connect with the Watcher.

The question was why. Was she attacking him? Was she somehow related to the strange green magic? Or was she trying to rescue him?

Only one way to find out.

Remaining far enough away to avoid alerting the mage to his presence, Azh focused his concentration on the power signature that hummed around the body of the Watcher. If he tried to force his way into the male's mind he might trigger a nasty defensive spell. Or worse, distract him from his battle with the evil magic. This way he could slide into the Watcher's thoughts using his own magic.

It was a trick he'd discovered in the early years of his hibernation. Unlike his mother, he hadn't wasted his time trying to plot how to break the treaty she'd been forced to sign. Instead, he kept a close watch on the vampires and demons, and later the humans, as they changed and molded the world. When the dragons returned they were going to have to find a way to fit into this new society. Or shatter it and start over, like the previous queen wanted.

Azh felt himself skimming along a tidal wave of magic as he slipped into the Watcher's mind, the sudden mist that surrounded him proving he was in the right place. Wynn had said she was taken into the mist when the Watcher had touched her. He mentally pushed his way through the thick fog, hissing in shock at the sight of the powerful male swathed from head to toe in a cocoon of green slime. The same slime that bubbled in a nearby pool.

"Stop." A female voice sliced through the mist, as a tall, slender woman moved to block his path. "Don't come any closer."

Azh recognized the mage kneeling next to the Watcher's unconscious body even as her magic smashed against him, a warning that she wasn't a harmless bystander. She was no match for a dragon, but she could cause him serious pain.

"I'm not a threat," he said, trying to keep the irritation from his voice.

Wynn was still downstairs and her presence was making him edgy. If this encounter went sideways he didn't want her anywhere close to this building.

"No?" the woman demanded, her expression grim. "Then why have you spent hours lurking at the edges of the mist instead of showing yourself?"

Azh scowled at the accusation. "I haven't been anywhere near this place."

She narrowed her gaze. "I've sensed your power. It's like nothing I've ever felt before. What are you?"

"Dragon." Azh stepped around her.

Magic slammed into him. "No. I won't let you near him."

"I told you, I'm not here to hurt anyone." Azh shattered the coils of power that had wrapped around him.

"Dragons already tried to break the treaty," she snapped. "Why should I trust you?"

Okay. She had a point. His mother had destroyed any hope of trust. It was something he was going to have to deal with at a much later date. For now, he forced himself to resist the urge to shove her out of his path.

"Allow me to ask my question and I'll disappear."

Her jaw tightened as she glanced over her shoulder at the male being squeezed by the slime.

"He's a little preoccupied."

"He's also losing the battle," Azh told her in hard tones. "Without finding a way to destroy the evil, it's going to consume him."

There was a long silence before she reluctantly stepped aside. "Ask."

Azh stepped forward, keeping a healthy distance from the spreading goo. "Watcher, is this the corruption that drove my people into exile?"

The answer whispered through his mind. *"Yes."*

Azh didn't know whether to be pleased or horrified his suspicions had been confirmed. On one hand, he at least knew what was infecting the demons. On the other, he had no idea how to stop it.

"It was trapped in Kazak when we came here," he muttered. "How did it follow us."

"The rift..."

"What about it?"

"It's failing."

Azh flinched. He shouldn't have been shocked by the answer. It was the most logical explanation. But he didn't want to accept the true depth of the danger they faced. If the corruption invaded this world...

No. He wouldn't let that happen.

"How do I repair it?" he demanded.

"Gabriela."

Azh growled at the worthless suggestion. "She's dead. She sacrificed herself to seal the opening."

"Her magic." The voice in his mind seemed to fade, as if the Watcher was growing weary. Or perhaps he was dying. A terrifying thought. *"Return it to the rift."*

Azh clenched his hands, resisting the futile urge to try to destroy the bubbling slime with his magic. There was every likelihood he would only make things worse.

"You mean the statue?"

"Hurry."

"How?" Azh growled. "I don't know where to find the statue." He grimaced. "Or the rift."

"Then we die."

The voice abruptly ended, the sense of the Watcher smothered beneath a pulse of evil that threatened to spill over Azh. He shuddered, turning to send the mage a warning glare.

"Stay with him."

She stiffened. Her face was pale, as if she'd felt the same pulse of evil, but her courage never faltered.

"I don't take orders from you," she snarled.

"If the corruption gets loose we all die. Right now he's the only thing holding back the magic."

"I didn't say I wasn't going to protect him, I just said I don't take orders from you."

Azh rolled his eyes. "Mages." He turned away, only to stop himself, glancing over his shoulder to deliver another warning. "If you did sense something in the mist, it wasn't me. Be careful."

Chapter 10

Azh returned to the hotel, pleasantly surprised to discover Wynn waiting for him. He had expected her to disappear while he was preoccupied. She made a habit of forcing him to track her down.

Pacing the cramped space, Azh shared his conversation with the Watcher word for word. Wynn leaned against the wall, her face pale as she absorbed the depths of the danger they were facing.

This was no longer a fun game of pursuit, while Wynn tried to get rid of a mysterious strand of magic. This was do or die. Perhaps literally.

She studied him with a worried expression. "What could weaken the rift?"

It was a question that gnawed at Azh. "It must be related to Gabriela. It was her magic that created the opening and sealed it after we came to this world. Something must have compromised her powers."

Wynn pushed away from the wall. "You think I'm responsible?"

Azh halted, confused by her sudden surge of anger. "Of course not. I don't know what's happened, but I think it's possible that the statue was stolen from the cavern where it was hidden and you crossed paths with it at some point."

Her anger slowly faded, as if realizing he hadn't been accusing her of deliberately attempting to open the rift.

"I agree," she said in low tones.

He arched a brow. "Thank you."

"I wasn't done," she chastised. "Even having a potential explanation doesn't help us."

"Why not?"

She spread her hands, her expression frustrated. "I've spent over a year searching for the object responsible for the mysterious magic. I returned to every vault and safe that I'd..." She took a second to find a word that didn't make her sound like a thief. It had to be habit. She couldn't be worried that he was concerned with her habit of taking stuff that didn't belong to her. He was a dragon. Stealing treasure was a long-honored tradition. "That I'd visited just before I absorbed the magic. When I couldn't find anything, I started searching through pawnshops and auction houses and private collectors in case it'd been stolen or sold since I touched it." She waved a hand around the cheap hotel room. "The past few weeks I've been stuck in this place, chasing down a dozen rumors of powerful objects. There's been nothing that resonates with the magic inside me."

"You can usually sense where the object is located?"

"Not necessarily, but most of the time I feel the magic as it's being absorbed so at least I know where I encountered the power. Especially if I absorb it by accident."

Azh studied his companion with a sudden burst of curiosity. He'd logically accepted that Wynn could absorb magic, but he hadn't considered the finer details of what that meant. Including the danger of being consumed by a magic she couldn't control.

"Does that happen very often?"

She made a face, as if recalling more than one unfortunate incident. "It did in the beginning, but I've developed shields to help avoid most unpleasant surprises."

Azh's gaze slid downward. That explained the heavy coat she wore despite the smothering heat in the cramped room. As he'd suspected, it was layered with spells of protection.

"But the dragon magic slipped past your defenses?" he asked.

"It must have."

It made sense. Dragon magic wasn't intended to be used by any other creature. Why should she be able to sense it?

Still, it was strange that she'd been able to absorb the power if she couldn't use it.

"How did you first notice the magic?" he asked.

"The strand just appeared one day." She pressed a hand against her stomach, as if she wanted to yank it out. "It was weird, but I ignored it."

"You ignored a mysterious magic that appeared inside you?"

"I ignore a lot of stuff. There's been too many strange things happening for the past two centuries to get worked up about everything. It wasn't until it started to expand and interfere with my other magic that I really noticed it. And then the nightmares started."

"The nightmares must have something to do with the corruption," Azh murmured.

"How?"

A good question. If she were a regular mage he would assume she had the power to tap into dreams, but he suspected her nightmares were a direct result of her brush with dragon magic.

"Maybe the dreams are trying to warn you. Are there any specific details you can remember?"

She shivered. "The glowing eyes."

"Beyond the glowing eyes."

There was a long pause, as if Wynn was afraid to speak the nightmares out loud.

"They're always the same," she eventually said. "I'm walking through the streets of London and I notice some demons walking toward me. As they get closer I can see the putrid green light in their eyes. I know they're infected with some sort of evil and that I can't let them touch me."

"Do you recognize the demons?"

She nodded. "Axton and his clan of goblins. They own a shop in Covent Garden. Or at least they did. I haven't been there in decades."

"It's a place to start," he abruptly decided.

Wynn looked confused. "Even if Axton has something to do with the corruption, how does it help to locate the dragon statue?"

Azh waved aside an inconvenient question. As a dragon he understood that patience was a virtue. How else could he endure endless eons of hibernation? But right now, the need to protect Wynn was vibrating through him with a painful intensity.

They had to figure out how to close the rift before the toxic magic could flood this world.

"Is it better to stay here and chase rumors?" he demanded.

She wrapped her arms around her waist, her eyes darkening with a sudden weariness.

"Right now I just want to find a dark hole and disappear for a few years."

Azh understood her exhaustion. She'd been fighting a battle she didn't understand for months. Every instinct inside him screamed for him to sweep her off her feet and carry her to his lair. Once she was away from this world she could have the peace she so desperately desired.

Unfortunately, the danger was all too real. For everyone, including the dragons. Right now all he could do was offer her support to face the enemy lurking in the mists.

"You'd never do that." He crossed to stand directly in front of her, cupping her cheek in his hand. "You're a fighter."

She thankfully didn't pull away. "I'm tired of fighting."

"Then lean on me," he urged in gentle tones. "Fate brought me to you for a reason."

The lavender eyes darkened, as if she were tempted to snuggle against him, but even as she swayed forward, her expression abruptly hardened. As if she suddenly remembered why she didn't trust him.

"You mean it was fate that brought you to Gabriela," she said in cold tones. "You're obsessed with her magic, not mine."

Ah. Azh was smart enough to hide his smile of satisfaction. She was jealous.

"I followed Gabriela's magic," he cautiously agreed. "But my obsession is with you, Wynn." He stepped closer, wrapping her in his heat as he allowed the flames to dance over his fingers before he smoothed them over her cheek. "The extraordinary lavender of your eyes. The soft silk of your skin." Hunger blasted through him as she shivered in response. It was perilously easy to imagine having her stretched beneath him as he pleasured her with the brush of his flames. And lips. And teeth... "I'm obsessed with the threads of gold in your hair," he continued, his arousal pressing painfully against his slacks as he lowered his head to stroke his lips over her brow and down the slender length of her nose. "And the sensual promise of your lips." He pressed a kiss against her mouth, growling as the taste of her seared through him. It wasn't dragon. Or demon. Or human. It was something utterly unique. "I've longed to devour you from the moment I first caught sight of you."

She reached up to grab his upper arms, as if her knees were weak. "Devour me?"

"Does that frighten you?"

"You are a dragon. I'm pretty sure you really could devour me."

Azh chuckled. There was curiosity in her scent. And desire. A blazing desire that matched his own. But no fear.

Inside him the dragon stirred awake, lured by Wynn's sweet floral scent and the sensation of soft, silken skin beneath his fingertips. Then, without warning, it released a low roar of possession, the flames erupting to flare around them in a cyclone of flames.

"I promise that my beast will give you nothing but pleasure," he assured her in a rough voice.

Wynn tilted back her head, her face flushed and her eyes shimmering with enchantment as she watched the sparks dance over her skin. But before Azh could sweep her in his arms and carry her to the nearby bed, she flattened her hands against his chest.

"Azh." She had to stop and clear the lump from her throat. "This isn't the time."

He pressed a hungry kiss against her parted lips. "No. It's not the time," he agreed.

She trembled. "Or the place."

"Definitely not the place." His fingers trailed down the curve of her neck.

"So what are we doing?" she rasped, her head tilting to the side to allow him greater access.

Unable to resist temptation, Azh skimmed his lips down the same path of his fingers, lingering on the rapid pulse at the base of her throat.

"A small taste of what's to come," he whispered.

Her nails dug into his chest, her breath ragged. "This doesn't feel small."

"No. It feels..."

Deep inside him, Azh's dragon parted its mouth to reveal the razor-sharp fangs, then with a smug contentment, it released a white blast of magic. Azh shuddered as the power raced through him, allowing the beast to absorb Wynn's essence until she was imprinted on his soul.

Wynn leaned back, eyeing him with a wary expression. "It feels what?"

"Earth-shattering."

"Azh."

"Ssh." He slid his arms beneath her coat and around her slender waist, pulling her tight against him. "I've got you."

"That's what I'm afraid of."

"Afraid?" He pressed a last, lingering kiss on her lips before reluctantly lifting his head to study her flushed face. "I don't believe you. You're the most courageous creature I've ever met. Courageous and reckless and stubbornly impervious to the fact you're mortal."

"I don't have any choice. Before last year I lived a very boring life. Well..." She wrinkled her nose at the blatant lie. "Mostly boring."

"You're an adrenaline junkie who lives on the edge." He wasn't teasing. This woman was a thrill seeker. He could only hope that taming a dragon would be enough of a challenge. "A trait that will no doubt give me an ulcer."

Her lips twitched as she accepted she couldn't fool him. "Can dragons get ulcers?"

"We'll find out."

"Hmm." Her hands smoothed over the muscles of his chest. "Why would you care if I put myself in danger?"

He tugged her hard against the aching length of his erection. "You know why, Wynn." He groaned at the feel of her soft temptation against his hardness. "We both know why," he rasped.

The rich scent of her desire swirled through the air, but she arched back as she realized how close they were to forgetting the danger just outside the door.

"Azh."

"Yes, I know. Wrong place, wrong time."

Azh clenched his teeth. It took more effort than he wanted to admit for him to lower his arms and step back. He'd spent eons indulging his various appetites, including sex, with a casual appreciation that didn't include clinging to anyone or anything.

The only thing he hoarded was his treasure.

And now...Wynn.

With a shake of his head, Azh forced himself to concentrate on his sketchy plan to locate Gabriela's statue. His dragon rumbled in frustration, but with a huff of annoyance the beast settled back to sleep.

"Do you have anything you want to take with us?" he asked.

She sent him a confused glance. "Where are we going?"

"London."

"Now?"

"The sooner the better."

She reached into her pocket to pull out a small rock. "My skipping stones won't take us that far. We'll have to book a flight. It's going to take a day or two to get things arranged. Always assuming you have a passport."

He snorted at her ridiculous words. "I have an easier way. Get whatever you want to take with you."

Turning, she headed toward the corner to grab her duffel bag that was obviously packed and ready to go at a moment's notice. He suspected she'd spent her entire life like that. Eager to run.

Could she be convinced to stay in one place? Or would she forever feel the need to roam?

A question for later.

She walked back to stand in front of him, a sudden frown tugging on her brows. "What's your easier way? You're not going to turn into your dragon, are you?"

He tried to imagine shifting into his natural form in the middle of New York City. It would be pure chaos. Not to mention warning every creature in the world that he'd left the confines of his lair.

Still, he couldn't resist teasing his companion. "Does the thought bother you?"

"It's a little intimidating," she admitted. "I mean I logically accept you're a dragon, but it doesn't feel real."

Azh held out his hand. "I have something that might help." He smiled as she hesitated. "Trust me."

"I don't trust anyone," she said, but she laid her hand against his open palm.

He squeezed her fingers. "Challenge accepted."

"That's not a challenge..." Her words dried on her lips, her eyes widening as the cheap hotel room began to fade and they were standing in the center of a marble corridor lined with fluted columns that soared toward the distant ceiling. She turned in a slow circle, her eyes wide. Everything was built on a grand scale fit for dragons. From the arched, stained-glass windows that soared ten feet off the ground to the alcoves carved into the thick marble walls large enough for a full-grown dragon to curl up for a nap. "Is this where your people are hibernating?"

He nodded. "Traveling through here is the fastest route to London."

She shivered, instinctively stepping closer to him as the chandelier overhead rattled and a blast of heat sizzled through the air.

"It might be the fastest, but I don't think I'm supposed to be here."

"You're with me. That's all the invitation you need."

"I hope so." Her eyes darted from side to side, as if expecting a beast to suddenly appear. "I don't want to end up a crispy critter because you enjoy breaking the rules." The chandelier rattled again as an ear-piercing screech echoed down the corridor. "What's that?"

"Do you want to see?"

She hesitated, then squared her shoulders. "Yes."

Still gripping her fingers, he headed down the long corridor, reaching the very end before turning into a side tunnel that led to a heavy iron door marked with layers of hexes. It was hard to imagine any creature stupid enough to sneak into a lair filled with dragons, but better safe than sorry. Every door was protected by a spell that would alert him if anyone tried to open it.

With a whisper of magic, the heavy door slid open, revealing a steep staircase heading into the darkness. He could hear Wynn's rapid heartbeat and the uneven breaths she was trying to disguise, but her steps never faltered as he led her into the depths of the vast cavern.

Surrounded by a thick darkness, Azh followed a narrow path that eventually opened to reveal an immense crater so deep the bottom couldn't be seen and wide enough that the dragon perched on the far side was little more than a smudge of shimmering scales.

In the center of the crater two dragons released precise bursts of fire as they veered and circled each other in elegant patterns. The larger white dragon with blue eyes was more powerful as he swooped down and sliced his claws along the scales of the emerald dragon. Not hard enough to penetrate, but enough to leave marks. The green dragon, however, had the advantage of speed as she performed a swift turn that allowed her to swoop over the top of her opponent and spray her liquid fire over his head.

The male bellowed in pain, slapping the younger dragon with a wing that was ten feet long. The female twirled away, something that sounded like laughter floating toward them.

Turning his head, Azh studied Wynn's tense profile. She appeared impervious to the fact she was standing on the edge of a sheer cliff. Her attention was locked on the dragons who continued their sparring with a dazzling display of power.

"Terrified?" he asked softly.

"Yes," she breathed, a fine layer of perspiration coating her skin. The searing heat from their blasts of fire could be felt even at a distance. "But only in the most beautiful way possible," she continued. "It's like a dance, only with fire and teeth and claws."

His clenched muscles relaxed at her captivated expression. She'd been right when she said that the idea of a dragon was different from seeing one in person. Their size alone was intimidating, but add in the thunderous power and their pleasure in testing their strength against each other...they weren't a species for the faint of heart.

There'd been a real possibility that she would see them in flight and run screaming in the opposite direction. The fact that she'd instead watched their skirmish with a blatant fascination not only assured him but the beast inside him.

"We've tried to minimize the damage we inflict on one another over the years. In the old days this sort of friendly sparring would often end in death," he admitted. She needed to know the full truth of his people.

The good, the bad, and the ugly.

She arched a brow. "Are you saying that the dragons are evolving?"

"It's that or become obsolete. A fact that has been difficult for some of my people to comprehend."

She abruptly turned to face him, her expression somber. "I hope they do survive."

He impulsively wrapped his arms around her waist, tugging her tight against him.

"I'm going to do whatever necessary to make sure they do."

He heard her breath catch, her eyes widening as his beast surged toward the surface. Having Wynn in this place, surrounding her in his scent, stirred his most primitive passions.

"Azh..." she breathed.

"What is it?"

"I see your dragon." She reached up to brush her fingertips gently over his eyes. "He's lurking just behind here. He looks like he really does want to devour me."

He tugged her closer, a growl rumbling in his throat. "From head to toe."

She shivered as he allowed his fire to dance over them, outlining the wings that were invisible in this form. In the background the dragons once again bellowed their battle cries.

Azh hissed as he struggled to control his pagan desires, sternly reminding himself that they were just passing through. Of course, that didn't mean they couldn't take a short detour.

"I have something else I want you to see."

She clicked her tongue, as if she thought he was teasing. "Seriously, you have to work on your cheesy lines."

He lifted her hand to press her fingers against his lips. "Trust me."

Before she could argue, he led her along the narrow pathway, heading toward an arched opening that led to the tunnels used by the servants who'd traveled with the dragons into hibernation. He wasn't trying to hide. Every dragon in the lair could feel his presence. Along with his companion's. This was simply the fastest route to where he was going.

Once inside the tunnel, they curved their way upward, heading to the layer of caverns directly above the arena. A few minutes later they stepped into another massive space. Azh stopped at the entrance, raising his hand to release a small flame that danced through the air, igniting the chandeliers that circled the coved ceiling.

The soft glow of light spilled over the endless rows of shelves that held the dragons' impressive library and the long wooden tables placed in the center of the marble floor. On the opposite side of the space were glass cases that held manuscripts and parchments collected over thousands of years. Lost in the shadows was a shimmering circle of magic. It was the entrance to the forbidden section, where the most fragile and dangerous books were stored.

Next to him Wynn released a small gasp, stepping forward to glance around the heavily stacked shelves with a bemused expression.

"You did this on purpose, didn't you?"

"Did what?"

"Brought me here to show off your library." She turned to send him a chiding glance. "You knew I would be enchanted."

He chuckled, shattering the illusion he'd wrapped around Gabriela's book. Now that the seal protecting Gabriela's hidden connection to the corruption had been broken, he wanted to make sure it was safely stored away. The history of the dragons was going to have to be rewritten.

Yet another worry for later.

With a word of power, he sent the heavy book spinning through the air, bypassing the glass cases to disappear through the swirling opening to the forbidden section.

Then he turned to study his companion with a faint smile. "Actually I assumed you'd be enchanted by the arena."

"They were kick-ass warriors. But this..." She spread her arms as if attempting to absorb the rich scent of leather and incense. "This is the true magic."

His dragon restlessly paced inside him as he stared down at the face that had captivated him from the beginning. The soft lavender eyes and delicate features were beautiful, but it was the bold, unbreakable spirit that called to his beast.

"Just like you," he whispered.

She swayed toward him, as if they were being pulled together by unseen forces. But even as he reached to pull her into his arms, the marble floor trembled beneath their feet.

"How dare you taint our home with that creature," a female voice roared, shattering the sense of peace.

Jumping back, Wynn shoved her hand into the pocket of her coat, no doubt grabbing her skipping stone in case she needed a quick exit.

"Someone's not happy," she said, her voice not quite steady.

Azh ground his teeth as his mother continued her angry tirade. "Destroy her or I will."

Dammit. He should have wrapped his mother's cell in layers that muffled her from sensing what was happening in the rest of the lair. Her unwelcomed interference wasn't going to stop until he made her understand that she was no longer queen.

"Time to go," he announced.

Not because he cared if his mother was angry that Wynn was in their lair. Zanna was always angry about something. But he didn't want Wynn to think she was anything but welcomed in his home.

"No shit," she agreed, hurrying toward the door.

Azh heaved a sigh and with a flick of his hand returned the library to darkness.

Chapter 11

Wynn released a silent breath of relief as they stepped through a thick layer of magic and into the early morning light. A quick glance around revealed they were standing on the Victoria Embankment near Blackfriars Bridge. The smell of the city along with the pungent stench of the nearby Thames hit her with a comforting familiarity. No matter where she traveled or how long she was gone, London would always be home.

It was in the steady pulse of magic from the powerful Gyre and the ancient sense of belonging that seeped into her soul. As if she'd been a part of this land for countless eons, not a couple of centuries.

Despite the early hour, the morning rush had already started, the sounds a reassuring background noise as Wynn sent her companion a quick glance to make sure he'd toned down his aura. The nuclear blasts that surrounded him would sound the alarm to every creature in England something dangerous had arrived. Even if the humans couldn't see it, the city had a large demon population, not to mention Saxton, the powerful vampire and current Cabal leader of the British Empire.

Once assured they weren't going to attract unwanted attention, she turned to head toward Farringdon Street.

"Want to tell me who's threatening to destroy me?" she at last demanded, proud when the words came out steady. She didn't want to reveal the booming voice had scared the crap out of her.

"Not really."

She glanced to the side, noting his clenched jaw. He truly didn't want to tell her. The knowledge did nothing to ease her raw nerves.

"Azh."

"My mother," he at last confessed.

Wynn flinched. No wonder he didn't want to confess the truth. It was bad enough to think that there was some unknown dragon who didn't want a stranger in the lair. But the fact it was Azh's mother made it a thousand times worse.

Was she pissed off because there was a stranger in the lair? Or because her son was there with a female who wasn't a dragon?

The anger thundering in the air had felt personal. As if it was a direct response to Wynn, not just a random intruder.

The thought made her gut twist with a vague sense of dread.

"Your mother. Great."

Wynn shuddered as they passed by Fleet Street, heading toward Holborn and Shoe Lane. Long ago this area had been the rookery, overrun with beggars and drunks who weaved their way through the narrow, filthy streets. On top of the hill she could just make out the square tower of St. Andrew's church. The one spot of hope in an otherwise dismal neighborhood.

Over the years the area had been invaded by the middle-class, who ruthlessly bulldozed away the mishmash of wooden structures and the open market where vendors had once stood next to cartloads of fruits, vegetables, and secondhand furniture. They'd replaced them with cement walkways and sleek new buildings.

Wynn supposed it was an improvement. Crime was down and it smelled a thousand times better, but the vibrant soul had disappeared. A tradeoff that most locals were no doubt prepared to accept.

"Don't take it personally," Azh said dryly. "My mother hates everyone. She would kill me if she got the opportunity."

"Seriously?"

"Dead serious."

She blinked. His expression warned he wasn't joking. Weirdly, that made her feel better.

"Why does she hate everyone?"

"Because I have her imprisoned for trying to break the treaty last year. She's not happy."

"I used to wonder what it would be like to have a family."

"Complicated," he admitted. "But despite my toxic relationship with my mother, I'm devoted to my people. They're my true family and I will do everything in my power to protect them."

She shrugged, pretending his words hadn't scraped against a raw nerve. "Being alone isn't so bad."

She could feel the weight of his gaze brush over her, as if he could sense her lie. "No?"

She shrugged. "My mother's not threatening to kill me."

"True."

"Of course, she might have and I don't remember it." Reaching the end of the block, Wynn glanced from side to side. "And speaking of not remembering."

A hot breeze wrapped around Wynn as Azh stepped close, flames coating his clenched fists.

"What's wrong?" he demanded. "Do you sense something?"

Wynn shook her head. "It's been years since I was in this neighborhood. It's changed." She at last pointed toward the street that sloped up the hill. "It must be this way."

They walked past glass shop fronts that were surprisingly elegant behind the steel shutters that hadn't been opened for the day. When Wynn had spent time in the neighborhood there had been pubs and cheap lodging houses shoved into the cramped spaces, not clothing stores. And the muddy streets had been clogged with horses, not expensive cars that zoomed past on their way to work.

"The pawnshop was at the end of the street," she said, shaking away the memories.

It was the gloss of time that made them seem less horrible. There was nothing romantic about standing on the corner begging for food. Or being splattered with mud when a carriage swept past. Not to mention dealing with the locals who would have brutalized her if she'd been a normal human.

She slowed her steps as they reached the corner, feeling a stab of unease.

The pawnshop was still there, or at least, the shell of the pawnshop was still there. The aged stone building was covered in black soot and the windows had been shattered. Even the heavy wooden door hung at a wonky angle, as if some power had tried to rip it from its hinges.

Had there been a fire? An explosion? A magical attack?

A steel barrier had been placed in front of the building, with large signs warning trespassers they would be fined or even imprisoned. A little over the top, she silently acknowledged, considering the place was a dump.

She assumed that it had been put there by the authorities to prevent anyone from dying when the building collapsed.

"I wouldn't get any closer if I was you," a voice warned from behind them.

The fact that Azh hadn't warned her there was danger approaching assured her that it must be a human.

She glanced over her shoulder at the young woman dressed in a narrow black skirt and sleeveless white sweater. Her dark hair was smoothed from her pale, oval face and her dark eyes were emphasized by her false eyelashes.

She had the look of an ambitious human on her way up the corporate ladder.

Wynn concentrated on the magic inside her, tapping into the pale-rose strand. Once she felt the familiar tingles she weaved a spell to change her identity. Gone were her blond hair and lavender eyes. Instead she was hidden behind an illusion of a sophisticated, older woman with silver hair pulled into a bun and wearing a beige trench coat. The sort of woman who would be employed in the elegant neighborhood.

Moving around Azh, she stood directly in front of the human, at the same time releasing a small spell of compulsion. It wouldn't force the woman to do anything against her will, but it would encourage her to talk.

"What happened?" Wynn asked.

"The official report was an explosion caused by a gas leak, but most people around here think it was an insurance scam."

"You believe the owners did this on purpose?"

"Maybe." She shrugged. "They were super creepy and the other business owners were constantly turning them in to the authorities for not keeping their building up to code." She glanced toward the building with a visible shudder. "This is actually an improvement."

Wynn wasn't surprised the neighborhood had been disgusted by Axton. He was rude, crude, and easily provoked to violence. Unfortunately for them, he had enough royal demon blood to make sure he was protected by the most powerful clans in the city. He could run his ratty pawnshop, so long as he didn't offend Saxton.

"I didn't hear anything about it. When did it happen?"

The woman's gaze started to swing back to Wynn only to be captured by Azh standing behind her. Wynn heard the poor girl's strangled gasp as she tried to absorb his shocking beauty. She sympathized. Even after spending a few days in his company she was still knocked off balance whenever she caught sight of him.

Wynn cleared her throat. "Do you remember when the explosion happened?"

With an effort, the woman forced herself to answer the question, although her bemused gaze remained locked on Azh.

"It must have been over year now."

A year? A chill inched down Wynn's spine. That couldn't be a coincidence, could it? Not when her dreams started at the same time.

"Do you know if they moved the pawnshop to a new location?"

"I think they took off. Probably to a place they can't be extradited."

"Why do you say that?"

The woman slowly peeled her gaze from Azh to send Wynn a warning frown.

"The site is toxic. Anyone who goes in there comes out sick."

"Like radiation?"

"I've heard radiation. If you ask me, I think it is some sort of nasty residue from illegal weapons. Everyone suspected that shop was a front for the drug cartel. Or worse. Whatever it is must be bad," she added. "Not even the authorities will go in there. If my job didn't pay so well I'd never come back to this street." The woman reached into her designer purse to pull out a key fob, directing it toward the glass door of the luxury leather goods shop. "Gotta go or I'll be late."

"Thanks."

Wynn waited while the woman gave Azh one last longing glance before disappearing into the store next door. Then, releasing her illusion, she turned back to study the pawnshop.

"Do you sense anything?" Azh asked as he stepped toward the metal barrier.

Wynn shuddered. The shields she'd woven into her coat protected her from the waves of magic that battered against her, but she could still sense them.

"Too much. The spells are all melted together into a weird glob." She grimaced. "What about you?"

The morning sunlight pooled over Azh, revealing a shimmer of scales on his exposed skin and a faint outline of folded wings. His inner dragon was lurking closer to the surface since they'd entered the lair. Or maybe it was responding to the danger that hummed in the air.

Her own spidey senses were definitely buzzing.

"There's a power that's separate from the other magic," he warned.

"Dragon?"

He shook his head. "It's something I've never felt before."

Something that a dragon had never felt before? She didn't know how old he was, but his years spanned several millennia. Long enough that he should have experienced everything this world had to offer.

"That's not good," she said.

"We'll find out." He grasped the protective fence, his fingers glowing with a heat that sliced through the metal as if it were butter. A second later a large section crashed to the ground, sending up a cloud of dust. Wynn coughed, instinctively stepping back. She didn't want to be there. And not just because this place had centered in her nightmares. There was a sense of "wrongness" that hung in the air. Azh turned, holding out his hand. "Together."

Forcing herself to take a deep breath, Wynn placed her hand in his. She expected it to be searing hot from the flames, but his skin was pleasantly warm. Comforting. An adjective she never expected to use in connection with a dragon.

"Yeah. Okay."

They stepped over the fence, careful to avoid the shards of glass spread over the ground. The tangle of magic thickened as they reached the busted door and stepped inside, feeling as if it was physically pushing them away.

Wynn gagged as she pressed through the barrier and into the shop, glancing around the shadowed interior. The heavy shelves had been toppled over, littering the wooden floor with piles of shattered figurines, crystal balls, and jars filled with potions. Even the heavy cases containing the more dangerous spells at the back had been pulled from the wall, as if someone had been searching for something in particular.

Whatever it was, she assumed they hadn't found it since the place had been ravaged by a fire that wasn't natural. It'd melted the magical items into unrecognizable lumps while leaving the walls and floor only lightly charred.

"Weirdly, it smells the same," she complained, waving a hand in front of her face. As if she hoped to chase away the stench that had been embedded in the shop over the centuries.

Azh sent his surroundings a disgusted glance. He was an elegant, lethal predator who was accustomed to soaring through the sky. Being stuck in this cramped, filthy space was no doubt making his skin crawl.

"Like a sewer?"

"Yup."

"Did you spend a lot of time here?"

Wynn pointed through the empty space where the front window used to be. "In the early days I survived by begging on that corner. Back then there was a pub nearby that would leave its doors open. It helped to keep me warm on the coldest nights. Plus, there was the hope one of the customers would get drunk enough to toss me a coin on their way home. Eventually I discovered that I could sense magic, and better yet, I could enter places no one else could go and steal the stuff inside. Axton would buy them from me."

With a small shake of her head, Wynn cautiously picked her way through the rubble. She didn't know what she hoped to find, but they'd come this far to get answers. Even if they couldn't locate Axton he might have left a clue behind.

"Eventually I refined my talents so I could locate artifacts that were powerful or rare. Or a combination of both. I could sell them for a lot more money and I stopped coming here. A pity I didn't bank some of that cash."

"What did you do with it?"

Wynn heaved a sigh. Her early days of poverty should have taught her to prepare for the future. Wasn't there some famous quote about learning from the past to avoid repeating the same mistakes over and over?

Instead, her deprivation had encouraged her to indulge her most excessive desires without concern for the future. Maybe because she knew in the back of her mind there was no guarantee she wouldn't once again lose her memories and be forced to start over. Or maybe she was just the sort of person who lived for the moment.

Whatever the reason, she'd gone through a fortune.

"Fancy hotels. Fancy clothes. The finest parties. In fact, I was at Queen Elizabeth's coronation. Good times." Her lips twitched, sensing Azh's disapproving gaze as she headed to the back of the shop. "Plus, I could never stay in one place too long. Eventually a demon or one of the Cabal would get grumpy about the number of their precious artifacts that were disappearing. Or sometimes I might sell them something that wasn't as powerful as I'd promised. I would have to disappear and start over in a new location. Usually somewhere across the Continent. Or even across the ocean." She shrugged.

It hadn't usually bothered her to take off and invent a new identity. There was something exciting about a clean slate. Why be stuck in one place for an eternity? Unless she was stuck in that place with a dangerously sexy dragon who could dance flames over her naked body and breathe fire...no. She abruptly shoved aside the distracting thought. The pawnshop might be abandoned, but there were plenty of things left behind that could kill her. "Although I never had to beg again," she continued, focusing on the shelves that had been ripped from the walls. "At least not yet."

Azh clicked his tongue. "You never have to worry again. Unlike you I've kept a close guard on my treasure."

Wynn chuckled, enjoying Azh's aversion to such lavish wastefulness. The knowledge he was willing to accept her own excesses by sharing his carefully preserved treasure was oddly endearing.

"So the cliché about a dragon being obsessed with his hoard is true?" she asked, stepping over a glob of magical items that had fallen from the shelf and melted together.

"The only thing more precious to a dragon is his mate," Azh assured her, then without warning, he sent a blast of flames directly in front of her, forcing her to leap backward. "Don't move, Wynn."

She sent him a startled glance. "What's wrong?"

"The power I sensed from outside is under the rubble at your feet."

The flames spun until they were a tiny tornado, searing away the upper layer of charred artifacts. Wynn lifted a hand to protect her face from the sudden blast of heat, her eyes narrowed as the flames created a blinding glow.

It took a moment for her vision to clear once the fire vanished. Slowly lowering her arm, she studied the spot that Azh had cleared away. The glob of artifacts had turned to liquid, draining away from the center of the flames. A shocking display of the raw heat that he'd released. Only one item remained on the blackened stone floor. A silver medallion in astonishingly pristine condition.

Hanging from a plain silver chain, the medallion was the size of a quarter and etched with a strange design. It pulsed with a soft silvery light in the dim shadows, as if it held a powerful magic.

Wynn gasped. Not because she was surprised that the medallion had survived the fire. But because she recognized it.

"My necklace," she rasped.

Azh moved to stand next to her. "You've seen it before?"

"I was wearing it when I first woke up on the banks of the river."

He sent her a startled glance. "That was yours?"

Wynn shrugged. "I guess it belonged to me. I was wearing it. Of course I could have stolen it, I suppose. Or whoever left me there could have put it on me."

When she'd awakened she'd been wearing a tattered robe that looked as if it'd come out of a trash heap and her hair had been coated with a thick layer of grime. Only the medallion around her neck assured her that she hadn't been dumped by her family who assumed she was dead. No one would have left a piece of jewelry that was pure silver on a corpse. Especially one that had been tossed away like trash.

Azh leaned forward to study the necklace. "How did it get here?"

"I pawned it to Axton the second night I came into London." At the time she hadn't realized that Axton was a demon. Or that the medallion might hold magic. She just knew that she was cold and hungry and in desperate need of shelter. "I was standing on the corner and he gave me enough money to eat and find lodging for an entire month. I should have known he was ripping me off." She snorted, trying to sense the magic that pulsed in the silver. It was there, but weirdly it didn't reach out to her. Was it because she'd already absorbed whatever magic was inside? Had she used it before she knew what she could do? She pursed her lips. "Axton would never have kept it all this time if it wasn't valuable."

"Or they kept it for their personal use," Azh suggested, cautiously reaching down to hold his fingers above the necklace. "There's a power attached to it."

Azh hissed, swiftly yanking his hand back as the medallion sizzled with warning.

Wynn arched her brows. What could make a dragon flinch?

"The demons must have done something to it," she said. "It was just a necklace when I was wearing it."

Straightening, Azh stepped back, nodding toward the medallion. "You try."

Wynn snorted. "Sure, have the fragile human touch the thing that you're afraid of."

"First, if you were ever human, that time has long past," Azh said dryly. "And second, I'd never associate the word fragile with you. You have the fierce spirit of a dragon." He returned his attention to the medallion. "I don't think it tried to hurt me. It was more a warning it didn't want to be touched. If you owned it in the past, I think it's possible it might recognize you."

His words made sense. Dammit.

She bent down, cautiously reaching toward the necklace. The last thing she wanted was to accidentally absorb another mysterious magic. On the other hand, there had to be a reason that Axton had kept the medallion for two centuries.

"I don't feel anything threatening."

She gathered her courage and plucked the medallion off the floor. The metal felt cool against her skin, the pulse of power barely noticeable. It was more a gentle welcome than a punishment.

"It's like the power recognizes you," Azh murmured.

Wynn studied the faint etchings on the medallion, a memory stirring in the back of her mind. There was pain. A screaming pain that enveloped her like a tidal wave. Then there was...nothing. A blessed darkness that wrapped her in peace.

She released a shuddering breath. Was the memory hers? Or the medallion?

"What power?" she muttered. "And what does it recognize?"

"Two questions that we need to answer." Azh used the tip of his boot to shove aside the rubble that had been on top of the necklace. "The destruction of this shop started where the medallion was lying and spread from there."

With a frown, Wynn stepped back. The floor where the medallion had been lying was untouched by fire, but everything around it was charred beyond recognition. She held the necklace by the silver chain, allowing the medallion to twirl in the muted light.

"You think this has something to do with the corruption?"

"There's a reason you were having nightmares about this particular shop. The medallion is the most obvious link to you."

"Maybe," she conceded. "But it's not much help. I don't know how I got it or what it does."

He shrugged. "Then let's go back to the beginning."

Wynn felt a stab of irritation. After a year of scouring her brain for anything that might explain her strange nightmares, she didn't want to waste time going over it again.

"I've told you everything I can remember."

"No, I meant let's physically go to the place you first woke up."

"Why?"

Azh arched a brow and Wynn abruptly realized she was sounding like a petulant child. Probably because she was tired, hungry, and frustrated that every time she thought they might get answers it led to a dead end. None of that was Azh's fault.

"Okay," she grudgingly agreed. "It's possible there's a reason I was dumped in that spot."

She tucked the necklace in her coat pocket, carefully retracing her steps out of the ruined pawnshop. She took a moment to wonder what happened to Axton and his clan, hoping they'd managed to escape. Sure, they were immoral opportunists, but they didn't deserve to be slaughtered because of her.

Making a mental note to see if she could track them down once she'd figured out what the hell was happening, Wynn headed back toward the river. She knew she should be studying the medallion, figuring out what the etching might mean. Or at least trying to discover why she'd remembered a crippling pain when she'd first picked it up.

Instead, she was forced to concentrate on planting one foot in front of the other. She was running on autopilot as the deep weariness clouded her mind, making it hard to think clearly.

"You're tired," Azh abruptly announced.

She didn't bother to argue. "Too many sleepless nights followed by running from one disaster to another."

"I think I can help with that."

"The sleepless nights or too many disasters?"

"Both."

Stepping into the shadows of a nearby building, Azh ignored the thickening crowd of pedestrians scurrying to work with various levels of dread and anticipation. Most had their attention glued to their phones. The few who bothered to notice them stumbled over their feet as they caught sight of Azh.

Male or female, it didn't matter. He was so brutally gorgeous it was impossible not to react.

Expecting him to pull open the door so they could enter the building, Wynn took a step back as she felt the heat of his magic. His hand was moving in a circle, as if he were opening a portal.

"Wait," she protested. "You're not going to feed me to your mother, are you?"

"Never." He stepped forward, disappearing into a soft silver mist.

Wynn followed, her steps reluctant. She didn't think he'd feed her to his mother. But his confidence in her courage meant he might lead her back to the lions' den...or rather the dragons' lair...without considering the fact his people might want her dead.

A few steps into the mist, she was forced to suddenly stop as she rammed into Azh's broad back. She grunted. She knew he was solid, but damn. He felt like a brick wall.

Regaining her balance, she rubbed her nose that had been squashed against his shoulder. "Is something wrong?"

He turned to study her with a faint smile. "This space is between our hidden lair and the world. The barrier is created to prevent anyone from using magic when they're here. That way no one can come in and no one can leave." He held up his hand as her lips parted to ask how he could pass through. "Unless the treaty allows them access. You're safe here."

She glanced around. She wasn't worried about the lack of a bed. She'd spent a lot of nights on the ground. But there was something unnerving about trying to sleep when she couldn't see the danger coming.

"Are you staying?"

The words escaped her lips before she could stop them, but before she could pretend she couldn't care less if the dragon decided to disappear into the mist, Azh stepped forward and cupped her face in his hands.

"I wouldn't be anywhere else." He brushed a kiss over her lips, his flames wrapping her in a possessive warmth. "Rest."

Chapter 12

Comforted by the heat from Azh's magic, Wynn tumbled into a deep sleep. It was the first time she'd felt truly safe for over a year. Strange, considering she was in a weird space between her world and the dragons' lair. Not to mention having a lethal predator watching over her. A creature who could destroy her with one stray hiccup.

Lost in the darkness, she floated in peace for what felt like hours. Then, slowly, the sense of floating changed to soaring.

She was no longer Wynn. She was Gabriela, soaring across the sky with her wings spread wide and her head tilted toward the suns that burned with a delicious heat.

Climbing higher than any dragon should dare, she folded her wings tight against her sleek body before tilting forward to plunge toward the ocean with an exhilarating speed. Pleasure shuddered through her as the wind whipped past her, the younger dragons scattering to give her room.

She tried to clear her mind. This was her happy place. Free from the grinding demands of her kingdom and the nagging worry that there were traitors plotting against her.

With a hiss that released a large cloud of steam, she angled her path toward the temple in the clouds. A second later she was transforming her shape to enter the forbidden chamber. She wrinkled her nose as she crossed the vast floor and climbed onto the dais before settling on her throne. The familiar scent of heavy metal that marked this world as Kazak, the dragon homeland, was nearly drowned out by a sour stench.

Not for long...

The voice whispered in the back of her mind. A silky soft voice that had appeared a century ago, warning her of the impending danger and urging her to take steps to protect herself and her people. This morning she'd accepted it was time.

If she listened to her royal council and waited to deal with the brewing trouble, it might very well be too late.

As if the thought of the aggravating male made him materialize out of thin air, she felt the brush of powerful magic before a tall, slender male dressed in a long robe stepped into the chamber. The elder dragon was bald with a narrow face marred by four scars that went from his left temple to his ear. The result of a battle with the former king that had left him on the verge of death for a millennium.

"Go away, Zion," she commanded.

The male bowed in a gesture of respect, but his expression was hard when he straightened. As one of the few dragons who'd survived the long-ago civil war that had shattered her people, he'd earned the right to speak.

And he used that privilege with annoying regularity.

"Not until I've had my say."

She clicked her tongue. "I've heard it all before."

"Then you'll hear it again. Don't do this, Gabriela. I beg of you."

"What choice do I have?" She waved a hand toward the river of green that bubbled in the crack in the floor. "Not even you can deny that the corruption is spreading."

Zion shrugged. "We've managed to keep it contained for eons."

No one knew precisely where the corruption had come from. It'd first appeared during the civil war, tiny rivulets of evil that would poison a river or taint a field so their crops would fail. Some claimed it was a punishment for the war. They pointed to the carcasses of the dragons who'd fallen to the ground and been left to rot. Not to mention the endless tears as their people mourned their families that had been mindlessly slaughtered.

When they'd finally realized the evil wasn't going to go away, they'd combined their magic to contain it in this temple, far away from the dragons.

"We can't keep it locked away forever. Besides, no one bothered to try and leash it," she argued. "Regardless of the taint it's still a powerful magic. Why waste it?"

"I haven't finished my experiments. I'm certain I can find a way to cleanse the corruption without you being exposed."

"It's too late. There are too many younger dragons who've become convinced that they can use the magic to challenge my authority."

The dark eyes regarded her with an unnerving intensity. This was one male who wasn't blinded by her beauty and raw power. To Zion, she would always be the young hatchling who'd recklessly battled her way to the top.

"And you fear they might succeed?"

Gabriela sniffed, pretending that the thought of having her throne stolen wasn't like a red-hot poker stabbing her in her heart.

"I fear their reckless hunger for power will destroy the shields that protect us."

"Then we'll face the threat when it happens."

"Why wait?"

"Why hurry?"

She rose to her feet, the voice whispering in her ear warning her that this male was trying to stop her from her duty. Why? Was he plotting with the rebels? It wouldn't be the first time he'd stood against the monarch. The last time had nearly killed him. This time he might hope for a chance to claim the crown for himself.

"If I can cleanse the magic, then they can't use it against me."

"Again, my queen, is this to protect your people or your crown?"

Fury raced through her. She was the ruler, not this interfering old lizard. "You can stand with me, Zion, or you can stand against me. The choice is yours."

"As always I remain your devoted servant." The male bowed again, his back stiff as he retreated from the cavern.

Gabriela waited until he disappeared before kneeling next to the crack. She hadn't become queen by simply hoping for the best. She'd used her enormous power to grab the crown and never looked back. It was the same way she intended to keep the crown.

By doing whatever was necessary.

Calling on her magic, she held out her hands, watching the flames burst to life. They blazed pure white, burning at a temperature that could melt solid granite. No other dragon could match her talent with fire. One of the reasons she'd never been challenged.

Until now, the voice reminded her. *With the evil power they will overthrow you and destroy the dragons. You have no choice.*

Dismissing Zion and his nagging warnings from her mind, Gabriela leaned forward to plunge her hands into the river of pure corruption. The only way to banish evil was to absorb it and use the power for good.

Closing her eyes, she tried to concentrate on the fire that burned inside her. It was harder than she expected as the corruption surged through her, the greedy magic scouring away her very essence. Mine. She released a blast of her flames. Nothing could contest her raw power, she reminded herself.

Nothing.

The magic roared through her like a raging torrent, filling the cavern with an emerald glow. It was...majestic. *This is what the power was meant to be*, a voice whispered in the back of her mind. It wasn't evil. It was a glorious celebration of dragons and their future without the petty rules.

She was Gabriela, Queen of the Dragons.

But even as she managed to leash the magic and bend it to her will, an unexpected pain smashed through her. No, it wasn't pain. It was a debilitating agony that cascaded through her like an avalanche, threatening to rip her apart. Her bones snapped and the skin began to peel from her flesh.

No, this was all wrong!

She had to get out of there. She had to flee before the magic destroyed her.

Gabriela tilted back her head to roar with a combination of fear and horror. "Release me."

* * * *

Azh remained on guard as Wynn curled into a ball and fell asleep. Behind this barrier they should be safe, but he wasn't taking any chances. They not only had to worry about the corruption that was seemingly able to infect demons with its evil magic, but now his mother had caught Wynn's scent and declared her an enemy.

Not that he regretted taking Wynn into his lair. A smug smile curved his lips as he glanced down at the delicate woman who he'd gently coated in weaves of fire.

He'd known she had courage. Enough courage to give him gray hairs. But there were few creatures who could have watched the sparring between the dragons and not cowered in fear. He needed to be sure that she could accept him in all his forms.

Savoring the rumbles of satisfaction from his inner beast, Azh was abruptly distracted as Wynn began to twitch in her sleep. Then the movements became bigger, her arms thrashing as if she were trying to hold off an unseen enemy.

Whatever nightmare she was experiencing was bad enough to cover her skin in a layer of perspiration.

Azh dropped to his knees, reaching out to wrap her in his arms. "Wynn, wake up." He gave her a gentle shake. "Wynn. Can you hear me?"

She fought against his hold, her breath coming in shallow gasps. Then her eyes snapped open to reveal a lingering terror.

"Azh."

"I've got you," he murmured, pressing her tight against his chest.

"It was her," she rasped.

"What?"

"Gabriela."

He studied her tense expression. "You were dreaming."

She shook her head. "It was more than a dream. I *was* Gabriela. I could feel everything that she felt. I soared through the air and plunged toward the ocean. I walked on two legs to enter the strange pyramid that we saw in the book and sat on her throne."

Azh would have dismissed her claim as simple weariness if it wasn't the dragon magic that pulsed inside her. Somehow she'd managed to tap into Gabriela's power. Why not tap into her memories?

He ran a soothing hand down her back. He could still feel the tremors that raced through her body.

"You were obviously disturbed by something. What happened?"

"She tried to leash the corruption. That's how it escaped."

Azh hissed. "Gabriela caused the destruction of our homeland?"

Wynn winced as if belatedly realizing the stark impact of her words. For countless eons Gabriela had been a folk hero out of legends. Even to those who weren't entirely convinced the mythical paradise was real. Now he had to consider the possibility that the savior of his people might actually be the villain.

"She didn't mean to. It was a mistake. That's why she sacrificed herself," she hurriedly added.

Azh shook his head, dismissing her fear that he was having a crisis of faith. Actually, he wasn't sure he was surprised. Gabriela the Savior was a fable. The real flesh-and-blood queen was no doubt as complicated and flawed as every other dragon.

He was far more concerned with the knowledge that Gabriela's memories were causing Wynn a pain that lingered in the depths of her lavender eyes.

"I'm sorry."

"Sorry about what?"

He waved a hand toward the surrounding mist. "I thought this place would protect you from the nightmares. I just made them worse."

"It wasn't this place," she assured him, sitting up and glancing around, as if reassuring herself they were alone in the mist. "I think she's trying to tell me something."

"About the corruption?"

"She was screaming to release her. I think she was sending me a warning." Wynn grimaced. "Not much help when I don't know how I'm supposed to do that."

"Did you see her come through the rift in your dream?"

"No. I felt her touch the corruption with the magic and everything went black."

Azh's brief hope that they might at least have a location to search for the rift was crushed before it could fully form. Annoying, but predictable. It couldn't be as simple as Gabriela coming to Wynn in a dream to tell her exactly where to go and how to end the threat.

Where was the fun in that?

"Then we continue with our original plan," he abruptly announced.

If Wynn was disappointed that he didn't have a better strategy, she didn't reveal it as she shoved herself to her feet and squared her shoulders.

"Okay." She pressed her hand to her stomach as it rumbled in a loud protest. "But first dinner. I'm starving."

Azh grasped her hand as he opened the portal and they stepped onto the streets of London that were now shadowed with the encroaching night. He paused as he absorbed their surroundings. The business offices had closed hours ago, but the locals and eager tourists were still strolling the streets in search of entertainment. Assuring himself that there was nothing but humans and a few demons in the area, he allowed Wynn to lead him toward the river.

"When you say dinner, do you mean donuts?" he demanded.

She hesitated at a corner, as if trying to remember her way. "Something a little more substantial than that," she assured him, abruptly turning to the left and picking up her pace. "My favorite chippie is just a few blocks away."

Azh smelled the hot grease and vinegar before she halted in front of a narrow building with a blue awning above the glass door. They walked into the brightly lit restaurant and stood in line, ignoring the curious glances from the crowd of customers.

More than a few of the gazes lingered on him, no doubt sensing the power that hummed in the air no matter how tightly he leashed his magic, but most of them openly stared at the woman next to him. Despite the old coat that hung on her slender frame and the strands of golden hair that had come lose from her braid, Wynn's luminous beauty was mesmerizing. The delicate features, the astonishing lavender eyes, and the don't-screw-with-me vibe.

And best of all, she didn't even seem to notice the stir she was causing. She was solely focused on feeding her belly before moving on.

Hiding his smile of pleasure at simply being near Wynn, he remained silent as she ordered enough to satisfy two hungry dragons. She remained distracted as she handed him a box of food and headed out of the shop and down the street.

Popping the lid off her dinner, she grabbed one of the deep-fried fish, shoving it into her mouth as if she truly was starving.

"Mmm." She closed her eyes in bliss. "Divine."

A hunger that had nothing to do with fish and chips blasted through Azh, nearly sending him to his knees. Gods above, she was glorious. No wonder she was quickly driving him to the edge of sanity.

"Agreed," he growled.

She opened her eyes, easily sensing his desire. How could she miss it? The heat blasted through the air like a furnace. A faint blush stained her cheeks, but she pretended to be oblivious as she glanced toward his untouched meal.

"I didn't even think to ask," she said.

"Ask what?"

"Do dragons eat human food?"

"We eat humans."

She blinked. "Seriously?"

"Of course not." He paused, realizing he wasn't being entirely honest. His ancestors hadn't been choosy when it came to snack time. "At least, not anymore." Opening the box, Azh tasted the fish and then a handful of the chips. The salt, vinegar, and hot grease hit his tongue with a burst of savory goodness. "You're right, this is divine."

They consumed the food in large bites before dumping the empty boxes in the nearest trash bin. Wynn licked her fingers as they crossed the bridge and headed along the south bank. She appeared lost in thought as they strolled toward Battersea.

Azh was content to allow the silence to wrap around them as he concentrated on the small groups of humans and demons that spilled out of the pubs and restaurants that lined the streets. He assumed he'd sensed if any of them were carrying the corruption, but he couldn't be sure. He intended to kill anything acting weird and ask questions later.

"Are you bothered by my dream?" Wynn abruptly broke the silence.

Ah. That's why she'd been distracted. She'd been worried that her revelations had hurt him.

"I regret you were forced to endure it. You've had enough nightmares," he said.

"Agreed, but I was talking about the possibility that Gabriela released the corruption."

"It's important that we discover the truth. The more information we have, the easier it will be to find the statue and close the rift." His tone was firm. He wasn't going to let her spend a second worried he blamed her for revealing Gabriela's blunder.

"But you—"

"No one is perfect," he overrode her protest. "And whatever her mistakes, she did sacrifice herself to protect her people."

She met his steady gaze, giving a slow nod of her head. "True."

"Gabriela is a legend among the dragons, but the reality of her will always be lost to the mists of time. Where she belongs."

As he said the words, Azh felt something click inside him. As if a missing piece had settled into place. Or maybe it was the end of his childish fantasies. His mother had a point when she'd accused him of being obsessed with fairytales. Especially the ones where Gabriela rescued them from certain death.

But it was remarkably easy to accept that the truth was more complicated. He was more than ready to close the door on the past and concentrate on the future. A future that included the lovely woman walking next to him.

"I hope you're right," she said, her voice lowering to a soft whisper. "Her magic is growing stronger every day. I'm afraid it might eventually consume me."

A growl rumbled in his throat. There wasn't fear in her voice, but he could sense her churning concern. A concern that he shared, even if he didn't want to admit it.

The magic inside her wasn't meant for mages. Or humans. Or...anyone.

"I won't let that happen," he swore, meaning every word.

"You might not be able to stop it."

He reached out to grasp her hand, tugging her to a stop. He'd started this journey with the intention of locating and destroying whoever dared to tamper with dragon powers, but now he knew he'd do whatever necessary to protect Wynn. She'd become a necessary reason for his existence.

"Trust me," he urged.

"I..." Wynn's words died on her lips, her eyes widening. "Azh."

"What?" Azh glanced around, searching for what had startled her. He couldn't see anything beyond the dark streets and closed businesses. Was it the magic inside her? "What's wrong?"

"We triggered a fissure spell."

"Shit." Keeping a tight hold on her fingers, Azh released the weaves that muted his magic, allowing his power to boom through the air with concussive force. Instantly the ground began to shake and the nearby windows shattered. "Hold on, Wynn," he commanded.

His flames whipped out, surrounding them in a layer of fiery protection, but it was too late. The trap had already opened, sucking Wynn into a gaping hole of darkness.

Azh roared in fury at the feel of Wynn's fingers sliding from his grasp, her expression one of terror as she disappeared.

He was going to kill someone. Maybe a whole lot of someones.

And then he was going to burn shit to the ground.

Ignoring the flames that continued to whirl around him like a fiery tornado, Azh stomped to the end of the block. He could smell the gathered demons crammed into the small pub.

It had to be one of the royal fey who'd created the fissure. They were the only creatures who possessed the magic to rip a small hole in the fabric of space to create a gateway. When they were at their full powers in the ancient past they could travel from place to place with the openings or escape from their enemies. These days the magic was too unstable for personal use. They tended to crash without warning, trapping the user inside. But they could set a trap for an unwary enemy. And if the fey was truly gifted they could set tiny fissures around a large area that could only be triggered when a specific prey stepped into it.

A fey that powerful would be well known, even in a city as large as London. Unfortunately, the locals would no doubt be reluctant to snitch on a fellow demon. Especially one that could make their life a misery.

Azh didn't doubt he could eventually force them to talk, but he didn't have time to figure out who had information and how to get the truth out of them. It was easier to go to the top of the food chain. The one creature absolutely certain to know everyone and everything happening in the city.

Saxton, the Cabal leader of Britain.

Ducking his head to get through the door of the noisy pub, Azh was relieved to discover the ceiling was much taller than most older establishments in the city. Probably because the gathered goblins and fey were much larger than normal humans, even if their blood had been thinned over the years. He still towered over the crowd, his gaze impatiently scanning for the owner. It took a moment to pick out the large goblin in the corner. The square-faced male was wearing a white dress shirt that was unbuttoned to reveal his hairy chest, as if compensating for the lack of hair on his bald head, and black leather pants. He had small dark eyes that glittered with satisfaction at the numerous customers squeezed into the cramped space.

Currently, he was leaning back in a wooden chair with a heavy club lying across his lap, although it was his dark crimson aura that warned most demons not to piss him off.

At Azh's entrance the place went quiet. Not the quiet of a group of friends suddenly confronted by a stranger. This was the terrified quiet of prey realizing that a predator had just strolled into their den. Even the loud music screeched to a halt.

No one wanted to attract his attention.

Unaware of Azh's entrance, the owner abruptly shoved himself out of his chair and swaggered forward, the club held tight in his fist.

"What's going on here?" he bellowed. "Turn the music back on."

Azh moved to stand in the direct path of the approaching demon. "Contact your master."

Jerking to a stop as he nearly plowed into Azh, the male's square face flushed with fury. "What the... Get out before I rip off your head and shove it up your ass."

Azh narrowed his gaze. "I will ask one more time before I burn this place to the ground. Call your master."

"Ah. You want to go?" Too stupid to sense his danger, the goblin lifted his weapon. "Okay, then, let's go."

Azh snapped out his arm, wrapping his fingers around the male's thick neck. Then, releasing his flames, he allowed them to crawl over the goblin from head to toe.

The male screamed. The fire was hot enough to scorch his skin, although Azh was careful not to do any permanent damage. Not yet.

"Last time," he snarled. "Contact your master. Now."

"Right. Yeah, just calm down," the goblin choked out, dropping his club to reach into the pocket of his slacks and pull out a phone. "I'm calling right now. See?"

Azh sensed movement behind him. Slowly turning his head he watched as a female goblin tried to creep toward him, her fingers wrapped around a long dagger that shimmered with powerful hexes. The owner's mate? No. He studied the bright crimson aura. She was the true power. With a hiss, Azh released a bolt of lightning, splintering the floor planks just inches from her toes.

The female froze, her eyes flashing crimson as the shoulder-length black hair floated on the electrical currents that sizzled in the air.

"Easy, dude. I just have to take a piss," she hastily lied, trying to hide the dagger behind her back.

"Don't move," he warned, his attention shifting toward the open door.

The sharp chill slicing through the air warned a vampire was approaching. A very powerful vampire.

That was quick.

It was no surprise that the goblin had sent a frantic SOS to the Cabal leader, but it was amazing the leech had managed to get here so quickly. Either he'd been in the neighborhood or he'd sensed Azh's presence in the city and had been keeping a close watch on him.

He was betting on the latter.

Frost coated the large front windows a second before a slender male wearing an expensive gray suit and silver tie stepped over the threshold. His dark hair was brushed from his narrow face and his black eyes smoldered with a commanding power.

He looked like an elegant aristocrat who'd been polished by the finest boarding schools that money could buy, not a monster who sucked the blood of his victims.

"You're the leader of this Gyre?" Azh demanded, not giving the male the opportunity to gain control of the confrontation.

The vampire gave a stiff nod of his head. "Saxton. Leader of the British Empire and member of the Cabal."

Satisfied, Azh glanced back at the goblin who trembled in pain as the fire swirled over him. Dousing the flames, Azh shoved him away.

"Leave."

The male licked his cracked lips, glancing nervously toward his master.

"Go," Saxton said, the soft word enough to send the host of demons scurrying for the exit.

A couple of scuffles impeded their progress as they fought to get out the door. Clearly no one wanted to be the last one out, but eventually the pub was empty and Saxton was regarding him with an icy displeasure.

"I assume this was a way to gain my attention?"

"Yes."

Saxton arched a brow at Azh's blunt admission. "I heard rumors there was a dragon who left hibernation to creep around the world."

Azh snorted. "Hardly creeping."

"True." Saxton narrowed his gaze. "You have some balls breaking the treaty and coming here alone."

"I didn't break the treaty and I'm not here to cause trouble." Azh held up a hand. He didn't have time to squabble with the leech, no matter how fun it might be. "There's a threat to this world. One that's great enough that the treaty allowed me to leave my lair."

Saxton bared his fangs. They were long and sharp and lethal to most creatures. Not Azh. The invisible scales that coated his skin made it impossible for the fangs to penetrate. Not to mention the fact he could char his ass with a burst of fire.

"I've been warned not to interfere, which is the only reason you aren't in my dungeons," the leech growled.

Azh spread his arms in a mocking gesture. "You're welcomed to try." The air filled with an icy mist as Saxton's power rammed into Azh's fiery aura. The two glared at one another, violence beckoning in an age-old battle for supremacy. Then the image of Wynn's terrified expression as she was sucked into the fissure had Azh hissing in frustration. What was he doing? His pride wasn't more important than finding the woman who'd captured the heart of his beast. "I need your help." He nearly choked on the words, but they allowed him to leash his powers.

A second later, Saxton did the same. The potential for battle was temporarily muted.

"What do you need?"

"Wynn..." Azh hesitated, not sure if this male was aware of Wynn's unique talents. "The female I was traveling with has been kidnapped. I need her back. Immediately."

"What happened?"

"She said it was a fissure just moments before she disappeared."

The vampire scowled. Was he suspicious of Azh's explanation? He'd be a fool not to be cautious. And you didn't become a leader in the Cabal by being stupid.

"Take me to the spot it happened," he abruptly commanded.

Azh stepped forward, his aura flaring with a blinding intensity. "Word of warning. I don't want to kill anyone, but I will if I'm threatened."

Another flash of snowy-white fangs. "Same."

Careful to keep a respectful distance from each other, the two predators left the pub and hurried through the dark streets. There was the sound of footsteps as the demons who'd lingered to enjoy the brewing battle scurried away.

By the time they reached the location where Wynn had disappeared, there was a heavy silence that suggested they'd managed to frighten away the demons, humans, and even the rats that hunted for scraps in the gutters. They might not know Azh's precise species, but they understood they didn't want to piss him off.

"Here." Azh stopped, pointing at the pavement. There was no visible trace of the spell that had stolen Wynn, but there was no way to completely erase the remnants of magic.

Bending down, Saxton closed his eyes as he absorbed their surroundings. Vampires possessed unrivaled tracking skills, even better than dragons. They could sort through hundreds of scents and sounds to locate a specific prey.

Saxton at last opened his eyes and straightened. His expression was grim.

"The magic was concealed. Probably because I prohibited the use of fissures after the royal fey families used them as weapons during a dispute over land, but there's a familiar power that is connected to the spell."

Azh curled his fingers into tight fists. "You know who it is?"

"I can make an educated guess."

Flames burst from his fists. "Where can I find them?"

"I have an easier solution. Come with me."

"No."

Saxton muttered something in an ancient language. Azh sensed it had something to do with pig-headed dragons.

"Do you want to find your female or not?" the leech demanded.

Azh held his ground. "Where do you intend to go?"

"Back to my lair." Saxton sent Azh a glare before he could protest. "The demon we're searching for has a dozen different estates spread through England. The fastest way to find him is to send out my servants to track him down. Once we have his exact location you can do all the rescuing you want. Deal?"

Did he have a choice? Without a trail to follow, Azh would be wandering the streets with no clue where to even start his search. In the meantime Wynn would be alone and at the mercy of whatever creature had kidnapped her.

"Let's go," he snapped.

Chapter 13

Tia was concentrating on her mental connection to the male stretched next to her as he battled against the nasty slime. She was weary to the bone, but then she sensed she was no longer alone in the mist. Shoving away the weariness that pressed against her with a tangible force, she watched a shadowed form begin to creep toward Joe.

Refusing to panic, she sucked in a slow, deep breath and reached up to touch the choker around her neck. She'd infused each pearl with an extra boost of magic that would help her trap whatever or whoever had been sneaking around. Or maybe she would just destroy the creature, she decided as a heavy throb of power pulsed through the air. A swift, killing blow might be her only hope of defeating it.

Silently mouthing a spell designed to strike with lethal force, Tia clenched her teeth as the power gathered inside her, feeling like sharp shards as it fused into a knot in the center of her being. The magic was warning her that it was dangerous to use. Both for her and her intended victim.

Waiting until the form passed close enough for her to see a vague outline of a tall, slender figure, Tia released her spell.

The magic flared with a blinding brightness, aiming straight for the intruder like an arrow. A second later she heard a low growl. It sounded as if it came from an animal, assuring her that she'd hit the mark.

"Gotcha," she rasped, leaping to her feet.

As quick as the light had flared, it was gone. In fact, everything including Tia was plunged in an impenetrable darkness. It had to be magic, but Tia didn't recognize the spell. Was it connected to the strange creature attacking Joe?

Expecting a retaliatory attack, Tia silently moved to the side, preparing a spell. She didn't have enough magic left for a second strike, but she could wrap the creature in a snare. It might be enough to hold them so she could call for backup.

The mist rippled, as if the creature was moving away. Tia prepared to release her spell. She couldn't let the thing escape.

"You think you can defeat me, worthless mortal?" a harsh voice whispered behind her.

Tia swiveled, the hair on her nape rising. How did the creature move so fast?

"I'm going to feast on your bones."

Tia released the snare, backing toward Joe as she heard an unnerving chuckle echo through the darkness. The sound began to fade away, but Tia wasn't taking any chances. It might be trying to fool her into lowering her guard only to circle back.

She was close enough to Joe to feel the creepy pulses of power from the evil pool of slime when an agonizing pain exploded in the back of her mind. At first she assumed the creature was attacking her. She couldn't see the aggravating intruder, but that didn't mean it wasn't lurking in the mist.

Squeezing her head in her hands, she tried to locate the source of the pain. It wasn't until she heard the scream from downstairs that she realized she wasn't the one being hurt. It was Maya.

With a hiss of fear, Tia shut off her mental connection to Joe, feeling disoriented as she opened her eyes and glanced around the empty apartment. She was still kneeling next to the unconscious male, her legs numb and her neck muscles cramped from sitting in one position for so long. She needed a mattress and blanket if she was going to stay for another night.

Another scream interrupted her foggy thoughts, and forcing herself to her feet, Tia stumbled out of the apartment and down the outside stairs. It was light enough to easily see the alleyway was empty, but she could hear heavy traffic out front. It had to be evening rush hour. Raising her hand, she sent out a pulse of magic, busting through the back door of the pawnshop.

Another scream ripped through the air, and without pausing to see if she was rushing into a trap, Tia ran through the storage area and into the front shop. The space was empty. There was nothing to see beyond a shabby counter and one metal stool.

With a frown, Tia darted toward the counter, at last finding Maya on the filthy floor, curled into a tight ball as a reddish magic surrounded her like a blanket. Dammit. Tia glanced toward the counter, relieved to spot Maya's satchel. Her own magic had been depleted by her attempt to kill the mysterious attacker. She needed help.

Lunging toward the satchel, she shoved her hand in to grab the first vial she could wrap her fingers around. Without bothering to glance at it, she tossed the potion toward the magic. Maya's screams warned her that the spell was doing serious damage. She couldn't worry whether the potions might cause additional injury or not.

There was a sizzling sound as the vial burst against the malicious magic and the glow momentarily dimmed. Without hesitation Tia grabbed another vial and tossed it. This one coated Maya in a layer of ice.

Perfect.

Stepping forward, Tia called on her fading powers and muttered the words to a healing spell. She stumbled through the words more than once. Her magic was devoted to collecting power and punishing her enemies, not curing the ill. At last she managed to mutter the right incantation and with a desperate mental push she released her magic.

It started with a low hum. A gentle vibration that spread over the frozen shell of magic. Once Tia was certain it was entirely surrounded, she intensified the hum, increasing the volume along with the speed. Nothing happened as Maya continued to scream, her eyes squeezed shut as if trying to block out the pain.

Tia clenched her teeth. This would work. As long as she didn't panic.

The vibrations continued, the sound becoming more of a high-pitched squeal than a hum. Tia winced as the noise threatened to pierce her eardrum, but the spell at last reached the perfect resonance, and with a thud that sent her stumbling backward, the spell surrounding Maya abruptly shattered.

Regaining her balance, Tia rushed forward as Maya slowly sat up, her hand pressing against her heart as if making sure she was still alive.

"What the hell was that?" she rasped.

Tia's breath hissed between her clenched teeth. "It has to be the creature from the mist."

Maya sent her a confused glance. "The toxic magic that's attacking Joe? It's spreading?"

Tia took a second to recall her brief battle with the shrouded form. The magic had been unfamiliar, but it didn't have the same clinging evil as the stuff that was currently wrapped around Joe.

"It doesn't feel the same," she admitted, "but they must be working together."

Maya shuddered. "Great."

Tia placed a hand on her friend's shoulder. "You have to leave."

"What?"

"The creature is using your presence to distract me from protecting Joe." Tia glanced at the ceiling, her instincts clamoring for her to return to the male who was alone and vulnerable on the upstairs floor.

"Then we face the threat together," Maya insisted.

"We can't. Whatever it is has the ability to disappear into the mist. We can't follow or stop them."

"I won't leave you unprotected."

Tia felt a burst of warmth at Maya's determination to keep her safe. It'd been decades since she'd allowed herself to care what anyone else thought about her. She'd told herself that her independence made her stronger. Back then she would have willingly sacrificed Maya if it meant she got what she wanted.

Now she knew that arrogance just made her lonely.

She wasn't going to let her friend remain a target for the mystery assailant.

"The barrier will stay in place even if you leave."

"Yeah, they've been fairly worthless," Maya said dryly, obviously referring to the dragon and thief who'd managed to slip through their shields. "But that's all the more reason I need to stay."

Tia shook her head. The intrusion by the mysterious male dragon had been a shock, but she would worry about that later. She was far more concerned with his warning that if they didn't stop the evil magic from spreading, the entire world might be consumed. "We're losing, Maya. Unless we figure out what's attacking Joe and how to stop it, the magic is going to overwhelm us."

Maya's lips parted as if she intended to insist on staying, then with a heavy sigh she glanced toward the large front window.

"You might be right, but I don't know where to start if this threat really is connected to the dragons. I've never run across any information that goes into any detail. Everything is always rumors and speculation from scholars. Unless you have some unknown manuscript hidden in your library?"

Tia shook her head. "I have nothing. The dragons erased all information before going into hibernation."

"Then how am I supposed to—"

"I have to return to Joe," Tia abruptly interrupted, sensing his call of warning. The creature had returned and was circling closer to him. "Find the source of the magic and how to get rid of it," she commanded, turning to head out the back of the shop.

"Right. Sure. Just produce a miracle out of thin air," Maya called out, clearly frustrated by the herculean task. "No problem."

"Make it a fast miracle," Tia called back, marching up the steps, preparing to head into battle. "The clock's ticking."

* * * *

Wynn slowly regained consciousness, her body aching from the violent whiplash of being jerked through a fissure. It was her first time being caught in the powerful snare and she had to admit she wasn't a fan.

Her bones and muscles ached, as if she'd been stretched too far and snapped rudely back into place. Like being sucked through a black hole.

Slowly opening her eyes, Wynn wasn't surprised to find that she was trapped in a dank dungeon with empty cells along one wall and the old-fashioned implements of torture piled on the other side. Just as she wasn't surprised to feel the manacles that were locked around her wrists and wedged into a stone wall behind her.

The only good news was that she suspected that she was still in England. It wasn't the familiar scent of the air or the magic that hummed beneath her feet that gave her hope. It was the boring construction of the dungeon. She'd spent more than a few nights in dank cells being tortured with hot pokers.

They all looked tediously similar.

Tossing back her hair that had unraveled from the braid during her violent trip through the fissure, Wynn took an inventory of her surroundings. There were a couple of torches burning in the corners, but they didn't offer more than a splotch of glowing light, leaving the majority of the room in shadows. Without the ability to see in the dark, she couldn't locate anyone in the dungeon with her, but she could sense them.

"I know you're watching me, you sleazebag," she called out. It probably wasn't super smart to challenge a demon who was powerful enough to create a rip in space, especially when she was chained to the wall, but she wasn't in the mood to play nice. She was in the mood to kick someone in the nuts. "Come out and face me like a man."

There was a soft, musical laugh before a slender fey male stepped into the glow of torchlight. He was taller than most fairies, with deep red hair that was cut short and carefully mussed to give him a sleepy, sexy vibe. His eyes were green with flecks of gold and his features were finely chiseled. He would have been beautiful if it wasn't for the arrogant sneer that was perpetually attached to his lips.

Sir Pheral Gardner.

A member of the fey aristocracy who routinely dabbled in the black market, smuggled illegal goods, and treated his servants like slaves.

She'd had dealings with him off and on over the past century, but while she'd cheated him a few times and he'd cheated her even more times, they'd never been enemies. So why had he gone to the considerable effort to design a fissure to capture her?

"Ah, Wynn," he drawled. "It's good to know that time hasn't dulled your sharp edges. The same obnoxious bitch I remember."

"Pheral." She flicked a dismissive glance over his expensive cashmere sweater and black slacks. He looked like he was headed out to dinner at The Ritz, not about to torture his latest captive.

"Miss me?"

"Like the plague."

Pheral clicked his tongue, strolling closer. As he neared, his impressive emerald aura spilled across the flagstone floor.

"I thought we had something special."

Wynn rolled her eyes. "The only thing special about you is your remarkable lack of anything resembling morals."

He pressed a slender hand over his heart. "You wound me, love."

Wynn snorted. "Just the opposite. I haven't done anything to you, which is why I don't understand why you kidnapped me."

"It is a shame." He halted a few inches from her, trailing a finger down the line of her jaw. "I always liked you, Wynn. Remember when we borrowed the queen's carriage to escape from the horde of goblins chasing us?"

She didn't have any trouble digging up the memory. It'd been a state banquet at Buckingham Palace with Queen Victoria and the Prince of Wales. The sort of swanky party that Wynn adored. Plus, a perfect opportunity to make a tidy fortune.

"They were chasing you, not me," she reminded him in cold tones. "I was at the palace as a guest."

He tapped the tip of her nose. "Liar. You were there to steal the opal pendant being worn by the mystic who was entertaining the guests."

Wynn shrugged. No use pretending she hadn't been there in a professional capacity. "Madame Swan claimed it allowed her to speak to the dead."

"You didn't believe that nonsense."

"No, but my client did. And she was willing to pay whatever I asked to get her hands on it." Wynn narrowed her eyes. "Then you ruined the detailed plot I'd spent weeks creating when you insulted Ambassador Bauer's wife."

"It's not my fault she resembled the stuffed boar head mounted above the fireplace," Pheral protested.

Wynn tilted her head away from his lingering touch. He might have been handsome and wealthy, but he'd always revolted her.

"You didn't kidnap me to rehash our past, did you?"

His gaze lowered to her lips. "I wish, but sadly this is a business arrangement."

A chill pierced Wynn's heart. That was exactly what she feared. If she was just dealing with Pheral she could find a way to pay him off. The fairy was always for sale. Or better yet, she could use her skipping stones to escape.

But if he was doing this for someone else, then she was in trouble.

"Business with who?" she demanded.

"The mysterious creature who offered an impressive reward for anyone capable of capturing you. It's taken a full year for you to finally wander into one of my traps. Where the hell have you been?"

Wynn ignored the question. She was more interested in the fact that whoever was searching for her must be in England. Did that mean she'd encountered the dragon magic while she was here? Maybe Azh was right. Maybe she had to go back to the beginning.

And where was that aggravating dragon? Was he looking for her?

With a shake of her head, she dismissed the pang of yearning to have Azh burst into the dungeon and sweep her away. She'd been taking care of herself for a long time. She didn't need anyone to ride to the rescue.

Not even a gorgeous, sexy dragon.

She glowered at her captor. "There's a reward out for me?"

"There's always a reward out for you, love," he reminded her. "But this one paid substantially more than usual."

"Who's offering it?"

"Malis."

"Malis?" Wynn searched through her memories only to come up empty. "Should I recognize the name?"

"I didn't," Pheral confessed. "I never heard of him. Not until I found this hanging in my favorite gentlemen's club." The fairy reached into the pocket of his slacks to pull out a folded piece of paper. With a flick of his wrist, he had it snapped open to reveal a charcoal sketch of her along with a reward that was large enough to make her queasy.

Studying the sketch, Wynn frowned. It was a better-than-average likeness of her, but not from today. Over the decades she hadn't aged, but her face had matured and thinned while her hair had lightened from a mousy brown to a lighter shade of gold. It was her eyes, however, that had changed the most dramatically. They'd gone from a pale blue to a strange shade of lavender.

"What makes you think this is me?" she asked.

"I remember watching you beg on the street corner when you first arrived in London. I knew even then there was something different about you. I was right."

Ew. She didn't like the thought this creep had been keeping an eye on her when she was so young. Unfortunately, he wasn't the only one.

"Fine. What did I do to this Malis?"

"I don't know, but whatever it was must have been bad." Pheral tossed aside the Wanted poster, a mocking smile playing around his lips. "You don't offer that sort of reward unless you're truly pissed."

No shit. A shiver raced through Wynn.

"It's a lot," she agreed, "but I can match it."

Pheral rolled his eyes. "Right."

"It's true. I can also add in a bonus if you return me to London tonight."

He pursed his lips, pretending to consider her offer. "Tempting, and not just because of the bonus. I don't like the thought of you being tortured and killed, Wynn. You were always causing some sort of delightful chaos. I've never seen my fellow demons so flustered as when they were trying to figure out who had stolen some rare artifact or scrambling to get invited to one of the underground auctions when those same artifacts went up for sale. It's sad but true that the city is boring when you're not around."

She held his gaze even as she concentrated on the strands of magic inside her. She located the only strand that might help her. A pale-yellow magic that would create tiny fractures in the stone wall behind her. It was her best hope of tugging the manacles free.

"Then let me go," she said.

"I can't."

She tapped into the magic, frustration blasting through her when nothing happened.

"I told you I would pay," she reminded the fairy, an edge of desperation in her voice. "I have the money—"

"It's not that," Pheral interrupted.

"Then what do you want?"

"To survive long enough to enjoy my rare stroke of good luck. Something I doubt would happen if I released you."

"You're scared?" Wynn taunted, trying to hide her own stab of fear. She'd seen this fairy fight his way through a rabid pack of goblins with nothing but a hexed dagger with a smile on his lips.

What could make him turn away from a promise of more money?

"Damned right, I'm scared," he admitted. "When I called the number on the poster to say I'd captured you I could feel the demon's power." He grimaced. "It gave me the heebie-jeebies."

"Through the phone?"

"I can't explain it, but I'm not stupid enough to ignore what I felt. I'm going to get my money and disappear."

Wynn sent him a glare, still struggling to release her magic. Dammit. Now wasn't the time for a dud.

"Coward," she accused.

"Guilty." Pheral stepped closer, once again running his fingers down the line of her jaw. "But the mystery demon warned me it might take some time for him to get here. We might as well have some fun until then."

Wynn gagged in disgust. "Fun?"

"You're a beautiful woman and I don't mind your vicious attitude." He traced her lips. "I think sassy females are sexy."

Wynn clenched her muscles. She was going to knee the bastard hard enough to knock his balls into his throat. Her leg was lifting when she felt the sudden tingle of magic trying to breech her barriers. She froze, recognizing the spell. Pheral had his famed hexed dagger hidden beneath his sweater.

The hex had been created by a powerful fey who'd used blood sacrifices to infuse the blade with the magic. Usually she was careful to avoid absorbing that sort of magic. There was always the risk of being cursed when a spell was created at the moment of death.

Now, she was willing to take a chance.

Lowering her shields, Wynn allowed the magic to seep into her, creating a thick twisted strand that looked dead next to the other vibrant weaves of power. Despite its appearance, Wynn could feel the dull, heavy thud of magic.

Queasiness rolled through her stomach, but she forced herself to continue absorbing the hex.

"Sassy?" she forced herself to ask, lowering her leg. The closer the dagger was to her, the quicker she could deplete the magic.

Unaware he was losing his most treasured possession, Pheral wrapped his fingers around her neck.

"Sassy and mouthy and unpredictable."

"I get that a lot." The fingers tightened around her neck. Wynn had heard that this male enjoyed hurting his lovers. Even killing them during sex.

"Probably because it's true."

The thick stench of the fairy's arousal nearly choked Wynn. "Are you going to release me so I can participate?"

"Not a chance in hell."

"That's not fair."

"You don't need your hands for what I'm going to do to you."

"And what's that?"

"This." The fingers tightened until Wynn could barely breathe as Pheral rubbed his stiff cock against her hip. "You like that?" He pretended her shudder of disgust was pleasure. "Yeah, you do. I'm going to..."

His rough words faded as the dungeon was filled with a weird, greenish glow. Visibly confused, the fairy released his hold on Wynn and started to turn toward the entrance.

He was still moving when a dart of green magic appeared from the darkness, arrowing straight at Pheral's head. Wynn thought she heard him gasp in pain, but there was no other sound as the fairy crumpled to the floor, his dead eyes staring up at Wynn with grim resignation.

Wynn parted her lips and screamed.

Chapter 14

Seemingly impervious to her shrieks that echoed with a piercing intensity through the dungeon, the intruder strolled forward wearing a floor-length robe. He was tall, but painfully thin for a goblin and oddly hairless. Like a weird, elongated maggot. Worse, his eyes burned with that malignant green fire.

"At last," he hissed, forcing Wynn to reconsider her first impression. He was more like a snake than a maggot. "You have eluded me for far too long."

Struggling not to puke as a rancid stench of rotting flesh swept through the dungeon, Wynn eyed the demon with a raw sense of horror. There was something so very wrong about him.

"Malis, I presume?" she managed to rasp.

Halting in front of her, the creature offered an old-fashioned bow. He moved with a strange, boneless grace. At the same time, something shimmered on his skin. Not scales, but something hard and brittle with hints of green.

Yup. Definitely snakelike.

"At your service," he murmured.

"You can be of service by releasing me," Wynn said. She'd be damned if she let the creature sense the fear churning inside her.

"As you wish." The glowing gaze moved to study the manacles that pinned her to the stone wall. A second later, they clicked open and Wynn cautiously lowered her arms. "Better?"

"Marginally." She rubbed her chafed wrists, remaining pressed against the wall. She knew beyond a shadow of a doubt she would only have one shot to escape. Which meant she had to have a clear plan in mind before she made the attempt. "I'd be better if I was out of this dungeon."

The male shrugged. "In good time. First we have some overdue business to complete."

"Doubtful. I don't do business with strangers."

"Strangers?" Malis clicked his tongue. "You wound me."

"Have we met?" Wynn pretended to study the male standing in front of her.

She was already certain that she didn't recognize him. He wasn't the sort of demon anyone could forget. His stench alone would have lingered in her mind for years. But it gave her an opportunity to study the dungeon behind him, memorizing the quickest path to the open doorway. She could use her spell that could create complete darkness. That might give her an advantage when she was ready to make a run for it.

"It's more than that. We are intwined in the most intimate way possible," the creature drawled, the fetid green glow deepening, as if savoring some distant memory.

Wynn shuddered. Was that why she lost her memory? To black out whatever had happened between her and this demon? It seemed a legit explanation. But it didn't tell her if she'd encountered him before he'd been infected with the corruption that made him glow with that awful green or after.

"Sorry, I don't remember. But maybe we can catch up later." She forced a smile to her lips. "Let's do coffee next week."

The demon's expression never changed. She wasn't sure if he was capable of moving his pale features. They looked frozen in place.

"I must insist we do it now. I've wasted too much time chasing you."

Wynn's heart missed a beat. The mere thought this...maggoty, glowing demon had been lurking behind her made her flesh crawl.

"Why are you chasing me?"

"You have something I need."

Wynn flinched. This had to have something to do with the dragon statue. The fact he was infected proved that much, but why couldn't he sense she didn't possess the actual artifact? And what was his connection to the corruption? Was he just another creature under the sway of the evil magic? Or was he something more?

Right now, it didn't matter. Once she was out of the dungeon with plenty of space between her and Malis, she would consider the various possibilities. Or maybe she would simply find the nearest pub and drink herself into oblivion.

"I don't think so." The words came out stiff, her lips refusing to work right. "You must have the wrong gal."

"Impossible. I never make mistakes."

"Never?"

"Never."

Wynn once again glanced over the male's shoulder, judging the distance to the door.

"Check for yourself, then. I don't have anything," she said, trying not to shudder at the thought of the demon getting closer. She wanted him distracted when she prepared to run.

"Your pocket," Malis said.

"What?"

"You have something in your pocket."

"The skipping stone?" Wynn returned her attention to the pale, unnervingly gaunt face. Could it all be that easy? "That's what you want? Okay."

He shook his head. "The other item."

Confused, Wynn reached into the pocket of her coat, surprised when her fingers brushed a metal object. It wasn't until she felt the delicate chain that she remembered she'd kept the medallion they found in the rubble of the pawnshop.

Pulling it out of her pocket, she held it up, grimacing as the polished silver reflected the ghoulish glow from the male's eyes.

"You mean this old necklace?"

"You found it."

The words were a statement, not a question. As if Malis was...not pleased but satisfied...she was holding the medallion.

Her plot to escape was put on a momentary hold. "You recognize this?"

"You wore it when we were together," he admitted. "That's how I tracked you to London. The goblin who was holding it was very unhelpful. A pity he escaped. I intended to punish him for leading me to his shop only to disappoint me when you weren't there."

Wynn clenched her teeth. Where had the medallion come from? And why had she been wearing it? And why had Axton kept it all those years?

The questions suddenly seemed important.

"Like I said, I don't remember." Frustration sharpened her tone. "Where did we spend time together?"

Malis stepped closer, ignoring Wynn's instinctive hiss of revulsion. "Perhaps I can help you with your missing memories."

"No—"

Wynn's protest was cut short as the red strand of magic inside her abruptly flared with power. She assumed it was about to punish the male who'd moved too close for comfort. Or maybe destroy the black magic she'd absorbed from Pheral's hexed dagger that ran like a sluggish toxin through her blood. Instead, the dungeon began to fray, as if it was an illusion that was fading.

Wait. Was it possible that this was all a nightmare and she was about to wake up? Could she be that lucky?

No, of course not.

The dungeon disappeared, but she didn't return to a cozy bed. Or even to the weird misty place where she'd spent the night with Azh. And thinking of Azh, where was the aggravating dragon? He'd followed her for days. Now, when she needed him the most, he was MIA.

Shaking away her petulant annoyance, she concentrated on her surroundings as the last of the dungeon disappeared.

The first thing she noticed was the breeze that tugged at her long hair and the thin robe that was the only thing she was wearing. She sucked in a shocked breath as she glanced down, realizing it was the same robe she'd been wearing when she woke on the banks of the Thames two hundred years ago. Confused, she lifted her head and glanced around the sundrenched pastoral countryside. She was standing on the crest of a hill, miles away from London, but she sensed she was still in England. There was something vaguely familiar about the thatch-roofed cottages clustered together in the distance and the neatly trimmed hedgerows that framed the fields.

She frowned as the babble of angry voices shattered the peace. It sounded like a mob was approaching. Turning her head, Wynn watched in confusion as a group of women walked out of the nearby trees, heading in her direction. They were various ages, from mid-teens to a few elderly women with gray hair and wrinkled faces. The one thing they had in common was their long robes that brushed the dirt pathway and heavy black boots.

Why were they wearing matching outfits like they were in some sort of cult? Was this a memory? Had she actually been standing on this hill as the women marched toward her?

For a moment she felt a stab of hope. Was she about to discover who she was and what had happened to her? Maybe she could endure Malis's vile stench if she could finally learn the truth.

Then the hope shattered, replaced by a surge of horror as there was a weird ripple in the air, like the blurred waves of a mirage, and suddenly all of the women were holding torches in their hands that burned with a white-hot fire. They marched toward her, the angry babble becoming an organized chant as they reached the top of the hill. Magic suddenly hummed in the air, warning Wynn that the women weren't in a weird cult. They were part of a coven. And they were about to unleash a spell.

She desperately turned to flee, only to discover she was too late. She managed less than a dozen steps when the magic lashed out, wrapping her in bonds that were impossible to break. A scream was ripped from her throat as she felt herself lifted off the ground, floating several feet in the air as the women moved to form a circle around her struggling form.

"Stop! Please. Let me go."

The women ignored her pleas as they closed their eyes and continued to chant. The bonds around Wynn tightened until she felt a rib crack from the pressure.

"Why?" she rasped, tears running down her cheeks. "Why are you doing this?"

An elderly woman stepped forward, her expression one of twisted loathing. Then she opened her eyes and Wynn caught sight of the smoldering envy she couldn't completely hide.

"You have been judged and marked unholy by the coven," she rasped. "Your profane magic is a gift from the devil. You are an affront to those who worship the mother earth. For that, you must die."

Wynn frantically shook her head. "No, I didn't do anything. I swear."

The woman hissed, raising her torch higher. "We witnessed the magic burst out of you. The very ground shook in outrage at your blasphemy."

Wynn struggled to think clearly as the women continued to chant, moving forward with their torches held outward. She didn't remember these women or any devilish burst of magic. But she did remember Maya telling her that she was some sort of Void. Which meant she must have been the daughter of a woman who could use magic, maybe even one of the torch-carrying lunatics surrounding her. And her wild magic must have flared only to burn out before she could use it.

Typical. Obviously her luck had always been shitty.

On the edge of a full-blown panic attack, Wynn forced herself to stop her futile struggles and concentrate on the threads of magic inside her. The witches' combined power was strong, but she had a few weapons of her own. She just had to be able to concentrate long enough to find the proper strand...

Wynn released a stifled sob as she realized that there were no magical threads. Not even the stupid dragon one that had been causing her such problems. It was as if they'd been stripped away. Or wait...maybe she just hadn't collected them yet.

If this was the past, then she hadn't had an opportunity to encounter the artifacts she needed to absorb their powers.

"She's calling on her devil magic!" the older woman cried. "Look at the medallion around her neck. It glows with an unholy light."

With a roar of anticipation, the women lifted the torches over their heads and threw them at Wynn with obvious glee. Wynn watched in helpless horror as they hit the spell surrounding her, igniting a wall of flames that swirled around her like a tornado. She was trapped as the flames swirled closer and closer, threatening to burn her alive, the medallion around her neck searing into her skin.

There was no way out. No way to escape. Not unless she could somehow wake up from this horrifying blast from the past. A damned shame she didn't have a clue how she was supposed to do that.

The flames were starting to sear a path of agonizing heat over her body when the ground beneath her dangling feet began to undulate, as if there was something beneath the thick layer of soil struggling to get out. The witches didn't seem to notice as they continued to chant and bask in the sight of her being tormented by their magic.

Wynn blinked. The world was blurry through her tears of pain, but she was certain that there was something happening beneath her. The massive surge of power felt like a volcano about to erupt. How could the witches be so oblivious?

Unless it was demon magic, a voice whispered through her tortured mind. The humans had no idea that paranormal creatures walked among them.

Another wave of flames whipped around her, searing deep into her flesh, and Wynn shrieked in pain. It was so overwhelming she nearly missed the sight of the ground abruptly bursting open like an overripe watermelon. It was at last the bright silver light bursting out of the massive hole that alerted her to the changes beneath her. A split second later she was abruptly sucked downward, caught in a funnel of air that reached up and grabbed her.

She heard the distant sounds of the coven's fury as their prey was snatched from their clutches, but she was too intent on her free fall through empty space to appreciate their bleating.

Waving her arms as if she could learn to fly in the next two seconds, Wynn fell through the blinding light, landing on a stone floor with enough impact to snap her spine in two and crack several ribs. The pain should have been overwhelming, but she felt nothing. Either she was paralyzed, or she was already dead.

Both seemed legit possibilities.

Laying spread-eagle on the ground, Wynn closed her eyes as she felt a presence approaching. She didn't want to know what awful thing was about to happen next. She was tired and nauseous and incapable of stirring up the urge to fight.

Expecting the worst, Wynn flinched as warmth spread over her. But there was no pain this time. In fact, the warmth seemed to be knitting together her broken bones and even healing the burns on her face.

What was happening?

Cautiously she cracked opened her eyes, unable to see anything beyond the white glow surrounding her. There was a vague outline of someone or something hovering above her, but she couldn't make out the features. Whoever it was might be using their powerful magic to repair her broken body, but that didn't mean they had sucked her into the hole out of kindness.

They might have even worse plans for her.

As if to reinforce her fears, the white glow was suddenly threaded with a familiar green slime, and the stench of rotting flesh wafted past her nose. Was the magic being infected before her eyes? Was the corruption in this hole?

Trapped by her sheer terror, Wynn was unable to move as the green threads pulsed their way toward her. Then a voice calling her name jolted her out of her stupor, and with a grim determination, Wynn forced herself to scramble to her feet.

She groaned as her muscles protested. She might be healed, but her body had taken a beating and it wasn't ready to be pushed. Too bad. She had already convinced herself that having the sickly green magic touch her would be a fate worse than death.

Stumbling backward, she felt a pile of loose dirt behind her. She assumed it was the ground that had collapsed when the hole had appeared at the top of the hill. Was it high enough for her to escape?

Without giving herself the opportunity to consider the wisdom of fleeing the healing magic to return to the coven of angry witches who'd already tried to kill her, Wynn spun around to desperately claw her way up the mound of dirt and rocks.

Ignoring the skin being scraped from her palms and the mud coating her from head to toe, Wynn hauled herself upward, her back stiff as she braced herself for a burst of killing magic. Her heavy panting was the only sound to break the thick silence, along with the occasional rock that tumbled down to crash against the stone floor beneath her.

Fiercely concentrating on pulling herself up inch by inch, Wynn didn't dare look down. Why would she want to know if she was about to be destroyed? It wasn't until she was finally forced to halt and catch her breath that she reluctantly glanced over her shoulder.

Fully expecting to discover the magic directly behind her, Wynn released a shaky sigh of relief as she watched the white glow battling against a wave of shimmering magic that had surged into the pit from a crack in the wall. Was that Gabriela's magic? Wynn had no idea, but the two powers churned and pulsed together, as if they were locked in an epic war of supremacy.

It was the distraction she needed to escape, but it was only temporary. She had to get out of there and disappear before the mysterious magic tried to suck her back down. Returning her attention to the top of the hole, Wynn judged the distance. It looked to be a couple of feet above her head. Not an impossible leap, but it was going to take everything she had to make it.

Luckily, the adrenaline surging through her body added an extra boost of power as she bent her knees and jumped upward. The tips of her fingers managed to grip the edge of the hole, and ignoring the screaming protest of the muscles in her upper arms, she dragged herself up and over the ledge.

She lay panting on the ground, straining to hear any sound of the witches. When there was nothing but silence, she wearily lifted her head to discover she was alone. Had the cave-in scared them away? Or had they finally sensed the magic bubbling beneath their feet?

Not that it mattered. They would eventually come back to search for her. Always assuming the glowing white power didn't manage to get her first. She had to get away from there.

Far, far away.

Managing to climb to her feet, Wynn was attempting to decide which way to run when she felt the ground trembling beneath her. Her heart stopped at the low rumbles that echoed through the air, watching the large cracks split open. It felt like the entire hill was about to collapse. Or explode.

Fear gave her an extra burst of power as she stumbled and rolled her way down the hill. Once at the bottom, she limped in the opposite direction, heading away from the coven as well as the distant village. She had no idea where she was going, but every step took her further away from her enemies. She continued through the empty fields, at last reaching the soggy banks of the river.

Too exhausted to take another step, Wynn collapsed into the sticky mud, needing to rest before she could search for a raft or boat to take her away from the godforsaken place. She closed her eyes and darkness claimed her.

"You remember?"

The words were whispered directly into Wynn's ear, and with a violent jerk that left her disoriented, she lurched from the countryside back to the dungeon. Her head was spinning as she tried to adjust to the sudden shift, but as her mind cleared she realized the demon was standing just inches away, bathing her in the vile green glow from his eyes.

That evil magic had to have come from the pit, right? So had this demon been dropped into the same place? Or had he been infected by someone else? And did it have anything to do with the dragon statue? Had it been down there too?

She shook away the gnawing questions. This demon admitted he'd been following her for months. It wasn't for any good reason. Once she'd escaped she would worry about the who, what, where, and why.

"I remember the coven," she cautiously admitted, not sure why the demon had returned her memories. Was he searching for information she'd forgotten? If that was the case, then she didn't intend to give him anything that might help. "Those bitches were trying to burn me alive."

"Humans are very dramatic when they're scared. Idiotic creatures."

"I remember them." She shrugged. "But I don't remember you."

There were no visible cues of the creature's annoyance, but Wynn could sense it in the stiffness of the gaunt body.

"Of course you remember. I was the one to save you."

Save her? The green slime hadn't done anything to help, had it? Maybe it distracted the white glowing thing long enough for her to escape, but that wasn't anything to cheer about. She was quite certain it had intended to infect her with evil.

"Nope." Another shrug. "No one saved me. I climbed out of the hole and then a few hours later I woke up on the banks of the river near London. There were no demons or saviors around. Just me doing what I had to do."

There was a hissing sound, as if the demon was offended by her refusal to show appreciation for being rescued from the coven.

"Fine, deny the truth. It no longer matters. This game is about to end."

"What game?" Wynn shook her head. "I think you've made a mistake. I—"

"Shut up," the demon rasped, abruptly leaning forward as a familiar metallic scent floated through the air. "What is that?"

Wynn's heart missed a beat. She knew exactly what it was. The sharp male scent belonged to one person. Or more precisely, one dragon. Her personal pain-in-the-neck stalker who finally decided to make his appearance.

Better late than never, she silently acknowledged, even as she forced herself to lift her hands and press them against the demon's chest. She was not only anxious to get some space between them, but she didn't want the creature to realize that Azh was lurking in the shadows.

"What are you doing?" She shuddered as a sickening sensation crawled up her arms. It was warm, but not the welcomed warmth she felt when she touched Azh. This was more like the hotness from a fever. A fetid virus that she desperately wanted to wash off. "Ew. Stop sniffing me."

"I told you to shut up," Malis snapped, turning his head toward the front of the dungeon as the ground shook. "Azh." The name came out like a curse. "That dragon is beginning to annoy me. Once I'm done with you I intend to devote special attention to his destruction."

Wynn curled her fingers into the thick material of the man's robe, frantically trying to keep him from moving.

"No."

The burning green gaze snapped back to stab her with an intense glare. "You're right. I can't be distracted," Malis muttered. "We still have business to finish."

Wynn pressed herself against the wall as Malis reached up to grab her chin with his bony fingers. He pressed hard enough to leave bruises, but

Wynn didn't struggle. The demon might look frail, but she wasn't deceived. There was no way she could physically overpower him.

"Why did you run from me?" he cooed, his breath putrid, as if he were rotting from inside out. "We need each other."

Wynn battled back the urge to panic. She was no longer in the past. She had magic she could use, right? Or at least, she had magic if it was willing to cooperate. Recently that was a fifty-fifty shot. Still, there was no way to know until she tried.

Blocking out the creepy demon who was now stroking his fingers over her cheek, Wynn concentrated on the threads of magic that twirled deep inside her. As always the crimson strand was the largest, as if demanding that she tap into the mysterious power, but for once, it wasn't the magic that floated closest to the surface.

Wynn had almost forgotten the hex that she'd absorbed from Pheral's dagger. Not surprising considering she'd been attacked by an emaciated demon with glowing green eyes and transported to the past. But now she reached for the tainted power, grudgingly allowing it to flow through her veins with a grimace.

At the moment, all she had was bad choices. As much as she hated releasing the evil power, it was the best she had.

Closing her eyes, Wynn blew out a shaky breath, then with grim determination, she twirled the hex into a tight ball of magic. Once it was squeezed as compact as possible, Wynn released the hex with one powerful blast.

She didn't know exactly what curse was contained in the hex, but she was hoping it was a crippling pain that would momentarily incapacitate the demon. Or at least send him stumbling backward. Something that would give Azh the opportunity to enter the dungeon without being immediately attacked.

But as usual, the crimson strand of magic decided to interfere, and instead of a condensed burst of power, she sent out a tidal wave of energy that lifted the demon off his feet and slammed him against the ceiling before dropping him back onto the stone floor. At the same time, the nearby cells shattered into lethal shards of iron that sliced deep into the demon's flesh. He looked like a bloody pincushion as he sprawled on the floor, but the green magic glowed as strong as ever in his eyes.

* * * *

Azh stormed down the shallow stairs dug into the bedrock. He'd entered the sprawling castle near the cliffs of Dover just moments ago, easily catching Wynn's scent as he'd burned his way through the heavy wooden doors guarded by two large demons. Nothing but ash remained in his wake, ensuring that the remaining guards were quick to toss themselves out the nearest windows.

They might not recognize the creature with an aura that glowed like the sun and fire that blasted from his fingertips, but they understood they were going to end up crispy critters if they were stupid enough to stand in his way.

Next to him, Saxton strolled with an elegant grace, still wearing his suit and tie as he allowed his own icy power to sweep through the vast estate. Vampires and dragons were natural adversaries, but for now they were tied together by a common enemy. Which meant the leech had not only sent out his minions to discover the current location of Sir Pheral Gardner, but he'd personally agreed to join in the rescue of Wynn.

Whether Azh wanted his help or not.

Ignoring the male who coated the walls with frost as they passed, Azh leaped forward, landing on the stony ground. Just ahead was an open door leading to what looked like a dungeon.

"Wait." Saxton was abruptly standing in front of him. "You can't just charge in there. This could be a trap."

Azh shoved the leech to the side. "I don't care."

With a speed not even Azh could match, the male was once again standing in the center of the narrow tunnel.

"I always suspected dragons were all brawn and no brain," Saxton hissed.

"We have fire in our veins, not ice."

The dark eyes flared with anger. "Rushing into danger might make you feel better, but it's putting your female at risk."

The damned leech was probably right, but Azh was in no mood to listen. The past few hours had scraped his nerves raw. In this moment he was prepared to burn down this world and every creature in it to get to Wynn.

"She's in trouble. I can sense it."

About to shove the leech aside once again, they both froze as a powerful magic blasted past them.

"What the hell was that?" Saxton turned toward the tunnel wall crisscrossed with thin fractures. As if a bomb had been detonated beneath the bedrock, sending shattering quakes through the earth. "Did you do that?"

Azh shook his head. "Wynn."

Shock rippled over the vampire's face. And not a happy shock. He didn't like the thought he not only had a dragon in his territory but a creature who could knock a castle off its foundation.

With an effort, Saxton smoothed away his unease. "I'm guessing she doesn't need you rushing to the rescue," he said dryly.

"That's not going to stop me." Azh sprinted toward the arched doorway, feeling Saxton inches behind him.

"I never for a second thought it would," the leech muttered.

Charging through the opening, Azh's gaze swept over the dungeon that looked as if it'd been hit by an earthquake. The walls were cracked and stone had been sheared off the ceiling. On the far side of the dungeon there was an empty space that he assumed had once held a line of cells, but there was nothing left. Not unless you counted the gouges in the stone floor where the bars had once been anchored.

With a shake of his head at the amount of power that must have been released, Azh glanced toward the back of the dungeon where Wynn was pressed against the wall, her eyes wide as if she were as stunned as everyone else by the chain reaction she'd set off.

His heart clenched as he headed toward her. She looked exhausted, with her hair released from the braid to frame her pale face and her shoulders slumped with exhaustion.

He had reached the middle of the dungeon before she noticed his arrival. "Azh." She pointed toward the floor a few feet from him. "Look out."

He glanced down, belatedly realizing that the lump of rags was actually a demon. The creature looked as if he'd gone through a woodchipper, with deep gashes in his flesh and his face a bloody mess, but that wasn't the strangest thing. It was the fact that Azh hadn't noticed the demon's presence the moment he'd entered the dungeon. And even standing this close, his senses were convinced he was looking at a corpse.

It wasn't until the head jerked to the side and Azh caught sight of the glowing green eyes that he realized the danger.

"You will pay for this," the demon hissed, then with an obvious desire to create a dramatic exit, the green glow vanished from the male's eyes and seeped into the ground.

For a second, it spread toward Azh, forcing him to jump back before it reached a crack in the stone floor and disappeared.

"What the hell was that?" Saxton rasped, his icy calm destroyed as the demon's body abruptly collapsed into a pile of dust.

It looked as if the creature had been an empty husk for months, no doubt animated by the evil magic. A walking zombie.

"The magic we're chasing," Azh rasped, stepping over the second dead demon on the ground. This one was wearing an expensive suit and looked too fresh to have been infected, at least not for very long.

Just a regular corpse, not a zombie.

With a grimace, he pulled Wynn into his arms. She was trembling, but he didn't smell the terror he'd been expecting. Instead her floral scent was threaded with a fierce determination. As if she were plotting her revenge and nothing was going to stand in her way.

The thought sent a chill down his spine.

"If it's incorporeal, how are we supposed to destroy it?" Saxton demanded from behind him.

"A good question," Azh said.

"And the answer?" the leech pressed.

Azh released a low growl. He understood the vampire's outrage at being confronted with an evil that seemingly had the ability to infect any demon and then disappear when it was cornered. Especially when that magic was preying on the demons living in his territory, but right now Azh was too distracted by his relief at having Wynn alive and well and in his arms to concentrate.

"A work in progress."

"Seriously? That's all you have?" An icy blast swirled through the dungeon as Saxton struggled to leash his temper, but before he could do something stupid, the vampire released a string of ancient profanities. "Get out of here, the foundation is going to collapse."

Azh didn't hesitate. Vampires had a profound bond with the earth. Probably because they had spent eons in caves and tunnels during their endless war with the dragons. Saxton would sense the instability in the rock before Azh.

Tightening his hold on Wynn, he swept her up and over his shoulder as he raced toward the door. He ignored the fist that landed in the middle of his back along with her angry protests.

He admired her independence, but he wasn't going to risk having the castle fall on her head because she was too stubborn to admit he was faster and stronger.

Saxton was a black blur as he raced up the stairs and led them toward the side door that opened into the formal gardens. Even then he continued to race through the neatly trimmed hedges, leaping over the wide moat to land lightly on the stone wall that skirted the castle grounds.

They turned back just in time to see the turrets crumble into heaps of shattered rock, followed by the large central keep that collapsed with enough force to send clouds of dirt billowing into the air.

Waiting until the dust cleared so he could make sure there was no sign of the corruption, Azh at last lowered the struggling Wynn to her feet. She glared at him as she straightened her coat and shoved the hair from her face, but she didn't bother to chastise him. They both knew he would do it again if he thought she was in danger.

"I'll send my warriors in search of the..." Saxton allowed his words to trail away with a low hiss. "Whatever the hell was in the dungeon."

"The corruption," Azh said, his gaze skimming the countryside for any hint of danger.

"Corruption?" Saxton demanded, his voice edged with disdain.

"You prefer that we call it the green slimy magic?"

"I'm going to sound like an idiot."

Azh turned his head to stare at the leech with raised brows. "And?"

Saxton shook his head, clearly realizing it was a stupid argument. "I want to stay in the area and question the locals. They might have heard rumors about Pheral meeting with strange demons." He tilted back his head to glance toward the sky that was beginning to glow with the promise of dawn. "Plus, I need to find a place to spend the day."

"Warn them not to get near enough for the magic to touch them," Azh insisted. "Just keep it in sight so we can try to track it."

Saxton nodded toward the road behind them where a stretch limo was waiting. "You can use my car to return to my lair in London to rest."

Azh started to nod his agreement, only to have Wynn take command of the situation. "I need to return to London, but I don't have time to rest."

He scowled, easily able to sense her fatigue. "Wynn."

"I'm fine. I'll rest later. I promise."

"What do you need in London?"

Her features hardened with a grim determination. "Axton and his clan."

"Axton." The vampire studied Wynn with a sudden frown. "I haven't seen or heard anything from Axton since his business exploded. I assume he's dead. Or at the very least he's left the Gyre."

Wynn stubbornly shook her head. "I know Axton. He wouldn't leave London even if the hounds of hell were chasing him."

Saxton narrowed his dark eyes. "You're familiar with the goblin?"

"We've met," Wynn admitted vaguely.

Saxton stilled, recognition spreading over his too-handsome features. "Wait. I remember that scent."

The leech started to step forward, but Azh was swiftly reaching out to place a warning hand in the center of the male's chest.

"Stay there."

Saxton's attention never wavered from Wynn. "You're the thief who's been terrorizing London for years."

Wynn shrugged. "Hardly terrorizing. I stole a few baubles here and there."

"A few." Saxton sent an impatient glare toward Azh. "Stop growling at me. If I wanted to hurt her I would have done something a long time ago," he snapped, forcing Azh to realize that he was indeed growling. Or rather, his beast was rumbling with annoyance. Right now, it was just grumbles. If the leech did anything to threaten Wynn, it would get a whole lot worse. With blatant disregard that he was poking the sleeping dragon, Saxton leaned toward Wynn, as if testing her scent. "What are you?"

"I don't have a clue," Wynn admitted. "Not yet."

Azh wrapped an arm around her shoulders, tugging her close. "She's completely unique."

Saxton wasn't satisfied, but he was smart enough not to press the issue. "At some point we're going to discuss your habit of taking things that don't belong to you. But for now, we have bigger problems," he conceded, once again glancing toward the impeding dawn. "I need to get going."

"Don't try to battle the power on your own," Azh reminded the vampire. "Call for me if you get it cornered."

Chapter 15

Wynn melted into the buttery-soft cushions of the limo as the demon driver put the car in gear and headed down the narrow path. Her body was so drained she'd barely managed to walk the short distance from the destroyed castle to the waiting vehicle. Not that she was going to let Azh carry her like a helpless damsel in distress again.

Not unless they were headed to a soft bed with satin sheets...

She swiftly shoved away the tempting image. There was still too much to do to think about the things she wanted to do to Azh. When she finally got the dragon naked, she wanted to make sure she had plenty of time to explore and savor and indulge in their heated passion.

"How did you make friends with Saxton?" she asked, as much to keep herself awake as out of genuine interest.

"Hardly friends. More like enemies temporarily forced to work together," Azh corrected. "It was Saxton's demons who discovered where you'd been taken."

She shuddered. Memories of being trapped in the dungeon with Malis were going to give her nightmares for years to come.

"I'm glad they did."

"Tell me what happened," Azh commanded.

"It was Pheral who created the fissure that took me to the castle."

"Why?"

"He spotted a poster hanging in one of the demon bars offering a huge reward to locate me." She made a sound of disgust. "Luckily it had an image of me from my earliest days in London. Not many demons knew about me back then, which is the only reason I wasn't captured before I realized I was being hunted."

"Was he infected?"

"I couldn't detect any corruption. He's just a greedy jerk." Wynn's words faltered as she recalled Pheral collapsing at her feet. She didn't know what sort of spell had been used against him, but he'd died instantly. "Or he was until Malis killed him."

"Malis is the demon who put up the Wanted poster?"

"Yes. I think he's been infected for a long time."

Azh tapped a slender finger on his leg, frustration smoldering in his stormy gray eyes as her words reminded him that Pheral and Malis might be dead, but the evil magic had escaped.

"But he's not the original source of the magic?" he asked.

Wynn shook her head. "Not the original source, but he was something more than the zombie demons that have been popping up," she said.

"Why do you say that?"

"I think he's been infected for so long that the magic is able to communicate through him." She struggled to find the words to explain the sensation that she'd been talking to something inside Malis, not to the actual demon. "It was like he was an empty shell that the corruption was using to move through the world."

He stilled, as if shocked by her words. "You were talking to the corruption?"

She wrinkled her nose. "It sounds ridiculous, but he claimed that we'd been together long ago and that he'd rescued me. And then he did something that allowed me to remember my past. Or at least a portion of my past."

"You remember?"

She held up her hand, sensing his surge of hope. "I'm not sure if the memories are mine or if they were put there by the magic," she warned, "but yeah, I suddenly had a vision of when I was still human."

"Tell me," he insisted, leaning toward her as he struggled to contain his eagerness to know more about his people's nemesis.

"I was on a hill. In the distance I could see the river, but I wasn't near London. The air was too clean. And I could see a village below me," she told him.

"Do you know the location?"

"Not exactly. I don't even remember my original name, but I do know that I was surrounded by a coven of angry witches."

His excitement faded at the edge of pain in her voice. "Were you attacked?"

She shuddered. The bitter fury of the women condemning her to death might have happened two hundred years ago, but it felt agonizingly fresh. Probably because the memory had just been exposed. Her ability to process and heal from what had happened to her would take time.

"I was trapped and burned at the stake."

Heat blasted through the limo as Azh's eyes swirled with thunderclouds. "Who?"

"I don't know any names, but I'm sure it was a coven of witches. I think they were pissed that my magic had flared and I was becoming a mage." Her lips twisted into a bitter smile. "Although it turned out to be worthless. I might as well have stayed human."

With a low growl, Azh reached to frame her face in his hands, gazing down at her with a fierce expression.

"Never say that you're worthless," he rasped. "You have more power than any mage I've ever encountered."

Wynn tilted back her head, easily becoming distracted by the lightning that danced at the back of the smoky gray eyes. So much raw power. So much raw passion. So much raw...dragon. Glorious, sexy, and possessive.

With an effort, she forced herself to finish revealing her memories. "Anyway, I had a vision of being surrounded by the flames and then falling into a deep pit. I think I was dying but then I was surrounded by a silver light that healed my burns."

"A silver light?" He considered the various possibilities. "That must have been Gabriela," he at last concluded.

She shrugged. "Maybe."

"What do you remember about the pit?"

"Nothing much. A lot of barren rock. And of course, the silver light was there." She took a minute to consider what else she'd seen. Her vision had been limited by the blinding glow. And worse, the memories were beginning to fade. As if they were being slowly erased again. "After I was healed I noticed the silver light was threaded with streaks of green. I assume it had to be the corruption attacking it."

"Was there a statue?" he pressed.

"I didn't see one, but I wasn't really looking," she admitted. "Oh, and there was also another magic. I could see the shimmer of it coming through a crack in the wall."

"Dragon magic?"

"I wasn't paying enough attention to do more than get a glimpse of it," she admitted. "I was too busy trying to get out of the pit while the weird powers were distracted fighting each other." She paused again. "I think I heard the pit collapsing behind me, but I don't know why. My next memory is stumbling toward the river."

Azh studied her with a fierce intensity, visibly trying to imagine what had happened to her all those years ago, and why.

"Maybe you didn't get your magic from an artifact," he at last suggested, as if the thought was just forming in his mind. "Maybe Gabriela shared a portion of her powers to heal you and your particular ability allowed you to absorb the magic."

Wynn jerked her face out of his grasp, still not comfortable with the thought the dragon magic was inside her. Especially not when it might be the sole reason Azh was so interested in her.

"I've never been able to absorb the magic directly from the user," she stubbornly protested.

Easily sensing she didn't want to discuss the bright light or Gabriela, Azh leaned back to regard her with a searching gaze.

"Okay, tell me why you want to find Axton."

Wynn readily latched onto the change in conversation. She didn't want to dwell on the creepy unease that there was more than an echo of distant magic inside her.

"Because of something Malis said about my medallion," she said, reaching into her pocket where she'd unconsciously shoved the necklace after she'd released the curse that destroyed the demon.

Azh arched a brow as he watched her pull it out. "He recognized it?"

"He claimed he used it to track me to the pawnshop. He wasn't happy when the medallion was there and I wasn't. I assume that's why he destroyed the place."

"Did he create it?" Azh demanded.

She shook her head. "I don't think so, but I was wearing the medallion while I was being burned. I could feel it melting into my skin, so that means I had it while I was still human."

"Then the corruption must have placed some sort of tracking spell on it while you were in the pit." Azh hesitated, as if struck by a sudden thought. "But if it had, why did it take so long to track you?"

Wynn shrugged. "I'm more concerned why it decided to track me at all," she said. "It implied that I had something it wanted."

"How do you imagine Axton can help?"

"This medallion is a clue to who I was and where I came from. There was a reason Axton bought it and why he kept it for two centuries."

He studied her for a long moment before giving a slow nod of his head. "You're right," he agreed. "For now, rest. I'll wake you when we reach London."

With a grateful sigh, Wynn closed her eyes and sank back into the soft leather seat. She could sense the effort it took Azh not to continue badgering her for answers about her encounter with Gabriela. It wasn't just his fascination with the legendary dragon. He was desperate to understand the danger to his people and how to protect them. For now, however, he put her needs above his own, pulling her close as she allowed the bone-deep exhaustion to claim her.

It felt like minutes passed, although it had to be a solid two hours, when she heard the muffled sounds of the city penetrating the hushed interior of the limo. With an effort, she forced open her eyes.

"Tell the driver to drop us off in Hackney," she croaked, pushing herself out of the comfort of Azh's arms.

Azh relayed the command, remaining silent as she struggled to clear the cobwebs from her brain.

It was still early, but the sun was up as they reached Mare Street. The neighborhood was an odd combination of old squat houses in the process of being restored by investors and colorful street fronts. There were dozens of trendy nightclubs that catered to the flocks of tourists who arrived in waves during the evenings as well as less well-known pubs that were the sole domain of the local demons.

The limo swerved to park next to the sidewalk, barely waiting for them to climb out before it was zooming away. Obviously Saxton had ordered the driver to deliver them to London, but that was the end of his duty. He made it clear he wanted to be far away from them.

Fair enough, Wynn silently conceded, glancing around the empty streets. She attracted enemies at a dizzying speed. If she didn't have to, she wouldn't want to spend any time around her either.

"Does Axton have a lair near here?" Azh demanded.

Wynn reached up to comb her fingers through her hair before quickly returning it to its usual braid. This area wasn't for the faint-hearted. Even in the morning hours.

"No, but if a demon wants to disappear in London this is the place to go."

Azh glanced around in confusion. "This looks like any other street in the city. Is there something special about it?"

Wynn glanced toward a nearby building where she could see the outline of a fairy in the upper window. She knew from experience he would be holding a crossbow pointed at her heart.

"The Vasiliki control Hackney. They're a powerful fey clan who've made a fortune by providing safe rooms for demons who need to disappear. Once you've paid their outrageous fee, they promise that no one will be able to track you to your hidden location."

"What if whoever is hunting them agrees to pay more to find them?"

"It's happened," Wynn admitted. "That's why they perform a public execution of any servant who is stupid enough to share more information than they should, just to remind everyone in the neighborhood to keep their mouths shut. Whether they're on the payroll or not. It's usually some sort of gory curse or a disembowelment that involves a lot of screaming."

Azh arched a brow. Was he shocked by her indifference to such gruesome tortures? If so it was probably best he realized she might have been invited to sophisticated parties, but she spent most of her life in the sewers with the rats.

"Have you used their service?" he demanded.

"More than once." With a shrug, she led him down the street, turning into a narrow alley that smelled like piss. "And since I've never trusted anyone, I made sure I had several escape routes prepared just in case."

"Of course you did," he said dryly.

Wynn paused as they reached the end of the alley, lifting her hand to press it against the brick wall in front of them.

"I'm hoping they're still protected by my magic."

Azh moved to stand next to her, the ground trembling as he allowed a portion of his off-the-charts magic to leak through his shields.

"If not I can find a way through the barriers."

She sent him a chiding glance. "Your way is too noisy."

He smiled. "Yes."

She rolled her eyes, returning her attention to the spell she'd left embedded in the brick. Once she could feel the warm pulse of the magic, she whispered the words that revealed the hidden tunnel.

With a shove, she pushed aside the wooden planks to reveal the narrow opening. "Follow me."

"Anywhere," he murmured, creating a flutter of butterflies in the pit of her stomach as his heat reached out to stroke over her like a caress.

With a click of her tongue at her giddy awareness, Wynn scurried down the narrow stairs that led to a cellar beneath the pub.

Azh followed, only to grunt in discomfort as he was forced to bend nearly double to avoid the low beams that were blackened with age. This particular pub had been ancient when Wynn first arrived in London. As far as she knew, it'd been there for as long as there'd been demons in the area.

Wynn crossed to the center of the stone floor, crouching down to once again search for the magic she'd left behind.

"The spell is still active," she said with a surge of relief. It'd been years since she'd been forced to go into hiding and she didn't know how long her magic would last. "We should be able to enter without anyone sensing the shields have been breached."

Azh frowned. "Tell me what we're about to walk into."

"Actually, we're going to drop into it." She ran her hand over the stones, revealing the outlines of a trapdoor. "There's a large space dug into the ground that can hold up to a dozen or more demons."

"A dozen?" Azh's frown deepened.

"We'll have the element of surprise." She grasped the iron ring and tugged the heavy stone aside before Azh could stop her. "Just don't cause a huge commotion. We don't want the Vasiliki clan to know we're here."

"No promises."

She tilted back her head, heaving a sigh at the sight of the nuclear aura that surrounded Azh and the beast that lurked in the depths of the storm-gray eyes. This male was custom-designed to attract attention.

"Never mind," she said. "Let's go."

The words had barely left her lips when Azh was moving to drop through the hole, the translucent shimmer of his wings folded tightly against his back revealing how close his dragon was to the surface. With a low growl of frustration, Wynn swiftly dropped in behind him, landing on the hard-packed earth with a jolt. She grunted, painfully reminded that she'd hurt her ankle leaping out of Hexx's window. It might have seemed like an eon ago, but it wasn't long enough to fully heal. Her ankle was still tender.

Swallowing her groan, Wynn quickly straightened, her gaze skimming over the cots shoved against the far wall. She counted six lumps that she assumed were demons.

"I told you to stay out," a groggy voice muttered from the shadows. "If we want something we'll..." The words trailed away and one of the lumps suddenly sat upright, as if he'd just caught her scent. "You." The blankets were shoved aside and a large goblin leaped off the cot and lunged toward her. "Bitch, this is all your fault."

The male was over six feet tall with a thick mane of black hair and a wide body covered in a thick layer of fur. Not thick enough, unfortunately, to disguise the fact he was naked. Or the fact that he was in dire need of a bath.

Wynn grimaced, not really worried as the male's aura pulsed with a furious red power. She was fully confident that Azh was prepared for the attack. A second later, he proved her right.

Axton had barely reached the center of the room when white-hot flames circled him, forcing him to halt or be consumed by the fire.

"Nobody move," Azh warned as the five other demons stumbled off their cots, looking around with wild eyes.

"Back off," Axton rasped, sweat already dripping down his square face as the flames danced close enough to singe his chest fur.

"Who are you?" Axton glared at Azh, almost as if he thought he could intimidate him. Then, easily sensing he was no match for the stranger, he swiveled his glare toward Wynn. "Damn you. I hope you're happy."

Wynn folded her arms over her chest. "Not particularly."

"You've cost me everything."

Wynn was pretty sure he wasn't exaggerating. The shop that had been in his family for centuries had been destroyed beyond repair. And worse, he couldn't know whether or not he was still being hunted.

She might tell him that Malis was dead and it was safe to leave the hidden lair. Eventually.

"What happened?"

"You tell me," he snapped, wiping his thick hand over his forehead. The sweat was running down his face and dripping from his chin. He was smart enough not to protest at the fire that burned and sizzled just inches from his face. "Some crazy dude came in with glowing green eyes tearing the place apart. I tried to stop him but he killed two of my nephews before he pulled your necklace out of the hidden vault under the floor and demanded to know where to find the owner. I assume he meant you."

"What did you tell him?"

Axton shrugged. "I gave him every address I could think of, plus a few I made up."

"Thanks," she said dryly.

"Hey!" Axton arched back as the flames flared. "I didn't have a choice. I was trying to save my skin. When it was obvious the dude wasn't happy with my answers I took off. Just in time, as it turned out. I barely got to the end of the block before the place exploded." Axton pressed his hand against the raw burn on the side of his face. "Who was that creature? And what the hell did you do to piss him off?"

"Just being my usual charming self," she admitted with complete honesty.

"That would do it." Axton made a sound of disgust. "Well, you buggered my life."

"You'll get over it."

"How? How am I going to get over it?" Axton's voice went up several octaves as he stomped a foot in frustration. "My shop is destroyed. My clan is scattered except for these handful of losers." He waved a hand toward the demons huddled together in the far corner. "And I'm terrified to leave this hole in the ground."

Wynn reached into her pocket to pull out her necklace, holding it out so the silver caught and reflected the light from Azh's fire.

"You can start by telling me why you wanted this medallion."

Axton froze, his eyes widening as if he were unnerved by the sight of the pendant. Was he worried it was going to bring back the demon who'd destroyed his shop? Or was there another reason for his concern?

"I didn't. Not really. I felt sorry for you, so I offered you a few quid for the thing."

Wynn rolled her eyes. Did Axton think she was stupid? He'd never done anything out of pity.

"Right." She snorted in disbelief. "You never cared about anyone but yourself. And you certainly never offered money unless you knew you were going to get something out of it."

Axton shrugged. "I told you, I felt sorry for you. Do you know how pathetic you looked on the street corner begging for a few scraps—" The taunting words were cut short as Axton's hair caught on fire. "Argh. Stop." Axton batted his hands against his head, desperately trying to put out the flames. "Please."

"We don't have time for this," Azh growled, his words rumbling through the hidden lair like thunder. "Why did you buy the necklace?"

Axton seemed to shrink beneath the force of Azh's power, looking ridiculous with his hair half burned away. Once, he'd strolled through the streets with his chest puffed out and his lips twisted into an arrogant sneer. He'd been the unchallenged cock of the walk and he'd rejoiced in keeping the lesser demons in their place. Either with violence or threats against their families. Now he looked like a sad, pathetic loser.

"I recognized the symbol etched onto the medallion," he at last admitted in sullen tones.

Wynn studied the carving on the silver. It was so worn she could barely make out more than a tree with branches spread wide and a crescent moon at the top.

"Is it a human crest?" she asked. The aristocracy in England were always stamping their family coat of arms on stuff.

"No. It's the symbol of the Graia Coven."

Wynn clenched her teeth. Of course. Obviously, her newfound memories were true. She had been connected to a coven. And they'd tried to burn her at the stake.

The bitches.

"Witches," she hissed.

"One of the most powerful covens in England," Axton added before he shrugged. "Or at least they used to be. They lost a lot of power over the years."

Wynn shoved the medallion back into her pocket. It was a painful reminder of what the coven had tried to do to her.

"Why would you be interested in human magic?"

"I could tell you weren't a witch, so I assumed you stole the medallion from them. I tried to sell it back to them for a tidy profit."

Wynn considered his explanation before giving a slow nod. Cheating a helpless woman to make a quick dollar was typical for Axton. He was a common street thug who had the imagination of a turnip.

"They didn't want it?" she demanded.

The demon visibly shuddered. "Not only did they not want it, they went into a panic the minute I showed up with it. They claimed the medallion was cursed, along with anyone who touched it."

Cursed? Wynn considered the powerful magic that had prevented Azh from touching the medallion. There was certainly something strange about the necklace, but it didn't feel like a normal spell. Maybe her lack of magic made it impossible for her to detect it.

"Do you believe it's cursed?" she asked Axton.

"Yes. And they were right. Look what happened." Axton glanced around the barren cellar with a bitter expression. "My bloody life is in ruins."

That wasn't actual proof of a curse, but she was willing to accept that the spell connected to the medallion was dangerous.

"Why keep it?"

"I thought I might be able to use it to destroy my enemies. But when I got back to London and finally had it locked in the vault I had a bad feeling. Just holding it during the journey had made me feel sick." Axton rubbed his fingers together as if he could still feel the taint from the medallion. "I was afraid there was something in the curse that would backfire if I tried to use it. Better to take the loss and forget about the stupid thing." Axton shook his head. "I should have tossed it into the sewer. Or better yet, I should never have bought it from you. This is all your fault."

Wynn waved away his petulant accusation. She still had no idea why the evil magic had waited two centuries to track her down, or why it wanted her dead, but it was obvious Axton didn't have any clue about Malis or why he'd burned down his shop.

All she could do was hope that he could lead her in the direction to find the truth.

"Tell me more about the coven. Are they still around?"

"Who knows." Axton sent a glare toward Azh as the flames danced closer. "I'm telling the truth. I haven't heard anything about them in years. Mortals come and go too fast to keep up with them. Besides, most covens try to stay below the radar these days. They don't like attracting attention."

Wynn swallowed her sigh of impatience. "Fine. Where was the original coven?"

"A remote area in Chiltern Hills. They used to have a tiny village hidden in the woods." Axton sent another glare toward Azh. "That's all I know. I swear."

Azh glanced at her with a lift of his brows. "Enough?"

"Yes." Wynn studied the bedraggled Axton with a surprising stab of sympathy. He was cruel and greedy and willing to sacrifice anyone to save his own furry skin, but he'd also allowed her to beg on the street corner without demanding a portion of her meager earnings. And his presence had kept away lesser demons who might have taken advantage of her innocence. She would at least give him a warning. "I'd leave London if I were you," she told him.

Axton's eyes widened with a burst of fear. "Does that dude know where I am?"

"No. I killed him." Wynn ignored Axton's shock at her blunt confession. She didn't have a single regret. "But there might be worse things hunting me. Probably best for you to get out of town before they come looking."

"Damn you, Wynn," Axton ground out.

Wynn shrugged, glancing toward a smirking Azh. "Let's get out of here."

Chapter 16

Maya entered the private lair of Micha and Skye hidden beneath the picture-perfect house built in the swamps outside of New Orleans. It didn't take her ability to sense the thick magic that pulsed in the air to realize that there was nothing normal about the vast spiderweb of caverns. It was impossible to dig beneath the bayous without them being flooded. Still, the amount of power it'd taken to create such a vast lair was impressive.

"I wondered what would finally lure you to visit my new home," Skye said as she moved forward to greet Maya, her summer dress floating around her slender legs and her golden curls bouncing around her face. She looked as beautiful and delicate as a butterfly about to take flight, but her ancient power pulsed against Maya with enough force to lift the hair on the nape of her neck. Had the native magic seeped deep into the bayous intensified Skye's special gifts? They certainly felt a lot more intense. "It turns out all it took was the end of the world. Again."

Maya gave her friend a tight hug. "I've been a little busy."

"And you didn't want to leave that delicious mate of yours," Skye teased.

Maya pulled back, her heart squeezing at the thought of Ravyr. She missed him. More than she ever dreamed possible.

"He is above-average delicious," she agreed, then turning in a slow circle she concentrated on the cavern that surrounded her. Ravyr would soon be home where he belonged. For now, she had more pressing worries.

Her eyes widened as she took in the polished perfection that surrounded her. A coved ceiling soared well above her head and the walls were framed by towering glass cabinets protected by thick weaves of magic.

Inside the cases she could make out rare manuscripts, scrolls, and various gem-encrusted weapons that were no doubt hexed. "Wow," she breathed, not having to pretend she was impressed by the extensive collection of magical items. Until this moment, she would have sworn that Tia had the largest library of rare books. Now she wasn't so sure. "This is spectacular. I assume Micha created this?"

Skye looked smug. "He possesses a talent for molding and altering earth. You should see the gardens he created for me at our hidden spot deep in the bayous. It steals my breath every time we enter our private oasis."

"It's no wonder he's always been a hermit." Maya's gaze skimmed over the tightly rolled scrolls and stone tablets etched with long-forgotten hieroglyphs. How long had it been since anyone beyond Micha had held those precious scrolls in their hands? Or tested the precise magic contained in the daggers and ivory figurines? "I wouldn't leave this place either."

"There's more," Skye promised, continuing to lead Maya across the open space.

They'd reached the middle of the cavern when Maya caught the sweet scent of lilies, and without warning invisible fingers stroked over the scars on her cheek, as if seeking to understand the source of the wounds.

"Magic." Maya shivered as electric tingles raced over her skin, as if someone was standing directly in front of her. "Arcane magic."

"Ah." Skye smiled as Maya stopped to concentrate on the invisible presence that continued to touch her face. "You must mean Adelle."

Maya shook her head. "This isn't a demon."

"Adelle is a spirit."

Maya sent her friend a worried glance. "A ghost?"

Skye shrugged. "A spirit. A ghost. A restless soul. It's hard to say. One thing I do know is that she was here long before Micha created this lair. She's kind enough to let us share her home."

Maya didn't have much experience with ghosts. Most were human spirits who avoided demons and vampires. But she knew that there were some that could be dangerous. Especially the ones who had been magic users when they were alive.

"Can you see her?" Maya demanded.

"Sometimes I catch a glimpse out of the corner of my eye, but she's never more than a misty form who floats through the rooms."

"She doesn't bother you?"

"Not usually, although she sometimes tosses books around when she's not happy," Skye admitted. "Or leaves behind unpleasant scents."

"You could probably have her exorcised if she's bothering you."

Skye's eyes widened with a genuine shock at the same time the scent of scorched lilies swirled through the air.

"Don't say that." Skye clicked her tongue. "She's part of our family. And like I said. This swamp was her home first. We're just visitors."

Maya's heart melted. This young mage had every reason to be bitter and jaded after her years of being used and abused by the demons who had held her captive. Instead she was filled with an infectious joy for life. Maya missed spending time with her dear friend.

"Oh, Skye," she breathed. "You and your odd collection of the lonely and abandoned."

Skye smiled. "You haven't seen anything yet. Follow me."

Maya nodded, allowing herself to be led through an opening in the far wall.

She shivered as she walked through a thick barrier that protected the inner chamber. Skye's pace never slowed as they passed by cupboards stuffed with magical artifacts that pulsed with a variety of hexes and curses. Maya hissed as the waves of evil washed over her. She understood why Micha took such care to keep the items out of the reach of potential enemies. They had the power to spread disease and plagues if they fell into the wrong hands.

Maya was relieved when they stepped through another opening and another layer of magic. The chamber was smaller and the power from the spellbooks gathered on the wood shelves snapped and sizzled in the air. Like standing in the middle of a lightning storm.

This magic, however, didn't have the thick tang of evil. This was raw power that strained to be released.

"I've searched for any information I could find on dragons and put them in this pile," Skye said, seemingly indifferent to the vast power raging around her as she strolled to the center of the room.

Maya followed more slowly, her brows pulling together as she studied the two piles on the table.

"That's it?" Maya counted the meager pile. "Seven books?"

Skye spread her hands. "Unfortunately there's only three books that directly refer to dragons."

"And the other four?"

"They contain magic that can transform into a sentient being."

Maya moved to stand next to the table, thumbing through the top few books. "These are all about the miasma," she said, referring to the evil magic that had attacked Peri a couple years before.

"It's the only thing similar to what you explained to me," Skye admitted. "The miasma gained enough power to think independently and to infect other creatures with its evil."

Maya had to admit that there were some similarities, but she'd been in the presence of both magics. They felt completely different.

"The power that attacked me wasn't any magic I recognized," she insisted.

"Maybe it's the dragon form of miasma," Skye suggested. "It wouldn't be exactly the same, would it?"

Maya tried to recall the magical attack when she'd been standing guard in Hexx's empty pawnshop. It hadn't felt evil. And it hadn't tried to infect her. Or at least, she didn't think she'd been infected.

It had been raw power pummeling her like a sledgehammer.

"I don't know." Maya heaved a harsh sigh. "We're grasping at straws, aren't we?"

"Do you have a better idea?"

"No." Maya shook her head, frustration storming through her. "And if this is some sort of dragon miasma, then I have no idea how we're supposed to stop it. Not even Peri's wild magic could battle against that sort of power."

"True, but maybe the dragon who is sneaking around the world will be able to stop it," she suggested. "There has to be a reason he was able to escape the bonds of the treaty."

Maya shook her head. She wasn't ready to trust the creature. They'd already discovered that dragons could reach into this world and cause havoc. If she had to depend on someone to save them from disaster, she would choose Joe every time.

Which only proved just how little faith she had in the dragons.

About to suggest they travel to Tia's library in Colorado, Maya jerked in shock when a heavy book tumbled off a nearby shelf.

Skye wrinkled her nose. "Adelle isn't happy."

The book flipped open, the pages fluttering in an unseen breeze. "Stop that," Maya snapped. "We're busy."

"Wait, Maya." Skye scurried to pick up the book, carrying it to the table. She carefully set it down, leaving it spread open to the page the ghost had chosen. "I think she's trying to help."

Maya blinked. "Seriously?"

"Quite serious."

With an effort, Maya leashed her smoldering irritation. She had no idea why an unknown spirit would be trying to assist them, but Skye wouldn't waste her time if she didn't truly believe that there was something in the manuscript that would prove helpful.

The beautiful young mage was eccentric, not irresponsible.

"Okay, I'll play along," Maya conceded, stepping forward. "What is the book?"

Skye skimmed her fingers over strange hieroglyphs etched on the parchment, easily deciphering the script that looked like a bunch of scribbles to Maya's untrained eye.

"A collection of ancient prophecies," Skye at last concluded.

"Dragon prophecies?"

"No, this is fey writing." Skye squashed Maya's brief flare of hope. "I thought I'd discovered and read through every book of prophecy in this library, but I've never seen these before." She sent Maya a strange glance. "I think there was some sort of spell hiding the book until Adelle revealed it."

"Why would anyone go to the effort of writing down a prophecy if they intended to hide it?"

"Most clairvoyants like me can catch glimpses of the future, but as we both know, they're just fragments of possibilities that usually offer more confusion than concrete answers." Skye tapped her finger on the book. "These are from an oracle. The seer has no context of what the words mean, but they can determine when the event will occur. Most oracles will wrap them in spells that will only allow the foretelling to be revealed when the time is right."

"Do you recognize the oracle?" Maya asked.

Skye shook her head. "These visions came from the days just after the dragons went into hibernation. I doubt whoever had the vision is still alive."

Maya sighed. Skye's predictions offered her warnings about things that were about to happen within minutes or days of the event. And they were usually so vague they did nothing to help. How could they trust something that had been foreseen eons ago?

Unfortunately, they didn't have any better options.

"Is there anything in them about the evil magic?"

Skye furrowed her brow as she slowly translated the glyphs. "Hard to say. The language is old enough to be different from modern fey, and it looks like there's a lot of mumbo jumbo mixed in." She silently mouthed the words, nearly reaching the bottom of the page when she abruptly stiffened. "Wait. This one mentions a corruption."

"Read it to me," Maya commanded.

Skye leaned over the book, clearly struggling to make out the words.

"*When the corruption bubbles in the bowels of the ground and violence spreads throughout the land, the heart of darkness will strike from beyond the prison walls. Those too blind to see will drown in the evil while the watchers will be devoured by fire. To survive, you must stand steady against the unseen traitor.*'"

"The watchers? That might refer to Joe." Maya clicked her tongue. "But the rest of it makes no sense. How do you stand steady against an unseen traitor? And are we going to be devoured by fire or the corruption? Typical prophecy nonsense."

Skye straightened, her face pale. Clearly she was disturbed by the oracle's vision. "Don't glare at me. I'm a seer, not a prophet."

Maya waved an impatient hand. "You're the only one to glare at."

"True." Skye tapped her finger against the book. "I know it sounds like gibberish, but I think we should share this with Joe."

Maya grimaced, recalling her glimpse of Joe through Tia's mind. He'd been covered from head to toe by the green, slimy magic.

"He's a little preoccupied and this vision doesn't really offer much clarity."

"If Adelle showed it to us, it has to be important," Skye stubbornly insisted. "And since Joe is the Watcher, this might mean something to him even if it sounds like nonsense to us. Maybe he's heard another prophecy that's similar to this one."

"Okay. You're right," Maya conceded with a small sigh of defeat, reaching for the book. "I'll take this back to Tia. She can share the prophecy with Joe."

"Hurry."

Maya stared at her friend, a strange unease creeping down her spine. There was a sharp urgency in Skye's voice that hadn't been there before.

"Did you see something?"

Skye shook her head, her curls bouncing. "Not a vision. But a feeling. Here." She pressed her hand over her heart. "Having you back in New York and close to Tia suddenly feels...important."

"She's in danger?"

"Yes."

"Now?"

"Yes."

"I need to warn her." Maya closed her eyes, ignoring the heavy press of magic that made it difficult to breathe as she tried to tap into her mental connection with the older mage. Immediately, she realized that it was going to be impossible. There was a familiar buzzing sound that echoed in her ears, and a thick mist repelled her efforts to break through. "I can't reach her." Maya opened her eyes, her frustration reaching a boiling point. Dammit, couldn't one thing be easy? "There's an interference that comes from being so close to that evil sludge."

"Then you have to go to her, Maya," Skye insisted. "I'll have Micha's jet ready and waiting at the airport."

Maya gave a slow nod. "You're right. So much for my plans to stay the night and catch up."

Skye moved forward to give Maya a quick hug. "Next time," she promised.

"Considering how often we're facing the end of the world, I assume I'll be here next week," Maya said dryly.

Skye offered a faint smile. "True. In the meantime, I'll continue to search for answers on how to stop the corruption."

"Call if you find something."

Chapter 17

Azh followed Wynn as they climbed out of the cellar and back down the alley to discover the streets now bustling with early morning commuters heading to work.

They didn't speak as they walked toward the river, both knowing their next step would be tracking down the coven who'd tried to burn Wynn at the stake. Even if the witches from two hundred years ago were dead, there had to be some record or stories left behind that gave a clue to who Wynn had been before her memories were stolen.

Plus, it was their best hope for finding the spot where Gabriela created the rift to this world and where the corruption was trying to enter.

What happened after they found it...well, he'd worry about that once they were standing in front of the rift. Until then he was far more concerned about Wynn and the toll the chase was taking on her.

She was still suffering from the hours she'd spent in Pheral's dungeon and the amount of magic she'd been forced to release in her battle with Malis. It was no wonder her face was pale and she could barely place one foot in front of the other. She was on the edge of a complete crash.

"Enough," he growled, reaching out to wrap an arm around her shoulders and tugging her tight against his side. "We know where we're going. It's time to rest."

She tilted back her head to send him a wry smile. "I feel like you say that to me a lot."

"Because you keep rushing into danger and draining your energy," he chided.

"I didn't rush into danger," she protested. Azh stared down at her with raised brows. "I stumbled into it," she clarified.

"The end result is the same. You can barely stay awake."

She wrinkled her nose. "I want to argue, but you're right. It's probably better to go to Chiltern Hills later tonight. I need some time to rest." She glanced around, her lips twisting as two women in expensive business suits and designer heels nearly stumbled over each other as they stared at Azh with wide, disbelieving eyes. "Besides, you attract too much attention during the daylight hours."

"Me?"

"You're overly gorgeous," she groused.

Azh abruptly stepped to the edge of the sidewalk, pulling Wynn behind a large potted plant in front of an organic bakery. Wrapping his arms around her waist, he gazed down at her upturned face, his heart clenching with an unfamiliar tenderness. In the early morning sunlight she looked unbearably fragile, the impression only emphasized by the pallor of her skin and the shadows beneath her lavender eyes. But there was a ruthless grit etched into her delicate features.

This woman was a force of nature who would face down any danger with a smile on her face. A knowledge that both impressed and horrified him. As much as he desired a strong partner at his side, he understood it came with a constant worry that she was about to leap headfirst into disaster.

"Overly gorgeous?" The words were a low rumble as his dragon prowled close to the surface. The sweet scent of this woman was like a siren call to his beast, stirring a hunger that had been dormant for endless centuries. "Is that even possible?"

She tilted back her head, sending him a wry smile. "Don't pretend you don't notice the women watching you like you're a tasty snack."

He shrugged. "I don't care about them. My only interest is whether or not *you* watch me like I'm a tasty snack," he assured her.

She sniffed. "I'm too busy."

Azh's nostrils flared as he caught the sweet spice of her desire. She could deny her attraction to him all she wanted, but her body gave away the truth. Her passions smoldered just below the surface.

"A pity." Slowly lowering his head, Azh stroked his lips along the curve of her throat. "And in case you're wondering. I *am* a tasty snack." He breathed out a soft flame, allowing it to caress her cheek with a warm promise of pleasure.

Wynn sighed, arching closer to his hardening body. She liked the feel of his fire. Satisfaction stabbed through him. Not every woman could handle a dragon lover. This one was more than strong enough.

"Maybe someday when I'm not so preoccupied I'll find out for myself," she whispered.

His dragon roared with impatience. The beast had waited for what felt like an eternity to discover a female who could not only stir his lust but fill the emptiness in his heart. A partner, a queen, a beloved mate.

His fingers spread across her lower back, pulling her tight against his thickening cock. "Why wait?"

"I..." The words trailed away, as if Wynn had forgotten exactly why she should say no to him. Then, shockingly, she reached up to trail her fingers along the line of his jaw. "You're right."

"I am?" He gazed down at her with wary disbelief. "That's a miracle."

She pulled out of his arms, but before he could protest, she grabbed his hand and urged him down the sidewalk.

"Come with me."

Azh smoothly fell into step next to her, using his large body to clear a path through the hustling crowd.

"Where are you taking me?"

"Do you trust me?"

"Without hesitation."

They turned onto a side street, heading toward the nearby park. Azh assumed that Wynn was hoping to avoid the worst of the rush hour crush on their way to wherever they were going, but she halted at the corner, nodding toward the faded brick building that looked as if it'd been standing in that exact position for several hundred years.

Azh studied the sturdy structure, catching the scent of several demons inside. Both goblin and fey.

"What is this place?" he demanded.

She reached into the pocket of her coat, pulling out a gold coin that she tossed toward the elderly fairy who was wearing a crimson-and-gold uniform and standing next to the rotating glass door.

"It's one of the few hotels in London that exclusively caters to demons," she said, leading him forward as the male tipped his hat and touched the wall to reveal a hidden opening.

Azh studied the magical entryway with a lift of his brows. "A friend of yours?"

She waved toward the fairy before heading through the narrow space. "I located a family treasure that had been stolen from the owner of the hotel years ago. In return they allow me to use the residential rooms to crash when I'm in the neighborhood."

"I'm starting to understand how you survived for so long," Azh said. "You've created your own personal network of allies and support staff."

"Not all of them are happy about the arrangement," she said in dry tones. "But I've avoided a knife in the back. So far."

Azh hid his smile at the satisfaction of providing her with a lair that would be protected by the fiercest warriors along with layers of magic that would make it impossible to breach. Once they were fully mated she would never have to worry about her safety again.

Not bothering to wonder when he'd gone from suspecting this female might be more than a passing pain in his ass to acceptance she was his destined mate, Azh glanced around the large sitting room that was stuffed with worn couches and puffy chairs that were designed for comfort, not beauty. The walls were paneled and covered by dozens of framed family photos and the windows hidden behind thick curtains. There was a dark scruffy warmth to the space that seemed to please Wynn.

"It's...cozy," he said.

She wrinkled her nose. "It's not as fancy as the rooms for the paying guests, but I like it."

Azh shrugged, his gaze sweeping over Wynn as she turned to lead him across the room and down a narrow hallway. She was wearing the oversized overcoat and her hair pulled into a lopsided braid and there were streaks of dust on her face from the hidden cellar they'd just climbed out of, but no woman had ever been so beautiful. Just the sight of her made his heart sing with joy.

"Fancy is overrated," he assured her in a rough voice, his hunger vibrating through him as she stopped at the door at the end of the hall and shoved it open.

"You don't miss your acres of marble and satin sheets?" she teased.

Azh stepped into the small room, scanning the shadows for any potential danger. Just because Wynn trusted the owner didn't mean they hadn't been infected by the evil magic. Or were treacherous rats who hoped to claim the reward money just like Pheral.

One glance was enough to assure him that nothing was hidden beneath the narrow bed or behind the dresser that was shoved against the far wall.

He could even see into the attached bathroom that was barely big enough for a walk-in shower and sink. It was empty.

"Marble and satin sheets are cold," he growled, slamming shut the door and abruptly pressing Wynn against the wall. "And lonely."

Wynn hissed in shock, but her arms readily lifted to wrap around his neck, her fingers threading through his hair.

"You're not cold."

"Not now." He wrapped them in his silver-blue flames, the heat scorching the wall but leaving Wynn's delicate skin unharmed. "My dragon burns hot when you're near."

She gazed deep into his eyes, undaunted by the fire that smoldered around her.

"I see him." Her hands stroked a restless path over his shoulders. "I want to see more."

The beast inside him purred with pleasure. The ancient creature was thoroughly enchanted by the delicate wisp of a female in his arms.

"Your wish is my command."

"Isn't it genies who make wishes come true?"

Azh pressed his thickening erection against her hip, a moan of pleasure rumbling in his throat.

"It depends on what you're wishing for." He nuzzled the tender spot below her ear. "Tell me what you desire, Wynn."

She trembled, but not from fear. Instead she boldly grabbed his face in her hands and pulled him down for a kiss that sent jolts of bliss ricocheting through him.

"This," she muttered against his lips.

"A wish I'm happy to grant." He returned her kiss with a fierce heat, his flames swirling around them like a tornado. "Anything else?"

"Yes." She nipped at his lower lip, as if savoring the taste of him. "What color are your scales?"

Azh blinked, caught off guard by the question. Then, with a low growl, he grabbed the silken material of his shirt and casually ripped it off his body. Wynn sucked in a sharp breath as he slowly released his magic, revealing the shimmer of crystal-blue scales tipped with silver.

"Stunning," she breathed, lowering her hands to run them over the translucent scales rippling over the muscles of his chest. "They remind me of the ocean on a winter night. The bluest of blues kissed with moonlight." She scraped her nails down his flat stomach to trace his clenched abs. Azh hissed in ecstasy, a soul-deep craving to claim this woman shuddering through him. "And your wings?"

Releasing another burst of power, Azh spread his wings just far enough to give Wynn a glimpse of the silvery leather that looked too thin to hold a full-grown dragon but were as strong as steel and capable of slicing through the scales of his enemies. Bluish flames danced over the edge of the folded sections, hinting at the enormous span that he kept tucked against his back. If he actually spread his wings to their full length, they would destroy the small hotel.

"Oh, Azh," Wynn murmured, her expression suddenly wistful.

Azh cupped her cheek in his hand, a sudden pang of worry slicing through him. Had she decided that he was too much? This was the first time she'd had a glimpse of his true nature. Was she worried he was more beast than man?

"What's wrong?"

"You're so beautiful. And powerful." Her hand moved to trace the outline of his wing, sending quivers of electric pleasure through Azh. "You're a god. And I'm a mere mortal."

Azh clenched his teeth as the ground seemed to crumble beneath his feet and he felt himself soaring through the emptiness on a surge of joyous relief. Wynn wasn't repelled by his true self. She called him a god. But even as he relished the awe in her voice, he was aggravated that she could ever consider herself less than astonishing.

"There's nothing *mere* about you," he rasped, lifting his head to glare down at her. "And I'm not a god. I'm just a male desperately hoping he can please his female."

She stubbornly shook her head. "Dragons are never just—"

Her protest died on her lips as Azh dropped to his knees, tilting back his head to meet her stunned gaze.

"Wynn, I'm captivated and bewitched and utterly at your mercy."

The uncertainty slowly faded from her magnificent eyes, replaced with a smoldering anticipation that sizzled through Azh.

"At my mercy? I like the sound of that."

Azh surged upright, capturing her lips in a searing kiss as he slowly slid her coat off her shoulders. The heavy material slid down her body, hitting the floor with a loud thud. He chuckled, wondering how many lethal objects she was carrying around with her. Then the warm scent of her desire blossomed in the air, adding fuel to the flames dancing over his skin, and he groaned.

"You like the sound of having me at your mercy?" he teased, hurriedly removing the rest of her clothing to reveal her delicate perfection.

Desire blasted through him, the heat so intense he struggled to keep from singeing the delicate skin.

"Yes. It's only fair," she chided. "You crashed into my world and forced me to remember that I'm more than a thief."

"Much more." He cupped his hands under her backside, lifting her off her feet as he pressed her tight against the wall. Instinctively she wrapped her legs around his waist. A moan was ripped from Azh's throat as he buried his face against her throat and sucked in her sweet scent. "You're a thief, and an elusive chameleon and a pain in the ass."

"Azh." Wynn arched back to grind herself against the hard length of his erection.

Azh hissed, nearly falling back to his knees. This beautiful, maddening creature was destroying him in the most fabulous way possible. He should no doubt be terrified at the ease with which she had slipped past his barriers and, worse, distracted him from his duty to his people, but he wasn't scared.

He was reveling in every moment he could be in her presence.

In her arms.

"You captivated me from the moment you managed to elude my grasp," he managed to mutter, blazing a path of kisses over her flushed face. "I followed you because I couldn't *not* follow you."

"I'm glad you did." She ran her hands down his chest, exploring him with the same bold intensity she did everything. "Most of the time."

Azh trailed his lips down the curve of her neck, savoring each satin inch as he reached her collarbone and down to the soft swell of her breast.

"Like now?" he moaned, teasing the tip of her nipple with his tongue.

"That has yet to be determined," she rasped, even as she trembled, the sound of her racing heart filling the room.

Azh laughed, moving to give proper attention to her other breast. He knew when a woman was drowning in passion.

"Harsh," he whispered.

"Mmm." Wynn reached down to fumble with the zipper of his slacks. Azh muttered an ancient profanity, embarrassingly close to losing control as her fingers wrapped around his thick arousal. "I have faith in you."

Azh had envisioned spending hours seducing this woman. He wanted to investigate her from the top of her satin hair to the tips of her toes. He wanted to use his fingers and teeth and tongue to set her ablaze with desire.

But as Wynn stroked his cock with an impatience that sent shockwaves down his spine, he knew that those fantasies would have to wait.

Kicking off his shoes, Azh managed to get rid of his slacks before he was carrying Wynn toward the bed. He bent down, setting her on the edge of the mattress before kneeling in front of her. Demand was battering against him with the force of a hurricane, but he'd promised himself when he finally got her naked, he was going to discover if the heat between her legs was as delicious as he imagined.

Skimming his fingers up her bare thighs, Azh glanced up to hold Wynn's darkened gaze as he tugged her legs over his shoulders. Her lips parted, her breath coming in short pants as he slowly leaned forward and stroked his tongue over her most sensitive flesh.

Wynn gasped and Azh grunted in pleasure. Blessed goddess. She was wet and hot and she tasted of nectar. Exactly as he'd imagined. Tightening his fingers on her thighs to hold her still, Azh tormented her with long strokes of his tongue and licks of flames that wrenched cries of pleasure from her lips.

"Azh, please," she rasped. "Now."

"Yes," he breathed, pressing her backward and wrapping her legs around his waist. Then, threading his fingers in her hair, he positioned his cock at her entrance and slid into her slick heat with one steady thrust. "Hold on tight, my fearless thief," he rasped, pumping deeper and deeper as the flames wrapped around them in a cyclone of passion.

Chapter 18

Wynn woke from a light slumber to discover she was still tightly wrapped in strong male arms. A sizzling heat danced over her skin as Azh cocooned them in his flames.

"You broke the bed." Azh's voice rumbled in her ear, his fingers brushing through the loose strands of her hair.

Wynn tilted back her head to study her companion. Her heart slammed against her ribs as she absorbed his impossible beauty. At the moment, his eyes were a soft smoky gray, but during their hours of intense lovemaking they'd flashed with dazzling strikes of lightning. As if a storm were raging through him as he brought her to the peaks of pleasure over and over.

That might explain why she'd barely noticed when the bed had splintered and buckled during their last intense bout of sex. Nothing mattered but the sensation of becoming one with the male who'd stormed his way into her heart.

"Me?" She smacked her open hand against his bare chest. It was as hard as steel. "You're twice my size. How can it be my fault?"

"You were on top when it broke."

She had been. And it had given her a whole new appreciation for riding a dragon. Glorious.

"It was your magic that lifted it off the floor," she reminded him.

"Only because you had me tied to the mattress."

"That's your fault. I wanted you to stay still so I could have my fun."

Strikes of lightning returned to his eyes. "You got me too excited. It's a miracle the hotel didn't collapse on our heads."

She rubbed her palm over the silky-smooth skin, enjoying the blue-and-silver hints of his scales.

"I like when you're too excited."

He bent forward to brush his lips over her brow. "The feeling is entirely mutual."

She snuggled closer. There was a comfort in being pressed close to his hard body. It wasn't lust. Or at least, it went beyond lust, she amended as his lips continued to nuzzle soft kisses over her face. It was the absolute confidence that she'd found a safe harbor in a world that had always been filled with unpredictable chaos.

It was peace. As if being in Azh's arms was fulfilling a glorious destiny she didn't know was waiting for her.

"Tell me about being a dragon," she murmured.

He pressed a lingering kiss against her lips before at last lifting his head to study her with a hint of amusement.

"What do you want to know?"

She studied his stunning features, abruptly acknowledging that she wanted to know everything. Every moment of his long life until this moment. His every thought and feeling. What made him happy, what made him sad, and his most cherished dreams. As if she could delve deep into his heart to discover his secrets.

Like a mate. A soul mate.

Dangerous, dangerous thoughts...

"Are you bored during your forced hibernation?"

He arched a brow, easily sensing she'd cowardly retreated from asking the questions that hovered on her lips. Questions that were treacherously intimate.

"Not really," he finally said. "Dragons routinely choose to retreat from the world. Sometimes because we've been injured and need to heal and other times because we prefer a few centuries of peace. Even when we lived in our homeland the histories reveal that we had personal lairs where we could disappear when we wanted time alone."

Wynn released a soft sigh. "A few centuries of peace in an isolated lair sounds perfect right now."

"Agreed." His gaze swept over her face, a hint of his beast flaring through the misty gray of his eyes. "As long as we're together."

An intoxicating heat brushed over her. Was the dragon reaching out to physically touch her? Wynn shivered, tempted to become lost in the sensuous pleasure that sizzled over her bare skin and warmed the blood flowing through her veins. Instead she distracted herself with more questions.

"What do you do with your time?"

"Personally or dragons in general?"

"Personally."

His fingers trailed up and down the curve of her spine in a gentle caress. "I spend most days in the library or keeping a watch on the humans and their evolving technology. Occasionally I spar with other dragons, although not enough to please my mother. She believes brute strength is the only measure of importance in a leader."

She studied him intently, genuinely curious. Despite the power of his dragon that thundered just below the surface, she'd discovered that Azh preferred to use his clever wits to overcome obstacles. Any bully could push around a weaker adversary, but you couldn't always depend on being the strongest creature in every fight. It took brains to avoid the conflict in the first place.

"And you?" she asked.

"I believe that knowledge is power. I also believe that the future will belong to those who understand that trust and respect are mightier than fear. Dragons who are united in a common cause can't be divided or broken. The only ones who can defeat us are ourselves. Something we have forgotten over the eons."

She smoothed her hands over his chest, relishing the hard muscles beneath her palms. She admired his preference for brain over brawn, but that didn't mean she couldn't appreciate his raw male power.

"Very lofty goals."

"Dream big, right?" He paused, studying her with a steady intensity. "What are your dreams?"

"I just want my life to go back to normal."

"And then?"

She pasted a stiff smile onto her lips. This wasn't a conversation she wanted to have. Not when she was still melty from her cataclysmic climax.

"I don't know. I've always been a live-in-the-moment kind of gal."

"There must be something you hope for the future," he insisted.

"To know who I am." She tried to divert him. "Or I suppose, who I was before I woke on the banks of the Thames. I'm not sure I can ever be that person again, but it would be nice to know if I ever had any family or someone who was worried after I ended up in the hands of the murderous witches."

"We're going to figure that out, Wynn. And then—"

"No," she interrupted.

He stilled, belatedly sensing her burst of unease. "Excuse me?"

"No talk of what happens after that," she insisted.

"Because you're a live-in-the-moment kind of gal?"

"Because once we destroy the evil magic, you'll return to your hibernation and I'll be returning to my normally scheduled program in this world."

"Wynn."

"No." She sent him a warning glare. This was what she'd been trying to avoid. "We have to concentrate on the now, not the later."

His nostrils flared and Wynn half expected to see smoke coming out as the dragon glared at her. It wasn't used to being denied what it desired. But at last, Azh released a low growl of frustration.

"You're right. First we defeat the corruption. And then we discuss the future."

She rolled her eyes. That was as close as she could get him to conceding their futures were in two different places.

"First things first." She wiggled out of his arms. "A shower, clean clothes, and dinner. In that order."

"This shower..." He gazed down at her with sudden anticipation. "Is it together?"

"Together."

With a laugh, Wynn was scrambling off the bed and running into the bathroom. She reached the shower first, but only because Azh allowed her to win. He stalked behind her like a predator, the lightning already dancing in his eyes. Wynn trembled with excitement as she hastily turned on the cold water at full blast. A second later Azh stepped into the small cubicle, his heat creating a thick steam that billowed around their entwined bodies.

Wrapping her arms around the dragon's neck, Wynn felt herself lifted off the ground and pressed against the slick tiled wall. A second later she was groaning in bliss as Azh entered her with one smooth thrust. Squeezing shut her eyes, Wynn allowed herself to become lost in the tidal wave of pleasure, surrounded by the steam and intoxicating blast of pure dragon magic.

Two hours later they returned to the bedroom to polish off a mound of takeout curry that was delivered by unobtrusive servants, and pulled on the clothes that had been in the bag with the food.

Wynn was in the bathroom braiding her damp hair when Azh appeared in the doorway, his expression one of annoyed disbelief.

"Seriously?" He spread his arms. "You expect me to be seen in public in this?"

Turning around, Wynn's lips twitched at the thin silk shirt that clung to his torso and the leather pants that revealed every delicious bulge. He looked like a fake pirate in a burlesque show. Or maybe a maître d' about to offer her a table at a trendy restaurant.

"I just gave your size. They must have assumed you were a male escort. Do you want me to order you something less..." She waved a hand over his too-tight outfit.

With a low growl, Azh created a narrow portal, disappearing into what she assumed was his private lair. A few seconds later he was back, wearing a pair of faded jeans and a plain gray sweatshirt.

The clothing did nothing to lessen the impact of his explosive sensuality. This male could be covered in a shroud and he would still be a sex magnet. It was annoyingly unfair, she acknowledged, glancing down at the cutoff jean shorts and scooped tee that emphasized her resemblance to a young boy, not a spicy vixen.

She clicked her tongue. Who cared? She was on the hunt for a toxic green sludge. Comfort was more important than glamour, right? Truthfully, as far as Wynn was concerned, comfort was *always* more important than glamour.

Thankfully unaware of her rambling thoughts, Azh pointed toward the center of the bedroom, creating yet another portal.

"Let's go," he commanded.

Wynn arched a brow as she pulled on her magically shielded coat. Better safe than sorry. "Are you going to feed me to your mother? I told you I didn't pick out those clothes."

"Tempting, but no," he assured her. "This is a shortcut to our destination."

He moved forward, disappearing into a thick fog. Wynn followed behind him, taking less than a dozen steps when a hand reached out to grasp her arm.

"Careful, Wynn, we can't be sure Axton didn't warn someone that we were asking questions about the coven." Azh lowered his head to whisper directly in her ear. "He already admitted he was willing to trade your location to save his own skin."

Belatedly realizing that they were no longer in the portal, despite the thick fog that continued to swirl around them, Wynn searched through her strands of magic to discover the slender silver thread. Tapping into the power, she grimly ignored the throbbing red strand that had grown thicker and more ominous in the past few days. As if it were trying to consume her.

Grinding her teeth against the blast of fear, Wynn forced herself to concentrate on the tingle of magic that flowed from the silver strand to create a chilled breeze. It wasn't as strong as she wanted, but after a struggle to get started, it managed to clear away the fog, revealing they were standing on the banks of the Thames. Around them the empty countryside was sleeping beneath the thick layer of darkness, the lights from a distant village the only visible sign of life.

"Axton would trade his own mother to save his skin," she said, her eyes darting from side to side in search of hidden dangers.

"Is anything familiar?"

"Not really." She shrugged. "It looks like every other rural part of the country."

Azh nodded toward the soft glow in the distance. "There's a village in that direction."

"It's a place to start."

They walked side by side, both on high alert as the heavy silence pressed against them. Wynn rarely spent time in the country, but she did know that she should be hearing the sounds of tiny animals scampering in the nearby fields or the croak of frogs from the river.

Had they been frightened off by Azh's powerful presence? Or was there something else that had sent them into hiding?

Rounding a curve in the pathway, Wynn felt a familiar tingle sweep over her. She came to an abrupt halt.

"Wait."

"Do you recognize something?"

"No, but I can feel magic."

Azh moved with blinding speed to stand next to her, his power sizzling through the air.

"Demon?"

"Human." She pointed toward a patch of oak trees that blocked the view of the rolling landscape. "There's a circle in that direction."

Reaching into the pocket of her coat, she pulled out the medallion they'd found in the destroyed pawnshop and slipped it over her head.

Azh studied her with a worried expression. "What are you doing?"

"Reclaiming my past."

His gaze lowered to the medallion that shimmered as if reacting to the magic that drifted on the soft breeze.

"Just..." His words trailed away with a heavy sigh. Smart dragon. He knew that trying to tell her to be careful was a waste of breath. "All right, let's go."

She sent him an encouraging smile, veering off the pathway to follow the scent of brewing herbs that was thick in the air. Whoever had created the circle was using it to add extra magic to a brewing potion. She wasn't familiar with the spell, but it had to be powerful for her to detect it from such a distance.

Entering the thickly wooded area, they instinctively slowed. Neither had forgotten the traps set by Pheral. The fissures should have been destroyed the moment the demon died, but it was always possible he'd tied the magic to one of his goons. Not to mention the fact there could be other traps set by completely unknown enemies.

At last reaching the center of the woods, they discovered a large clearing where the outline of an ancient circle was dug deep into the earth and surrounded by large rocks. Closer to the edge of the trees, there were a dozen cottages and outbuildings in various stages of decay. A few were still standing, although they were empty shells, and others had already crumbled into piles of rotting timbers. Whatever had happened to the small village had been a slow decline, not a quick desertion.

"It looks abandoned, but someone has to be close by." Wynn nodded toward the heavy cast iron cauldron bubbling over an open fire in the middle of the circle. "No one would leave such a potent brew unattended."

Azh tilted back his head, as if testing the air. "There's a cottage hidden behind the bushes," he at last announced. "I can smell a human inside."

"I think I should have a chat with them."

"*We* should have a chat."

Wynn turned to face her companion, meeting his stern gaze with a determined expression.

"I'm not trying to keep you away, Azh, but I need you to stay here to keep a watch on my back." She glanced toward the bubbling pot, a chill inching down her spine. She couldn't explain what she was feeling, but she sensed a dark magic hovering just out of sight. Like a monster preparing to leap from the shadows. "There's a heaviness in the atmosphere that's giving me the creeps."

Azh folded his arms over his chest. "And?"

She heaved a loud sigh. "And if it's a human they're going to be too distracted to get any sensible answers from them. They can't help themselves when you're around. They turn into babbling idiots."

His jaw tightened, but he didn't argue. Humans weren't prepared to be in the presence of a full-fledged dragon. They were either overcome with lust or fear when they caught sight of Azh. Many times both.

"Leave the door open," he instead commanded.

She rolled her eyes. "Like you couldn't huff and puff and blow down Buckingham Palace, let alone a puny cottage."

He held her gaze, his jaw tight with the effort to control the beast who smoldered deep in his eyes. The dragon wasn't happy with her demand that she face the unknown human on her own.

"I want to hear what she has to say," he explained between clenched teeth. "Fine."

On the point of turning away, Wynn found herself grabbed by the shoulders and hauled against Azh's hard body. She tilted back her head in surprise, barely given time to brace herself as he swooped his head down to kiss her with a savage hunger. Wynn instinctively grasped his sweatshirt, her knees going weak as heat blasted through her.

For a long moment they simply melted into the desire that instantly sizzled between them. It wasn't just need that brought an edge of urgency to the embrace. It was the whispering fear this might be their last kiss.

Eventually it was a whiff of something nasty coming from the cauldron in the center of the circle that brought Wynn back to her senses. This wasn't going to be her last kiss, she fiercely swore.

She didn't care what it took, she was going to defeat the dragon magic that was pulsing inside her, as if struggling to be released.

"Stay here," she commanded, turning away. One glance into that gorgeous face and she would be a goner.

Feeling his gaze burning into her back, Wynn walked along the edge of the circle until she was past the untrimmed hedge that hid the cottage from view. A quick glance assured her it was in better condition than the others, but it was still in dire need of repairs. The thatched roof was shabby and the windows coated in dust. Even the front step needed a good scrubbing, although there was a new sign next to it painted with the words:

Herbal Healing by Charlotte

With a shudder, Wynn walked up the narrow path and knocked on the wooden door. She hoped the herbal healing wasn't the stench coming from the cauldron. That stuff smelled nasty.

There was a long silence, as if whoever was inside was hoping that Wynn would assume the cottage was empty and leave. Wynn knocked again, this time with enough force to send a cloud of decaying straw drifting from the roof.

There was another long silence before the door cracked open to reveal an older woman with long, tangled gray hair that framed her gaunt face and wary blue eyes.

"Yes?" She glanced over Wynn's shoulder as if sensing Azh's presence in the distance. When she couldn't see any lurking danger, she returned her attention to Wynn. "What do you want?"

"Are you Charlotte?"

"Yes, but I don't take clients this late."

"That's okay. I'm not here for your healing."

Charlotte furrowed her brow. "Are you lost?"

"No." Wynn's lips twisted into a bitter smile. "I'm hoping that I'm finally home."

"Home? Are you from the village? Do I know you?"

"Perhaps." Wynn reached up to touch the glittering medallion.

The watery blue eyes widened as the woman pulled open the door wide enough to reveal the interior of the small cottage. Wynn caught a glimpse of a sofa with worn cushions pulled close to the stone fireplace and a wooden table with one chair. There were dozens of leatherbound books piled on the flagstone floor along with glass bottles filled with potions. The ceiling was low, with open beams that had bundles of herbs tied together hanging from them.

"Where did you get that?"

"It was seared into my flesh when your coven tried to burn me alive," Wynn said in blunt tones.

"What? I don't..." The words trailed away as the blue gaze locked on Wynn's face. Then she released a hiss of shock. "Oh, blessed goddess. Gwen? Gwen Winsor? How is this possible? I watched you die."

Wynn was briefly distracted by the woman's horrified words. Her name was Gwen Winsor? Ew. It sounded like a stuck up aristocrat. No way she was going back to that. She was Wynn. Magic thief, escape artist, and dragon lover. Wild and free.

With an effort, she returned her scattered thoughts to the reason she was standing outside the shabby cottage.

"So you were there when I was murdered?"

"No." Charlotte started to shake her head only to bite her lower lip as Wynn glared at her. The older woman had just admitted she'd watched Wynn die. "I mean I was hidden in the woods. I wasn't old enough to be an official member of the coven, but my mother and aunt were there. I followed them and watched from a distance. It was horrible."

"No shit."

Charlotte flinched. She looked old and miserable. As if she were decaying along with the isolated covenstead.

"Sorry. I don't understand," the woman said. "How did you survive?"

Wynn held up a hand. "First I want to know about the coven."

"Know what?"

Wynn shrugged. "I have no memory of the witches. Or my time here. I want you to fill in the gaps."

"Really?" Charlotte blinked. "No memory at all?"

"Only of my near death."

The woman winced again, then with a jerky motion she abruptly turned away and shuffled toward the fireplace.

"I have a book that might help."

Wynn cautiously stepped over the threshold, careful to leave the door open. "I'm not a traditional mage, Charlotte, but I'm not helpless," she warned. "Be very careful what you plan to do next."

The woman clicked her tongue, smoothing her palms down the threadbare fabric of her nightgown that looked to be at least three sizes too large. Had she recently lost weight or did it belong to someone else? Wynn couldn't sense any other presence in the area, but that didn't mean they couldn't be disguising themselves with a spell.

"My powers are for healing, and they have faded until I can barely brew a potion," Charlotte admitted. "The magic of the coven died a very long time ago." The woman bent over to study the books, at last choosing one from the middle of the stack. Grabbing it with gnarled fingers, she straightened and shuffled to the table. "This should answer some questions," she said, glancing back at Wynn.

"What is it?" Wynn demanded, tapping into the strand of magic that would create a blinding darkness so she could escape if things went sideways.

Right now, Charlotte was her only connection to the past. She didn't want to kill her unless she absolutely had to.

"The history of the Graia Coven." Charlotte tugged on the heavy leather cover of the book, tipping it open to reveal the spidery handwriting on the yellowed parchment. "Most of it's pretty boring. The earliest witches had a connection to the druids who first crafted the medallions that we all wear. It supposedly gave us a mystical power that other covens envied."

Charlotte stepped aside to allow Wynn room to stand in front of the book. With a frown, Wynn studied the faded illustrations of robed men forging the medallions before handing them to a circle of identically robed women. She flipped over the page, realizing that the scribbled text was written in a language she didn't understand. Ancient Celtic? A secret language only the coven understood?

"What's in the rest of the book?" she demanded.

"There's a brief explanation of how the witches were drawn to this location by a powerful magic that made the earth tremble," Charlotte said, thankfully not going into any boring details as Wynn continued to flip through the pages. When Wynn said she wanted to know about the coven, she didn't need a tedious history lesson. Wynn reached a page that was different. It looked like a long list. "What's this?"

"The rest of the book is a catalogue of the names of the witches who were members of the coven over the centuries."

Wynn skimmed her fingers over the names, more resigned than surprised that she didn't recognize any of them. So far nothing about this place had jogged her memories.

"Why are some of them written in purple?" she demanded as she reached the last page.

"Those are the witches that came from aristocratic families."

Wynn snorted. "Why would that matter?"

Charlotte hunched her narrow shoulders. "Many of them brought large dowries with them that helped to support the coven. One of the early founders even donated this land that extends from the river to beyond the woods along with the cottages." The woman heaved a heavy sigh. "At one time there was a large meeting hall in the meadow, but it collapsed long ago. I'm the last witch left, you see. Or at least I thought I was until you showed up."

Wynn shut the book. This wasn't the information she wanted. "Why are you the last one?"

Charlotte looked confused. "Because of what happened to you, of course."

"What does that mean?"

"You really have no memory?"

"Only of the day they tried to torch me. Hard to forget that," Wynn snapped, pretending that she hadn't just recently retrieved the memory. "Why do you blame me for what happened to the others?"

The witch twisted her hands together, as if bothered by the question.

Unless this was all an elaborate act, Wynn silently warned herself. Maybe Charlotte killed the other witches to absorb their power. It seemed unlikely, but Wynn wasn't going to take any chances. She was going to assume this witch was a dangerous threat.

"I don't," Charlotte muttered. "Not exactly. It's just..."

Wynn squashed her stab of irritation as the words died on the woman's lips. Charlotte was obviously disturbed by Wynn's return from the grave. Pressuring her wasn't going to help.

"Start at the beginning," Wynn urged, trying to soften her tone. "Not this beginning," she hastily added, closing the ancient book. "How did I end up in this place?"

"You were born here."

Wynn flinched. It was the obvious answer. Any mage, whether she was a Void or not, had a mother or grandmother who could use magic. Still, it was one thing to think that the coven stumbled across her and decided she needed to be burned alive. It was another to realize that the murderous mob chasing her with torches had been women who'd presumably loved and cared for her since she was a baby.

"My mother was a member of the coven?" she forced herself to ask.

"Yes. In fact, she was the leader at the time. That's the only reason you were allowed to stay here after you were born."

Wynn was confused. "Why? The coven didn't allow babies?"

Charlotte licked her lips, as if they were suddenly dry. "Most of them, but after your birth your mother called in a seer. I think she hoped to prove that you were the chosen one, destined to take over the coven after she retired."

Unease stabbed through Wynn's heart. "I assume that's not the future the seer revealed?"

"When she touched you she supposedly fainted," Charlotte said with a visible shiver. "When she finally woke up, your mother demanded to know your future, but the woman would only mutter the word 'destruction' over and over. The other witches wanted you banished, but your mother refused to listen to anyone who suggested you were putting the coven in danger."

Destruction? Wynn clenched her hands. Had she been cursed from the moment she'd been born? That hardly seemed fair.

"Obviously they convinced my mother they were right since they tried to kill me," she said in tight tones.

"Not for sixteen or seventeen years. I remember vividly the day it changed."

"What happened?"

Charlotte glanced toward the window, as if oblivious to the fact it was coated in dust. "You were standing in the middle of the circle helping to stir the potions brewing in the community cauldron." Her gaze moved to the open doorway. "I was playing in front of the cottage with my dolls. I remember I was pouting because my mother wouldn't let me go into the woods to play. She said that there was a strange magic buzzing in the air. She was worried danger was coming. And she was right."

Wynn studied the gaunt face that appeared ashen in the flickering firelight. As if the memory was making her physically ill.

"What was the danger?"

"At first I didn't know. I was still playing with my dolls when you suddenly cried out like you were in pain. Everyone started running toward you—we all thought you'd been burned—but before we could reach you, there was a weird humming sound and you started to glow with this terrible white light." Charlotte squinted, as if the mere thought of the light still bothered her. "It was so bright I squeezed my eyes shut. I'm not sure what happened next, but there was a lot of screaming and a few witches tried to cast spells and eventually I could smell smoke. Then the next thing I knew there was a huge explosion and I was flying through the air to land against the fireplace."

Wynn didn't have to wonder about the explosion. She'd heard enough stories about the wild magic that flared through women when they became mages to imagine the fear and chaos it'd created. The only difference was the fact that the magic hadn't bothered to stay around for her. And she had no memory of the event. Which meant that she got all the bad with none of the good.

Typical.

"What happened next?"

"When I opened my eyes I could see the witches lying on the ground bleeding from the chunks of metal that went flying when the cauldron exploded. There were even roofs blown off the cottages." Charlotte shook her head. "I'd never dreamed that one person could hold so much power. I was both horrified and jealous I would never have a fraction as much magic."

"Destruction," Wynn murmured.

"That's when your mother called the most powerful spellcasters to grab you while the others collected torches. I suppose they'd all been prepared for the day that one of the coven would release their wild magic and transform into a mage." Charlotte paused, as if struck by a sudden realization. "Or maybe they'd been preparing for you to fulfill the seer's prophecy," she abruptly suggested. "Anyway, they seemed to know exactly what they intended to do."

Wynn might have had some sympathy for the witches. Not only had she brought a curse to their coven, but her transition into an almost-mage had come with an explosion that had destroyed buildings and caused serious injuries. But any attempt to understand their panic was shattered by the one memory she did have. A group of women screaming for her death.

"Their plan was to burn me alive," she rasped.

"Unfortunately," Charlotte agreed, smart enough not to try to excuse the coven's murderous intent. "I was hiding in the woods and too far away to see exactly what happened after they'd forced you to the top of the hill, but they all looked anxious when they returned to the cottages and started to repair the damage. No one ever spoke of that day again, but it was the beginning of the end for the coven."

Charlotte once again implied that Wynn was somehow responsible for ruining the coven.

"Why do you say that?"

"It's the truth." The watery blue gaze swept over the cramped room. "No one died that day, but our powers began to fade. And worse, none of the witches could have children. I even left the area to find a lover thinking the curse might be isolated to our land, but I was still denied a baby. It was as if we were being punished for your death." Charlotte snapped her lips together, staring at Wynn in confusion. "But that can't be right, can it? You didn't die."

Wynn resisted the urge to continue to press for a reason that the coven had died out. Maybe the curse really had been caused by her birth. Or maybe it'd been brought on by the witches' evil attempt to kill an innocent girl. Or maybe it was simply natural selection.

"What about my mother?" she instead asked.

"She passed away decades ago. Along with the rest of the coven. I'm the only one left."

Wynn took a moment to absorb the realization that her mother was dead. No, not her mother. The woman who'd given birth to her. A real mother didn't try to torch their child.

Was she sad that she'd never have a relationship with the woman? Not really. The woman sounded like an overly ambitious bitch who was more interested in power than her own child.

Good riddance.

Not sure what else the witch could tell her that might help in the battle against the corruption, Wynn was on the point of turning away when she was struck by a sudden thought.

"If you're losing your magic, why do you stay?"

The woman blinked. "This is my home."

"There are other covens. I'm sure you could find a new—"

"No." Charlotte raised her hands to her throat, as if frightened by the mere suggestion of leaving. "I can't."

"Can't? Or won't?" Wynn studied the pale eyes that were darting from side to side. Was Charlotte afraid of the question? "Is there someone keeping you here? Or some sort of magic?"

The eyes continued to dart as Charlotte leaned toward Wynn. "They need me."

"Who?" Wynn demanded. "You said the rest of the witches were dead."

"They're still watching."

Wynn swiftly battled back the prickling sense of unseen eyes that crawled over her bare skin. Azh would have sensed anyone lurking in the dark. Obviously this woman was going mad from being alone for so long in this isolated cottage.

"I'm sure they do watch over you," she gently assured her.

"No, you don't understand." Charlotte abruptly reached out to grasp Wynn's arm in a painful grasp. "I hear them whispering at night."

Wynn started to yank her arm free, only to hesitate. There was a fierce intensity in the woman's voice that warned she fully believed the witches were talking to her. Was it possible she'd been tainted by the corruption? Wynn couldn't detect the evil magic, but maybe it was in the area, driving this woman to the edge.

"What do they whisper?"

"They beg for me to release them."

"Release them from what?"

"Death."

"You're trying to bring them back from the dead?" A new fear stabbed through Wynn, wiping away her suspicion that the corruption had caused Charlotte's madness.

Necromancy was strictly forbidden, no matter if you were a demon, a mage, or a witch. The practice went beyond evil to immoral and often destroyed the minds of those attempting the dark magic.

The witch nodded, seemingly indifferent to her danger. "They're on the other side. If I can get through the barrier I can bring them home. Then I won't be alone." The whispered words were still hanging in the air when a violent tremor rippled beneath the earth. As if the ground were trying to split in two. Books tumbled into messy heaps and the bottles of potions crashed to the flagstone floor. "There," Charlotte hissed, releasing Wynn's arm as she stumbled back. "You see? They're angry."

Wynn coughed, waving away the dust that rained from the thatched roof. The earth continued to tremble, threatening to bring the cottage down on their heads. She didn't know what was causing the quakes, but she didn't intend to stick around and find out.

"Listen to me," she commanded, holding out her hand. "You need to leave this place. It's not safe."

"No, no, no." The witch shook her head, her eyes wide with fear. "I have to stay. They need me."

Wynn's lips parted, but before she could continue her plea for the woman to leave, the sound of Azh's voice thundered through the air.

"Wynn!"

Chapter 19

Wynn bolted out of the cottage, awkwardly stumbling as the ground continued to surge and heave beneath her feet. It was like running on waves that were about to crash into the shore.

Passing by the overgrown hedges that blocked her view, Wynn had a glimpse of Azh battling against a blinding silver light that burst out of a crack forming along the edge of the circle.

"Azh!"

Her heart squeezed with terror as the crack widened and Azh was sucked into the pulsing glow. Scrambling forward, Wynn desperately sorted through her strands of magic, seeking something that could wrap around Azh to hold him in place until she could reach him.

She was still futilely racing forward when the light abruptly disappeared and the crack snapped shut. Wynn cried out as she reached the spot that Azh had disappeared from and fell to her knees.

Pressing her hands against the ground, she could feel the searing heat from the powerful magic, but there was nothing to reveal that the earth had been split open. Not unless you counted the charred bits of grass.

"Azh," she rasped, swallowing a sob as the tremors beneath her slowly faded.

A second later the night was silent, as if the violent quakes and blinding light had never happened.

Wynn resisted the urge to frantically dig through the dirt in the hopes of locating Azh. As desperate as she was to reach him, she clung to enough sanity to know that the magic that had taken him wasn't a common protection spell created by the witches. Azh wasn't being held in a pit a few feet underground. Whatever had captured him was powerful enough to trap a full-grown dragon. He could be anywhere.

The question was how did she follow him?

Wynn straightened, grimly refusing to give into the panic. She couldn't follow Azh through the closed crack, but that didn't mean there wasn't another entrance. And she knew exactly where to start looking.

Without giving herself time to consider the wisdom of running through the dark in search of the creature responsible for kidnapping Azh, Wynn headed into the nearby woods. The light that she saw wrapped around Azh reminded her of the glow that had split open the ground when she'd been attacked by the coven. It couldn't be a coincidence. Now she just had to find the spot where she'd fallen into the pit.

With no idea what she intended to do after she got there, even assuming she could find the precise location, she raced up the slope of the hill.

Right now this was her only plan. It made the decision easy.

Tripping over a hidden log, Wynn reluctantly slowed her hectic pace. She wasn't going to be any help if she broke her stupid neck. Besides, the rich scent of moss and thick green vegetation was starting to stir her faded memories.

They were nothing more than flickers of visions that danced too fast for her to entirely take them in, but she could catch images of herself as a child, walking among the trees to gather the mushrooms and herbs that grew wild in the fertile soil. There was a tall, stern-faced woman standing behind her, but Wynn didn't recognize her. Was this her mother? Possibly. She didn't feel any emotion as the woman waved for her to join her.

The memories flickered to an older version of herself as she secluded herself in the shelter of a blackberry bush, ignoring the sharp female voice calling out her name. Another flicker and she was dressed in a long robe, walking up a narrow pathway. She was carrying a basket of flowers to place on the altar at the top of the hill.

Yes. That's where she wanted to go.

Zigzagging through the trees, Wynn used the fragmented images to lead her to the narrow trail that carved through the woods. The ground was uneven and overgrown with weeds, but she picked up her pace. She trusted Azh to be able to defeat whatever magic had snatched him, but the fact that his presence had been muffled was unnerving.

Not that long ago she'd been furious at the sensation she was being followed by a mysterious stalker. And even after she'd accepted she needed Azh to get rid of the destructive magic ruining her life, she hadn't realized how accustomed she'd become to the constant pulse of his thunderous power.

Now her heart instinctively clung to the distant connection, as if he were a vital part of her soul.

Continuing upward, Wynn was huffing and puffing as she charged out of the trees and climbed the crest of the hill to reach the top of the peak. It was one thing to scamper through dark alleys and down city streets; it was another to battle against mother nature and a steep incline that made her calves burn from the effort.

Or maybe she was just getting old, she wryly acknowledged, panting as she came to a halt next to the tall pile of stones. She didn't know who'd originally stacked the rocks into the formation of a pyramid, or what it was supposed to do, but she had a vague impression that the coven had considered it a holy place. Was that the reason the witches had chosen the spot to burn her? Maybe. Right now, she didn't care.

Nothing mattered but finding Azh.

Falling to her knees, she pressed her hands against the ground, desperately seeking any hint of her dragon. Or even an echo of the magic that had saved her from the witches.

She cursed when she felt nothing.

No magic. No heat. No lingering quakes. There wasn't even a fault line visible from where the ground had been split open two centuries ago. It was as if it'd never happened.

There was...nothing.

No. Wait. That wasn't true. She leaned down to press her head against the mossy grass. She could hear something echoing through the earth. A distant thud, as if someone was banging a drum. Or something was pounding against a barrier.

Wynn sucked in a sharp breath, leaping to her feet as she was struck by a sudden realization.

She'd sensed that Charlotte was unhinged, but she'd allowed the woman's confession that she was trying to raise the dead distract her from her original suspicion that it had a connection to the corruption. That was the sort of thing a person did out of grief, not to gain power.

But what if the corruption was forcing her to open its prison? Or even using her as a conduit to spread his evil through the world? Charlotte was a witch who could channel magic and yet human enough to be easily manipulated. The perfect tool.

A sharp cry echoed through the air, and Wynn whirled around to run back down the hill. She didn't consider the fact that she might be rushing into a trap. She was convinced that Charlotte was the key. Not only to locating the magic that had abducted Azh, but the corruption that was spreading through the world.

When she'd fallen into the pit two hundred years ago, the white light and the green slimy magic had been imprisoned together. She was betting that they were still there, in an endless battle for dominance.

Reaching the edge of the trees, she skidded to a halt, discovering Charlotte in the center of the circle. The older woman was kneeling next to the cauldron, her head tilted back as she screamed in pain.

Wynn still held on to the strand of magic that contained the spell of darkness, but she had no idea what was causing the witch's pain. Any attempt to help her might make things even worse.

Glancing around to make sure there was nothing lurking in the shadows, Wynn slowly crept forward to step into the circle. The power of the magic hit her without warning, nearly driving her to her knees. She hissed. It was no wonder the witches had decided to build their coven in this spot. It wasn't a Gyre, but there was a core of magic directly below the circle that sent out shockwaves of energy. As if they were standing on top of a nuclear reactor.

Taking a second to regain her balance, Wynn was stepping toward the sobbing witch when the tremors returned. She braced herself, a surge of hope racing through her. This was exactly what was happening moments before Azh disappeared.

Charlotte lifted her head, as if belatedly sensing Wynn's cautious approach. Her features were frozen in an expression of sheer terror.

"Blessed goddess, what have I done?"

The words were still trembling in the air when Charlotte's eyes rolled back in her head and she tumbled to the side, as if she'd been knocked out by some unseen force.

Wynn didn't have time to worry about the witch as the ground buckled beneath the bubbling cauldron before it abruptly collapsed and the pot disappeared along with the fire. The hole continued to spread, dropping the unconscious witch into the empty space.

Wynn stumbled back, lifting her hand to shield her eyes as a blinding light abruptly burst out of the opening. At the same time, an intense heat washed over her, searing her skin until she felt blisters form. With a muttered curse, she tried to back out of the circle. The power was going to destroy her.

But despite her mental command to run away, her feet refused to budge. She glanced down in confusion. She was stuck in place, as if she'd stumbled into a magical quagmire.

Grimly struggling against the invisible bonds, Wynn felt another blast of heat. She lifted her head to glare at the light that was obviously determined to finish what the witches had started two hundred years ago, only to feel an unexpected stab of hope.

The light was shrinking. As if it'd reached a critical mass and was about to implode. Then her hope died as quickly as it appeared. The light wasn't shrinking, it was being sucked into the creature that was currently crawling out of the hole.

Wynn's mouth dried as the light continued to flicker around the slender form of a woman.

"Stay back," Wynn commanded, ignoring the massive surge of magic that swirled through the air.

This creature could destroy her with ridiculous ease.

"There's no reason to be afraid, child," a female voice assured her. "We are old friends."

"Are we?"

"Don't you remember?"

The glow dimmed to reveal the exquisitely beautiful woman wearing a translucent robe that did nothing to hide her muscular body. Her long hair shimmered like silver in the moonlight and was topped with a diamond crown that was worth a very large fortune. It was her skin, however, that revealed the truth of her heritage. Even from a distance Wynn could see the faint outline of scales that looked as if they'd been dusted with the luster of pearls. Oh, and of course, her eyes. They smoldered with crimson flames.

"You're Gabriela," Wynn breathed.

The woman cocked a brow, as if offended by Wynn's casual reference. "I am Queen Gabriela, ruler of the dragons and empress of the demon races."

For some reason, the arrogant edge in her voice scratched against Wynn's raw nerves. She should be delighted to have found this dragon. Hadn't they been searching for a connection to this female's power for days? They'd been desperate for any scrap of Gabriela's magic that might help them battle against the corruption.

And here she was...in the flesh. Or at least, sort of in the flesh. Certainly she should be able to offer the assistance they needed. Not only to destroy the evil magic but also to rescue Azh and to take away the unruly dragon magic that was ruining her life.

Still, she felt more wary than relieved as the female towered over her. And maybe a little annoyed that Gabriela was peering down her slender nose as if Wynn were a meddlesome pest she intended to squash.

"Not my queen," she said before she could stop the words.

The flames danced in the crimson eyes. "You will learn."

"Learn what?"

Gabriela waved a dismissive hand. "We'll discuss that later. We have more important matters to finish. You have something that belongs to me."

Wynn was distracted by a shimmer in the corner of her eye. Her gaze darted toward the gaping hole, tracing the slender strand of magic that was curling out of the darkness to connect to the back of Gabriela. The dragon seemed unaware of the strange thread that kept her tied to the pit. Or maybe she was too focused on Wynn to care.

There was something weird going on. If Gabriela was alive and well, then why had the corruption managed to seep into the world? And if she needed help, why hadn't she reached out to the dragons?

Was this a trick? Maybe Gabriela was an illusion created by the corruption to fool Wynn into releasing it into the world.

"First I have questions," Wynn said, ignoring the pounding urgency to demand the female track down Azh.

She didn't trust this dragon. Certainly not enough to reveal that Azh was missing and unable to rush to her rescue. Plus, deep in her heart she clung to the belief she would know if Azh was in trouble. He felt...distant. But not in pain. As if he were separated from her by a thick layer of magic.

For now, she had to discover if Gabriela was real or a clever deception designed to destroy her. Or Azh.

Gabriela scowled. "Your questions can wait."

"No." Wynn folded her arms over her chest. "They can't."

White-hot flames danced around the dragon, as if she were preparing to punish Wynn for her stubbornness, then with a visible effort, Gabriela managed to regain her temper.

"What questions?"

"Were you the light that healed me after I fell into the pit on top of the hill?"

Gabriela offered a regal nod of her head. "More than that. I brought you back from the brink of death."

Wynn shuddered at the memory of flames searing over her flesh and the unbearable pain that had felt as if it were sucking the very life from her. This female wasn't lying. She'd been close to death when she'd plunged into the pit.

"How?"

"I shared my magic with you. It was the only way to repair such grievous wounds."

Wynn took a moment to consider the explanation. Did that mean the magical healing had created the crimson strand that was now causing havoc in her life? But if that was the case, then why hadn't she noticed it until the past year? And what connection did it have to the corruption that was haunting her?

Just as importantly, did the fact this female had shared her dragon magic to save Wynn mean that this was truly Gabriela and not an imposter? That she really was the hero from legends?

Wynn remained wary. "Okay, now I know how. Now I want to know why."

"Why what?"

"Why did you save me?"

"I couldn't allow you to die."

Wynn glanced toward the decrepit cottages that looked as if they'd been empty for decades. Perhaps even longer.

"Obviously lots of people have died around here without you saving them."

Gabriela looked genuinely confused. "I had no interest in them."

"But you were interested in me?"

"Of course." Gabriela stepped closer, the flames continuing to dance over her shimmering skin. "You called to my magic."

Wynn would have fled if she wasn't stuck in place. The dragon didn't have Azh's nuclear aura, but it pressed against her like she was caught in a massive vise. Each pulse of power felt like it was going to crush her, making it harder and harder to breathe.

"How could I call to your magic? I don't have any." Wynn struggled to think clearly. Not easy when she was being squeezed to death. Then she abruptly realized why such a powerful creature would be interested in her. "Ah. Because I'm a Void."

Gabriela shrugged. "I don't know what that means. I only know I was lost in the darkness and you offered me salvation." She stepped closer, bringing a painful blast of heat to add to Wynn's discomfort. "You are the vessel I will use to escape this prison."

"Prison?" Wynn glanced toward the gaping hole. Her brows drew together. Was the strand connected to Gabriela thicker? It was certainly shimmering brighter in the moonlight. Was that what was keeping her stuck in this place? "I thought you willingly sacrificed yourself to close the rift?"

A cunning expression rippled over the beautiful features. "Of course I did. I would do whatever necessary to protect my people," she insisted. "But now it's time for me to leave this place so I can be the leader they need."

The smooth explanation only reignited Wynn's original suspicions. And it wasn't just a petty jealousy of Azh's fascination with the stories of Gabriela's valor. There was a burning hunger in the female's eyes that spoke of raw ambition, not concern for her people.

"So you sacrificed yourself, but now you want out of your sacrifice?"

"My people need me to control the corruption," she snapped. "I'm the only one capable of keeping it from infecting the world."

Impossible to argue with that.

"How did it get loose?" Wynn demanded. "Didn't you seal it on the other side of the rift?"

The crimson eyes narrowed. "The seals began to weaken centuries ago. I did my best to keep it contained, but it must have attached itself to you before you foolishly fled from this cavern."

Outrage threaded through the pain that pulsed through Wynn's body. "Are you blaming me for the corruption invading this world?"

"You shouldn't have run away. It's exactly what the evil wanted you to do."

"If that's true, then why didn't I sense it?"

Gabriela peered down her slender nose. "You're a mortal. How would you know if you were tainted?"

"I'm not human," Wynn argued. "Besides, I can feel and touch *your* magic."

Gabriela made a sound of impatience, the flames snapping and sizzling around her stiff body. She obviously wasn't accustomed to anyone questioning her.

"The evil obviously disguised itself so you wouldn't realize you were infected by its madness," she snapped.

Wynn tilted her chin, refusing to back down. "I've seen creatures who've been infected. They're all glowy and gross. I think I would notice if it was inside me."

"You know nothing." The earth trembled beneath the force of the dragon's anger. "How else could the evil appear wherever you happened to be? It had to have some means of tracking you."

Wynn's mouth parted, but the words froze on her lips as she swiftly reviewed the short conversation she'd had with this dragon. She hadn't mentioned being in close contact with the corruption.

"Wait. How did you know it was tracking me?"

There was a tense silence, as if Gabriela was caught off guard by the question. Then, with a shrug, she took another step forward.

"We're connected by my power inside you. I could feel when you were close to the magic."

Wynn hissed. The searing heat was becoming unbearable. Along with the sensation of being crushed. She wanted answers, but maybe it was time to consider how the hell she was going to get away from this dragon. She needed Azh to determine who she could trust.

Covertly she attempted to move her feet, not surprised when they were still trapped in the magic.

"If we're connected, then why didn't you help when the corruption was attacking me?" she demanded, trying to keep the dragon distracted as she sorted through her limited options.

Her *very* limited options.

Gabriela clicked her tongue. "Obviously I'm still trapped by the magical barrier that surrounds this place. Once I'm released I promise you'll never be in danger again."

Wynn wasn't comforted by the promise. "How do you intend to get released?"

"I'll store the remainder of my power inside you, and once you're away from this place, I can take it back." Gabriela curved her lips into a smile that sent a chill down Wynn's spine. "We'll both be free."

Wynn sucked in a sharp breath, recalling Gabriela's explanation for why she'd rescued Wynn from the bloodthirsty coven.

"That's what you meant when you said I could release you from your prison."

"You are the only vessel capable of containing so much magic."

Wynn shook her head. "I don't want it."

"It won't be yours for long. Once my power is fully transferred I can escape through the barrier and reclaim it. You'll be free to return to your life."

"And if I don't want to be your vessel?"

"You have no choice." The smile widened as Gabriela waved her hand toward the gaping hole. "I've gone to a lot of effort to bring you here."

Effort? What did she mean? The strand of magic that was growing inside Wynn? No. A tendril of smoke wafted through the air. A residue from the fire that had smoldered beneath the cauldron that was now at the bottom of the pit. Along with the witch who'd been haunted by the dead.

"Charlotte."

"She didn't have the power to shatter the barrier, but she was able to give me a small opening to reach out to you."

Wynn felt a pang of sympathy for the poor witch who'd been tormented into believing her coven was calling out to her, but it was quickly smothered. She'd worry about the various people the female had used and abused once she had some much-needed distance between them.

"That's why your power suddenly started interfering with my magic," she said, allowing the darkness spell she'd tapped into earlier to flow through her blood. She wasn't sure it was going to do anything but piss off the dragon, but it was all she had. She had to make it work. "And that was how the corruption got out. It was you."

There was a surge of white-hot air as Gabriela spread the translucent wings that she'd had tucked against her back. At the same time, her eyes blazed with a fiery determination.

"It doesn't matter. You're finally here where I need you and it's time to put an end to my confinement."

"No." Wynn held out her hands as if she were pleading for mercy. At the same time, she prepared to release the spell. "I'm not going to take any more of your magic. Not until I know for certain who and what you are."

"You don't have a choice." Gabriela snapped her fingers. "Come here."

Wynn smiled. "No one tells me what to do."

Releasing the spell, Wynn felt a surge of relief as the magic abruptly cloaked them in a thick darkness that not only hid her from view but shattered the invisible bonds holding her captive, as if Gabriela had been distracted by the unexpected attack.

Her relief, however, was brief. Turning to flee, she gasped as a wall of crimson flames erupted from the large rocks that formed the circle. The heat blasted through the air, searing against her skin that was still raw.

Wynn snarled in frustration. Unless she was willing to walk through dragon fire, she was trapped.

Spinning around, she could start to see the crimson outline of Gabriela. Dammit. The female was using her magic to cut through the thick shroud of darkness. Any minute and she would have battled through the darkness and Wynn would be completely at her mercy...

Wait. Wynn was distracted from her fatalistic thoughts as another faint glow pierced the shadows. It was a silvery light coming from the ground.

Briefly confused, Wynn suddenly realized the glow was coming from the pit where Gabriela had been hiding. The one that had recently swallowed Charlotte and perhaps even Azh.

It was the last place she wanted to go. But then again, did she have any choice? Right now she was caught between a dragon who intended to shove her full of magic before ripping it out of her, or being turned to ash by the inferno of flames.

Sucking in a deep breath, Wynn gave into her rash impulse, darting toward the open pit and diving in.

If she was lucky, she would find a tunnel beneath the ground to escape. If not...well, it wasn't the first time she'd faced death.

She just hoped that her sacrifice kept Gabriela trapped in this place for another thousand years.

The bitch.

Chapter 20

Azh was prepared as the ground crumbled beneath his feet. He'd assumed that there would be snares and traps waiting for them. The corruption—or whatever malignant force was currently tormenting Wynn—had been luring them to this particular spot for days. Maybe even months.

He'd be a fool not to suspect it had planned for their eventual arrival.

But falling through the darkness to land in the deep pit, Azh was still struggling to regain his balance when a shimmering portal opened directly in front of him.

"Come through," a harsh voice commanded. "I can't hold it forever."

Azh hissed, releasing his powerful magic at the same time shimmering strands whipped out of the portal to wrap around him. The next thing he knew, he was being jerked through the opening and tossed onto a stone floor that was hot beneath his body.

"What took you so long?" that same male voice demanded.

Azh surged to his feet, the beast inside him roaring with outrage. Never in his very long life had he been tossed around like he was a sack of potatoes. Not even when he was a newly hatched dragon.

Prepared to strike, he ran a furious gaze over the male wearing a long robe who was currently regarding him with a grim expression. The stranger was obviously a dragon although he was in human form with a slender body and bald head. The aura around him flared with a golden hue that was beginning to fade around the edges, as if he were ancient. Or maybe sick. But it was the thin face disfigured by four claw marks angling from his left temple to his ear that captured and held Azh's attention.

There was something about those scars that stirred a distant memory. He hadn't seen this male before, but he sensed he should recognize him.

"Who are you?" he asked.

"Zion, Royal Councilor."

Azh hissed. He recognized the name. Zion had been a renowned general during the dragon civil war and later the most trusted councilor to Gabriela. His name had been spoken in reverent whispers by the ancient dragons who'd told stories of the homeland. But Zion was supposed to be a legend. Not a living creature who was glaring at him with blatant impatience.

"Are you here to protect Gabriela...wait. It doesn't matter." Azh's confusion was quickly replaced by a sharp-edged urgency. He glanced toward the spot where he'd been hauled through the portal. His connection to Wynn was muffled, as if his trip through the opening had placed a barrier between them, but he could sense she was in danger. He had to get to her. "Take me back to where I came from."

The older male shook his head. "Impossible."

Azh instinctively lashed out, his flames sweeping over Zion. Not hot enough to kill, but an unspoken warning.

"Take me back."

The man lifted one slender finger, easily smothering the fire. He might have looked emaciated, as if he'd been worn to the bone, but he maintained a shocking amount of strength.

"The door is one-way," Zion said.

Azh released a low growl. "I don't believe you."

"Try for yourself." Zion stepped to the side, nodding toward the closed portal.

Azh didn't hesitate. Calling on his magic, he smashed it against the spot he'd entered the...well, actually he didn't know where he was. All he could see was smooth stone. As if he were in a pit. Or a dungeon. The magic hit the wall and exploded, sending him flying backward.

He cursed as he skidded across the smooth floor, his back at last slamming into a hard shelf that brought him to a painful halt. Glancing over his shoulder he realized it wasn't a shelf he'd hit. It was the edge of a marble dais with a gem-encrusted throne perched in the center.

"What is this place?" he asked, forcing himself to his feet.

"Kazak." Zion snapped his fingers and light cascaded from an unseen source to reveal a pyramid-shaped room with shimmering hieroglyphs carved into the soaring ceiling. Oddly, there was a deep crack in the floor, as if something had caused damage that couldn't be repaired.

Azh shuddered. There was something about that crack that warned he didn't want to get near it. He turned back to face his companion.

"This has to be an illusion," he accused.

"It's real enough." Zion snapped his fingers again and a series of heavy copper doors slid open to reveal a brilliant blue sky with two red-tinted suns and tiny puffs of clouds. "Abandoned, but real."

There was a hint of aching sadness in the male's voice, but Azh was less concerned with the fact that the skies were empty, and more concerned with the realization that it was still there. Had any of the stories he'd read been true?

"I've studied hundreds of history books. They all claim this place was destroyed by the corruption," he said, his feet carrying him to the opening to peer down at the lush green landscape and the distant ocean that sparkled in the sunlight.

"It was," Zion assured him as he moved to stand at Azh's side.

Azh snorted, pointing toward the rolling hills dotted with herds of antelope.

"This is destroyed?"

"Once the evil was removed, the land slowly began to heal. It took eons, but it's at last returned to the paradise it was meant to be."

Was this male saying that the corruption was gone? Azh struggled to comprehend what that would mean for his people. The consequences of having his homeland free of evil was so vast he could barely allow himself to hope.

"You did this?" he rasped. "You cleansed the magic?"

"No." Zion scowled, his scars twisting as if he were struggling against a powerful emotion. "That was the mistake I made for too long."

"What mistake?"

"Believing the magic could be cleansed."

Azh continued to stare at his homeland with a strange sense of bemusement. Of all the possible futures he'd considered for his people, he'd never once dreamed they would return to Kazak.

"Obviously you did something to repair the damage," Azh insisted.

"There was no repair." Zion pointed toward a cloud in the sky. He released a burst of magic to send the cloud scampering out of the way, revealing a jagged hole patched over by a shimmering magic. "I've imprisoned the source of the evil."

Azh knew instinctively what he was staring at. "That's the rift to the human world. The one created by Gabriela."

"It is. Once the evil followed Gabriela through the rift, I built a barrier to keep it trapped between the two worlds."

Azh glanced back at Zion. "You were the one who trapped the corruption?"

"Yes."

"Then the histories are wrong again. The ancestors were convinced that Gabriela sacrificed herself to close the rift and keep the corruption from following us."

"We were all wrong about a lot of things." Without warning, Zion closed the panel, sealing them in the pyramid. "You need to understand."

Azh blinked, jerked out of his weird stupor. Later he'd deal with the shocking revelation that his homeland was still here and gloriously healed. Right now, nothing mattered more than returning to Wynn.

"I don't have time for this now. I have to go back."

Zion moved, as if intending to physically hold him in place if necessary. "This is important, Azh. The survival of the dragons, along with your female, depend on you."

"How do you know my name?"

"I know everything," the male announced without arrogance. It was a simple statement of fact. "I've witnessed the early battles between dragons and vampires and the treaty that forced our people into hibernation. I witnessed your mother's betrayal and your own transformation from hatchling to unquestioned ruler of the dragons. That's why it has to be you that finishes this. *Only* you."

Azh's excruciating need to rush back to Wynn didn't lessen, but he grudgingly accepted he couldn't ignore the elder dragon's fierce warning. A part of him had known his entire life that he was ordained for this precise moment. That at some point he'd be called on to shoulder the fate of the dragons.

"What do I need to understand?" he snapped, vibrating with the urgency to get his duty done so he could be with Wynn.

Zion turned to nod toward the empty crack next to the glittering throne. "When the evil first contaminated the magic, we all assumed it was the after-effects of the civil war that ripped apart the dragons. It's not unusual for strong emotions to create a toxic brew that eventually takes on a power of its own."

Azh nodded. "In the world I come from it's known as a miasma."

Zion managed to look even more grim, his fingers trailing along the scars that marred his face.

"After all the death and suffering we endured it would have been shocking if our homeland wasn't tainted by the destruction we'd caused. It was an unbearable tragedy."

Azh had read the histories written about the civil war, but he no longer trusted what they claimed as truth. As Wynn had pointed out, those books were written by the victors and those in power. It was to their benefit to offer a distorted view of the causes and victims of any conflict.

Unfortunately, delving into the truth of the past was yet another thing that would have to wait.

"Why are you convinced that the war wasn't the cause of the corruption?"

"We did everything to purge the evil. Including the combination of magic by our most powerful dragons to destroy it. The best we could do was contain it within this royal temple."

Azh glanced around, belatedly realizing that this was more than a throne room perched in the sky.

It had become a prison.

His attention returned to the elder dragon. "Once the evil tainted the magic, your efforts might have made things worse, not better. It could have been feeding on whatever power you were using to destroy it."

Zion sent him an approving nod. "That was my thought as well. But first I wanted to test the theory."

"How?"

"I captured a portion of the magic in a lead container that had been wrapped in a binding spell and took it to an isolated spot in the mountains."

Azh arched a brow. He liked to think he was courageous, but the thought of gathering the green sludge and hauling it around sent shudders of horror through him.

"You went alone?"

"I had no choice. I wanted to eliminate any possibility it was capable of feeding from a dragon without them being aware of what was happening. And of course, there was the risk the corruption might infect any companion I brought with me. I'd taken precautions to ensure that if I was tainted I would be unable to leave the cavern I'd chosen." The male didn't have to explain that he'd triggered a doomsday countdown. Every dragon possessed the ability to destroy themselves in a worst-case scenario. It meant they couldn't be taken captive and imprisoned by their enemies or forced to use their enormous powers against their will. It was also used when they were too grievously injured to heal themselves. Zion shrugged. "Besides, I didn't truly expect anything to happen. It was more a desperate attempt to feel as if I was still trying to rid us of the evil than a truly scientific experiment."

Azh could sympathize. That's what he'd been doing the past weeks. Simply running around trying to stumble across the truth.

"But something did happen?" he asked.

Zion's expression remained calm, but he pressed his hands together, as if battling against a wave of emotions.

"Once I created a barrier to keep the corruption trapped and any outside magic from getting in, I settled in and prepared to wait."

"And?"

"And there was no need to wait. As soon as the barrier was fully in place, the magic was cleansed. I couldn't believe it had been that simple."

Azh was confused. He'd seen the evil with his own eyes. "The corruption was gone?"

"Completely."

"Wait. So does that mean the corruption feeds on magic?"

Zion held up his hand, as if urging Azh to remain patient. A task that was painfully difficult when every instinct screamed that Wynn was in trouble.

"I had to test the theory. First I removed the protective spells around the container. When nothing happened, I walked back down the mountain toward a small village. I remained a safe distance away, but there was enough power in the area to stir the corruption back to existence."

Azh's confusion deepened. "Still nothing?"

"Nothing. I was convinced I now had the answer to destroying the corruption. I rushed back to this temple to reveal what I had discovered to the queen." Zion glanced toward the empty throne, a hint of wistful regret in his voice. "I was about to become the savior of our people."

"That didn't happen?"

"No." Zion's jaw tightened, as if he were clenching his teeth. "As soon as I entered this room the corruption returned to the magic and I barely managed to dump it behind the original barriers before it could consume me."

Azh slowly glanced around the pyramid-shaped space. There was a mystic quality to the temple. As if it'd been created by an ancient, unknown magic. But there was no sense of impending doom.

"You think the evil is connected to this temple?"

"I couldn't be sure. It didn't make any sense at the time," the male admitted. "All I knew for certain was that I needed to do more research. But as the years passed Gabriela became more and more convinced that the younger dragons were plotting against her."

Azh arched a brow. "Were they?"

Zion brushed aside the question. "We're dragons. There is always some sort of plotting. But Gabriela was obsessed with the belief that she could leash the magic and use it as a weapon against her enemies."

Azh made a sound of shock. "She wanted to use the corruption as a weapon?"

"Yes."

"That's crazy."

"My thought exactly." Zion visibly shuddered. "I feared our entire world would be destroyed when she released the evil."

"And you were right," Azh said, not entirely surprised that Gabriela wasn't the hero from his legends. There'd already been clues the histories had been more myths than factual accounts of the past.

"No," Zion's tone was sharp. "I was wrong."

"Wrong about what?"

"Everything." A surge of anger destroyed Zion's pretense of calm. "As always, Gabriela did exactly as she wanted and touched her fire to the corruption contained in the crevice in the floor." He pointed to a spot behind the throne. "I was standing in the shadows over there and I could see the magic absorbing her fire. It swirled around her, as if it was becoming one with her magic, then it was spreading through the temple and out the open doors. Before I could stop it, the corruption had spilled across the land, destroying everything in its path. I can still remember the screams of our people." Zion was forced to pause and clear a lump from his throat. "That's when I finally saw the truth."

"What truth?" Azh braced himself, already prepared for the answer.

"The magic wasn't corrupted. Gabriela was."

Chapter 21

Wynn hit the ground with enough force to rattle her teeth, but ignoring the shockwaves of pain, she jumped to her feet and searched the shadows for the slimy green magic. She assumed that this was the pit where she'd seen Gabriela and the corruption battling two hundred years ago.

But she couldn't see any hint of the evil power. Instead, her gaze traced the shimmering strand that she'd seen attached to the back of Gabriela. It coiled over the stone floor and up the wall to disappear in a glowing portal.

Was that the rift? It had to be, right? The place where Gabriela had led her people from their homeland to this world? So what was the shimmering magic? And why was it attached to Gabriela?

The questions were spinning through her mind when she was abruptly distracted by a swirling mist across the pit. Another portal? Inching forward, Wynn realized that the thick fog was oddly familiar.

Keeping a safe distance to avoid being sucked into the opening, Wynn leaned forward, her heart stopping as the mist parted to reveal a pool of the bubbling green and the strands of the evil magic that had reached out to wrap around a large body lying on the ground.

She'd seen this image before. When the stranger had cornered her in Hexx's apartment and touched her with his powers.

"This is inside my mind." She blinked, grappling to accept the truth. The Watcher hadn't taken her into the mist. He'd simply stepped into her thoughts to confront the evil magic. "Just when I thought this couldn't get any creepier."

"It's the corruption," Gabriela said from behind her. "I'm using my powers to keep it from overwhelming you, but the strange demon is interfering in my efforts. If he would just die all this would be over."

With a muffled scream Wynn whirled around to confront the dragon who'd silently followed her into the pit. There was no use trying to tap into the magic she'd stored away for an emergency. She was too flustered to concentrate, not to mention the fact she didn't have any spells that could match the power of a dragon.

Besides, she was suddenly distracted by the greenish tint to Gabriela's aura. It was no longer veins of corruption weaving around her as if they were in a constant battle for supremacy. The power pulsed through her with every heartbeat.

The power wasn't attacking Gabriela. It was protecting her.

"It's you," she rasped. "The corruption has infected you."

The female's eyes smoldered with a strange hunger. As if she were combating the urge to swallow her like a tasty morsel.

"Perhaps you're right," the dragon purred.

"That would be a first." Goosebumps crawled over Wynn's skin. Something had changed in the air. A new sense of heaviness that pressed against her with a blatant threat. "You admit you've been tainted by the evil?"

Heat blasted over Wynn, blistering her skin as she stumbled back to evade the punishment.

"It's not evil. It's power. Raw power!" Gabriela roared. "And it's mine. It's always been mine. I was just too frightened to claim it."

"It's always been yours?" Wynn struggled to think through the pain. Her skin felt as if it were being flayed from her body. "Are you saying you're the corruption?"

"It was corrupted because I tried to deny my true destiny."

Wynn pressed against the wall as Gabriela towered over her, an iridescent magic silhouetting her as if she were about to shift into her dragon form. This was it. Wynn had spent two centuries living on the edge of disaster, always assuming that luck and sheer audacity would get her through. But somewhere in the back of her mind, she'd always known there would be a day when she took one too many risks.

And this was it.

She was about to be... Well, she didn't know exactly what the dragon intended to do, but it was going to be awful. And there was very little hope she'd survive the experience.

But even as she braced herself for the hideous death about to smash her into oblivion, she realized that the shimmer wasn't coming from Gabriela. It was coming from the strand of magic that snaked through the portal and attached to her back.

She didn't know why the magic was flaring, but she could sense the power was connected to a dragon. A dragon who wasn't Gabriela. And while there was no predicting if the mysterious shimmer was a good or bad thing, there was the possibility she could use it to her advantage.

"And what's your true destiny?" Wynn asked, playing for time as she tried to focus on the strands of magic inside her.

If she could tap into the unknown magic, she might be able to distract Gabriela and escape.

It wasn't a great plan, but it was better than nothing.

"I was created to rule *all* the worlds. Dragons. Demons. Vampires. Even the humans. That's why I was given the magic."

Wynn rolled her eyes as she cautiously inched to the side. She needed to get closer to the strand to see if it was even possible to absorb the magic.

"That's quite a destiny," she muttered, ignoring the blistering heat as she tried to skirt around Gabriela's pulsing aura. She didn't want that green taint touching her. "So why are you stuck in this pit?"

"Zion." The name came out in a hiss and Wynn had a sudden memory of the robed male who'd tried to keep Gabriela from unleashing the corruption. "I thought I could trust him. He'd been my most loyal servant for centuries. But as soon as I embraced the magic, he stabbed me in the back. I had no choice but to flee his vicious attack."

Wynn hid her shock as realization hit her. The strand belonged to Zion. That was the only reasonable explanation. *He* was the one who'd sacrificed himself to close the rift, not this egotistical bitch. She moved another step closer.

"And you brought the dragons with you?" she asked, more to keep Gabriela boasting about her glorious future than any interest in her answers.

"They belong to me."

"No." A male voice shook the air and Wynn was forced to squeeze shut her eyes as the shimmering magic became a blast of white light. "They are no longer pawns to be exploited by an overly ambitious bitch."

"You," Gabriela rasped in fury.

Wynn abruptly forced open her eyes, enduring the blinding glare as relief blasted through her.

"Azh."

Wynn barely resisted the urge to launch herself toward the male stepping through the portal. She'd sensed he was okay, but that didn't mean she didn't need to examine every inch of his hard, flawless body to assure herself that he was completely unharmed. Not to mention the fact that she was giddy with happiness that she wasn't going to have to face the dragon alone.

But an inner voice warned her not to disturb Azh's concentration. Not when she could feel the oppressive heat as their powers clashed in the confined space.

"I knew you were going to be a pain in the ass the moment you appeared," Gabriela rasped, her aura marbled with veins of sickly green magic.

Azh offered a mocking smile, his eyes filled with storm clouds as flames danced over his body. The scent of scorched metal swelled until the air was so thick it was hard for Wynn to breathe.

"I try my best," he taunted the female he'd once admired.

Gabriela spread her translucent wings, but she didn't attack. Was she worried that Azh was stronger? Or was she keeping him talking so she could finish stuffing Wynn with her magic to make her escape?

Wynn pressed against the wall of the pit, trying to focus on the strands of magic inside her. There had to be something she could use to protect herself if Gabriela suddenly attacked. But even as she tried to reach her stored magic, she hit a crimson barrier. Wynn muttered an obscenity. The damned dragon was already filling her with more of her essence, making it impossible to tap into her other magic.

"I suppose you've been promised to become the next king if you destroy me?" Gabriela demanded, her own flames appearing as she tried to intimidate Azh. "Is that why you're here?"

Azh's exquisite features were unreadable as he stared at the queen who'd betrayed everything and everyone who'd trusted her. And for what? Power? Greed? Vanity?

"I've already warned you that the dragons aren't pawns in your sick desire to become a petty tyrant. When the time comes they will choose their next leader," Azh responded, his calm confidence more threatening than any amount of bluster. "And they'll do it without threats or coercion."

Wynn's heart swelled. She'd never been so proud.

Gabriela wasn't nearly so impressed. Or maybe she was. Maybe she understood that she'd ruled out of fear and weakness and that's why she'd needed to lie and cheat and manipulate her people. Azh would never have to resort to nasty tricks to earn the trust of the dragons.

"Such a feeble coward," Gabriela snapped, sounding more like a petulant child than a hero from legends. "You're not worthy to rule such a proud species."

"At least I don't have to force them to bend the knee." Azh spread his arms. "Or destroy their homeland in an effort to control them."

"They will worship me," Gabriela snarled.

Wynn grunted, falling to her knees as an excruciating pain stabbed into her stomach. Glancing down, she could see the crimson strand of magic snaking out of her, heading straight toward Azh.

"Azh look out!" she cried, desperately trying to find a way to snap her connection to Gabriela.

Distantly she was aware of Azh shooting a blast of magic toward the female dragon, who countered with billowing flames that charred the air. Wynn felt sweat drip down her face, well aware if she'd been a normal human the heat would have killed her. Thankfully, her coat was wrapped with enough layers of magic to keep her from melting.

Unfortunately, the protection didn't help her control the dragon magic that continued to pulse out of her in sharp, agonizing bursts. It felt like Gabriela was digging her talons into Wynn's soul and yanking out her very essence.

Gabriela continued to pull on the crimson strand deep inside Wynn, but she didn't use it to attack. Instead, she absorbed the power to spread her greenish evil aura across the stone floor.

She must have realized she couldn't win in a fair fight against Azh.

Watching in horror as the evil crawled toward the male, Wynn shoved herself to a standing position. The pain continued to batter her, along with the unbearable heat, but she had to do something.

Frantic, utterly unfeasible plans were whirling through her brain when Azh abruptly swiveled away from Gabriela, aiming his magic toward the shimmering strand that ran from the portal to the female dragon.

"What are you doing?" Gabriela demanded, more annoyed than frightened. Then the shimmering strand started to expand, moving over her back and along the spread of her wings until they were encased in delicate threads. To Wynn, it looked as if the magic were wrapping the female in a spiderweb. Or a cocoon. "Stop," Gabriela commanded, blasting Azh with crimson flames.

Azh managed to deflect most of the fire, but Wynn didn't miss the stench of scorched flesh. He'd been wounded, she just didn't know how grievously. Grimly he continued to pump his magic into the strand.

"There's no escape," he warned Gabriela. "You'll be trapped here forever."

The female screeched in frustration, the greenish glow trying to battle against the silvery web that continued to coat her in a layer of magic. Then, accepting she was losing the battle, Gabriela abruptly turned to point toward Wynn.

"Release me or your female dies," she warned, the flames already dancing around her fingers.

Wynn sucked in a horrified breath, caught between the terror of dying in a fiery blast and the fear that Azh might sacrifice himself to save her. Instinctively she shoved her hands in the pockets of her coat, holding it tight against her body as if it could shield her from the dragon fire.

That was when her fingers curled around a familiar object and the half-baked plots still whirling around her brain coalesced into one perfectly crazy plan.

"Azh, end this," she called out at the same time she tossed the skipping stone through the open portal. Once it disappeared she grabbed the second stone in her pocket and rubbed it with a frantic urgency. For once, luck was on her side. With none of the usual lag time, the spell snapped into place. Magic lashed around her and the pit abruptly disappeared as she was jerked from the pit and into the brilliant blue sky of Kazak.

She'd gone so fast the stone hadn't had time to land, which meant she was left to free fall toward the rolling meadows far, far below her.

Oddly, Wynn wasn't alarmed. Maybe it was the endless danger she'd endured over the past weeks and months. She'd faced nightmares, zombies, green gooey evil, dragons, the memory of being burned alive, and now falling from the heavens with no parachute.

It was bound to numb her nerves at some point.

But as she watched the violent flashes that leaked through the rift above her, she realized she was waiting. And a few minutes later she watched as a massive, blue-and-silver dragon burst out of the portal to nosedive toward her with blinding speed.

She'd been confident that Azh would destroy Gabriela and appear just in time to rescue her from splatting onto the ground.

Swooping beneath her plummeting body, Azh angled upward, allowing her to land on his back before he was gently floating down and landing on a sandy beach next to the vast ocean.

"I've got you," Azh assured her, the words spoken directly in her mind even as his dragon tilted back its head to roar in triumph.

"I know. I've always known."

Wynn smiled, watching the greenish glow that leaked through the rift fading from view, a sure sign that Gabriela was finally destroyed. It was all the reassurance she needed before she allowed the bone-deep weariness to overcome her willpower and she slipped into a welcomed darkness.

* * * *

Maya was running on sheer adrenaline by the time Micha's jet landed in New York and she hurried through the early morning shadows to reach Hexx's apartment. Once inside she found Tia still kneeling next to the unconscious Joe, her face pale and her shoulders slumped with weariness.

Taking a second to sweep the cluttered apartment for a hidden enemy, Maya crouched next to her friend and closed her eyes. Then, concentrating on the mental connection she'd created with her friend centuries ago, she stepped into Tia's mind.

Nothing had changed since the last time she was there. The mist was still thick enough to make it impossible to see more than a few feet in front of her, except for the spot where Joe was wrapped in glowing green tentacles of magic next to a bubbling pool of sludge.

She was taking a step forward when Tia appeared next to her, grabbing Maya's arm in a tight grip.

"Stay back," she hissed. "Something's happening."

Confused, Maya stared at the image in front of her, belatedly realizing that she'd been wrong. There *was* something different. In the very center of the pool the sludge was changing shade from green to deep crimson. And the crimson was spreading. Was the evil growing in strength? Or was this a new enemy?

"That's why I'm here," Maya announced.

Tia sent her a hopeful glance. "You found the answer to stopping the corruption?"

Maya grimaced. "Not exactly. But there is a prophecy that we think speaks about the evil."

"A prophecy?" Tia studied her with a hard expression. "That's it?"

Maya shrugged. "I was sent by Skye. I think you should listen."

Tia's jaw tightened as she resisted the urge to tell Maya exactly what she could do with her stupid prophecy. As frustrated as Tia might be, the older woman couldn't have forgotten that Skye's premonitions had saved the world more than once.

"Fine. What's the prophecy?"

Maya had rehearsed the words until she had them memorized. *"When the corruption bubbles in the bowels of the ground and violence spreads throughout the land, the heart of darkness will strike from beyond the prison walls. Those too blind to see will drown in the evil while the watchers will be devoured by fire. To survive you must stand steady against the unseen traitor."*

Tia's eyes flared with annoyance. "Strike from beyond prison walls? Unseen traitor? How is that supposed to help?"

The older woman's petulant complaints were abruptly cut off as the ground shook beneath their feet and the center of the pool of bubbling magic exploded upward. Like Old Faithful erupting to send scalding water into the air. They stumbled backward to avoid the drops of evil magic splattering around them.

"What the hell was that?" Maya demanded.

"I have no idea." Tia was pulling a handful of small beads from her pocket, clearly preparing to throw the powerful potions at whatever new threat crawled out of the churning pool. But as the seconds passed there was nothing more sinister than a tendril of bluish-gray smoke that spread over the puddle of corruption, visibly destroying it. "Look at that," Tia rasped. "The sludge is dying."

"Is Joe doing that?" Maya asked. The healing magic felt as if it were coming from beneath the mist, but it was impossible to pinpoint the location.

"I don't know and I don't care." Tia cautiously inched toward the unconscious male being slowly revealed as the tendrils faded away. "I just want him out of here. Then I'm going to lock him in my castle and let the world take care of itself for a change."

Maya's lips twitched. Tia had loudly and proudly proclaimed her independence for years. She didn't need friends or allies, and she would have laughed herself silly if anyone suggested that she might find happiness in a romantic relationship.

It seemed fitting that when she at last accepted that she had room in her life for a lover, she would pick the most powerful being in the world. A male who would drive any sane person to the edge and who regularly wandered around the streets like a homeless vagrant. They were a perfect combination.

"Good for you," Maya announced, then a vague movement in the mist warned her that they weren't alone. "Tia."

Leaping forward, Maya knocked her friend to the ground, barely avoiding the blast of fire that sizzled an inch above their heads.

"Dragon," Tia hissed, rolling to the side and throwing her handful of potions toward the shadowed form that darted through the fog.

There was a roar of fury as the beads exploded to send nasty shards of magic sailing through the mist. The creature had been wounded, but it was doubtful it was more than an annoyance.

"Move out of my way or die," a female voice commanded from the mist, more flames flowing in their direction.

Maya lifted her hands to weave a complicated shield that diverted the fire to the side. The emerald that hung from the chain around her neck glowed in the darkness, amping up her power. Thank the goddess she'd taken the time to restore the magic stored in the gem before she left New Orleans.

"I'll shield, you kill," she said between clenched teeth.

Trusting in Maya's ability to keep the fierce flames from toasting them into tiny bits of charcoal, Tia rose to her feet and called on her magic. She whispered the ancient words as she released a mire spell, spinning the magic toward the form that suddenly halted as it was trapped in the silvery webs.

"No." The fire came again, but this time it was directed toward the unconscious male. "He's mine."

Maya barely managed to deflect the flames. "I'm guessing she's not a fan of your Watcher," she muttered.

The mist parted to reveal the tall female surrounded by a blindingly powerful aura. It was hard to imagine how she'd managed to keep herself hidden despite the thickness of the fog. Maya blinked, her eyes slowly adjusting so she could make out the sheer satin robe that the woman was wearing. It was flimsy enough to reveal the bronzed scales that protected the dragon skin while her brilliant red hair was left to hang down her back. Still stuck in the mire spell, she continued to send bursts of fire toward Joe.

"The bastard imprisoned my people and turned my own son against me," the female hissed. "I will destroy him for that."

"Zanna," Maya muttered in disbelief. She should have suspected when Azh showed up that his mother wouldn't be far behind. The one-time Queen of the Dragons had made it her ambition to destroy the Watchers since they had forced her to sign the dragon/vampire treaty eons ago. And nothing was going to stop her. "How do you keep escaping out of hibernation?"

Zanna shrugged. "I used the magic I could sense attacking that annoying creature." Her too-beautiful features twisted into an expression of evil anticipation. "It allowed me to slip through the barrier. Now I at last will have my revenge."

Tia sent another weave of magic toward the dragon, but with a wave of her hand Zanna managed to unravel the spell. At the same time, she broke free of the webs holding her captive.

Maya barely noticed. Instead she glanced back at the pool of sludge that was fading to a sickly shade of ash. More importantly, it no longer bubbled with power. It was being sucked back into whatever hole had allowed it to enter the mist.

"You're connected to the sludge?" she asked.

"Sludge? It's dragon magic," Zanna snarled. "The most powerful I've ever felt."

"Yeah, well, it's also dying." Maya pointed out the obvious.

"What?" Zanna's brows snapped together as she glared toward the pool. Then her eyes widened, genuine fear rippling over her face. "No."

"Maya, get out of the way!"

It was Tia's turn to knock Maya to the ground as Zanna screamed in fury. The dragon unfurled her wings that had been tucked against her back, in an effort to halt being pulled into the rapidly emptying pool. Maya was forced to turn her head as the wings beat with enough force to send clouds of choking dust in her direction. She didn't see the moment that Zanna was sucked into the hole, but she knew when it happened.

One second she was covering her face with her arm, the searing heat squeezing the air from her lungs, and the next she was lying on a filthy linoleum floor next to Tia.

With a groan, she sat up and glanced around, her nose wrinkling at the smell of moldy food and old sneakers. Thankfully the stench of evil magic, along with the metallic tang of dragon, was completely and blissfully gone.

Turning her head, she watched as Tia scrambled across the sticky floor to lean over Joe, who was just opening his eyes.

"Good thing Skye sent me, right?" Maya demanded, cautiously rising to her feet.

It was a relief when her knees held her weight and the dizziness slowly receded from her weary brain.

Tia didn't glance in her direction. Instead she brushed her fingers over the strange man in flannel PJs, clearly searching for injuries.

"Go away," she commanded.

Maya smiled, not blaming her friend for needing to reassure herself the man she loved had survived yet another disaster.

"Gladly." Maya headed toward the door. Soon Ravyr would be home and she intended to spend every minute reacquainting herself with his delicious body. Until then...it was time to relax and recover. "I'm finally going to have that hot bubble bath and glass of wine I've been promising myself. If there's another disaster, don't call me."

Epilogue

Wynn stood next to Azh, wrapped in a sense of blissful peace. Odd, considering she was standing on the edge of a massive pyramid floating hundreds of feet off the ground. Not to mention the fact dozens of lethal dragons were zooming past the open doorway, occasionally sending blasts of scorching flames through the air along with ear-splitting roars.

It'd been a couple of weeks since she'd awakened in a four-poster bed in the secluded lair at the back of the royal temple. Since then she'd watched with smug satisfaction as Azh stepped into his role as King of the Dragons, assisting his people in their return to their homeland.

It hadn't always been easy. The large beasts were ill-tempered after their long hibernation and easily provoked to violence when things didn't go their way. And there was still the mystery of what had happened to Zanna, Azh's mother. She'd disappeared along with Gabriela and there was a faint fear that they might be lurking in some dark pit, waiting to stir up trouble again. But gradually they were settling into their various lairs and absorbing the potent magic that had been fully cleansed of the corruption.

Which meant that Azh could at last spend some time enjoying the freedom that he'd earned for his people.

Wynn leaned against his hard body covered by a long satin robe stitched with silver thread and held together with massive sapphires that marked his position as royalty. She'd been surprised when he'd presented her with a matching robe, insisting that his people had offered them as gifts to thank them for their battle against Gabriela.

"It's beautiful," Wynn murmured, her gaze locked on the black dragon who swept past the doorway of the pyramid, opening his claws to drop a delicate gold box that was no doubt filled with priceless gems. The dragons had been leaving tributes on the ledge of the temple for days. It was a display of approval for Azh's leadership.

"Yes," Azh agreed in soft tones. "Exquisite."

Wynn turned her head, smiling as she realized he was staring at her with the eyes of his dragon, his expression hungry. If she were a humble creature, she would wonder how she'd ever been lucky enough to attract the notice of this amazing, deliciously sexy beast. Instead she simply accepted that fate had brought them together. And she wasn't going to argue.

Not when it meant spending her nights wrapped in the arms of this male.

Tilting back her head, Wynn savored the pure perfection of his features. "You explained how Zion used his magic to imprison Gabriela before she could spread the corruption to our world, but how did he recognize you were the dragon destined to defeat her? I mean, I always knew you were special..."

Azh snorted, no doubt remembering her early efforts to evade his ruthless stalking.

"But how did Zion know?"

"It was proclaimed by the oracles." Azh pointed toward the soaring walls that angled to meet in a sharp point at the top. As he continued to point upward, one of the elaborate hieroglyphs etched onto the wall suddenly blazed with a bluish fire. "That's me. And beneath it is written the death of Gabriela. Zion said that it appeared shortly after I first hatched."

Wynn arched her brows. Zion had retired to a private lair in the mountains, earning a well-deserved rest after his eons of protecting the dragons.

"You have your own symbol?" she teased.

"Not just me." Azh pointed toward the braided lines that circled his hieroglyph. They abruptly glowed with a blinding silver light. "Those belong to you."

"Me?" Wynn's breath caught in her throat. "No way."

Azh lowered his arm to wrap it around her waist, tugging her close as he gazed down at her with an unbearable tenderness.

"I knew from the moment our paths crossed that destiny had brought you into my life. And now it's confirmed. Two symbols that are intertwined to create a new beginning for our people."

"But I'm not a dragon," Wynn protested, even though she still possessed the crimson strand of magic. Thankfully it had diminished to the point it no longer interfered with her other spells, but she was only now learning how to use the impressive power.

"Don't tell them that." Azh nodded toward the opening where the dragons continued to fly past, nodding their heads in gestures of respect. "They've already accepted you as one of their own."

Wynn released a slow breath of pure contentment. This was exactly where she wanted to be. Of course, a tiny voice whispered in the back of her mind, it wouldn't be entirely awful to return home to see her friends.

She glanced toward the rift in the sky that shimmered with Azh's blue-tinted magic. "Will you close the portal?"

"Not yet." He shrugged. "I'm not sure it's healthy to be isolated. We need to develop a tolerance and appreciation for other species that was sadly missing when we were banished from our homeland. Until it's proven we can't find a way to live in harmony with our neighbors, the doorway will remain open."

"Good." She leaned her head against his broad chest. "There might be times I'd like to go back and visit."

"Quick visits," he growled, pressing a kiss to the top of her head. "I don't want to be parted from you a moment longer than necessary."

A shiver raced through Wynn, stirring the passions that she was quite certain would never be fully sated.

"You know. I was thinking." Her fingers brushed over the silken texture of his robe, feeling his muscles clench beneath her light caress.

"Yes?" The word came out as a growl, the metallic scent of his dragon swirling through the air.

"I'm feeling much stronger since my battle with Gabriela, but I probably shouldn't risk being out of bed so soon," she murmured, unhooking the sapphire buttons on her robe to expose the bare skin beneath. "In fact I'm thinking I might go back there right now."

Heat swept over her, igniting her desire until she trembled with anticipation.

"My clever thief. Where you lead, I will follow." With a sharp wave of his hand, the opening to the temple slid shut. A less than discreet way to tell the dragons they didn't want to be bothered. The beast watched her from the depths of Azh's smoky eyes. "Always."

Blowing him a kiss, Wynn turned to race toward the back of the temple, heading for their private lair.

"Follow quickly."

Enjoy this preview of
ETERNAL MAGIC
by Alexandra Ivy

Chapter 1

Spring was springing. Or at least there was a faint promise of spring in the air, luring the winter-weary citizens of Linden, New Jersey, out of their homes. Who cared if the wind whipping through the narrow streets was more frigid than refreshing? Or that darkness was already gathering as they headed out of their offices after a long day of work? Or even that it was a random Tuesday in mid-April. Tonight they eagerly celebrated happy hour at the local bars and jammed the sidewalks as they wandered in and out of the various shops.

Including the Witch's Brew.

The brightly lit coffee shop with a white tiled floor and lavender walls wasn't the largest in town, and it wasn't part of a chain, but it was always packed with customers who crowded into the narrow space and battled to claim one of the small tables set near the large front window. Most were eager to munch on the variety of muffins and scones and brownies, not to mention enjoy the freshly brewed coffee. But there were a few who wandered into the attached bookstore in search of a good novel to enjoy during a quiet evening alone.

The private office at the back of the shop, however, was strictly off limits. The only customers allowed through the door were by appointment. And only for those select few clients who could afford Maya Rosen's outrageous fees. As one of the most powerful mages in the world, Maya could name her price.

And she did.

Plus, she only offered her considerable skills to demons. They were split into two categories. The goblins who had long ago been giants, ogres, and trolls. And the fey creatures who had been fairies, sprites, and imps.

She never worked for vampires. Ever. And, of course, the local humans didn't have a clue that she was anything other than a successful businesswoman who was always generous with the neighborhood charities. Just as they didn't know that they were living on the outskirts of a pool of ancient magic called a Gyre that fueled the demons who infested New York City. Or that the territory was ruled by Valen, a powerful member of the Vampire Cabal.

Ignorance could definitely be bliss, Maya wryly acknowledged as she calmly watched a male demon storm around the barren office like a caged lion, waving his arms as he vented his seething fury. At first glance, the intruder appeared to be a regular guy in a tailored gray suit with his dark hair smoothed from his square face. Maya, however, could see the dark crimson aura that throbbed around his large body. It revealed that he was a goblin, but also that his blood hadn't been diluted over the centuries.

She could also smell the sour stench of his fear that he was trying to hide beneath his loud bluster.

Understandable. She had, after all, created a truth potion that had caused him to blurt out the fact that he'd been routinely overbilling vendors and pocketing the money during a meeting with his manager. Plus he'd shared his nasty habit of forcing himself on his young female employees.

Now he was out of his job as an accountant at the glitzy nightclub in New York City, and soon he'd be facing Valen's wrath for his sexual harassment. Something no demon wanted.

"Who was it?" he ground out as he stomped past her desk, his face an interesting shade of purple.

Maya pretended to be confused by his question. "Excuse me?"

"Who paid the contract to have my coffee spiked with a truth potion?"

Maya shrugged, not surprised he'd managed to figure out she was responsible for the potion in his coffee. But that's all he'd ever know. There was no way in hell she would reveal that the contract had been negotiated by his last victim. The pretty fairy had sold everything she owned, plus taken a loan from the bank, to ensure that the goblin was exposed and punished for his crimes.

The payment would be returned to the fairy through some covert means. Maya had too much respect for the female to refuse the stack of cash she'd proudly handed over. Just as she hadn't told the younger woman that she intended to add a secret layer to the potion. A layer that hadn't kicked in yet.

A week from now the demon was going to develop a mysterious rash with oozing pus and a disgusting odor. It wouldn't kill him, but it was going to make him miserable for several days.

"My clients are guaranteed confidentiality," she informed the seething demon. "Unless they specifically request I share their name."

"I don't give a flying fuck about your—"

"Enough," Maya snapped. She'd allowed the idiot to indulge his rabid temper—which was more than he deserved—but she was done. Beyond done. Opening the top drawer of her desk, she pulled out a small glass vial. "This meeting is over."

"What do you mean, over?" His face darkened from purple to puce as the male moved to slam his palms on her desk, spittle hanging at the corner of his mouth. "I'll tell you when it's over, bitch." The threat was unmistakable, but Maya didn't flinch. Instead she calmly pulled the stopper out of the top of the vial. The demon stiffened, the fury fogging his brain penetrated by the acrid odor that abruptly stained the air. "What's that?"

"A very powerful potion."

The male scowled. "Are you threatening me?"

"I'm giving you an opportunity," Maya corrected in a soft voice.

"An opportunity for what?"

"You can walk out of here, and never return. Or I can toss the contents of this vial on you and various parts of your body are going to start shriveling." She paused, studying the liquid that was beginning to bubble inside the glass container. "Perhaps even fall off," she conceded with a small shrug. "I haven't used this recipe before so it's hard to say how bad things might get for you."

The male stumbled backward, his jaw bulging as he clenched his teeth in frustration. He was a cliché bully who used bluster and intimidation to manipulate others. The fact that he couldn't terrorize her was pissing him off as much as the knowledge that he'd lost everything.

"You wouldn't do it," he snarled. "Those potions are illegal."

They were. And the foaming liquid in the vial was nothing more than a harmless cleansing potion, but he didn't know that. Maya slowly rose to her feet, stretching out her arm as if preparing to launch a spell.

"So is stealing. And lying. And being a pervert," she reminded him in overly sweet tones. "Should I go on?"

The male smacked into the wall with a heavy thud. "I hope you rot in hell, you...you witch," he rasped, his insult ruined as he hastily turned to wrench open the door and flee like a coward.

With a roll of her eyes, Maya tossed the contents of the vial onto the floor, allowing the potion to spread through the office and purify the air. The demons couldn't touch their ancient powers when they were outside the magic of the Gyre, but that didn't mean they couldn't buy hexes and leave them behind.

Better safe than sorry. That was her motto.

Then, moving toward the open door, Maya paused to wipe her hands down her yellow cashmere sweater that she'd matched with a pair of ivory slacks. The meeting had gone pretty much as expected, but this was her least favorite part of her mage-for-hire business. Next, she combed her fingers through her shoulder-length black hair that framed her face. There was no gray to be seen in the silken strands, just as there were no lines on her oval face. As a mage, she stopped aging around thirty, but there was no mistaking the hard-earned wisdom in her bright green eyes.

The only visible mar to her polished beauty was the silvery spiderweb of scars that ran from her ear along the line of her jaw. The remnants of the magic that had nearly destroyed her.

Once she was confident that her composure was firmly in place, she walked through the empty bookstore and into the coffee shop that was serving the last of the customers. It was after six o'clock and the shop was officially closed, but even on a Tuesday it was closer to seven before the staff could shut off the lights and call it a day.

nsington Publishing Corp.
yce Kaplan
0 Third Avenue, 26th Floor
-NY, 10022

aplan@kensingtonbooks.com
2-407-1515

e authorized representative in the EU for product safety and compliance is

comply OÜ
arko Novkovic
arnu mnt 139b-14
Z, 11317

tps://www.eucompliancepartner.com
llo@eucompliancepartner.com
72 536 865 02

BN: 9781516112104
elease ID: 154969777

www.ingramcontent.com/pod-product-compliance
Lightning Source LLC
Chambersburg PA
CBHW031120030726
47496CB00002BA/623